**ROB
SMITH**

NIGHT FIGHTERS

For Brie and Aidan

Prologue

May, 1941

There was no moon the night the war changed.

Flying Officer Dunn checked his instrument panel for the hundredth time and thought again of the warm bed that awaited him in England. It was bitterly cold in the cockpit and he shivered despite his fleece lined jacket and boots. He forced himself to concentrate.

At twelve thousand feet the darkness of the summer sky seemed infinite, broken only occasionally by faint patches of cloud. It never failed to amaze Dunn how peaceful the night could seem, in stark contrast to the painful noise within the cockpit. The Wellington bomber had two engines. Tonight one was damaged and silent, but the vibration in the airframe still shook Dunn's body and was bringing on a familiar headache.

He glanced over at Allen, who sat tiredly nodding in his own seat. The co-pilot snapped back instantly to full alertness when Dunn shook his shoulder. He had been impressed with Allen this sortie, only their second together. The Australian had been calm over the target, despite the adrenaline that would have been pumping through him. That same adrenaline would have seeped away now, leaving the younger man drained. Dunn felt the same way. He wondered if they had scored any successful hits. With just one functioning engine they hadn't been able to keep pace with the rest of the formation on the homeward leg, but it could have been much worse. He shook his head at the memory of the pre-flight brief which had told them to expect only light resistance, and wondered how many of the one hundred and fourteen bombers in tonight's stream would make it home.

Allen tapped his watch and gave him a quizzical look.

"Captain to Observer," Dunn said into his intercom. "Are you on headset, Forbes?"

"Yes, sir. We're on course and twenty minutes from home." It didn't surprise Dunn that he hadn't even had to ask any questions. Forbes was always efficient. As observer, the Scotsman counted both navigator and bomb aimer among his duties, and in their four flights together Dunn had developed a strong respect for his abilities in both roles.

"We'll start descending soon. Freddy, have you made contact yet?"

"Not yet," the radio operator responded. "I'm still trying, sir."

Allen looked out at the silent engine with its feathered propeller, the blades edge on to the airflow to reduce drag. "She's done well, hasn't she?"

"She's a tough old bird," Dunn said. He knew what Allen meant. He was feeling quietly satisfied. Two hours earlier there had been nothing but fear. The sky over the lightless city of Hamburg had been busy with the bursts from heavy flak shells, and as they started their attack run red hot shrapnel from one near miss had struck the starboard engine. Somehow they had held the aircraft steady, allowing Forbes to get the bombs away on cue. Dunn was doing his best not to think about the flak.

"We'll have earned our pint tonight," Allen said, obviously thinking about the same thing.

"I'll be asleep before I can drink it," Dunn told him. "I'm…"

"Fighter!"

It was Perry's voice, terse over the intercom from his seat in the rear turret. Dunn hesitated. His eyes were drawn to the tiny streaks of light that seemed to pass within a few feet of the cockpit. He struggled to clear his mind before yanking at the controls and throwing the bomber into a tight bank to port. The straps of his harness dug painfully into his shoulders. A shadow, barely darker than the night, momentarily filled his vision and then was gone. There was the sound of machine gun fire and several flashes from the end of the long nose of the bomber.

"Is everyone okay?" Forbes said.

"What happened?" Allen asked, scanning the sky ahead. There was nothing to be seen now except the smothering darkness.

"I think he overshot," Dunn told him.

"The bastard must be new," Forbes growled. "Bloody amateur." It was a common enough mistake for new fighter pilots to make, Dunn knew, particularly at night. They would come in too fast, misjudging the difference in speed between them and their slower prey, unprepared for the violent evasive manoeuvre which was the bomber's first defence. Dunn glanced towards the starboard engine. There was no smoke or flame to give their position away. The engine was inert, the fire extinguished and the props motionless. With no moon and little starlight, it was unlikely the fighter would find them again.

"Everybody stay alert," Forbes added unnecessarily. No one was going to relax now.

"I had a go at him," Roberts said excitedly from the front turret.

"What was it?"

"I didn't get a good look, but I think it was a 110." Dunn caught Allen's look and nodded. That made sense. The Messerschmitt Bf-110 was one of the mainstays of the Luftwaffe's night fighter fleet. He took the Wellington down another thousand feet, his hands damp with sweat within his gloves, and kept the aircraft jinking for a few more minutes.

"Try not to put too much pressure on that engine, sir," Forbes warned from somewhere within the aircraft.

"Do you think he'll find us again?" Allen asked.

"I doubt it," Forbes said. "It's far too dark a night. He was lucky to find us the first time."

"We were lucky he missed."

It was unusual, Dunn reflected, to find a night fighter this far out over the Channel. Forbes was right; finding the bomber had to have been a monumental stroke of good fortune for the fighter's pilot. The German had probably caught a glimpse of an unknown shadow, taken his shot and headed home. It was fortunate for the British aircrew that the fighter had not been able to capitalise on his unexpected chance.

The second attack came just as they began to relax.

The rear gunner's warning shout in Dunn's headset was drowned out by an anguished scream and the sound of cannon shells ripping through the airframe. Dunn felt a sharp pain in his face, followed by a sudden breeze. Two large holes had appeared in the instrument panel, and at least one cannon or machine gun round had torn through the Perspex next to him. His face felt cold and wet in the airflow.

This time the fighter didn't overshoot. A second burst of fire hammered into the fuselage. Dunn put the aircraft into a shallow dive, frantically searching the sky below. The scream in his ears had now reduced to a constant monotone groan, abruptly cut short. Finally spotting a band of cloud, Dunn banked and increased the rate of dive. More tracers flashed past the starboard wing. The fighter was following them.

The Wellington was a sturdy aircraft but it couldn't take much more of this dive. The controls shook violently in Dunn's hands. He held them tight, his body tensed as he waited for the final killing burst from the fighter or the awful rending sound that would accompany the airframe breaking up. Neither came. The aircraft plunged into the safety of the cloud bank.

Dunn brought the Wellington level. One look at Allen was enough. The Australian was dead, slumped forward in his chair. The Perspex and instruments ahead of him were spattered with blood.

"Forbes to Captain. The radio is in bits, and Freddy's in a bad way."

Dunn tore his eyes away from the seat next to him. "Where is he hit?" he managed to say.

"High in both legs," Forbes replied grimly. "I've given him morphine, but he's losing a lot of blood. There's not much I can do for him."

Dunn rubbed his face with his gloved hand and took a deep breath. He felt vomit rising in his throat and swallowed it down, turning slightly in his seat so that he would not have to see the body still strapped in next to him.

"What about Roberts?" he said, trying to sound calm, knowing he was failing.

"He took one in the back of the head."

"Perry?"

"I'm okay, sir, but the turret's jammed. I can't get out." There was an edge of panic in the tail gunner's voice.

"Can you still use your guns?"

"Only if he comes straight at them. I can't see a thing in here. There's oil all over the place and my electric gun sight's out. Sorry I couldn't give you any more warning. The bloody thing came from nowhere."

"I think he's gone now."

"I hope so. I got a few rounds off. They weren't even in his direction but he sheared off as soon as I opened fire."

There was movement behind Dunn and he turned to see Forbes entering the cockpit. The observer barely glanced at Allen.

"Are we burning?"

Dunn looked out of both windows and then scanned his instruments. As far as he could tell the port engine was still running sweetly and they were not losing fuel. Most importantly there was no fire to spread to the rest of the aircraft. "We're okay," he said.

"At least there's no light for him to follow," Forbes said, "but we should probably stay in these clouds, just in case."

"How did he find us again?"

"Luck."

Dunn took a long look at the sky around them, careful to avoid letting his eyes linger on the glistening spots on the instrument panel. He wondered why the fighter had broken off the engagement so easily. Perhaps it was understandable, given the dangers of the two machine guns in the rear turret.

"He must be miles away by now," Dunn said. He felt oddly disconnected. He didn't even feel cold any more, simply numb.

"The bastard's probably already marked us down as a kill," Forbes said bitterly. "We're pissing hydraulic fluid all over the place down the back. How's she flying?"

"Seems fine," Dunn said. He had to regain control of himself and his aircraft. He turned to Forbes. "Take the emergency axe and see if you can get Perry out." The observer couldn't help in the cockpit. They had been in cloud for several minutes and the English coast was close. Even if the enemy had remained in the area, it would never find the bomber again. It was simply too dark.

The last shreds of cloud melted away. Dunn checked his watch. It was nearly two o'clock.

When he looked up again, the fighter was there.

The shark-like form was scarcely visible barely a hundred yards away. It surely could not have followed them, yet it was there. Dunn's hope that it had not seen them lasted only seconds. Even as he watched the night fighter slowed and positioned itself to fire.

The thin nose lit up with tiny flashes. Tracers slammed into the body of the Wellington and, after a slight pause for adjustment, into the port engine. The whole wing seemed to disappear in a shower of sparks, followed by a shocking flash as the engine burst into flames. The light of the fire flickered on the canopy of the fighter.

"Captain to crew, bail out." He fought to keep his voice calm, but it was hopeless. "Everybody get the hell out." He punched the release button on his harness with his right hand as his left instinctively felt for his parachute.

The night fighter was still effortlessly keeping formation with them as he stumbled towards the emergency escape hatch. A fire had started amongst the reconnaissance flares amidships, dangerously close to the oxygen bottles. The glow of the flames combined with thick smoke gave a grimly surreal effect. Dunn slipped on something and fell heavily against the side of the fuselage. Looking down, he saw that he had stepped on Freddy the radio operator, or rather the sodden and pulped remains of his legs. Forbes was lying on the canvas crew-rest bed where he had been hurled by the impact of a shell, the axe still dangling from nerveless fingers. He looked as if he were asleep, except for the blackened, sunken crater that had once been his face.

Dunn's eyes were stinging as he began to choke on the burning acrid smoke. At the very end of the fuselage the tiny door of the rear turret was jammed ajar, and he saw Perry's arm reach through the narrow gap as the gunner desperately tried to free himself.

He dropped to his knees, knowing the fumes were overcoming him, and started to crawl. Behind him there was the sound of something splintering, and then he felt an impact that forced the last pockets of air from his lungs. He slumped to the floor, all pain and feeling gone. His final emotion was frustration, that he'd never know how the night fighter had found them again.

The German fighter's last burst had been unnecessary. It stayed to observe the burning bomber as it slowly slipped to port and dropped inexorably towards the Channel below. Even as it became a bright disintegrating mass, the turret at its tail sent out defiant tracers until eventually the aircraft ploughed into the sea. The flames continued to burn after impact, a slick of unused fuel covering the calm water. The fighter circled the fires in a slow pattern, until finally it turned its tail towards the English coast just a few miles away and headed back towards the distant shore of Europe. Of the one hundred and fourteen aircraft that had left England that night, eleven aircraft and their crews did not return, but no other engagement that night was as significant.

The Vulture had claimed his first kill.

"We'll have to make this quick," the Fat Man said, itching at the collar of his dark suit. "I'm lunching at Mansion House with the Canadian PM. You'll take a drink?"

"If there's time, sir."

"There's always time for a drink, Quentin. Mackenzie King will wait."

Quentin Quiet watched as the Fat Man walked to the sideboard that dominated one wall of the expensively-furnished office. In truth he was not particularly fat, simply a big man who despite questionable levels of alcohol consumption remained surprisingly fit for a man of his age. Quiet often wondered if his host knew of the nickname, but decided it didn't really matter. He was confident that he was one of only half a dozen men in England who could get away with it.

Quickly and efficiently the Fat Man poured himself a glass of brandy, and moved to pour a second.

"I'd prefer whisky, if you have it," Quiet said.

"Ah, yes. I always forget." The Fat Man poured him a generous measure of expensive Scotch, and sat down in a leather armchair. He placed his drink on the table in front of him and reached into his pocket. "You'll forgive me smoking," he said, without attempting to make it sound like a question. "Somehow every time you ask to meet me I end up needing a drink and a smoke."

Quiet ignored the second armchair and remained standing, one arm resting lightly on the mantelpiece above the open fire. His host produced a Cuban cigar, lit it with a long match, and gave Quiet a quizzical look. "Do you ever take that hat off?"

Quiet smiled tolerantly. The brown trilby stayed where it was. Instead he reached into his rumpled suit and withdrew a thin sepia file binder.

"Is that the finished study?" A trickle of smoke escaped from the side of the Fat Man's mouth.

"Yes. With my recommendations."

The Fat Man sighed and sank back in his chair. "The Air Staff sent me the latest figures for the strategic bombing campaign yesterday. I'm not sure how long we can sustain this level of losses."

"It will get worse before it gets better, believe me."

"You were right about this Hun fellow, then? What are we calling him now, the Vulture?"

"Yes, sir. We believe he has somewhere in the region of twenty kills so far, apparently always targeting damaged or isolated aircraft."

"The bastard," the Fat Man said with real venom.

"That's in less than three months. No one else on either side is getting close to that kill rate at night."

"We could have used someone like him during the Blitz. How do you know it's the same man each time?" He paused, and a look of contempt passed across his face. "Presumably that little rat Goebbels and his propaganda cronies are milking it for all it's worth?"

"No, oddly enough. Not yet. We've been piecing it together from aircrew reports. A few of the aircraft put up enough of a fight to scare him off and make it home, and in a couple of cases other crews saw him attacking a nearby bomber. All the reports mention the same thing, a crest on the aircraft's tail. Some sort of bird."

The Fat Man blew a smoke ring, his face thoughtful. "It doesn't sound like you've got much to go on."

"I have my other sources too, sir. The ones you prefer not to know about."

"The sources you don't want me to know about, you mean?"

"It amounts to the same thing," Quiet said blandly. "There's more bad news. The Germans are training up a special squadron, to be led by the Vulture. Once that becomes operational, no RAF bomber operating anywhere in north-west Europe will be safe."

"So what are you suggesting?"

"We form a squadron of our own."

"Using what?"

Quiet stepped forward and placed the opened binder onto the polished wood of the table. There was only a single sheet inside, hand-written on brown paper. The Fat Man leaned forward, resting the cigar in a trough at the top of his silver ashtray. For several minutes he was silent as he read the notes, his eyes widening before flicking back to the top of the page and reading it again.

"Are you serious?" he said finally.

"Always." Quiet reached down and took the binder, closing it without a glance at the contents. "Twelve months ago I wouldn't have believed it myself. Since then certain things have come to light, or in this case, not come to light. Does the name Morgan Bale mean anything to you?"

"I can't say it does."

"He's Sir William Bale's son."

"The industrialist? Yes, I remember now. You don't mean to say that strange looking boy of his was…"

"I do mean to say that, yes."

"My God."

Quiet reached into the binder and pulled out the sheet of paper. He looked at his own hand-writing for a few seconds, then reached for his whisky glass and downed it in a single go. "As always the whole affair would be above Top Secret. There would be no records." He dropped the sheet into the fire. "Everything is in place, ready to go. All I need is your authorisation."

The Fat Man took a large swig of brandy, the shock on his face quickly fading to be replaced by a wary acceptance. "I don't know," he said finally. "This is outlandish, even by your department's standards."

"I will admit that it's…" Quiet paused for a few moments, trying to think of the correct word to use, before finally adding "unconventional. But I've never misled you."

The Fat Man looked up from his seat and raised an eyebrow.

"Well, I've never let you down, sir," the man in the hat said with a straight face.

"No, I suppose you haven't. Very well, then. Consider it authorised under the usual terms." The Fat Man stood and finished his drink, and looked down forlornly at his barely-lit cigar. "I hate to leave so soon, but if you'll excuse me, I must get to this damned luncheon. Keep me informed, will you?"

"Of course, Prime Minister."

October 1941

The only light in the barn came from a handful of battered oil lamps hanging on the walls, but for the seventy or so men crowded inside to see the spectacle the dim glow wasn't a problem. Bright lights drew attention, and none of them wanted attention drawn to their sport. There would have been panic if the crowd of farmers and munitions workers had known how close the police were to raiding the barn that night. As it was, only one man knew. It was down to him that efforts to close down illegal fighting dens in the area had been delayed.

13

Quentin Quiet watched from the back of the crowd as the fighters walked out. A makeshift ring had been constructed in the centre of the room. The crowd parted briefly to let the two men through before closing in again. The lucky ones at the front rested their arms on the ropes, while those further from the action stood on benches to look down into the ring.

Quiet squeezed onto a bench, ignoring the suspicious looks sent his way. He'd been to enough fights recently to know that the sort of person who came to watch bare-knuckle fighting would always be nervous. The war had ruled out many legitimate sources of entertainment, and there were a number of men who were making a lot of money from this business. As he watched, bookies weaved through the spectators, taking ever larger bets.

Had Quiet been a betting man, he would have found it easy to spot the favourite. The confidence of the first fighter was palpable even across the room. He was well over six feet tall, and wore flamboyant blood-red shorts. There were tattoos visible on his thick forearms and chest. His face and knuckles bore the scars of dozens of contests. Only the excess weight around his waistline suggested any weakness.

"In the red shorts," the promoter called, "the fan's favourite, Harry 'The Hammer' Morrell!" There was a cheer from a large section of the crowd, which Morrell acknowledged with a pump of his fist and a grin.

From beneath his trilby Quiet watched with interest as the second fighter climbed unhurriedly through the ropes. He wondered briefly if he had been misled; the fighter did not look like a man with such a reputation. He had a naturally stocky build from which it seemed all fat had been stripped. His hair was long and unruly, and even from across the ring Quiet could see it was matted by dirt and lack of care. There was a stark contrast between the paleness of his skin and his battered, dirty black trousers. The fighter looked drawn and unhealthy as he moved slowly about the ring without paying any obvious attention to the crowd or his opponent.

The one detail that truly stood out was enough to overshadow the rest of his appearance. Despite the dim light, the smaller fighter's eyes were covered with several layers of thin material that were wrapped around his head above the nose and tied at the back of his skull.

"In the black trousers," the promoter called with less enthusiasm, "back from retirement, it's the man you love to hate; Crowe!"

14

Whistling and booing filled the barn. The promoter gave Crowe a wide berth as he climbed out of the ring. Crowe didn't seem to notice. He had begun pacing in his corner, and Quiet was struck by the sudden thought that, more than anything, Crowe reminded him of an attack dog, one which had been starved and angered.

Perhaps his sources could have been right about this man.

The referee called the two men together. The fighter in the red shorts towered over his opponent, and laughed as the referee spoke to them. There was a late flurry of betting. It was all on the man called Crowe.

The bell rang.

The Hammer rushed forward and swung a huge right hand. The smaller man swayed easily away. Morrell stumbled with the momentum, causing a few chuckles around the arena, but he regained his balance and threw a heavy jab. Crowe stepped casually to one side and watched the hand fly past. There were impatient shouts from the crowd now, as the fighters circled warily.

Then, as if suddenly freed from a leash, Crowe attacked. From well out of range he took two quick steps forward. His hands were a blur, slamming two fast jabs into Morrell's face. Before the big man could even begin to cover up Crowe's left hook whipped around with vicious intent, driving into the side of Morrell's head with an audible crack of bone on bone. Morrell stumbled back, blood streaming down his face where his opponent's fist had sliced open the soft flesh above the eye. Crowe gave him no respite. As the crowd roared in approval he slipped beneath Morrell's despairing jab and drove the air out of the bigger man's lungs with a brutal uppercut that ripped into him below the sternum.

Morrell wrapped his arms around Crowe, trying to use his weight. His opponent simply shrugged him off. Twisting from the hips he sent first a left hook and then a right thudding into Morrell's ribs. Morrell was starting to go down, his breath gone. Crowe stepped back, let him begin to sag, and then threw a right hand with all his weight behind it. It landed flush on the bridge of Morrell's nose, pulping it into a thickly-spread mess. The fight was over. Morrell dropped to one knee and then curled into a ball on the cold floor, clutching his face as he gasped helplessly for air.

Quiet could feel the turmoil in the crowd, the bench shaking under his feet with the fury of their reaction. A handful cheered, happy with the blood they had seen for their money, but the majority screamed their displeasure. It seemed that the fight had been simply too short for their tastes. Many of those who booed had won money on Crowe's victory, but that wasn't the point. Some began to hurl coins, which tinkled incongruously as they struck on the stones. A group of men dragged the groaning Morrell away, leaving blood on the floor to join the faded stains from earlier contests.

"Crowe wins," the promoter called apologetically.

The winner stood alone in the centre of the ring, head bowed. He seemed to be looking intently at his fist. His knuckles were dripping blood, his hand and whole body shaking slightly, as if under great strain. A coin struck his shoulder, and in an instant he looked up. The offender backed hurriedly away into the crowd.

With a smile Crowe turned and walked back towards the side door from which he had first emerged. The crowd parted ahead of him.

Quiet stepped carefully down off the bench and wordlessly threaded his way through the angry spectators towards the exit. He had seen enough. Everything he had been told was true.

He heard the threats being hurled towards the promoter fade behind him as he walked out into the cool night air, and pulled a battery powered flashlight from his coat. He looked around slowly at the silent farmyard, and then flashed the torch, once, twice, until on the third flash the night came alive with the sound of whistles as the fifty policemen who had waited so patiently finally closed in to get their reward.

The ensuing brawl lasted far longer than the fight the crowd had just seen. Many of the spectators were aggressively drunk, and as happy to be in a scrap as to watch one. The police had come prepared, though. Arrests were made with the liberal use of truncheons and boots.

The grin on the Chief Inspector's face seemed cadaverous in the torchlight. He was nominally in charge of this operation. Both men knew the truth of it. "I'd call that a success," the Chief Inspector said as the brawl finally subsided and the last of the prisoners were led out to waiting police vans. "It's an impressive haul, though it looks like a fair few got away into the fields."

"Never mind that," Quiet said. "Did you get him?"

"Of course. He put up a fight, though. Three of my men will have to spend the night in hospital."

"What about him?"

"Crowe? He's something of a legend on the bare-knuckle circuit. I've heard some remarkable stories. Apparently he-"

16

"Is he hurt?"

The Chief Inspector frowned at the interruption. He clearly wasn't used to such lack of respect for his authority. "No," he replied. "A few bruises, but nothing he won't survive. He's on his way to a cell now."

"Make sure the cell has a window."

"It will be arranged."

Quiet nodded and walked away without another word. He regretted the necessity of involving the police, and felt little urge to be polite to them now that they had served their purpose. He had provided the tip off; the Chief Inspector's prize would be the praise for nearly thirty successful arrests. Quiet's own prize waited in the police station.

He left Crowe alone in his cell for several hours, occasionally checking his watch. There were only two hours until dawn when he finally walked in, ensuring that the four constables on duty locked the door behind him.

"Wait at the end of the corridor," he told them through the door grille. "No one comes past."

"The Chief Inspector said to wait outside," one of the policemen said.

Quiet gave him a look, and after a few seconds the constable mumbled something with a respectful nod and they walked away, their polished shoes echoing in the corridor. Quiet turned and looked around the room.

It took a few moments for his eyes to adjust to the semi-darkness, even as he breathed in the stench of stale sweat. The harsh electric light from the corridor through the grille was the only illumination, except for a thin shaft of moonlight coming from the high window. It was enough to see that it was a simple room with only a bench along one wall and a filthy sink. The bowl of the sink was spattered with blood. The meagre light reflected faintly from the drying, brownish droplets, and from fragments of glass on the stone floor. The wire cage that had been meant to protect the light bulb above had been twisted apart to gain access to it.

The victorious fighter was slumped on the bench in the darkest corner of the room, still dressed only in his blood stained trousers. He looked up as Quiet walked in. The fighter's eyes were still obscured behind cloth, but even in the shadows his face showed his wariness. His breath was visible in the cold air, but he gave no indication of any discomfort. Strangely, for a man who had recently been heavily beaten by half a dozen policemen with truncheons, his abnormally pale skin looked unmarked. There was dried blood on his chest, but it wasn't his.

"You don't seem very happy for a winner," Quiet said, amiably. "But I suppose your night has taken an unfortunate turn."

"How long are you going to keep me here?" the man he knew as Crowe said.

"Why? Do you need to be somewhere else?"

"What do you want?"

"Just a few words."

"Unless they're 'you're free to go', don't bother."

"Crowe, isn't it?" There was no response. "The name suits you. What's your real name?"

"Who says that isn't my real name?"

"I may be wrong. I doubt it, though. Just as I doubt you were called Crowe when you were a patient at Bedford Sands."

The fighter froze. The surprise registered on his face for only an instant before the mask of disinterest returned. "I don't know what you're talking about."

"Of course not. Just as you wouldn't know anything about the death of a patient called William Hunter in 1927, or of an unlicensed boxer in Clapham about twelve months ago."

"I've never been to Clapham," Crowe replied, but Quiet couldn't help noticing the telltale reaction this time. For all his talents, Crowe hadn't mastered the art of hiding his feelings. That, thought Quiet, would come in time. Life had a way of forcing feelings to hide themselves.

"Relax, Crowe. I'm not with the police. I've been looking for you, though."

"What are you after, then?" the fighter growled. He turned his head slightly towards the door. "Let's hear it. I'm a busy man."

"No, you're not. I am. But I know you're keen to be gone," Quiet added with a pointed look towards the window, "so I'll make this quick. Tell me, have you ever flown an aircraft?"

"No."

"Ever wanted to?"

There was no response, only a disinterested sigh.

"You really should try it," Quiet continued. "It would suit a man of your talents."

"Why?" Crowe muttered. "Do they need pilots who can beat people half to death?"

"Sometimes." He took a step forward. When he spoke again, his casual manner was gone, his voice lower. "I'm talking about your other talents. There aren't many men who can see in the dark."

This time there was no concealing the surprise on the man's pale face. "I think it's time I left," he said, standing up.

"How exactly do you plan to do that?"

Crowe looked at him with a faint smile. "I'm going to ask you to open the door. Politely, of course." The smile faded. "And you're going to do it."

Quiet shrugged, unconcerned by the implied threat. "There are four policemen just down the corridor," he said reasonably, "and another twenty in earshot. You've been arrested for illegal boxing. That's a serious charge, not to mention the three policemen you've put in the hospital. They might even call it attempted murder."

"They'll live," Crowe said. "You might not. One way or another, I'm leaving this cell now."

"Before the sun comes up, you mean?" He smiled at the flicker of concern on the fighter's face. "When was the last time you saw daylight?"

Crowe didn't respond. His head turned first to the window above him, then to the locked steel of the door, and finally back to the man in front of him. His eyes were unreadable behind the bandages.

"Where would you go anyway? Back to some alleyway to hide until nightfall? From what I understand you've been living on the streets for some time now. It shows. What then? Another meaningless fight? That's not the life you want."

"What would you know about it?"

"More than you realise," Quiet told him calmly.

Crowe's response was a short laugh, a harsh sound devoid of amusement or emotion. "You don't know anything about my life."

"Perhaps not. But there are others who do."

"Others?"

"Oh, yes." He crossed his arms, totally relaxed now that he knew he'd succeeded, that this man would be recruited just as easily as the others. Everything was going exactly according to plan. "I know a number of other gentlemen like you. Pale skin, lightning reflexes, marked aversion to sunlight. Did you think it was just you?"

"You're lying."

"They cover their eyes, too."

"Who are they?"

"They work for me, Crowe. I work for the British Government."

"Doing what?"

"You'll find out in time." Quiet looked at his watch. "Time, of course, is something neither of us has right now. I trust you're interested in this...opportunity?"

"Maybe," Crowe said, still staring. "But why should I trust you?"

Quiet smiled. "You shouldn't," he said. "But if you turn me down, you'll be watching the sunrise in a couple of hours." He turned and rapped on the door three times, and waited until the sound of bolts sliding open echoed harshly in the cold cell.

"The choice is yours."

Chapter One

Crowe awoke. The bus had stopped, unlike the rain which continued to beat a steady rhythm on the windows. Outside in the night there were soldiers with flashlights in their hands and rifles slung over their shoulders.

"We're here," Morgan said, squeezing his shoulder softly. Crowe turned in his seat and looked around the bus. The others were waking, stretching and rubbing their eyes beneath their smoked sunglasses. Someone coughed at the back and Crowe saw it was Hinde, his pale face looking more nervous than ever. The Swiss saw him and smiled, the edges of his slightly feminine mouth curling up to reveal tobacco stained teeth. Lieberwitz, sitting directly behind Crowe, caught his eye and nodded slightly. At the back of the bus Gorecki continued to sleep, his head resting against the window and a book lying open in his lap.

"You were moaning in your sleep," Morgan said, gently. "Dreaming again?"

Crowe grunted a non-committal reply.

"Are you okay?"

Crowe nodded. "What's the hold up?"

Morgan shrugged. "Checking our papers, I guess." He looked around, clearly unimpressed. Ahead of them the road was barred by a heavy iron mesh gate, and away to each side stretched a high fence, topped with barbed wire. There was no guardroom, just a handful of trees beyond the four soaked and miserable looking guards. One of them was talking to the pretty WAAF driver, the man's low tones lost in the rattle of the rain on the thin metal roof of the bus. "So this is it, then. Charney Breach, our new home. Doesn't look like much, does it?"

"Maybe we got lost?"

"I wish. Did you see that town we passed a few miles back? I think it was called Staverton."

"Staverton St Mary," Hinde said in his rough voice, his English precise as always.

"That's it. Didn't exactly look like the party capital of East Anglia, did it?"

"What does it matter?" Werner said, stirring in the seat opposite. "We're not here for party. We're here to kill Nazis."

Morgan sighed. "That's all you ever think about. Personally, I'd like to think we might find time for the odd drink or two, though God alone knows where we could get a decent bottle of wine around here. Of course, it's only a couple of hours to London, and I know some great places there." He nudged Crowe. "Maybe you could take us to some of your old haunts, eh?"

"You wouldn't want to go to them."

Hinde reached into the pocket of his plain suit, drew out a cigarillo case and placed a cigarette in his mouth. He lit it and took a long, nervous drag. The acrid smoke drifted through the bus and woke Gorecki. The Pole sat bolt upright, looking startled. His book fell to the floor with a thud.

"Do you have to smoke those stinking things in here?" Werner said, his thick Teutonic accent smothering the words. Crowe could imagine the German's one remaining eye staring menacingly beneath the sunglasses.

"Sorry," Hinde rasped, hurriedly inhaling again before stubbing the cigarette out.

The guard moved away from the bus and made a motion with his hand. With a squeal of metal against metal the gates were pushed open, and the bus began to move forward.

"About time," Crowe said, cracking his knuckles.

Hinde coughed, bringing a slightly pained gasp with it. "Do you think Raithe will be here already?"

"He ought to be," Morgan said. "That car of his looked a lot faster than this bus."

"I could walk faster than this coffin," Werner said bitterly, rubbing his shaven scalp with one thin hand.

"Why was he allowed to travel by car? Why didn't he travel with us?" There was the faintest trace of a whine in Hinde's voice, which he tried to hide with another cough.

"Didn't you know?" Morgan said, feigning surprise. "He's too good to travel with the rest of us. What a dive," he added after a few more moments of appraising their surroundings. They were driving alongside the airfield, passing a number of temporary-looking buildings. The blackout was in force throughout England, as it had been every night since the war began, and none of the buildings showed any light. Through the darkness Crowe could clearly see the half-dozen simple blister hangars a short distance from the buildings. On the far side of the airfield was a much larger hangar, close to the trees and obscured beneath camouflage netting. There were vehicles and piles of building materials scattered around the place, seemingly at random.

"Like a building site," Werner said.

"Maybe they haven't finished it yet?" Hinde suggested. His hands were already rolling another cigarette.

"It's probably a ruse," Morgan said. "In case Jerry day fighters come over. They won't waste their efforts on a half-finished base."

Morgan stood, smoothed down his civilian travel clothing and grabbed his bags. Ahead now was a larger single-storey building, and Crowe guessed from its modern brick-construction that this must be the headquarters. The bus pulled up opposite the double doors at the front, and the driver sounded the horn once.

"Alright, boys, follow me," Morgan said. "Make sure you've got everything because the bus won't be coming back." The door opened and Morgan thanked the driver with a low word and a generous smile, his perfect teeth flashing. Crowe sensed the girl's apprehension but could still tell from her reaction that she found Morgan attractive. He felt the slightest familiar pang of jealousy, though not surprise. Morgan had always had the looks to match his self-confidence. He was taller and slimmer than Crowe and, by his own generous admission, much better looking. His face, seemingly perpetually happy and open, was framed by pleasantly untidy brown hair.

With one large bag in his hand and another slung over his broad shoulders, Morgan stepped out into the rain, his sunglasses looking incongruous in the darkness of the early October night. Crowe followed with his solitary kitbag. He gave the driver a sideways glance as he passed, and saw her flinch slightly before she turned away. It did little to improve his mood.

The doors swung open, revealing for an instant a painful flash of light. A short, well-fed man of about sixty walked out smiling broadly behind his unruly black beard, with a half-filled glass in his left hand while his right brushed crumbs from the front of his woollen sweater.

"Dr Madeley, I presume?" Morgan said with a delighted grin.

"My dear Morgan," the man said, embracing him warmly. Behind them the bus driver barely hesitated long enough for the last of the men to disembark before she closed the doors and accelerated away.

Dr Byron Madeley shook hands with the new arrivals in turn, greeting each of them with obvious pleasure. Crowe hung back.

"How are you, Crowe?" Dr Madeley asked, quietly.

Crowe shrugged. "I'm here."

"Are you still refusing to drink?" The doctor looked him directly in the eyes but kept his tone neutral. "We really should talk, dear boy," he added when Crowe didn't respond. "Will you come and see me sometime over the next few days?"

"Is there any danger of us getting out of the rain, gents?" Morgan called to them.

"Marvellous idea," Dr Madeley said, "I'm getting water in my Cognac." He turned back to Crowe. "Come and see me. Let me help you."

"I've told you before. I don't need help."

The doctor sighed, turned and walked to the front of the group. "Okay, chaps, I appreciate you've had a long journey over from Wales and you probably just want to have a rest, but there are still three hours until dawn and your new squadron mates are keen to meet you."

"Are you sure keen is the right word?" Morgan interrupted to general smiles. Hinde chuckled nervously until Werner silenced him with a glance.

"They've heard a little about you," Dr Madeley said carefully, "so be prepared for some odd looks. We're going to go through to the bar. I'm afraid it's a little bright in there. I'll try and get something done about the lighting tomorrow but until then I suggest you all keep your eyes covered."

Dr Madeley led them inside, where a long central corridor ran the length of the building with numerous doors on each side. The lights on the ceiling were not bright by normal standards, but they were enough to make Crowe glad for his sunglasses. Morgan fell automatically into step next to him, the two of them leading the group as usual. They could hear the growing hubbub of conversation, of raised voices and laughter.

"This is it," Morgan said. He turned to Crowe. "Try not to start any fights, okay?"

"I don't know what you mean," Crowe replied innocently as Dr Madeley opened the second door on the right and ushered them into the bar.

The rush of sound that accompanied the opening of the door died as Crowe and Morgan entered. The room was not large, and the harsh glow of two thin electric lights was enough to light it all. The décor was simple and cheap, with furniture that looked old and battered. There was a wooden bar top along the inside wall and several heavily curtained windows along the other. The dozen men in the room were enough to make it seem busy. Most had drinks in their hands, and all were dressed in neatly-pressed RAF uniforms except for a balding, white-shirted barman. Crowe felt every pair of eyes looking at him, felt the tension in the room, and resisted the urge to smile. He knew how these people were feeling now. He recognised the mixture of fear and discomfort they would be experiencing. He had known it all his adult life. Part of him was disgusted by it. Part of him revelled in it.

No one spoke as they filed in, until eventually the six men in their sunglasses stood by the near end of the bar. Hinde coughed. The sound echoed hollowly in the silent room.

"Well," Morgan said, confidently, "I need a drink." He walked past the nearest of the men towards the barman, Crowe following a couple of feet behind. One of the RAF officers, a big, good-looking Flight Lieutenant with pilot's wings on his chest and black hair slick with Brylcreem, watched as Morgan went past.

"Freaks," the man muttered. Morgan ignored him. It wasn't in Crowe's nature to do the same.

"Did you say something?" Crowe spoke quietly, but in the still of the room it was loud enough for all to hear. He stepped in close to the bigger man. Crowe could see the arrogance in the man's eyes, but he knew what to look for and saw the flicker of fear behind the posturing. He wanted to drive his forehead into the man's nose, and felt his hand starting to curl into a fist. Instead he slowly moved his hand up to his face and pulled his sunglasses down his nose, not more than half an inch but enough to reveal the eyes behind them. The man inhaled sharply in surprise and took the smallest step back.

Morgan put one hand on his arm, gripping firmly enough to make his point. "Why don't you have a drink? You can chat with your new friend later."

A single bead of sweat ran down the big man's temple, and Crowe smiled. For a second longer he held the stare, and then turned away dismissively, pushing his sunglasses back into place.

"Mine's a pint of Best," he said lightly.

The conversation returned to the room, soft and hesitant for a few moments but quickly regaining its former volume. Crowe knew the only talk would all be about the new arrivals, but he didn't really care. He'd heard it all before. His colleagues were left to talk amongst themselves.

"Did you even hear a word I said?" Morgan asked. "I might as well talk to a brick wall."

"You should try it. Maybe the wall will care."

"Funny man. Now stop showing off and pay attention. I'd like to at least try to fit in here before you ruin it for all of us with your tried, tested and increasingly boring hard man act." Morgan signalled to the barman, who walked reluctantly towards them. He was in his forties, Crowe decided, with a heavy build now turning to fat and eyes that were unfriendly behind his round glasses.

"Good evening," Morgan said. "Or should that be good morning now?" Undeterred by the lack of any response, Morgan added, "Could I have a pint of Best Bitter and a glass of red wine, please? Maybe a decent Bordeaux?"

"What?" the man said loudly, leaning towards them.

"Three pints of Best, Barry," a friendly voice said from behind them. Crowe turned and was surprised to see a hand being offered to him by a solidly built man with dark, slightly greying hair and a bushy but neatly cultivated moustache. "Ignore Barry's rudeness. He's half-deaf. And you won't find any bloody wine around here, lads. Hello, I'm Harry Stead."

"Crowe." He shook hands, noting that the man's grip was firmer than he expected. Harry Stead was clearly the oldest of the aircrew in the room, but his eyes seemed out of place, bright and enthusiastic and looking like they belonged in a much younger face.

"Morgan Bale. Pleased to meet you, sir," Morgan said, obviously noting the Squadron Leader rank braids on the wrists of the man's jacket.

"Call me Harry, son," Stead said genially. "Only the young lads call me sir and while you both look young enough all right, from what I hear from Dr Madeley I guess you're both a lot older than you look. Am I right?"

26

"Well, I'm only twenty-two," Morgan said. "But Crowe is thirty, and ageing at a frightening rate."

"You both look so young," Stead sighed. "I'll be forty bloody years old at Christmas and I'm showing every last year of it. Anyway, welcome to RAF Charney Breach. I couldn't help noticing the sunglasses. We've put in some weaker lights but I take it that it's still too bright?"

"It is a bit, yes."

"Well, I'm sorry. I'm Station Operations Officer around here so that's probably my mistake. I also answer to Station Intelligence Officer, and between those two job titles it means anything menial the boss needs doing winds up on my desk."

"Is the boss here tonight?" Morgan said, looking around.

"I'm afraid Group Captain Noone is far too busy. I don't know exactly what he's doing," he added, "but I'm sure he's very busy. You'll meet him tomorrow night when he briefs the squadron. Ah, Barry's excelled himself. He's actually managed to fetch the drinks. You can't always take that for granted."

The barman deposited three pint mugs of bitter onto the bar top and waited sullenly until Stead paid him. "I can't say everyone here is pleased to see you," Stead said, "but I bloody well am. We've lost a lot of good men in the last twelve months and your arrival has saved us from being disbanded, even if that does mean major changes in the way we do business. But if you'll excuse me, lads, I'd better see if your friends need a drink. It was good to meet you." He smiled and moved slowly away towards the others, clearly favouring his left leg.

"No wine," Morgan said, stunned. "I had no idea the situation was so bad."

"Yes, desperate," Crowe muttered sarcastically.

"I suppose we all have to make sacrifices for our country. Harry Stead seems friendly enough, at least. Mind you, I suspect he's the only one."

There was no disguising the looks that were being sent their way. It didn't surprise Crowe. People had been looking at him that way for twenty years.

Morgan shook his head sadly at the unfamiliar drink in his hand, and then looked towards Stead, who was introducing himself to the rest of the newly-arrived pilots. "How do you think he got that limp?"

"He was shot down last year," Dr Madeley said, joining them. "Return fire from a German bomber. I'm told he refused to be cut free from the wreckage until his wounded navigator was safely out. Harry was one of the top night intruder pilots in the RAF but the crash messed up his back pretty badly, so he doesn't get to fly much these days and he's stuck with that nasty limp. He's a marvellous chap, by the way. He wants this business to succeed. It's a shame that the same can't be said for some of the others."

"Like the Group Captain?" Crowe said.

"I'll let you make your own opinions about him, old boy."

"So," Morgan said, "any sign of Raithe yet?"

"He's arriving tomorrow."

"Are you serious? Why?"

"Does Raithe need a reason why? He does pretty much what he pleases. He probably just wanted to avoid spending time with his new colleagues tonight. You know how he feels about ordinary people."

The bar was beginning to empty. One by one the pilots were finishing their drinks and slipping away to their accommodation. "Looks like our new squadron mates weren't all that keen to meet us after all," Crowe observed.

"It will take time," Dr Madeley said. "Wait until you've flown some missions and proved what you can do. You'll win them over."

"You've already made a big impression on one of them, anyway," Morgan added. The big pilot was talking with two other men, and seeing them looking muttered something to his grinning companions.

"Shaun Clark," Dr Madeley said. "He's one of the squadron personalities, though sadly not in a good way. By all accounts he was lined up to be a flight commander here until we got involved and he was passed over. He could be a dangerous enemy."

"Enemies aren't fun if they're not dangerous," Morgan replied brightly.

"I'm merely suggesting you be careful."

"I looked in his eyes," Crowe said. "He's nothing."

"I'm sure he speaks very highly of you," Morgan said with a friendly nudge.

"We're not welcome here, Morgan," Crowe said without smiling. "We might be flying with them, but that won't stop them hating us."

Morgan opened his mouth to respond, but kept silent. Crowe saw the look in his eyes, knew that it hurt Morgan that his friend bore so much anger and resentment towards normal people. Even after a year Morgan did not understand. He'd never had to fight just to survive, or to hide from the daylight in foul-smelling sewers and abandoned houses. No, thought Crowe, that was unfair. It wasn't Morgan's fault that he'd had a privileged upbringing. No one with their condition ever had it easy.

"Well, gentlemen," Dr Madeley said, breaking the awkward silence, "you must be exhausted and the sun will be up soon. How about you finish those drinks and I'll show you to your quarters? It's not much, but for the next few months it's home."

"We should get some sleep," Morgan agreed. "We've got a lot of work to do from tomorrow onwards."

Crowe cracked his knuckles, picked up his pint glass and emptied it. Across the room, all but a handful of the pilots had already gone. Shaun Clark and his two companions were the last of them, and as Crowe watched, they finished their drinks. There was no mistaking the menace in the look Clark gave them as he left.

"Oh yes," Morgan said, smiling. "A lot of work..."

Chapter Two

"Make no mistake about it, gentlemen," Group Captain Raymond Noone said, "this is not a normal squadron."

Crowe's first impression of the Station Commander was hardly flattering. Of average size, with brown curly hair and a slightly weak chin, Noone did not look particularly military despite his immaculate uniform, razor-sharp creases and well-polished shoes. To Crowe he looked more like a librarian. The Group Captain's eyes scanned the assembled aircrew, looking first towards the fourteen neatly-turned out and experienced pilots and navigators who sat on one side of the briefing room, and then towards the six pale men in sunglasses and well-worn black overalls on the other. It was clear from the look of disdain on his face that Noone's first impression of the new arrivals was as poor as theirs of him.

"They tell me that our new colleagues can see in the dark," he continued, his voice dripping with scepticism, "that they are better than radar. They also tell me that they are excellent pilots. At this moment I have seen nothing to prove any of these claims. If you want my respect you must earn it. That goes for all of you, but especially those of you that require, let us say, special considerations." Crowe felt as much as heard the familiar murmur of distaste that spread around the room.

Crowe looked around him. The briefing room was not large and was close to capacity. The main lights were switched off, the room lit instead by a number of lamps placed along the side walls. By conventional standards it was dimly-lit, but Crowe knew that his own eyes would have been hurting from the brightness if it were not for his sunglasses. Behind the Group Captain was a large chalkboard, and there was a telephone on a small table. Of more interest were the other three men who sat against the wall in armchairs that looked far more comfortable than his own wooden seat. There was Harry Stead, looking slightly uncomfortable with the Group Captain's manner.

Next to him sat Dr Madeley, scribbling notes in a small black book and paying little attention to Noone's opening address. It was the third man, though, who really interested Crowe. The man's features were obscured by a tilted brown hat, which rose and fell slightly as he dozed, but Crowe did not need to see his face. He recognised the hat, as he did the crumpled brown suit. He'd only met the man a few times, but each meeting had been interesting. One had been life-changing. What was he doing here now?

"What do you think?" Crowe murmured as Noone continued his speech, referring to the slumbering figure as much as the speaker.

"I think the Group Captain likes us, don't you?" Morgan said. "If only he knew what lovely people we are when you get to know us. Apart from Raithe, obviously. I can't believe he's still not graced us with his presence."

"You really find that hard to believe?"

"Of course, I'm forgetting that in his mind the word 'grace' is meant literally."

"Am I interrupting your conversation, gentlemen?" Noone asked loudly. Virtually the whole room turned to look at them.

"Not at all, sir," Morgan said. "Please carry on."

Noone's eyes narrowed. "I understand that our newly-arrived and specially-gifted pilots have not received the full military education that the rest of us take for granted," he said. "I do not know how you conducted yourself during your training, but you are now allegedly officers in His Majesty's Royal Air Force, and while you are here I expect you to conduct yourself with the appropriate bearing. I appreciate for some of you that will be asking too much." His eyes were focused firmly on Crowe and Morgan, sitting at the back of the room.

"That is all," the Group Captain said.

"Room 'shun!" said Clark, rising to attention, the rest of his colleagues following with instant precision. The new men followed their lead, though slightly alarmed and with infinitely less enthusiasm. The difference in their responses was not quite as obvious as the contrast between the established pilots' blue-grey battle dress and the faded overalls of the new crews, but it did not go unnoticed. Noone, with a muttered word to Harry Stead, walked quickly from the room, his head turning to deliver a final poisonous stare towards Morgan.

"Oh," Morgan said, "he definitely likes us."

"Good evening, lads," Stead said pleasantly as he limped to the front of the room. In contrast to his commanding officer, Stead seemed at ease and happy to see them all. "I hope you slept well. For our new arrivals, I'm sorry your accommodation is not much and that we can't provide single rooms. Hopefully the double occupancy isn't too taxing." Crowe hadn't slept well, but it wasn't because of the double occupancy. He'd grown used to sharing with Morgan during the months of training in Wales. The new pilots shared a single storey hut, divided into four bedrooms plus ablutions and a small common room. The regular crews had a similar set-up, although due to their greater numbers they had two buildings. Their room had proved sparse with just a couple of side tables, one wardrobe and two comfortless beds, plus a single heavily shaded lamp. There was also a light switch on the wall for an electric bulb that hung unnecessarily from the ceiling. Crowe had suggested smashing it. Morgan, always the optimist, had wanted to keep it in case he ever had the chance to 'entertain'.

Dr Madeley was particularly unhappy with their domestic arrangements, as the rooms all had windows. Despite the heavy blackout curtains the doctor was concerned about the risk of accidental exposure to daylight.

"A few admin notices from me before we start," Stead said, drawing a sheet of paper from his pocket. "We've not had much time to work on this place since we took it over from the Yanks so the construction's a bit half-arsed, but with luck we'll be too busy hammering the Hun to care."

"I like him already," Werner murmured.

"The Mess is all-ranks. Breakfast will be served in the dining room from 1700 to 1900. Other meals will be dependent on the flying programme. Please take the time to read Station Routine Orders each day. There is a lot to take in but as we're an unusual station we have some unusual rules." There was a collective groan from the aircrew, and Morgan stifled a yawn.

"The engineers and support staffs are housed on the other side of the airfield. That is intentional. We're operating with a skeleton staff on this base and we want to segregate the aircrew as much as possible. Staverton and other local towns are off-limits to everyone."

"God, this is going to be fun," muttered Morgan.

Stead talked on for a few more minutes, trying to keep the audience interested.

"Harry," Dr Madeley interrupted, putting down his black book and rising with some difficulty from his chair. "Is it about time I said a few words? I'm sure your chaps have lots of questions."

Stead shook his head. "There's been a change of plan," he said, looking at the dozing figure in the hat. "We're to go ahead with a short test first. Two of my best, with radar, against two of your new boys."

"That's our cue," Morgan told Crowe, standing up.

"About time."

"Who's going up for us, Harry?" said one of the pilots, a thick-set Flight Lieutenant with a weather beaten face.

"You and Clark," Stead said. "And don't go easy on them, Geordie. We need to see what they can do."

"I must protest," the doctor said sternly. "My boys are tired. They've not recovered from their journey yet and they haven't flown in a week."

"Don't worry, doc," Morgan said. "We're ready."

"Shouldn't we at least have some idea what we're up against?" Clark said. "Not that I'm worried, but before we fly against them it would be nice to know what these freaks can do."

Morgan gave Crowe a look to warn him against responding, but Stead acted quickly to cut off the angry mutters from the new arrivals. "You'll find out, Clark," he said with a note of scorn in his voice. "If you're only half as good as you think you are you've got nothing to worry about."

"I'm going to enjoy this," Crowe said.

"There are four fuelled up aircraft waiting at dispersal," Stead continued. "Crowe and Morgan, you'll be flying Spitfires. Clark and Hulse, you'll be in your old NF-Two's with Barton and Lomax as your navigators. Make the most of your radar. If this test goes well, you won't be using it again. Your transport's waiting, so grab your kit and get up there. We'll see you in two hours for debriefing."

Throughout the whole discussion, the man in the hat hadn't said a word. It seemed he had simply slept on, but somehow Crowe knew he hadn't missed a thing.

The drive out to dispersal was unpleasant. The six men were crammed together with their flying kit into the canvas-covered rear compartment, and the atmosphere was less than friendly as the small lorry bounced uncomfortably on the uneven ground. Clark sat as far as possible away from the two new pilots, staring moodily out over the back ramp.

"Who was that bloke in the corner, anyway?" Geordie Hulse asked finally, breaking the silence.

"He recruited us," Crowe said. He cracked his knuckles.

"Oh." The silence descended again, until finally the truck came to a halt. The driver banged on the wooden partition and someone unhooked the rear ramp. Clark jumped down and walked away towards his aircraft.

Morgan reached into the thigh pocket of his black flying overalls, pulled out a monogrammed silver hip flask and offered it to Crowe. "Try some. It will improve your flying."

"Why do you always offer me that?"

"I'm hoping one day you'll accept," Morgan told him, a note of sadness in his voice, and then when Crowe shook his head he unscrewed the cap and took a sip. Even as he placed the flask back in his pocket his eyes closed and he began to shake slightly. Crowe looked away in slight disgust, and heard his friend's sharp intake of breath and the faintest of moans.

"Five hours until dawn," Crowe said. "Don't get lost."

"Don't worry about me," Morgan said, his eyes slowly opening. "Be lucky."

"I've never been lucky," Crowe said with a smile, and walked to his Spitfire.

There were few things that Crowe found beautiful, but the sleek Spitfire was definitely one of them. There was just something about the purity of its design. Every part of it, from the single Merlin engine to the long slim fuselage and the unmistakeable elliptical wings, seemed perfectly in balance and proportion. There was menace too, a sense of power that was focused in the partially obscured cannon and machine gun barrels in the wings. He had known the Spitfire by reputation long before he'd flown it, the fighter already a legend even before Crowe had been approached and recruited. Though he'd tried to ignore the war that raged on above London during the summer and autumn of 1940, he could not ignore the Londoners who seemed to speak of little else at night than the Spitfires they had seen by day.

The ground engineer was waiting with a clipboard, and helped Crowe strap himself into the tight cockpit. Crowe was polite to the man but otherwise ignored him, concentrating on his pre-flight checks. It had been months since he'd flown a Spitfire. They'd only had two of them in Wales, but he remembered how much fun they'd been to fly after the lumbering Harvard trainers. His first instructor, the normal one, had told them all how difficult the Spitfire was to land in the dark with its long nose and all that mass of engine obscuring the view to the faint landing lights. Difficult, that was, for a normal man, not for men like Crowe. That instructor hadn't lasted long; he'd been a good pilot but after three months every one of his pupils was better than he would ever be.

There was an exchange of gestures with the engineer. Crowe fired up the engine with a touch of the starter button. There was a cloud of smoke and a stab of flame which stung his eyes despite the thin aluminium flare dampers, designed to prevent the engine glow from blinding the pilot at night. They also did a job of keeping the glow concealed from the enemy, but Crowe would have preferred the proper flare dampers found on twin-engined aircraft. To his right he saw Morgan taxiing towards the runway. The two Mosquitoes were slowly coming to life, their propellers flickering in the dim light.

He thumbed the Receiver/Transmitter switch for his radio and contacted the tower. "Belfry from Blue Two," he said, "permission to taxi?" Belfry was the codename for Charney Breach's Control Tower.

"Okay Blue Two." That was it. Obviously the Controller wasn't feeling chatty tonight. Crowe followed Morgan out towards the runway, feeling the aircraft reverberating around him from the noise and power of the Merlin engine. He swung the aircraft from side to side as he taxied. The distinctive long nose had a habit of obstructing forward vision, and he didn't want to embarrass himself by ploughing into another aircraft before they were even in the air. Something was different about the aircraft, a few of the controls unfamiliar. "Morgan, are you reading me?"

"Blue Two from Blue One, yes I am. Surely we taught you better radio discipline than that?"

"Bollocks to it, we're just going out for a play. It's been a long time since I've flown one of these. I could only just remember how to start the thing."

"Blue Two from Blue One," Morgan persevered, "there are a few changes. This is the latest model, the Mark Nine. I've not flown one yet either. It should be fun."

They reached the runway and a quick call to the control tower gained them permission to take off. The two Mosquitoes were just beginning their taxi. Pulling up alongside Morgan on the runway,

Crowe gave him a smile. Morgan returned it with a thumbs-up, and then both opened the throttles and the Spitfires lurched forward in unison, bouncing slightly over the Pierced Steel Planking of the runway.

Crowe felt it the moment the wheels left the ground, the familiar sense of peace, of comfort. Nothing in his life had prepared him for the first time he took control of an aircraft, and the joy he had felt then had not dissipated with all the flying hours since. The sky waited above for him, vast and empty, and the night air extended its welcome to him. There was no sun to hide from here, no cold stone walls or damp earth enclosing him. Twenty years of living in the city and fleeing from the daylight was forgotten the instant the Spitfire was airborne, the moment he felt the graceful aircraft respond to his slow pull on the control stick.

At three hundred feet he closed the Perspex canopy. This was why he was here, why he put up with all the bullshit. This, he knew, would be the reason that whatever happened, he would try to put up with people like Clark, and why he would fly their missions for them, so that they would never have a reason to take this away from him. He looked over at Morgan, and remembered how their friendship had started, the shared delight in flying. He closed his eyes, took a deep breath, savouring the smell of leather and aviation fuel, before slowly letting it seep out and opening his eyes once more.

From the air his first impressions of Charney Breach were confirmed. The base lay on a virtual peninsula, surrounded on three sides by the marshy ground of the fens. The site had been chosen well. Though the small town of Staverton St Mary was only a few miles away, the area was otherwise uninhabited but for a few isolated farms.

For several minutes neither man spoke, content merely to enjoy the sensation of flying that both loved so much. They gained altitude quickly and comfortably, occasionally glancing down as Charney Breach dwindled beneath them, the Norfolk coast and Lowestoft ten miles to their east and the urban smudge of Norwich visible to the north. The weather, which had been awful for several days, was fairly clear, though there was little moon. It was cold in the cockpit, the cotton twill overalls unable to keep the frigid night air at bay, but Crowe hardly noticed it and knew Morgan wouldn't either.

"What do you think?" Crowe said finally, reluctantly breaking the silence as they passed twelve thousand feet.

"This is good. Oh, yes, this is good." Morgan didn't elaborate, but his breathless tone left no doubt that he was as happy with the Spitfire as Crowe was.

"Blue One from Forge One," Geordie Hulse said over the squadron frequency. "We are flying a search pattern south of home base and ready to begin the test."

"Roger Forge One, commencing test now."

Out there in the night, Crowe thought, was a pair of radar-equipped Mosquitoes, flown by two of the most experienced and battle-hardened pilots in the Royal Air Force, each veterans of fifty or more night combat missions. He was in an aircraft he had only flown a dozen times, about to fly against a live target for the first time in his life. It was a mismatch. He smiled, and looked over towards Morgan's cockpit, the other Spitfire almost close enough to touch. Morgan returned his smile, and nodded.

"Let's show them what we can do."

The two Spitfires pulled into a tight starboard turn, keeping close formation as they headed back towards the airfield. Crowe had never flown in a radar equipped aircraft but he knew enough about them to be able to envisage what the Mosquito crews would be doing now. They would not be flying in close formation like the Spitfires. To do so would risk a mid-air collision. Instead they would operate individually, each pilot relying on ground control and his radar operator's calls to guide him towards his target. For a regular pilot, Crowe had been told, visual range at night was rarely more than a thousand yards, and on a fairly dull night like this, probably five hundred.

Morgan spotted the first Mosquito at about four miles range. It was flying a slow zigzag at ten thousand feet. A few seconds later Crowe spotted the second, above them at fourteen thousand feet and three miles to the east.

"Belfry from Blue One, visual contact with both targets made," Morgan announced. Crowe smiled at the thought of the confusion this would cause at Charney Breach. The Control Tower staff had been briefed that the Squadron would be trialling new night vision equipment, and they would be stunned, breathlessly debating what manner of pilot aid could allow visual contact to be made at a range they knew to be several miles even as they tried even harder to bring Hulse and Clark to bear on their targets.

"Which one do you want, Blue Two?" Morgan asked.

"I'll go high, you go low."

Crowe pulled the Spitfire into a steep climb, hoping his target would be Clark. His finger twitched slightly, and with a sigh of disappointment he checked his weapons were in the 'safe' position. The Mosquito was about two miles and closing, still jinking slightly as it swept the sky. Crowe turned across its front, giving himself a little more time to gain altitude, watching as the Mosquito stopped turning and pointed straight at him. He must have made radar contact, but it didn't worry Crowe, not at this range. He had passed fifteen thousand feet now and banked sharply to bring his aircraft over the top of his opponent, still climbing. The Mosquito did not follow and in a few more seconds resumed its sweep pattern, the fleeting contact lost.

Crowe passed over the Mosquito and turned the Spitfire through a slow descending bank to bring him behind the target at a range of about eight hundred yards, thirty yards below it in the aircraft's blind-spot. He slowed the Spitfire down, aware of the risk of overshooting and content to slowly close on his target. There was no hurry, after all. At six hundred yards Crowe found himself admiring, not for the first time, the smooth and pretty lines of the Mosquito, the uncluttered profile and simple black paint scheme. The glow from the engine exhausts, invisibly dim by normal standards, was to his eyes a flaming beacon that was painful to look at. Two hundred yards now. Crowe regretfully noted that the aircraft's markings identified it as Hulse's.

The range was down to one hundred yards. He checked his pace to match the cruising Mosquito exactly, and waited. A glance to his left, to where two aircraft could be seen three miles away, one close behind the other, showed him he wouldn't have to wait long.

"Hello Forge Two, this is Blue One," Morgan said. "I'm awfully sorry to have to tell you this, but you just bought it."

"What?" Crowe could hear the confusion in Clark's voice. "You're lying."

"Forge Two, check your six o'clock high position." Morgan was obviously trying to conceal the triumph in his voice but was failing dramatically, and the stream of curses that filled the radio suggested that Clark had spotted the dark shadow fifty yards behind him. Crowe smiled. Clark would have been even more annoyed if he could have seen Morgan's victory roll in the darkness.

He turned back to his own target. "Forge One from Blue Two, claiming kill."

"Nothing seen, Blue Two." Crowe caught a glimpse of Lomax, Hulse's navigator, peering out into the night. Even at one hundred yards they were struggling to pick out the Spitfire against the dark carpet of the countryside below.

"Hold your course," Crowe said, releasing the full power of the Merlin engine. The Spitfire sprang forward like an unleashed animal and Crowe brought it over the top of the Mosquito, less than twenty yards above the crew's heads.

"Jesus!" he heard Hulse exclaim. "I never saw a thing!"

"They got lucky, Geordie," Clark said. "That's all."

"Shall we do it again?" Morgan asked. All pretence at radio discipline had gone now, washed away by the joy that rang in his voice.

Second time around the Mosquitoes were more alert, regularly weaving and breaking in an attempt to make themselves more elusive targets. It merely added to the difficulties faced by their navigators in attempting to pinpoint the target 'blip' on their radar screen. Crowe was disappointed to find himself targeting Hulse again but there was no radar contact with him this time. He quickly claimed his kill, Hulse accepting his victory call without demur. If anything Clark was even more outraged this time when Morgan secured his victory, the obscenities intensifying when his opponent dropped in front of him and performed a second elated victory roll.

"All call-signs from Belfry, return to base," came the order from the Control Tower.

"Spoilsports," Morgan sighed. "I was really starting to enjoy that."

They allowed the Mosquitoes to land first, enjoying the last chance to play with the new Spitfires. By the time Clark and Hulse had cleared the runway dawn was less than two hours away, and they were not kept waiting long before being directed in to land.

As Crowe clambered out of his aircraft he found Morgan waiting, a beaming smile on his face which hardly faded during the silent drive back. Again the seething Clark refused to acknowledge them, but twice Crowe caught Hulse looking at him quizzically. Both times the stocky man maintained Crowe's eye contact without any apparent nervousness.

The rest of the squadron was gathered in two distinct groups outside the main building when they arrived, waiting for news of the engagement. Clark was first out of the vehicle. He paused as he stepped down, looking up at Morgan with barely concealed hatred.

"Very impressive," he said. "It's a different business in a real fight, though. Good thing for you we weren't using our guns." He smiled, looking at his navigator. Bobby Barton, small and slim, laughed nervously at the remark, stopping abruptly the moment Clark was out of sight. He glanced at them, and Crowe saw the apologetic look in his eyes.

"Can we refuel and go up again?" Crowe said.

Morgan looked wistfully at the distant parked aircraft. "That would be nice. I really have missed it. But I don't think our friends would be up for it, do you?"

"They're embarrassed."

"Speaking of which," Morgan said, "we should go and make sure everyone knows how we got on." He smiled triumphantly at the thought.

"You go ahead," Crowe said. "I'm sure you'll enjoy it more."

"Too right I will. Don't take too long, you'll miss all the fun."

"Crowe," Geordie Hulse said as he stepped down last from the truck, "have you got a moment?"

"What is it?"

"Clark's going to be pissed off for a while. He's not happy that you beat him."

"Poor Clark. What about you?"

"Me? I don't like being beaten by anybody." Hulse smiled. "But you didn't just beat us. That was murder, pure and simple. Greg Lomax is one of the best radar operators around, and he never saw a thing."

"I think you spotted me briefly first time around."

"Maybe. It didn't do us any good. How far away did you see us?"

"Three miles. Maybe four. It would be further on a moonlit night."

"Jesus," Hulse said. "If you could see a German bomber at that range, at night," he added thoughtfully, his voice dwindling away.

"Was there anything else, Geordie? The doctor's going to tell you everything you need to know."

"One last thing," Hulse said, hesitating for a moment, but his eyes direct. "What is it like, when you see at night? Is it like how one of us would see during the day?"

From inside the building drifted the sounds of excited conversation, although Crowe barely heard them. Memories flashed across his mind, vague but insistent. A country park, a garden, a street, a childish game played with friends. His parents. And above them all, linking every dimly recollected scene, was the sun, its pleasant warmth upon his skin.

"I wouldn't know," Crowe told Hulse shortly, and walked away towards the waiting briefing room.

"Bloody hell!"

"I take it you're impressed, Harry?" Dr Madeley said with a satisfied smile after Hulse and Morgan had calmly relayed the details of the engagement to the waiting audience. Stead was professional enough to keep his shock mostly under wraps. His eyes, though, glowed with enthusiasm.

"The Germans aren't going to know what's hit them. I'd hoped all this bloody secrecy would be justified," he said, "and I reckon it is and then some. Can you imagine if the Germans found out we had…" Stead stopped, looking a little embarrassed. "I'm sorry; I don't have a bloody clue what to call you."

"Vampire is fine."

It was Werner who answered for them all, his accent as thick as ever. The immediate response was about what Crowe had expected. There was an audible intake of breath from the regular crews. They seemed surprised but not stunned, and Crowe guessed that the rumour mill on the station must have been going at full speed over the preceding days. He wondered how many of them wanted to walk out of the room right now in disgust, but he knew none of them would, not because they were too professional but because they wanted to know more.

"It is not something we're ashamed of," Werner added.

Morgan raised his hand. "We also answer to chaps, gents, guys, boys, fellers…"

"Lads…" Hinde suggested meekly.

"Thank you. Lads, mates, muckers…"

"They get it, Morgan," Crowe said.

"We don't really want any special treatment," Morgan continued. "We're all just men, after all."

There was a stifled titter, and Crowe saw the smile on Clark's face. How good it would feel to smash that smile away, dislodge some of those gleaming teeth with a right hook.

"Of course," Doctor Madeley said, "there are some differences. I think you should let me speak to them now, Harry."

"Be my guest, Byron."

41

Looking portly in his white woollen top and a pair of flannel trousers that struggled to contain his bulk, Doctor Madeley smiled warmly at the gathered aircrew. Every man in the room seemed poised on the edge of his seat.

"Good evening, all. Some of you will already know me, others will not. My name is Dr Byron Madeley, and I will be the Medical Officer for the Station. I've been a practicing doctor for over forty years. Recently, however, I have become the nation's leading expert on vampirism." He paused, as if thinking about that statement. "You may think me arrogant, but believe me I am not exaggerating. Experts on vampirism are really rather few and far between."

The rumours were being confirmed. Crowe could tell every man in the room was giving the doctor his full attention. No, he corrected himself, there was one exception. The man in the hat had not stirred.

"Dispel any ideas you might have about vampires. What you may have gleaned from Bram Stoker's Dracula or Bela Lugosi movies bears no resemblance to the truth. The single most important thing to recognise is that vampirism is a medical condition. However, you won't find it in any medical textbook and don't ask me the scientific name for it because there isn't one yet. No study has ever been published. What we do know is that it is hereditary. Some people are born with the condition, others develop it as they get older, but all suffer the same rather drastic symptoms, which become more acute the longer the condition continues. Some of these symptoms will directly affect their relationship with the rest of the squadron.

"Firstly, the skin becomes incredibly photo-sensitive. Basically, sunlight kills. It burns and blisters the skin at an incredible rate, causing massive damage, terrible pain and, depending on the brightness and directness of the light, death through shock within a matter of minutes. That's why you won't see any of the vampires during daytime, and why their rooms have such thick blackout curtains. The second symptom is the eyes. Morgan, would you lower your glasses for a moment?"

Morgan slipped his sunglasses down so his unshielded eyes were visible. At first there was little reaction as people struggled to see in the dimly-lit room. Then, predictably, there were gasps. A few recoiled. The majority, though, seemed to lean towards Morgan as one, keen to get a closer look at the dark orbs and the elongated feline pupils that were already contracting tightly in the harsh light.

"The eyes become much like those of a nocturnal animal," Dr Madeley told them, their eyes still on Morgan. "Within the eye there are what we call rods and cones. Without getting too technical, cones work in bright light and register detail, while rods work in low light and detect motion and basic visual information. The ratio of rods to cones in a vampire eye is about seven times that in a normal human eye. This has drawbacks; vampire eyes are immensely sensitive to light, hence the sunglasses, and the picture they provide lacks definition. Vampires are largely colour-blind. That said, a vampire's eyes are at least as effective at night as yours are during the day."

Even though that had already been demonstrated to them, the dawning understanding of how much difference this would make to their effectiveness as night fighter pilots was gratifying. Hulse in particular seemed enthused by the prospect. Clark tried to look disinterested.

Morgan's eyes were watering from the light, but he maintained his posture until finally, with the doctor's thanks, he slipped the glasses back into place. Crowe could see his facial muscles twitching as he tried to blink away the pain.

"Thank you, Morgan," Dr Madeley said. He was smiling at the effect the revelation was having on his audience. "The third important symptom is the reflexes. Cat-like would be a minor exaggeration but a vampire can generally process information and react to stimuli at least twice as fast as any ordinary man. This is part of the reason why they make such naturally gifted pilots."

They were definitely intrigued now, chattering amongst themselves. Dr Madeley was forced to raise his voice to be heard. "I will be available in my office down the corridor each night if anyone wants more details. In the meantime are there any questions?

Geordie Hulse stood up respectfully. "I'm sorry if this is a daft question, but in the myths, vampires drink blood. What about this lot?"

"Would you smile for me, Morgan?" Morgan grinned easily, looking comfortable with the attention. "Thanks again. As you can see, the whole sharp fangs thing is just folklore. There is however some truth in it. For some reason science cannot yet explain, the drinking of fresh blood provides a boost to an already quite remarkable constitution and capacity for regeneration. It also feeds certain basic nourishment requirements that, for whatever reason, vampires cannot effectively provide through a normal human diet.

43

Animal blood is sufficient but human blood works most effectively, rather like the difference between cow's milk and mother's milk. For the last year I've been providing enough blood, through medical sources, to satisfy their needs. Does that answer the question?"

Hulse opened his mouth to answer but Clark cut him off. "Can we get infected?"

"Excuse me?"

"This condition," Clark said shortly. He did not stand. "Is it contagious? Could we get infected?"

Dr Madeley frowned. "Did I not say it was hereditary? It is not an infection. Don't worry, Clark, you won't become a vampire."

"You are not worthy to be a vampire," a voice said harshly. All eyes turned towards the speaker.

The seventh vampire stood framed in the doorway. He was a tall man, with long dark hair, and while all the vampires were pale, the complexion of the new arrival was close to marble and his features harsh enough to have been carved from it. He was clearly older than the other vampires, with only the Austrian Lieberwitz seeming close to him in age. His thin face gave him the look of a forty year old. He was as close in appearance to the archetypal vampire of legend as could be imagined. On his right hand he wore an ostentatious silver ring; Crowe also caught a brief glimpse of the thick silver chain he wore around his neck, below the flying suit. With an arrogance that was palpable even from across the room, he slowly turned his head as he scanned the audience.

"Ah, Raithe," Dr Madeley said. "It's so nice of you to join us. Where have you been?"

"Listening. Watching. It was an interesting presentation, Madeley. As usual you focused only on the negatives."

"I believe I made it clear that the symptoms of vampirism can be useful?"

"Useful to them, you mean?" the vampire sneered.

Morgan stood up. "Why don't you take a seat, Raithe?" he asked reasonably, though not entirely able to conceal his dislike.

Raithe smiled, without any such attempt at concealment. "Of course, Bale. I would not miss your pathetic attempts to impress your beloved humans."

"Raithe." The word was spoken in a pleasant enough tone, but the faint note of warning was enough. The man in the hat was no longer sleeping. He rose slowly to his feet, and as he did so Raithe silently took a seat on the back row, his face cold and emotionless.

With a nod to Dr Madeley, the man took his place in the centre of the room. As always, Crowe found himself both puzzled and amused by his appearance. He was a big man, and would have been taller but for a slight stoop. He could have been anywhere between forty and sixty, his lined face suggesting age but the thick forearms and neck hinting at a still-formidable physical power. Beneath the shadow of the hat his cheeks and nose carried a suggestive redness, but his voice was precise and the hand that picked up a piece of chalk and began to write on the board was faultlessly steady.

When he had finished, he turned his back to the simple message and stood gazing dispassionately at the men before him. Behind him the words 'K Department' stood out in large bleak letters.

"Who knows what this means?"

Seven pale vampire hands went slowly up. No one said a word.

"Good," the man said. "That's the way it is supposed to be. None of you will ever mention those words to anyone other than Noone and the others sitting here. To do so would not be," and for several seconds he paused, as if concentrating intently on finding the right word, "tolerated."

Morgan glanced at Crowe, his expression a familiar blend of respect and amusement. The man turned again and erased the words from the board.

"My name is Quentin Quiet," he said, "and I work for the British Government. On one side of this room sit the top pilots and navigators of one of the finest night fighter squadrons the RAF has produced in three years of war. On the other side sit a group of people you probably thought existed only in fairy tales and cheap novels. Together you will be the most dangerous night fighter squadron in the world."

It was not a stirring speech. It was simply a statement of fact. Crowe could see, though, that they all instantly believed it.

Quiet smiled. "I don't believe in motivational speeches. I don't believe in wasting your time, and you won't waste mine. In three days this squadron will be operational again with a new name, and some of you are probably wondering how things are going to work. Tomorrow we will take delivery of three new navigators and six of the latest model Mosquitoes. Want to know what you'll be flying in? Pay attention now."

Without any hesitation or recourse to notes, Quiet began to reel off names. "Bale, Clark, Crowe, Werner, Hulse and Masters, you will be flying Mosquitoes. Mosquito Leader will be Bale." Morgan grinned at Crowe, seemingly oblivious to the mutterings from the established two-seater pilots and navigators, outraged that a vampire had been put in charge of them. Clark looked stunned.

Hinde leaned towards Crowe, the smell of tobacco hanging unpleasantly on him. "Look at Clark's face," the Swiss whispered. "He looks like someone slapped him."

"The Spitfires," Quiet continued, "will be flown by Raithe, Gorecki, Mills, Barnes, Lieberwitz, Mortimer, Rhys-Jones, Slater, Hinde, Owen, Farnham and Sullivan." He could have simply said 'everyone else', thought Crowe, but then that wouldn't have been half as impressive. A mischievous glint came into Quiet's eyes. "Spitfire Leader," he said, pausing long enough to gain their undivided attention, "will be Raithe."

Where Morgan's appointment had met with suppressed annoyance, Raithe's was met with open dismay. Not one of the original squadron had met Raithe until three minutes earlier. Clearly he'd made an instant impression. Several of the pilots protested loudly to Quiet, although without effect. Even some of the vampires shifted uneasily, though most made certain to hide their uneasiness from Raithe. The new Spitfire Leader didn't even blink, aloof to the mutterings and cries around him.

"Congratulations," Crowe murmured to Morgan. "Can you handle the pressure?"

"Less of your insolence. I was your instructor, remember? Have some respect." He smiled. "I'm a bit disappointed to get Mosquitoes. That Spitfire was so good. I almost wish I was going to be flying one of those instead."

"Maybe you could swap with Raithe?"

"What, and inflict him on some poor navigator? You're the cruel one, not me."

"Enough," Quiet said finally, holding up a hand. "If anyone has any burning issues with the personnel allotment they can take them up with Noone. I can assure you," he added with subtle but undeniable emphasis, "it won't make an ounce of difference."

Quiet looked out over the audience, his eyes hidden in shadow. The squadron in front of him had been together for twenty-four hours but, as Crowe looked over at the faces of his new colleagues, he knew they were a long way from being united. It seemed Quiet knew it too. For a long time he stood in silence, his face unreadable, his body relaxed as if he were enjoying the tension in the room.

"Combat ops start tomorrow night." And with that, leaving the regular pilots and the vampires eyeing each other in a wary silence, Quiet turned and walked from the room.

Chapter Three

"Good God," Morgan said, "they've sent us schoolboys."

"They are a bit young," Stead admitted as Crowe and Werner followed him into the deserted mess hall. The rows of tables still showed the detritus of the evening's breakfast. "Some bugger at Fighter Command must think we're not important enough to waste experienced navigators on. But they all come with top-notch reports from their training establishment."

"None of them have flown any operational sorties at all?" Crowe asked incredulously as the three young Sergeants stood to attention.

"Neither have we, to be fair," Morgan said. "I'm sure they'll do just fine. Which one's mine?"

Stead looked down at his list. "Danny Baggers."

"That's me, sir," said a small, wiry figure, stepping forward. "Everybody calls me Bags." Crowe saw Stead frown slightly, presumably at the state of Baggers' hair, which was blond and scruffy.

"Morgan Bale," said the vampire, stepping forward and offering a hand.

"Nice to meet you, sir," Baggers said with a smile. "If you don't mind me saying, you all look pretty normal to me. I mean, you're not as weird looking as they said."

"Who said?" Werner asked with a note of danger in his voice.

"The other pilots. They said you were right weird looking freaks." Baggers winced at his own words. "Sir," he added.

"Well," Morgan smiled, "it's nice to be noticed."

"But it is true, though? That you're vampires?"

Morgan dropped his sunglasses to show his eyes. All three were clearly startled. The plump Sergeant on Baggers' left visibly shrank away.

"Bugger me," Baggers said.

"I'd rather not."

"Nice sunglasses though. Where can I get a pair?"

"If I get shot down, you can have mine."

"Won't I be with you at the time?"

"Not if you're this cheeky in the cockpit. You'll be out of the side window and still trying to climb back in when you hit the ground."

"Right," Stead said, "which one of you is Ronnie Hall?" A tall dark navigator stepped smartly forward. He looked like the oldest of the three, and had about him an air of competence which appealed to Crowe.

"At ease, lad. You'll be flying with Werner."

"Damn it," Crowe exclaimed, far more loudly than he'd intended. The others turned to him in surprise. The plump navigator looked close to tears.

Werner stepped forward, silently looking Hall up and down. The young man stayed rigidly at attention as the German paced slowly around him before halting a few inches away, staring at him, with his shaven head bowed forward so close as to almost touch foreheads. The vampire was an intimidating sight at the best of times, but now he pushed back his own sunglasses and the three navigators jumped as they saw the empty socket where his left eye had once been.

"Bloody hell," Stead muttered. "What happened to him?"

"We don't know. He's never told us," Morgan whispered.

"Can he shoot straight with only one eye?"

"If you ever see me miss," Werner said without turning, "you ask again." His eye never left his new navigator. "What do you think of Nazis, Hall?"

"Hate them, sir," Hall said, his eyes still on the dark ravaged hole. "My brother was killed in the Battle of Britain."

Werner nodded, and let the sunglasses drop back into place. "He will do," he said. The sound of Hall exhaling in relief could probably have been heard a mile away at dispersal.

"I guess that's us," Crowe said wearily to the final navigator. "What's your name?"

"Jones, sir," the boy stammered. "Stephen Jones." Crowe looked at him more closely, ignoring the hand that the navigator tentatively offered. Jones looked even younger than his companions. He was visibly shaking. His uniform was neatly pressed, but Crowe could see tramlines on his dark blue trousers where the front crease had been missed one too many times.

"How old are you, Jones?"

"Nineteen, sir."

"Nineteen?" Crowe turned to the others in mock disbelief, winking at the grinning Morgan. "You look about twelve. Are you a vampire?"

"No, sir," Jones said, a little too quickly for Crowe's liking.

"Have you got something against vampires, Jones?"

"No, sir," Jones squeaked, his hand still hovering between them as if frozen in place.

"You know it's true, Crowe," Morgan said languorously, "you really are a nasty bastard."

Danny Baggers leaned over, and nudged Jones. "I told you you'd need that spare flying suit, didn't I?" he whispered as Crowe walked over to where Stead stood waiting by the door.

"Come on," Crowe said, being careful to lower his voice. "There's got to be more experienced navigators available."

"I'm sorry, son. Go easy on them, will you? Everybody has to start somewhere."

"He's got a point, Harry," Morgan said, joining them. "We start combat sorties tonight. We're going to be busy flying the planes, and if we have to try and bring our navigators up to speed too it's going to put a hell of a strain on the pilot. I'm not worried about myself, you understand, but a lesser pilot, like Crowe, could really struggle."

"It's bollocks, I know," Stead said as Crowe gave Morgan a threatening look, "but it's out of our hands. From what I hear Quentin Quiet has really put Fighter Command's noses out of joint, taking over this squadron. I mean, we were one of the best they had. I don't think we can expect any real help from them."

"Politics," Crowe said contemptuously.

"You said it," Morgan agreed. "Toys thrown out of the pram all 'round."

"These lads are all good, though," Stead said. "All they need is a bit of confidence and they'll be fine. Don't complain too much, Crowe, you've got the one with the best report."

"Lucky me."

"Unlucky him," Morgan added. The two vampires looked forlornly over at the three navigators. Werner, pleased with Hall's commitment to his anti-Nazi crusade, now appeared to be questioning Jones, leaving the young man wearing an expression of bemused terror.

"Right, then," Stead said loudly, "if you've quite finished scaring the life out of the new boys, I think it's time you met your new aircraft. They arrived this afternoon."

"The Mosquito NF II, Special Duties variant," said the moon-faced chief technician proudly when Crowe and Jones reached their aircraft. "It's the latest model. In fact, it isn't even officially ready yet. The rest of the RAF won't be getting hold of this beauty for at least another three months. Somebody up there loves you."

"How's it different from the bomber version?" Crowe asked.

The man snorted. "Where do I start? It's been developed from the night fighter variant, so it's as manoeuvrable as you could want and will still outrun anything the Germans can put in the sky, but it can also carry four two hundred and fifty pound bombs. And it's got one hell of a punch. Four machine guns in the nose, and four of these." He pointed to the dull steel barrels jutting out from the fuselage beneath the cockpit. "Twenty millimetre Hispano cannons, guaranteed to ruin Jerry's day."

"Have you flown in Mosquitoes before?" Crowe asked Jones as he adjusted the leather chin strap of his helmet.

"Yes, sir, a few times. We did a conversion course."

"This uniform means nothing to me. My name is Crowe. Not 'sir', Crowe. Understand?"

"Yes, sir," Jones squeaked.

The Chief Tech walked away to talk to Morgan. It was left to Dom, a short, slightly rounded man who was one of the ground crew, to sign their aircraft over to Crowe and to see them off. Crowe did a quick circuit of the aircraft to make sure everything looked okay. A handful of men scurried around him, ensuring the battery cart was in position and that all their checks were complete. Dom was standing under the starboard wing, his hands tight on the ladder leading up to the cockpit. Crowe turned away while he slipped his sunglasses off, shielding his eyes from the glow of the belly light which allowed others on the ground to see them but which was invisible from above. He clambered up and squeezed through the narrow doorway into his seat on the port side, scanning the controls in front of him and familiarising himself with them once again. There were a few changes from the versions he had flown before but, he decided, nothing to get too excited about. The two main throttle levers were still there to his left with their black handles, with the two white-topped levers for RPM control just right of them. Two large push buttons on a panel mounted just right of centre and at the top of the console were used for feathering and stopping the propellers in mid-flight. Centre mounted below the windscreen were three pull-down switches, which were the radiator shutter and air-intake filter switches. To their immediate right he recognised the rudder trimming tab and indicator, and just below the right bottom corner of the central instrument panel were two levers; the left for bomb doors selection and the other for undercarriage. All fuel and general electrics switches were on the starboard side of the cockpit, by the navigator's right hand, or at least where the navigator's right hand would have been if he had been anywhere to be seen.

"Are you coming?" Crowe called, and heard the frantic scrambling on the ladder as Jones hurriedly boarded, his Mae West life preserver snagging on the doorway. Crowe's own preserver was still in the dispersal hut. None of the vampires would take them. Better to drown than be caught floating in the sea when dawn came.

He secured himself in his seat, pulling two straps over his shoulders and two up from the sides of his seat. He locked them together with the brass pin. Jones did the same, fidgeting uncomfortably in his seat, mounted slightly lower than Crowe's. The Mosquito's cockpit was just as snug as Crowe remembered it. He slipped on his flame-retardant black leather flying gloves.

"Have you got all your maps?"

"Yes, sir," Jones said, double checking the small box at his right knee before noticing the look on the vampire's face and adding "Crowe." A mixed look of fascination and trepidation appeared on the navigator's round face, and Crowe knew that Jones was looking at his eyes, seeing them properly for the first time.

"Relax," Crowe said. "This is a practice flight. Just remember your training." He knew that the prospect of facing the Germans was not foremost in the boy's mind at that moment, but Crowe wanted it to be. They might not be looking for trouble, but there were still enough German night intruders and hit-and-run bombers over Britain each night to make it possible that they would find something. The boy looked so young that Crowe wondered if he would be up to the job. If not he would have to be replaced, and soon.

Dom pulled the ladder away. "Okay, Crowe?" he called.

"Okay."

The door was slammed shut and the latch turned from the outside. Crowe plugged in his intercom and opened the small panel in the Perspex next to him. "Contact," he yelled through the gap. The call was returned by the man at the battery cart. With what he hoped was a reassuring smile to Jones, Crowe pressed hard on the start button for the port engine. The prop turned lazily twice and then the engine burst into life with a roar. A second later and he pressed the button for the starboard engine, which misfired before catching properly. Crowe winced at the flash of light from the exhaust before the flare dampers kicked in.

He brought the engines to taxi speed and requested permission to taxi from Control. He decided against reminding Jones of any of the matters he needed to attend to, wanting to see if the navigator could get them right first time without prompting. There would be time to complain later, but in the meantime this was supposed to be a practice flight. Better that Jones made his mistakes now and learned from them, while there was still time.

A word from Control and the chocks were pulled away by the ground crew. Dom signalled to them, his hands empty where normally he would have needed flashlights, beckoning them to pull out onto the taxi strip. Crowe followed the signals, until within less than a minute they were at the end of the runway and ready to go. He made sure the brakes were on and then pushed the throttles slowly forward until the revolutions per minute reached three thousand and the wooden frame of Mosquito shuddered with the suppressed power.

"Mosquito Three, you are cleared for take off." At Morgan and Raithe's behest the control tower had abandoned the previous unwieldy call-signs. The night missions they would be flying would be quite unlike anything ever seen before, and fast simple communication was going to be crucial.

Crowe released the brakes, and the aircraft lurched forward. He caught a glimpse of Werner's Mosquito taxiing alongside and then the speed was increasing rapidly and the other aircraft was left behind. The tail came up just as they roared past the control tower. At just under one hundred miles an hour Crowe pulled back and the aircraft lifted, soaring over the twisted trees at the end of the runway. Crowe noted with some satisfaction that Jones reached out to switch off the belly light at just the right moment, and then he himself reached forward and yanked up on the undercarriage lever.

They were airborne. Crowe held the aircraft steady as he slowly gained height and altitude. He had heard of Mosquitoes crashing due to unnecessarily violent manoeuvres at low speeds and altitudes. Twisting in his seat he saw that Werner was airborne, with Morgan barrelling down the runway behind him.

Looking past the two Mosquitoes, he was struck again by how basic the setup at Charney Breach was. The nature of the operation meant that personnel numbers were minimal, with barely fifty engineers and forty support staff employed. There weren't many buildings. Other than the Station Headquarters there were just Spartan huts to provide accommodation, assorted hangers and a control tower that was easily the tallest building on the site. From this simple base, though, the squadron could intercept any German bomber raid against London or the east coast. Ultimately, that was all that mattered.

"How are we doing?" he asked Jones.

"Good, I think," Jones said, the words punctuated with exaggerated nodding. "Everything looks fine. What course did you want setting?"

"I don't care. You choose."

"Me?"

"Where do you want to go?"

Jones looked stunned at the question. "Well," he said finally, "my family are from Hull. My Mum sends me letters saying the Germans have been bombing them, but I haven't been home for ages." He paused for a few seconds. "I miss it," he added quietly.

"Let's go, then. Set us a course and we'll have a bit of a play on the way." He thumbed the transmitter switch on his radio. "Mosquito Leader from Mosquito Three, are you receiving?"

"Ah, radio discipline at last," came the laconic reply. "Maybe you're brighter than you look."

Crowe ignored that. "We're going to Hull. You coming?"

"What the hell do you want to go to Hull for?"

"Jones says it's lovely there this time of year. I'll race you."

"You're on, little man. Just don't expect to win."

Crowe opened the throttles fully and took the aircraft up to its maximum cruising speed. The Mosquito's performance was already legendary after only a year in service, but it was still a pleasant experience to be reminded of it. Behind him he saw that Morgan and Werner were closing the gap, and so he took the aircraft up to full speed, the engines roaring as their considerable horsepower propelled the lightweight airframe across the sky. In what seemed like only a few minutes Crowe found himself looking down through a layer of patchy cloud onto the English coast, the Humber estuary and the sleeping, blacked out city of Hull. Even from ten thousand feet, Crowe could see the areas of severe damage inflicted by the "Baedeker" raids the previous April, German revenge attacks for the increasing civilian casualties being inflicted on the Fatherland by Bomber Command.

Crowe slowed the Mosquito and made a gentle turn above the city. Werner dived towards the buildings below and then pulled his aircraft into a steep climb which brought him within a few hundred feet of Crowe's idling aircraft. Crowe saw the German wave cheerily at him as he passed. Morgan closed into formation off Crowe's starboard wing, startling Jones when he drifted to within fifty yards.

"I take it all back," Morgan said. "There's nothing I'd rather fly than a Mossie. What a machine!" He flicked the aircraft into a quick roll, holding it perfectly steady on its axis. Crowe, as always, watched Morgan show off his natural flying skills with envy. The gap between their abilities had narrowed massively since those first days the previous winter when Morgan had begun teaching the other vampires, but Crowe knew he could only dream of matching Morgan's skill. "Hey," Morgan added, a boyish enthusiasm in his voice, "have you tried it on one engine yet?"

"What do you mean?"

"Give it a try. Switch off your starboard engine and see what you think."

Jones didn't look too impressed at the prospect as Crowe reached out without hesitation and pressed the button to kill the engine. The starboard prop swung slowly to a halt, and Crowe put the aircraft into a shallow dive to maintain his airspeed. To his surprise, though, the effect of losing one engine was relatively minimal. The aircraft lost a little speed, and did not turn with quite the same grace, but it handled and flew well. He pulled up and found he could still climb, and swung the aircraft around to bring his nose to bear on Morgan's aircraft with little fuss from the remaining engine. "Unbelievable," he murmured.

"Good, isn't it? I wouldn't want to take on half a dozen fighters on only one engine, but it's rather nice to know I'd still get home."

Crowe noticed that since he had feathered the propellers, Jones had been gripping the edge of his seat with such force that his fingers were in danger of ripping the leather. He reached out and pushed the starboard restart button. The props began to turn once more and the engine caught. He looked idly down to watch Werner throwing his Mosquito through a series of increasingly violent turns, and caught sight of a flash of movement well beyond the vampire's aircraft.

"Unidentified aircraft, my four o'clock low."

"I see them," Morgan said. "Four bandits, angels one."

"Speak English," Werner muttered, sounding more German than ever.

"Four enemy aircraft, one thousand feet," Morgan translated impatiently.

"I can't see them," Jones said, pressing his face to the Perspex, but Crowe ignored him.

"Are they British?" Werner said.

"Not likely. Not at that altitude, anyway. My guess is Dornier bombers out of Holland."

"Excellent," muttered Werner. "We report the sighting?"

"No point. Someone would just ask awkward questions about how we'd spotted them."

"*Gut.* Then we do not have to share."

"Okay, boys. Remember your training. Nothing fancy. Just get in close and give them the good news."

"Let's get on with it," Crowe said.

"Follow my lead," Morgan said, and put his aircraft into a dive.

Crowe was already ahead of him. He felt a rush of exhilaration as they plunged towards the four tiny blobs in the distance. Twelve months of training had led him to this. He felt no fear, nor even the possibility of fear, only a growing desire to engage the targets and to carry out the task which nature and his training had prepared him for so well.

The four bombers began to climb as they closed in on the unsuspecting city. In a few short minutes they would be over the houses below and would empty their bomb loads onto the sleeping civilians beneath. Crowe felt the aggression rising in him. He didn't think of the enemy crews as people. At that moment they were an opponent, not to be hated or pitied but simply to be crushed. The Mosquito was shaking slightly with the buffeting from the air, the hands on his altimeter spinning as he dropped altitude towards the four bombers. He could see them more clearly now, each about five hundred yards from its neighbour, long, skinny aircraft with two engines, bigger than the Mosquito and lacking its beauty. Morgan had been right. They were Dorniers, with a crew of four men. One man in each crew would be scanning the sky behind them, hunched over a machine gun. For a moment Crowe contemplated attacking them head on, but with such a high approach speed he knew he'd probably miss. Instead he pulled the Mosquito out of its dive, passed by them at about a mile's distance, and then pulled the aircraft in a sharp turn to get behind them. Werner, he saw, had kept pace with him throughout and was less than a hundred yards behind them now. For a moment he'd lost sight of Morgan, and then saw his friend's Mosquito drop down from above to take up a position close behind the bombers.

"How the hell did he get there?" Crowe said into the intercom, annoyed yet impressed. Jones, who had seen nothing but the spinning altimeter since they started their dive, looked like he might vomit.

"I'll take the two on the right," said Morgan. "Werner, the one on the extreme left is yours. Crowe, take the middle left. Hold your fire until I open up. There's no sense in letting them know we're here, eh?"

"Why do you have two?" Werner asked, but Morgan ignored him. They were six hundred yards away and closing fairly quickly, and Crowe's mind flashed back to the practice engagement against Hulse. The gap was still shortening, and he began to worry about the risk of overshooting. But he trusted Morgan, and resisted the urge to open fire as the bombers loomed closer, oblivious to the three killers lurking in the darkness just behind them.

"I can see them," Jones announced excitedly, and although Morgan could not have heard his schoolboy voice on their internal intercom, it was as if that was the signal he had been waiting for.

With a sudden shocking flash the four machine guns in his Mosquito's nose and the four cannon beneath opened up simultaneously. At two hundred yards range against a target flying straight and level, Morgan could hardly miss. It took only a short burst. Even as Crowe pressed his firing stud, Morgan's target crumpled and burst into flames, falling to the right towards the waiting sea.

The first few rounds passed beneath the Dornier's port wing, but in an instant Crowe corrected and brought his aim up just as the bomber tried to evade. A stream of cannon shells ripped through the aircraft's fuselage and canopy, and Crowe saw the stunned look on the rearmost gunner's face as the cockpit and crew members around him simply dissolved in the hail of impacting rounds. The bomber dropped slowly away.

Crowe looked away to his left and saw that Werner was still closing in on his target and had not yet fired. The bomber's pilot must have seen the attacks on his comrades and was now weaving from side to side, but it did him little good. Werner closed to within fifty yards before opening up, and his rounds smashed through the aircraft's starboard wing. Crowe blinked as sudden light flared from the engine. Werner ceased his firing as the flames spread but stayed close as the stricken bomber began to burn along its whole length. Crowe could not understand the words that Werner muttered into the radio, but the harshness and venom of his tone was unmistakeable.

Morgan was closing fast on the final bomber, whose crew had clearly decided enough was enough and had turned back towards the open sea as soon as the firing had begun. The bomber was at full throttle but it had no hope against the faster and more agile Mosquito. Darkness, the night bomber's greatest ally, was no longer any protection. Morgan only closed to within three hundreds yards this time, before firing a perfectly judged burst of fire which must have struck something vital, as the Dornier exploded with sudden violence. Morgan gave a cry of elation as he put the aircraft into a victory roll. The burning fragments tumbled through the air before splashing down into the sea.

"I'm still not sure what happened," Jones admitted as they sat in the dispersal hut waiting for Harry Stead. The building was little more than a shed, with sparse furnishings. On one wall a board listed crews and their assignments, although for the moment it was blank. There were maps on the walls for the navigators, two telephones, some chairs and a large table for working out flight plans. On a normal station, Crowe guessed, this room would probably be a lot busier. It was where crews gathered to plan their ops and to await the call to run to their waiting aircraft and get airborne. At Charney Breach it was little more than a debriefing room.

"Why were they flying so low?" Jones mused aloud. "Weren't they scared of crashing into the sea?"

"Not as scared as they were of radar-guided night fighters," Morgan said. "They knew that radar would struggle to pick them out at such a low altitude."

"It didn't help them," Werner said, his joy unmistakeable. He looked over at Morgan. "I still don't understand why you get to have two and we only get one each."

"I'm Mosquito Leader," Morgan said, proudly. "That means, my murderous Teutonic chum, that I get first dibs on any extras. However," he added, seeing the sour look of rebellion on the German's face, "I suppose you can have the extra one next time."

"What was that you said up there, Werner?" Crowe said. "When you shot your bomber down?"

"Favri curse," Werner replied simply.

Crowe wanted to press him further, but at that moment Harry Stead walked in, a broad smile on his face. "I'm told you boys had some trade tonight? I thought it was supposed to be just a practice sortie."

"Well," Morgan said, "you could say we got some practice, couldn't you? That reminds me, I meant to ask the engineers how many rounds I'd used."

"Why?"

"I hate to waste them. Get close and be accurate, that's my motto."

"Spot on," Stead said, nodding appreciatively. "Now lads, I know you'll want to get back and celebrate, but business first. As you know, I'm the Intelligence Officer here as well as just about every other job title under the sun, so I'll try to see you after every sortie. So," he said, taking out his notebook, "make yourselves comfortable and talk me through it."

"Well," began Morgan, "we were flying over Hull."

"Hull? What on earth possessed you to go there?"

"Who wouldn't want to go there?" Morgan said dryly with a glance at Jones, before talking Stead through the mission.

"You got all four?" Stead said, shocked.

"Two for him," Werner said sourly with a nod at Morgan. "One for me, one for Crowe."

"Four," Stead repeated. "My God, we're not even operational yet and you've just got more kills in one night than the entire squadron managed in the last two months before we were grounded. Dorniers, you say?"

There were more questions, about the formation the enemy had been flying, their altitude, their manoeuvres on reaction to enemy fire, the effectiveness of the brand new Mosquito's armament and its stability as a gun platform. Crowe let Morgan handle the enquiries. He was thinking back to his Dornier, and the look of terror on the gunner's face as the damaged aircraft plunged towards the waves, his three colleagues already dead. He still felt no anger towards them. His overriding emotion was a sense of satisfaction. He'd seen them at three miles range or more, and yet the tail gunner had not been able to see the fighter that condemned him to death even a few hundred yards away, as he was carried down to the sea below.

He realised that the others had stood and were making their way to the transport outside. As Crowe rose to his feet and made to follow, he saw Stead's eyes watching him.

"First time you ever killed someone?"

Crowe didn't reply. The Squadron Leader, he noted, wrongly took that as a yes.

"It gets easier, I assure you," Stead told him gently. "I don't know if that is a good thing or a bad thing. I find it helps if you don't think about the crew. Just think about the aircraft. You shot down one bomber, and you and all your colleagues came home alive. Consider it a job well done."

Crowe nodded, but remained silent.

Stead sighed. "You know, son, I've got fifteen kills. Fifteen aircraft destroyed, some single seat, some bombers, maybe thirty men dead? I'm not proud of that. But I'd rather thirty of them than ten of my colleagues or, most importantly of all, one of me." He smiled. "Come on, let's get a beer before they drink the bloody place dry."

By the time they reached the Mess Stead had regained his joviality. He had personally congratulated each of them at least twice, while the three navigators were beaming with pride that their first sortie should have been so successful. Werner had apparently forgiven Morgan for his gluttony and the two continued busily discussing the details of their kills as they clambered from the truck and led the way into the bar.

Crowe trailed in their wake. A couple of drinks and he would sleep well, at least until the dreams started. No amount of alcohol stopped his dreams.

The bar was close to full. Most of the non-vampire pilots were gathered in small groups, and Crowe could hear them discussing their new aircraft. A few looked intrigued as the three black-clad vampires walked in. Clark was stood at the bar talking to the girl behind it. He tried to appear oblivious to the new arrivals, but was unable to hide the look of disgust on his face as they were greeted with triumphant smiles and handshakes from their vampire colleagues. Dr Madeley hustled past Clark to join them, his beaming smile visible beneath the tangled mass of his beard.

"Marvellous," the doctor said, "simply marvellous stuff. Well done, my boys, well done."

"Yes, well done," Raithe said loudly, clapping slowly. "I think you've proved a point. That's four kills for us, and none," he added with a disdainful look across the room, "for the humans."

"Don't forget we had three of those humans with us," Morgan said, with a protective glance at Jones, Baggers and Hall.

"Ah. I forgot you had some of them flying with you. Such a shame." The pale vampire turned away.

"Right," Dr Madeley said, "what can I get everyone? I think this is a time for celebration, don't you?"

"Hey, new lads," Clark called loudly. He sounded slightly drunk. "Why don't you come and stand over here with us? You don't have to stand with them."

The bar fell silent. The three young navigators looked around, slightly confused. They could clearly sense the tension, and were far from oblivious to the dirty looks they were getting from the rest of the crews. Crowe saw the look of indecision on Jones' face. "Go on over," he told him quietly. "They're your people." For a moment Jones hesitated, and then the three of them walked timidly over to join the regular crews in their blue-grey aircrew suits.

Slowly, tentatively, the conversations resumed. Morgan gave Crowe a quizzical look.

"You didn't expect them to socialise with us, did you?" Crowe asked him. "They're human." He couldn't help noticing the cold smile that passed over Raithe's thin features.

"That Clark really is the most colossal idiot," Dr Madeley said.

"He'll get his." Crowe glanced over at the slick haired pilot. Clark, his work done, had turned back to the bar, and Crowe watched the smile fade from his face as he realised the girl had walked away to serve Harry Stead. Crowe looked at her as she pulled a pint of bitter and chatted happily to the Squadron Leader. From the way Stead leaned forward, subconsciously stroking his moustache, Crowe could tell the old man was smitten. He looked closer at the girl, noting the confidence in her stance, the open posture of someone who felt sure of her looks, not that he could blame her. She was certainly pretty, with large eyes and light-coloured hair that she wore loose about her shoulders. Her figure was slim with just a trace of lingering youthful plumpness, the attractively low cut of her top revealing a tantalising glimpse of firm breasts. He wondered who she was and how old she was. For a moment he felt a stirring of desire, but it was as fleeting as it was surprising.

He didn't need to know the slightest thing about her to know she wouldn't be interested, that it could never work, that she would be just like all the others. He couldn't remember every time he'd been with a woman but he didn't need to, because they were all the same; reluctance, feigned arousal, the fear they tried to hide. She would think him a freak. She would see his eyes and her reaction would be just like everyone else. "Monster." He heard the word echo in his ears, though he knew no one had spoken. It seemed like he'd heard it a thousand times, in a hundred different voices, but he still recognised the familiar tones.

Dr Madeley thrust a pint into Crowe's hand, and with a grateful smile the vampire downed it in one. It seemed like it had been a long night, and somewhere in Germany sixteen different families would be sleeping, unaware that their sons and husbands lay blackened and shredded in the dull waters off England's east coast. Stead was right about one thing, thought Crowe. Better them than him. But the kindly Squadron Leader had totally misjudged him. It wasn't the first time Crowe had killed, and he certainly wasn't upset about it. He remembered the pleasure he'd felt when his rounds struck his target, the sense of power as he'd adjusted his aim.

Perhaps they weren't so wrong, he thought. Maybe he was a monster after all. The guilt would come later, of course, the way it usually did, but for the moment it could wait. There were three hours to go until dawn, he was with the only friends he'd ever known, and the vampires had claimed their first successes.

Chapter Four

Crowe turned for home as the last Heinkel bomber dropped away towards the English countryside below, thick smoke billowing from its burning wing. Morgan and Werner were waiting for him, circling a thousand feet above against a backdrop of two more grey columns that wound up from the smouldering woods and joined seamlessly into the clouds.

"That makes four in total for me," Crowe said into his radio.

"You're taking your time, aren't you?" Morgan said. "I'm on six already. They don't seem so hard to bring down as they did in 1940, but maybe I'm just getting even better."

"You had no cannon then," Werner reminded him. "And you are also so lucky. I have only three."

"It could have been four if you hadn't wasted all your ammo on that Ju-88."

Werner made a grunting sound. "Let's land and reload. Raithe got three last night. Maybe I fly with him."

"Help yourself," Morgan said dismissively. "He won't keep that rate up. No chance."

"You're not jealous, are you?" Crowe said.

"Of Raithe? I've got six kills in ten nights, mate. Weren't you listening?"

"He has eight in nine nights," Werner pointed out wistfully.

"Yeah, but he's flying alone. He doesn't have to share his kills with the likes of you, Werner."

"If I had two eyes I would get more kills than you."

"You couldn't get more kills than me if you had two planes."

"Can I ask a question?" Jones asked on the Mosquito's intercom.

Crowe turned and nodded. It was the first time the navigator had spoken in an hour, except to give timid navigational instructions as they swept up and down the Suffolk and Kent coasts.

"Why does Werner hate the Germans so much?"

"He doesn't hate the Germans. He is one."

"Really?"

"The accent gives it away," Crowe said dryly. "But he hates the Nazis with a passion."

"Doesn't everybody?"

"Not like him. Werner's a German Favrio."

"A what?"

"One of the Favri. They're like gypsies," Crowe said. He didn't feel this was the time to go into greater detail. He knew Werner would not thank him for comparing him and his ancient, secretive people to the more populous Romany, with whom they had fought a brutal, secret war for centuries.

"Oh," Jones said. "But why would that make him hate the Nazis?"

"Because the Nazis are trying to wipe out the gypsies, and anyone like them. They sent soldiers to his family's campsite. He managed to escape but his mother and sisters were locked in their caravan. They set the wagons on fire and burned the whole family." Crowe looked at Jones. The colour had drained from the young man's face. "Does that answer your question?"

Jones could only nod speechlessly.

"How far are we from home?"

Jones fumbled for his maps. "About twelve minutes."

Ahead of them Morgan and Werner were beginning to descend, and Crowe followed suit.

"What about Hinde?"

"What about him?"

"Well, you know, he just doesn't seem the type."

"Neither do you," Crowe told him. "Hinde was a banker in Switzerland. He got involved in the financing of the Westphalia Trust."

"The what?"

"The Westphalia Trust. It's some kind of Europe wide society of vampires. Like a bloody co-operative or something."

"What do they do?"

"Don't ask me, I've never been in it. Raithe's pretty high up in it though."

"Oh," said Jones, his expression changing at the mention of Raithe, as if he had just tasted something unpleasant.

"Anyway," Crowe continued, keen to keep clear of the subject of Raithe, "Hinde got bored of banking and volunteered to train as a pilot for K Department. He made the wrong decision."

"What do you mean?"

"He's even more nervous than you. He smells worse, though, thanks to those cigarettes of his."

"It seems strange that a banker should end up flying fighter planes."

"Gorecki was a poet back in Poland. It didn't stop him from joining us either, and now they're both good pilots. All of us are. It comes with the condition. Now stop talking and get your pre-landing checks done."

All three pilots made first time landings, wanting to get rearmed and refuelled as quickly as possible. However, as they taxied to a halt and the first of the ground crew ran out to their aircraft, Crowe saw that Harry Stead was waiting for them.

"What's going on?" Crowe called to him as he clambered down from the aircraft.

"Grab your stuff and get in the lorry. There's a briefing going to start in ten minutes."

"We got another three," Morgan called as he and Werner ran up to join them.

"Give me the details later, son," Stead said tersely. "The Group Captain has called a briefing. You're going up again, lads. All of you."

"The whole squadron?"

"Yes, everyone; vampires and non-vampires. In a few hours we'll know if you can actually work together despite the physical differences. Jump in."

They raced across the airfield, the vehicle bouncing violently as the driver took them as fast as he dared back to the ops building. The other crews were already in the briefing room. Noone stood impatiently at the front. Dr Madeley smiled as the seven men stumbled through the door, Stead limping at the rear in obvious discomfort.

"Gentlemen," Noone said as they fell into their seats, "this is it. In half an hour you take off on your first joint sortie and this squadron becomes operational again. We've made a decision and you have your new squadron number. I think you'll find it apt." He smirked and with chalk wrote "666 Squadron" on the board behind him.

Danny Baggers immediately raised a hand.

"Yes? What is it?"

"Sir," Baggers began, "have you ever read any of the Biggles books?"

"What?"

"Treble Six is the name of Biggles' squadron. My little brother's got all the books."

Noone turned to Stead, unamused. Stead shrugged apologetically. "We chose it because it sounds sinister. It's the Number of the Beast, after all."

"It's fucking Biggles, sir."

There were a few nervous smiles around the room. "Bags," Morgan said in a warning tone.

"Sorry, sir," Baggers said formally. The glint of mischief remained resolutely placed in his eye.

"Thank you for that insight, Sergeant," Noone snapped. "Now, as you know we've already got more kills in two weeks than most night fighter squadrons have got this year. Tonight, though, is when the real work begins. This squadron was put together so that our experienced fighter pilots could be better directed to their targets, and that's what I expect to see – vampires guiding our pilots to the bombers."

As the Group Captain began to run through the minutiae of the sortie, covering the usual allocations of crew, radio frequencies and meteorological conditions, Werner leaned towards Morgan and Crowe. "He is serious?" he whispered.

Morgan sighed. "Apparently twenty-three kills in eleven nights doesn't count for anything."

"...low cloud base," Noone said, winding down. "This is where the vampires earn their pay." He paused to observe the faces watching him. "I expect full reports from all crews on my desk within an hour of landing. That is all."

Without another word the Group Captain walked from the room, leaving the regular pilots nervously excited and the vampires indignant.

"Right lads," Harry Stead said. "You all know who you're flying with. Good luck up there. Control will keep you updated on the radar feed and get you close to your targets, and then the rest is up to you. Don't stay up too long; the weather is likely to get worse as the night goes on. And don't worry too much about those reports – just give me a few details when you land. I'll make the rest up." He smiled benevolently. "Give them hell."

Dom had pretty much the same thing to say when he helped Crowe into the Mosquito's tight interior. "Give them hell for us, sir." He gestured towards the rest of the ground-crew.

Crowe nodded briskly and began strapping himself in as Jones followed him up the crew ladder. All around them the night air was broken with the sound of Merlin engines. It was an awesome sight. Every aircraft the squadron possessed was preparing for take off, twelve Spitfires and six Mosquitoes. Once in the air they would split into smaller groups but, Crowe thought, it was an impressive display of the squadron's power. He flicked the tiny, improvised switch on his control power that turned on his rear lights. They were only small bulbs and would be invisible more than one thousand yards away or from the front, but they would be the main way of ensuring that the regular pilots were able to keep track of their vampire guides, particularly on a night like this one where the cloud was quite low and thick.

Once airborne he turned the Mosquito to the east, as pre-arranged with Morgan and Werner. The Spitfires would stay quite close to Charney Breach, flying patrols over Norwich, which had been hit twice in the last month, and further south over the mass of London. Morgan, as Mosquito Leader, wanted to use the range and greater navigation of the two-seater aircraft to patrol the Channel. There were German mine-laying aircraft operating over the sea every night, flying low to avoid detection. Morgan had wished him luck before take off, as always; Crowe knew they'd all need luck if this first joint sortie were to be a success.

"A couple of Navy destroyers ran into mines not far from here yesterday," Morgan said. "Let's try to stop that happening again for a while, eh?"

For a long time, though, it seemed as if his ambition was going to be denied. Perhaps it was the weather, but there seemed to be little activity. At one point Werner saw a lone aircraft at eleven thousand feet to the south, but as they got closer they saw that it was a British Halifax, returning from a raid. The aircraft appeared undamaged and safely on course, so they ignored it and returned to their frustrated search pattern.

Three times their radios crackled into life to inform them of successes elsewhere. Lieberwitz had successfully directed Michael

Rhys-Jones and Steve Slater in Spitfires Seven and Eight onto a lone Ju-88, and Slater had gratefully claimed the kill, the first by a regular pilot for Treble-Six Squadron. Hinde had gone one better, directing Peter Owen in Spitfire Ten and Ian Sullivan in Eleven onto a pair of Heinkels with lethal results. Not everything was going so smoothly. Gorecki, despite his poor English, had managed to direct Archie Mills in Spitfire Three onto a lone Bf-110 intruder, but before Mills could close into firing range, Raithe had swept down and blown the German aircraft out of the sky. Crowe had a feeling that Raithe's actions would lead to trouble, but for the moment the news of Spitfire kills simply frustrated the Mosquito crews more.

"Looks like everyone else managed to find something," Clark said bitterly. "Who chose this patrol area anyway?"

"There's still time," Geordie Hulse told him firmly. "Just keep your eyes open."

"I thought that's what they were here to do," Clark sneered.

"Hello, Mosquito Leader, this is Control." The monotone voice of Charney Breach's duty controller filled all twelve men's ears.

"Mosquito Leader, receiving."

"Ack-Ack at Kings Lynn reports they've just been hit by at least four bombers, last reported five minutes heading east, Angels Four on heading zero-eight-zero."

"Zero-eight-zero," Morgan repeated.

"Have we got time to catch them?" Crowe asked hopefully.

"If we hurry. Everyone on me." Morgan's Mosquito turned sharply towards the north and accelerated into a shallow dive. The others followed, the regular crews following the small lights on the trailing wing edges of the aircraft ahead. The cloud base was at about six thousand feet and the six aircraft plunged through it without hesitation.

"Crowe," murmured Jones, "I think we're going to miss them."

"What? Why?"

Jones dragged his map onto his knee, and shone his pencil torch on the area to the north and east of Kings Lynn. The torch had been altered so that only the narrowest pinprick of light was visible, but it was still enough to sting Crowe's eyes. "We're here," Jones pointed out, ignoring the fact that Crowe was looking away from the torch with a pained grimace on his face. "We're heading towards the spot where we would intercept them if they stayed on their last reported course."

"So? Isn't that right?"

"No, because I don't think they will stay on that course. Once clear of the land they'll turn back towards bases in Northern France or southern Belgium. That would put them in this area here, to our east. We're heading north."

Crowe risked a glimpse at the map, wincing. "You're sure they'll be in that area?"

"No, I'm not," Jones said after a few moments. "But I'm certain they won't be where we're heading now."

Crowe gave him a long look. Jones looked nervous, as always, but the young man didn't turn away from the vampire's stare.

"Morgan," Crowe said, "turn to heading zero-eight-five."

"Why?"

"Trust me. And don't slow down or we'll miss them."

The six Mosquitoes altered course and headed towards the area Jones had indicated. Crowe turned to his navigator again but Jones was staring resolutely out of the window to his side, diligently searching the darkness below. Crowe kept the Mosquito at maximum cruise, keeping pace with Morgan. A glance behind showed that the others were close at hand.

"There they are," Morgan cried exultantly. "Three miles at three thousand feet."

It took several more seconds for Crowe to spot them. It was much darker beneath the cloud layer and Morgan had always had better eyes, but he saw them at two and a half miles, and with a surge of pleasure realised that the gunners at Kings Lynn had been wrong. There were six, not four, and as they continued to drop towards them he saw that they were all Heinkels, well spaced but cruising at a leisurely pace.

"What's going on?" Clark asked. "I can't see a thing."

"Six bombers," Morgan told them.

"Perfect," Werner murmured.

"Clark, you come with me. Hulse, you go with Crowe, Masters with Werner. When we hit the first one they'll all scatter. Let's make sure we get them all. Clark, we're coming in very fast. Be sure you don't overshoot."

"I've done this before, okay?" Clark snapped. "Just worry about your own kill." His anger was clear but he remained close to Morgan's tail.

"There's one each, now," Morgan said. "Werner, Crowe, let your wingmen get their kills before you take your shot."

"Geordie, are you hearing me okay?" Crowe said.

"Yes, Crowe. How far out are we?"

"There's a Heinkel about a mile and a half to your front. I'm going to lead you in until you confirm visual. You need to descend another four hundred feet."

"Roger." Hulse dropped away from Crowe, trusting in the vampire's instructions. The Mosquitoes were within a mile.

"Slow it down a little," Crowe murmured.

"I've got a visual on the target," Hulse said calmly. "One Heinkel, nine hundred yards and closing." The man had good eyesight, Crowe noted. A few seconds later Clark and Masters confirmed their sightings too. Crowe pulled up slightly, scanned the positions of the aircraft below him, and saw that one Heinkel was flying some distance apart from the others. He altered course.

"Taking my shot," Hulse announced. It was a good one, too. For a moment the tracers seemed to hang in the air, a glittering stream of light passing slowly through the darkness, and then they slammed into the bomber. It burst into flame instantly, the fire quickly spreading along the fuselage and sending thick cloying streams of smoke into the sky behind it as it began to disintegrate. Clark didn't take the time to announce his shot but his rounds were as accurate as Hulse's, and from a greater distance. His target broke apart. Whatever faults Clark had as a person, there was nothing wrong with his gunnery.

Crowe turned to his own bomber. The crew must have been dozing, content that they were out of danger, because they seemed somehow to have missed the incongruous beauty of the battle behind them. Crowe closed the distance quickly and fired a short burst into the bomber's right engine. For a second he thought he had missed, but then a sheet of flame burst from the cowling and spread quickly to the wing. He felt a surge of elation. The aircraft was as good as finished, but he kept above it as the flames spread and the bomber plunged in a fireball towards the sea. There were no parachutes, and he banked tightly back towards the others.

He watched and listened as Werner impatiently guided Masters onto another bomber, the Favrio pausing only long enough to see the first sparkling impacts of shells on the target before turning towards his own prey. The fifth Heinkel had been the leader, and was now desperately jinking and twisting through the sky in an attempt to lose his pursuer. The tactic might have worked in the past, but against a vampire it provided nothing more than a slight delay to the inevitable. Werner effortlessly followed it, but seemed in no hurry to finish it.

"Stop toying with it," Morgan told him.

"That is the fun," Werner replied cheerfully. He gave a small mutter of discontent and fired. His first attempt was enough to accurately finish the Heinkel, but he continued to fire burst after burst of cannon and machine gun rounds into the stricken aircraft as it slipped away downwards, the crew already dead.

"*Mulo mukat tuv ratesa, bengu tuv anav.*" This time the words of Werner's Favri curse were clear.

The fight, if it could be called that, was almost over. Where moments before there had been twelve aircraft there were now seven, and as he watched Morgan chased down the final bomber and dispatched it with a short but lethal burst which sent huge chunks of the fuselage and wings tumbling to the water as a plume of smoke poured from its burning mass. Mosquito Leader passed through the smoke, rolling in celebration of victory as he did so.

"That makes six," Morgan said with some satisfaction. "Now let's get home and start the celebrations."

Chapter Five

It turned out the celebrations were already in full swing. Harry Stead was buying the drinks as they walked in, and from the noise in the bar it appeared he had already bought more than one. Barry was struggling to cope with the rush and was becoming more and more flustered. Taking grateful delivery of a pint, Crowe looked down to the far end of the bar. The girl was standing there, talking to Clark, who was clearly describing his kill while she pleaded with him to let her get on with her job. Finally she managed to extricate herself and walked towards Barry. For a moment she looked at Crowe. A friendly smile crossed her face.

Kevin Masters had followed Clark's lead and quickly left the vampires once they were in the bar, but Hulse hesitated. "I just wanted to say thanks," he said gruffly. "We wouldn't have found them without you."

"It was Jones who found them," Crowe said.

Morgan looked over with interest. "Really? I wondered why we changed course. Good bit of navigation that, Stevie." Jones blushed, clearly embarrassed.

"Good work," Hulse echoed, and then with a nod to Morgan he walked away to join the group of men listening to an excited Steve Slater's account of his victory.

"Thank you? Good work?" Dr Madeley pushed in next to Crowe, a Cognac in his hand and the remains of another dampening his pullover. "Whatever's next? Looks like you may win them over yet." When Crowe merely grunted, the doctor smiled. "It's a start, anyway."

"Who cares if they like us, as long as we keep getting kills?"

Dr Madeley shook his head at the renewed bitterness in Crowe's voice. "You still haven't been to see me," he said sadly. "Do I need to ask Harry Stead to order you?"

Crowe was about to suggest what Harry Stead could do with his orders when the Squadron Leader appeared, a gloss of beer foam on his moustache. "Ah, Crowe," he said. "Another kill for you, eh?"

"Two. We got three more earlier."

"Two for me, also," Werner interrupted.

"I almost forgot those. You'll have to give me a full account later."

"It looks like you're empty, Harry," Morgan said. "Same again, is it?"

"I'll get these," Crowe said. Morgan gave him an odd, slightly crafty look but he hardly noticed. For some reason he needed to get away from the group. He felt tired, and the others were radiating a happiness he did not feel comfortable with. He collected their empty glasses and made his way to the bar.

The girl was waiting. Crowe placed the glasses down on the wood, the clink of glass drowned out by Morgan's laughter. He turned to see his friend chatting to Stead and Werner, his expression relaxed, and Crowe felt a sharp pang of envy. Morgan knew what he wanted from life. He didn't worry about the past or the future, content just with the moment. He was living his dream every time he flew.

"Do you know what you want?" the girl said softly.

"What?"

She smiled. Now that he was closer he could see that her mouth was slightly too wide and her nose a little too small, but the imperfections only improved the whole.

"Do you know what you want to drink?" she said.

"Oh. Yeah. Three pints of Best and a Cognac."

"Which one is for you?"

"One of the pints."

"Shame," the girl said, before adding "I love Cognac," with a direct, slightly challenging look.

"Oh." He didn't really know what to say.

She poured a generous shot of Cognac without asking whether he wanted ice in it. Taking a pint mug she began to pour the first bitter. The top few buttons of her blouse were unfastened, and he found the view much improved as she leaned forward over the pump.

"What do you think?" she asked without looking up.

"Huh?"

"Of Charney Breach?"

He swallowed. "Interesting," he said, glad that his sunglasses covered the direction of his eyes.

"And the people?" she said, looking up with a knowing glint in her eye.

"I meant the people." Crowe managed to pry his gaze away. Clark was glaring at him with ill-concealed loathing.

"Shaun Clark doesn't like you," the girl said.

"I won't lose sleep over it."

"His bark's worse than his bite." She leaned towards him. "His bark isn't that impressive, either," she whispered.

"You know him?"

Crowe saw a strange expression pass across the girl's face, but it was gone in a moment. "I know all of the pilots, Crowe. I work in the bar three or four nights a week, and you may have noticed that there's not a lot else to do around here but drink."

"You know my name. I won't ask how."

"And I won't tell," she said. "I'm Cassie." She reached out a slim hand and he took it, her skin feeling soft against his palm. He could feel her pulse and the warmth of her veins where his fingertips rested against the back of her hand. She held the contact for a few moments longer than she needed to and then slowly drew away.

"It's nice to meet you, finally," she said, looking at him as she poured his final pint. "Hopefully we'll see a lot more of each other."

"Like you say, there aren't many other places to go around here."

"You never know," she said as she placed his drinks in front of him and took the note he offered her.

"Thanks," he said as she placed, rather than dropped, his change into his hand. He felt awkward. He opened his mouth but couldn't think of anything to add, and instead gave her a slightly formal nod and picked up his drinks.

"Well, hark at you," Morgan said as Crowe rejoined them.

"What?"

"You," Morgan said with a grin, "getting friendly with the barmaid. You're a dark horse, aren't you?"

"Hardly. She's all yours if you want her."

"Well, it would be rude not to at least try." He gave a sly nod to the group and walked confidently towards the girl, who was cleaning glasses. Crowe caught her eye as Morgan approached. She smiled.

"It's probably for the best, anyway," Dr Madeley told him.

"Excuse me?"

"It's probably best that you don't get too friendly with Cassie. My dear chap, you do know who she is, don't you?"

74

"Should I?"

"Her name is Cassie Noone. She's the Group Captain's daughter."

Crowe shrugged, trying to appear disinterested.

"Crowe and Noone's little girl?" Werner said, and laughed sharply.

"It would annoy him, wouldn't it?" Crowe said thoughtfully.

"Don't you dare," Dr Madeley squeaked in outrage.

Morgan was chatting happily to the girl. Crowe couldn't hear them in the busy bar, but he could tell from her smile that Morgan's charms were not entirely wasted on her. He thought her eyes flicked towards him briefly, but the harsh lighting meant he couldn't be sure, and a moment later she was looking at his friend again.

"Morgan," Werner said with a baffled shake of his head. "How does he do this?"

"Practice," Dr Madeley said. "Before the war I'd take him down to London for the occasional night out. He was quite a hit with the girls on the winter social scene, I can assure you. Hello, old bean, where are you off to?"

Crowe had drained his glass again and placed it firmly on the table. "The toilet," he said bluntly. "Is that okay?"

"Of course," the doctor said, taken aback. Werner raised an eyebrow but said nothing as Crowe threaded his way through the gathered aircrew and walked out of the room.

Crowe had not lied. Nevertheless, he did not return to the bar. He paused in the corridor on his way back, and one look was enough to see that the room was still full, the vampires were still largely left alone, and Morgan was still talking to Cassie. The Group Captain's daughter, he corrected himself, and before he knew it, without ever having really thought about it, Crowe found himself outside. The rain had finally arrived, as promised. It bounced off his skull and ran into his eyes. He walked slowly back to his room, took a long look at the simple furnishings of his new home, and dropped heavily onto the hard bed. The wet flying suit clung to his body. It was an hour until dawn.

Although he was tired and had been drinking, sleep remained mockingly distant. He was still awake, hands clasped behind his head, when Morgan finally crept in. He whispered an apology when he saw Crowe's eyes open.

"Cutting it a bit fine, weren't you?" Crowe asked, forcing a smile.

"It's just starting to get light now," Morgan said, then added, "Are you okay? I didn't see you leave."

75

"You were distracted."

"Cassie, you mean? She's a lovely girl."

"I half-expected you to bring her back with you."

"I wish," Morgan snorted. "Sadly she didn't seem all that interested. Oh, we got on well enough, don't get me wrong, but I rather think she's taken with someone else."

Crowe felt a sudden jolt in his chest, and dismissed it in the same instant. You're a fool, he told himself, if you think she could ever be interested in you.

"Still," Morgan said, climbing into bed and pulling the thick blankets over him, "I'll keep trying. Goodnight."

"Goodnight," Crowe replied, his voice barely audible. He heard Morgan's breathing slip into the steady rhythm of sleep, but he remained no closer himself. Instead he kept thinking of the way Cassie had looked at him, of the genuine interest he thought he'd seen in her eyes.

"You're a bloody idiot," he told himself again, aloud this time. He pulled up his own blanket and rolled onto his side, but still sleep would not come. Outside, beyond the thick blackout curtains, the sun was coming up.

The lone Halifax heavy bomber was close to home now, another mission over Germany behind them and less than an hour of flying to go before they were back in the Mess, celebrating another day of life. The crew had survived near-disaster over the target, but even now they could not relax. Not with the Boss watching them. For the young men who made up his crew the Boss was a near- mythical figure, with his calm manner and effortless skill. He was a legend, a man who'd gone from bombers to night fighters and back and excelled in every aircraft he'd ever flown, earning just about every decoration his country had to offer in the process. He was also the Squadron Commander, but that wasn't why they listened when he spoke. The Boss knew that this was as dangerous a time as any. Relaxing too soon could kill as surely as the flak that had bracketed them over the Ruhr, knocking out the number four engine. Quick action had extinguished the flames. A fine trail of fuel still leaked from the damaged section and lingered in the air behind them.

It was the rear gunner who caught a glimpse of the faint shadow closing just beneath them. His hoarse shout gave the Boss an instant's warning, and with his years of experience that was all he needed. He kicked hard on the port rudder, keeping them on their course but making the nose point left even as the aircraft crabbed sideways. He knew the night fighter would think they were turning to the left. It worked. The Boss saw the first burst from the fighter zip past their port wing tip, and hurled the aircraft into a series of violent turns, hoping to lose the fighter in the darkness.

A calm enquiry to his rear gunner ended that hope. The fighter was still there, struggling with the evasive manoeuvres but staying just within range. The Boss knew the difficulties of following a target in the dark and was a little surprised that the fighter could track them so well. He didn't allow it to slow his actions.

He put the aircraft into a corkscrew. It was a tactic he'd used four times before, rolling and diving at the same time to make the fighter's aiming impossibly hard. It had worked every time. He'd never tried it on three engines but felt sure the reliable Halifax would cope. It was not the Boss's job to engage in battle with fighters, but simply to convince them that there were easier pickings available. He increased engine power, holding the tight roll for several seconds. Then he rolled to the opposite side and started upwards, using the aircraft's momentum to climb, feeling the remaining three engines straining under the effort.

The fighter was still there. Usually it should have overshot by now, or retreated out of fear of the Halifax's phalanx of heavy machine guns. But the fighter remained near, slowly and calmly keeping close to them. The Boss reached the top of his spiral and for an instant the aircraft hung in the air before he began the process again.

This time he pushed even harder. He knew the risks of overstressing the airframe or slipping into a spin, but he also knew he could control them. He admired the German's skill, but they had enough fuel left to outlast the fighter if need be. He reached the bottom of the dive and brought the aircraft back up again, calling to his gunners for constant updates on the fighter's position, but apparently it had gone. One more time to be sure, the Boss decided as they reached the top of the spiral.

The Vulture was waiting. The first burst killed the Boss instantly, wounded four of the crew and set the aircraft on fire. The second sheared off the wing, and as the flames spread to consume the surviving airmen the wreckage spun slowly towards the uncaring sea below.

It was kill number one hundred and thirty five.

Chapter Six

So this was what impending death felt like.

Twenty-three hours earlier the squadron had taken its tally to thirty-five kills in a little over three weeks, and Crowe had claimed his sixth kill. The aircraft had been another Dornier but this time, as the burning bomber plummeted towards the Kent countryside, a burst of machine gun bullets from the rear upper gunner had zipped past his cockpit. It had been a sudden reminder of his mortality, but the mild concern he'd felt as the tracers seemed to creep towards them was nothing compared to this.

It was not that Morgan couldn't handle the car. He drove the big Bentley with the same verve with which he flew his Mosquito, throwing it through the bends on this Hampshire road with total control, but his skill wouldn't help if they hurtled around a corner and found another vehicle in front of them.

"Relax," Morgan had told him. "There won't be anything else on the roads. The blackout's on, isn't it?" So far, the younger vampire had been proved right. With only the dimmest of downward pointing headlamps allowed, very few people felt safe venturing onto the roads at night. Morgan had left the lights on to warn others but found them distracting, his unshielded eyes providing perfect vision of the road ahead.

Although he would never have admitted it, Crowe felt a surge of relief when the car pulled into a long tree-lined drive and came to a halt outside the sprawling manor house.

"You can let go now."

Crowe released his fingers from the death grip they had taken on the window frame of the door, and wiggled the circulation back into them.

"I can't believe that a little car journey worries you. I've seen your flying."

"Flying only worries me when you're the pilot."

They climbed out of the car. The house was even larger than he'd imagined from Morgan's description, an elegantly plain building made pretty by the fine detailing around the windows and the ivy clinging to the brickwork. Above the black painted door the word "Ravenswood" was carved into the stone.

"Nice, isn't it?" Morgan said.

They took their bags and walked towards the house, boots crunching in the gravel. A middle-aged man with neat brown hair and a thick well-groomed moustache stood waiting in the dimly lit doorway.

"Father," Morgan said with a smile, awkwardly embracing the man.

"It's good to have you home, son."

"Father, this is Crowe. Crowe, this is my dad, William Bale."

"It's a pleasure to meet you, Crowe." William Bale said formally, shaking his hand with a firmness of grip that matched his solid build. Crowe saw the traces of a welcoming smile on his otherwise stern face. "Let's go inside. Your mother has been looking forward to seeing you, Morgan."

Within the house there were only a couple of masked candles to provide light, but Bale moved with the confidence of a man used to navigating his home in darkness. This, after all, was the home where an established society family had secretly raised a vampire son, safe from the eyes of the outside world. Bale took their bags from them.

"Did you send the servants away for the night?" Morgan said.

"I thought it was for the best."

"Do the servants know about Morgan's condition?" Crowe asked.

"They know he can't go out in the daylight," Bale said. "One or two of the older ones may know about the blood, but if they do they aren't going to mention it to anyone else. They're loyal people." Crowe got the impression that Bale was a man used to being surrounded by loyal people.

"They might be surprised if they found out there were others with the same condition, though," Morgan said. They moved further into the labyrinthine interior. William Bale was limping slightly as he carried their bags.

"Souvenir from the Turks," Bale replied casually when Crowe mentioned it. "Aches in the winter a little." Crowe realised he could quickly grow to admire this man, understanding why Morgan was so proud of a father who, despite his age, had only been persuaded not to rejoin the army at the outbreak of war by the protests of his family.

The house was huge, and it seemed a long time before Bale finally led them into a tidy kitchen with a huge oven against one wall and an oak table dominating the centre of the room. The ceilings were low, accentuating the darkness. Various utensils hung from a wall where the only window had been bricked up. Bale put down their bags and motioned for them to sit before turning on a small side lamp, which brought a faint glow to the room.

The kitchen door opened again behind them, and a woman walked in.

Crowe knew in an instant that this was Morgan's mother, but Morgan had only inherited a fraction of her looks. Catherine Bale was quite extraordinarily beautiful. She must have been in her forties and yet her face and tall, full-figured body would have been amazing for a woman half her age. The effect of her long raven hair and piercing eyes was startling. It never even occurred to Crowe to find her attractive; she was beyond that.

She gave a cry of joy and embraced Morgan, holding him tightly before kissing him with fervour on both cheeks. Crowe saw the look of absolute adoration in William Bale's eyes. Catherine was probably a full twenty years younger than her husband, and he could imagine how proud the older man must be to have her as his wife. The moment she had entered the room, Crowe had understood what had led a wealthy battalion commander in the British Army with two young sons to romance a Budapest professor's daughter barely half his age, and to stay devoted to her when their child was born a vampire.

"Morgan," Catherine said with mock anger, "how dare you stay away so long?"

"I've been busy, Mum," Morgan said sheepishly. "There is a war on, you know."

"So? What business of mine is that? Your brother John comes home every month, and he has a whole squadron to command."

"I call on the telephone."

"Every two weeks if I'm lucky, and even then you're not allowed to talk about what you've been doing!"

"Sorry."

"You will be if you don't start visiting more often." She embraced him again.

80

"Forgive me," she said finally, releasing Morgan. "You must be Crowe." He could hear the faintest trace of a European accent in her speech as he took her outstretched hand. Her skin was soft, but there was real strength in her touch. "Morgan has told us so much about you."

"Really?"

"All of it true," Morgan said, "none of it good."

"Does anyone want tea?" William Bale asked, filling the kettle.

"Since when does Morgan drink tea, Will?" Catherine said. "There's blood in the pantry, Morgan. It's fresh; I got it today from the butcher's in the village."

"What sort is it?"

"Beef."

"My favourite," Morgan said with relish, but one look at Crowe and he hurriedly changed his mind. "Maybe later."

"Crowe?" Catherine turned to him. She was taller than him, which only added to the intimidating effect of her beauty. She looked directly at him, deep into his eyes. It made him feel naked. He looked away.

"No," he said neutrally.

"Well," Catherine said, sounding disappointed, "I suppose we'd better put that tea on after all. Morgan, you look tired. Have you been drinking enough? Is Byron taking proper care of you?"

William Bale prepared four cups of steaming tea while they talked. Catherine wanted to know everything that had happened to Morgan since she had last seen him, about the months spent training in Wales, his relationship with the other vampires and with the rest of the squadron, the details of the journey down. Even as he answered her questions she would look over at Crowe, her eyes watching him openly without embarrassment. He felt as if she was trying to read his mind. It scared him. There was too much he didn't want this woman to know, and yet he was hypnotised, unable to turn away from her.

Morgan left no detail unexplained. He told her about the six months of hard work it had taken him to turn five vampires into combat-ready pilots, able to work together or alone, against enemy fighters or bombers or even against ground targets, each possessed of an effectiveness that an ordinary pilot would need a decade to acquire.

"Five vampires?" she said. "I thought you said there were six others?"

"There are," Morgan said. "But Raithe didn't join us until later, and he was already fully-trained. It's just that no one knows quite where he got his training. Is something wrong?"

"Did you say Raithe?"

"Yes. Why?"

Catherine paused, her eyes distant, but then the moment had passed. She shrugged. "It just seems a strange name. That's all." She continued to listen to Morgan's stories as if the thought had never even occurred to her. Her eyes remained unreadable when Morgan told her of his seven kills.

"I'm so proud of you," Catherine said finally, touching his cheek lovingly.

"What do you think of this Group Captain of yours, Crowe?" William Bale asked gruffly. It was, Crowe realised, the first word he had managed to get in since they had sat down. Having shared a home for so long with the ever-loquacious Morgan and his mother, it probably wouldn't be a new situation for Bale.

"Not a lot," Crowe said.

"I suspected as much. Morgan told me the same thing on the telephone last week, so I made a few enquiries. I may be retired but I still have a few friends in the right places." This was something of an understatement, Crowe knew. Whatever influence William Bale had once wielded as a Lieutenant-Colonel was dwarfed by the power he now held as one of the most important figures in the munitions industry. "Seems this character Noone was promoted quite rapidly before the war. No one knows exactly why, but they all agree that he had an amazing ability for pleasing his bosses, or as we used to call it, brown-nosing." Bale's face crumpled with contempt as he poured the tea. "Anyway, he made a complete balls-up of his first squadron command, but rather than sack him they moved him to Fighter Command headquarters."

"How on earth did he end up in charge of Treble-Six?" Morgan said. "The man's hardly the stuff of military legend. Of course, they may have employed him purely for his daughter. She really is quite lovely," Morgan assured his mother. "Isn't she, Crowe?"

"Yes," Crowe murmured.

"Now Morgan," Catherine said, "I'm not going to hear that you've got in trouble again like you did with Lord Aberbodie's daughter, am I?"

"Of course not, mother dearest. I wouldn't dream of letting you hear about it. Besides, I imagine Noone keeps a close eye on her to make sure she's not getting too friendly with the staff." Morgan made a face. "I just don't understand how he got appointed. Surely they'd have wanted someone at least halfway decent for such a sensitive job?"

"You mean someone like Mark Wolsey, the fellow Noone replaced?" William Bale said. "Popular, effective, and with a VC in his pocket? That's what I thought too, but apparently not. Fighter Command were so furious about losing some of their top pilots to one of Quentin Quiet's special projects that they picked Noone for the job. How is Quiet, by the way?"

"He drops in every now and then to mutter something cryptic. We don't see a lot of him."

"Good. I never trusted the man. Does he always wear that hat?"

"Always," Crowe said.

"Strange fellow. Here's your tea."

"Thanks."

"Still," Bale said after a moment's consideration, "I'd rather him than Raymond Noone. Apparently the good Group Captain has been promised a promotion if he can prove that Quiet's special squadron is an expensive waste of time."

"Fat chance of that," Morgan said. "We've got nearly forty kills already. They gave us a few days off because the German attacks have dried up; they simply can't take the casualty rate we've been inflicting. It's a shame. Flying really is so much more fun if you can get a good fight in too."

"Morgan," Catherine said, shaking her head, "why do you always have to be so bloodthirsty?"

"Probably because I'm a vampire, mum."

"Quiet's got Churchill's backing," Crowe said to Bale.

"A lot of senior officers are getting tired of Churchill meddling in military business. They see this as a chance to give him a bloody nose." Bale paused. "All this is deniable, of course."

"The whole thing is deniable," Crowe said quietly.

"How were you recruited, Crowe?" Catherine said, turning her body towards Crowe. Once again he felt the strange sensation of being laid wide open for her eyes to read at will.

"Crowe was…"

"Shush, Morgan," Catherine told him distractedly. "I want to hear Crowe."

"There's not really a lot to tell," Crowe lied. "I was working in London."

"What were you doing?"

"Stuff," he said simply. She took the hint without as much as a blink. "I had a reputation amongst a certain type of person. Quiet heard about me, about what I could do. He made me an offer. He described it as an opportunity."

"You would describe it differently?"

"Let's just say I didn't have much choice."

"And now?" She leaned forward slightly, her eyes showing their interest even as they unnerved him.

"I love flying. I have friends. I have no regrets."

"Morgan tells me you weren't born a vampire."

"No. I started developing symptoms when I was seven."

William Bale announced that he was going to take the vampires' bags to the guest bedrooms. Catherine gave him a fond smile but otherwise didn't stir. "Morgan has told me about your parents. How they rejected you. I'm sorry if it offends you that I know."

"It doesn't."

"Your mother would have been of the bloodline, of course. You know that the vampire heritage always flows in the blood of the women of the Favri?"

"No, I didn't."

"It can skip three or more generations, but always it is carried within the female. And yet only male children could be born with the gift. As a child, listening to my mother's stories, it always seemed unfair that I carried the bloodline but could never have the honour of being a vampire."

"Honour," Crowe murmured. "Gift. You sound like Raithe." He said it deliberately, watching her. There might have been a hint of a reaction in her eyes, but it could have been his imagination.

"How much do you know of your heritage? Of the Favri?"

"Not much," he said. What little he did know came mostly from Dr Madeley's years of research, with a smattering from Werner and Morgan. The Romany called them *Mulo*, the unclean dead, and spoke in hushed tones of their cruelty and evil. In time, as the stories of the *Mulo* spread, the Favri had been forced into hiding, always trying to conceal their true heritage from others while keeping their own beliefs

84

and history alive. And every now and then, somewhere amongst the hidden Favri communities scattered throughout Europe, a new *Mulo* would be born.

Crowe didn't know where he fitted in.

"And you have never wanted to know more?" Catherine said, sipping her tea. She paused, waiting for his reaction. "We are related, did you know that?"

"No," he said, taken aback.

"Not closely, perhaps, but all Favri are related. The *Mulo* line is a narrow one. I'm surprised that Byron hasn't told you more about it, or Morgan. But then Byron was always more interested in the science, not the history, and Morgan was always too busy having fun to worry about his heritage." Catherine's face glowed with warmth as she looked across at her son. "But it is such a glorious history that I only wish we did not have to keep it secret. That is the way of this world, I suppose. Your mother was Eastern European, like me?"

"I don't remember much about her. I was a boy when they....left. She may have had your accent, I don't remember. I know she wasn't beautiful like you."

There was the sound of liquid splattering behind him as Morgan coughed violently and sprayed the last of his tea onto the kitchen floor.

"Morgan," Catherine said softly, "why don't you help your father with the bags?" Her son took the hint, giving Crowe a shocked look as he left.

"Sorry," Crowe said when they were alone.

Her eyes sparkled with amusement. "You're sorry for flattering me?"

"I'm sorry if I embarrassed you."

"You didn't," she said softly. "And I hope I haven't offended you with my questions."

"No. But I can't help feeling you already know the answers." He looked directly back into her eyes.

"The second sight, you mean? Perhaps. It's always run in my family. But it doesn't take supernatural powers to see that you have been hurt. It's in everything you do. The way you speak, the way you hold yourself. It's part of you."

"Except when I fly."

"Except when you fly," she agreed. "Morgan told me about your love of flying. He and you are not so different."

85

Crowe looked at the kitchen, thinking of the huge house around them, the grounds beyond and the absent servants. "I'm not so sure about that."

"It means nothing to him, you know," she said, and he was again conscious of her eyes boring into him, reading his thoughts as plainly as if he had spoken. "This house, the Bentley, all his father's wealth. He'd give it all up in an instant if that was what it took to keep flying or to do the right thing. It meant nothing to me, either, although I will admit I have become used to the luxury." She smiled with self-deprecating good humour. "When I met William I took him for just another officer, but I knew he was a brave and good man."

"Morgan takes after him."

"I know, and I'm so proud of him for it. Morgan is more impulsive, though. I'm afraid he inherited that part of his spirit from me. Sometimes he does things without thinking of the consequences."

"And you have done the same?" Crowe said, prompted by her tone.

"It is a shame you do not know about your heritage," Catherine said again. She paused to finish her tea before pushing the empty cup slowly away from her. "I knew everything there is to know about the Favri before I was seven years old. How my people began their days in the East, like the Romany and the Sinti. How we became dispersed as we headed ever further west. How the stigma of the bloodline and the ignorance of the other tribes led them to wage war against us, and to hunt us wherever they could find us."

Crowe watched her, transfixed by the power of her eyes. Her voice hadn't changed but her eyes seemed ablaze with pride and suppressed anger.

"My father was a Professor, a respected man, and yet all his life he had to hide the truth of his family's heritage. My mother was of the pure bloodline, the ancient bloodline. She could trace her Favri ancestry for a thousand years. When she died, my father could never hide his disappointment that she had not borne a *Mulo* son. Still, he loved me. All my life he told me I would grow up to marry a Favrio and keep the bloodline pure." She paused. "It broke his heart when I married William."

"Do you regret it?"

She smiled. The passion in her eyes subsided, replaced by contentment. "I married a wonderful man, and had a wonderful son. Maybe I could have done things differently, but I would not have been so happy, and I would not have had Morgan. He adores you, though of course he won't say it. Don't let anything ever come between you."

"I don't plan to," Crowe said, surprised. "He's the best friend I've ever known. I'd die for him." He thought about that statement for a moment, and knew before that moment had passed that it was true. "I really would."

He took a deep breath. He didn't want to look at her anymore, didn't want to have her reading him through his eyes. "I do envy him, though," he said. "Not for the house or the money. I envy him for you. I envy him for his father, and for the way he talks about his brothers." He tried to stop the sudden bitterness that was building in his words, but the words kept coming, shocking him with their honesty as the emotional walls he tried to build up around him crumbled. "That's what I envy. Because all I ever had is a mother and father who gave birth to a monster."

"They didn't." Her voice throbbed with conviction. "They gave birth to you."

Crowe looked back at her, into her perfect eyes. "If I met them tomorrow," he said in a steady voice, "I'd kill them. I wouldn't hesitate, not for a second. Isn't that enough to make me a monster?"

She didn't reply. She didn't even flinch this time. Catherine Bale simply reached out a slim hand and placed it on his, and Crowe saw the tears that gathered in her eyes. Now that the words had passed his lips, he wondered what it was that had made him speak. He felt better for saying them, though. They had been hidden inside him too long. Even as he looked at her, though, he knew that she might understand him but others never would.

"I'm sorry," he said. "I don't…"

"I know," she said. That she knew what he was going to say was already familiar enough that he didn't feel surprised. "It is not something you talk about. I am honoured. That's twice today that you have flattered me. I am starting to see why Morgan likes you so much." She raised fingers adorned with rings to brush away a tear and smiled brilliantly at him, and despite everything he felt his tension disappear. He smiled back.

The conversation never returned to such serious territory. They were discussing Morgan's somewhat spontaneous instructional technique when the man himself returned.

"Crowe," he said from the doorway, "can you come with me? I've got something to show you."

Catherine gave him a stern look. "Morgan, can't you see we're talking?"

"But Mum," he protested, "I need to show Crowe his surprise gift."

"Oh," she said. "Of course. You'd better go with him," she told Crowe. "He's been very excited about this. But we will talk again."

"I hope so."

"You'll like this," Morgan said as he led the way down a long corridor towards the back of the house.

"What is it?" Crowe could smell the freshly-sipped blood on Morgan's breath, and felt the familiar craving inside him.

Morgan grinned back over his shoulder. "It wouldn't be much of a surprise if I told you, would it?" Crowe followed him into a small stone room with an oak door on the far side. There were no windows, and the room was bare except for a low bench and two coat-pegs. From each hung what looked like a flying suit and a pair of large smoked goggles.

"The left one is for you."

"I already have a flying suit, Morgan."

"This is a bit more complicated." Morgan took down the longer of the two suits and began to slip it on over his clothes. "Put it on," he said. "We're going outside."

Crowe didn't need to look at his watch. His body always knew when dawn was coming. "Are you serious? The sun will be up in a few minutes."

"That's the point." Morgan pulled his flying suit over his broad shoulders and smoothly zipped it up at the front. Then, reaching over his shoulder, he pulled a hood over the top of his head and fastened a trailing flap across his face so that only his eyes were visible deep within the shadow of the material. He drew gloves from the pockets and donned them, and then finally pulled a pair of goggles over the top of the hood. There wasn't an inch of his skin visible.

"Dr Madeley made me my first suit when I was four," Morgan said, the words muffled by the material. "It was the first time I'd ever been outside in the daylight. I still couldn't go out on a bright day, and even on an overcast day the light hurt my eyes through the glasses. But it was worth it, to be able to see the sun. He's made me another one every year since then. It has to fit just right, you see."

He pointed to the other suit. "He made that one for you."

Crowe pulled the suit on slowly as if in a daze, feeling how closely it fitted and how heavy the material was. He did not speak. The gloves were snug to his hands and passed over the sleeves so as to eliminate the risk of a slice of wrist or forearm being exposed even for an instant. Pulling the hood on was like plunging his head underwater, all external sound disappearing. He fumbled at the catches on the face flap. Morgan reached out wordlessly to seal them in place.

"The glasses have two settings," he heard Morgan say, his voice dull as if he were in another room. "Pushing this lever flicks between a thin lens and a much darker one. I suggest you keep it on the darker setting. Otherwise it will hurt." Crowe pulled the goggles on and toggled the settings. With the darker setting chosen he was virtually blind in the unlit room.

"Are you ready for this?"

Crowe nodded. Morgan opened the door.

The sun was only just starting to lighten the horizon, but the glow seemed utterly alien to him. He followed Morgan out into a wide, well-tended garden. They skirted around the edge of the lawn, past a small but ornate fishpond. The water flickered in the growing light. Three small birds fluttered between the branches of the nearby trees. He could not hear them, but he knew they were singing. He looked down at the grass beneath his feet, and saw that the trees were starting to cast a gentle shadow as the sky grew lighter.

He felt fear growing inside him. He had dreaded this moment for most of his life, the terror of being caught in the open as dawn arrived. He remembered his skin burning when exposed for even a second to daylight through a broken window or an unexpectedly opened door. There were other memories too, worse even than that. Doctors in white coats, holding him still as the sun brightened his cell, watching him, calmly making notes while his skin smoked and blackened and his scream echoed from the walls.

The sky ahead was ablaze with colour now, its brightness beginning to hurt even as he raised one hand to cover his eyes. The fear was fading. His excitement grew. More images came to his mind now, older and happier. He was a small child again, playing in a park with his loving parents, feeding the ducks, running and laughing. He remembered the comforting warmth of the sun on his skin. He reached up with one hand and switched the goggles to the lighter setting, and kept them like that until his eyes stung and the tears rolled down his face.

For the first time in twenty-three years, Crowe watched the sun rise.

Chapter Seven

"So he got away then?"

"Ach, Crowe, you disappoint me."

"Will you two let me finish the story?" Crowe snapped, ignoring the grin that Morgan and Werner exchanged. "I must have hit him five times. I could see the holes in his wings but he wouldn't go down, and now my ammunition's all gone."

"The Ju-88 is a tough aircraft," Werner said.

"Plus you can't shoot straight," Morgan added.

They were sat in the room that served as their messing hall. It was nearly midnight, and their aircraft were being refuelled in advance of another sortie.

"I wasn't going to let him go," Crowe said.

"Even though you were out of bullets?"

"He didn't know that."

"You're insane."

"I kept chasing him, but we were coming up on Norwich and we were starting to run short of fuel. Jones convinced me to give up."

"So he got away, then," Morgan repeated with a note of triumph.

"Not really," Crowe said, sipping his tea. "He flew into the side of a factory."

"I like that," Werner said approvingly.

"I'm claiming it as a kill."

"Are you drunk?" Morgan said. "You can have half."

"Half a kill?"

"And you'll be grateful for it."

"Bollocks. That should count double."

"The factory wall gets the other half. Making it," Morgan paused, pretending to ponder it, "eight kills to me, six and a half to you, four to Werner."

The German muttered something indeterminately foul-sounding. Crowe looked at his watch. To his left he could hear Clark loudly

90

complaining about the dimness of the lighting, but ignored him. He found that was the easiest way to deal with the big, arrogant Flight Lieutenant, although twice in the last few days he'd stepped in to defend the young navigators from Clark's bullying. Idly, he plucked at the collar of his pullover.

"Stop that," Morgan said.

"What?"

"That." He gestured towards Crowe's new clothing. "You'll damage the wool."

"What are you, the clothing Gestapo? We look daft." All the aircrew now wore the same blue-grey flying suits, with their rank slides attached and identical blue sweaters underneath. It had been the Group Captain's idea, and it had quickly proved unpopular. The original crews resented the inference that the vampires were in any way *proper* aircrew, while the vampires would have been happy to remain in the black overalls that, like so many other things, set them apart. Crowe took no satisfaction from the Flight Lieutenant rank slides he now wore.

"They'll be warmer for flying in," Morgan pointed out. "Besides, if we look like them, maybe they'll accept us a little sooner." He reached into his own flying suit and pulled out a crumpled brown envelope.

"What's that?"

"It's a letter from my father. I haven't had the chance to look at it yet." Sipping at his tea, Morgan read it, occasionally smiling at something on the page. He had a very expressive face.

"Well," he said, "that is interesting."

"What's that?"

"You remember Dad said he'd do some digging into Noone and Quentin Quiet? Apparently, he dug up a lot. Noone was sent here to ensure the squadron fails, preferably without any losses to us. It looks like Fighter Command is even less happy with Quiet and Churchill than we thought."

"I'm not surprised. They must hate their precious fighters being flown by vampires."

"The RAF top brass don't know anything about vampires. All they know is that they've lost a squadron to K Department, it's a special squadron and we're doing something odd. Even Noone didn't know what we were until a few days before we arrived."

"Surely he's told them by now?"

Morgan shook his head. "It's above Top Secret and strictly need to know. If he tells them anything about vampires or K Department, it will be a career stopper. The Government might even do him for treason."

"It would never get to court."

"Obviously. Quiet would see to that. Besides, who'd believe him anyway? Noone isn't going to tell them, but he's desperate to report that we're failing."

"You can't argue with our results," Crowe said, thoughtfully.

"No. And by the sound of it, our stock with Fighter Command is going up all the time, because we're doing their job for them by getting all these kills and they're starting to think maybe we're worthwhile after all. But Noone's reputation is plummeting. He was supposed to prove we were useless."

"That must be frustrating."

"Incredibly frustrating," Morgan agreed gleefully. The smile faded as Harry Stead walked in. "This doesn't look good." Crowe, seeing Stead's expression, knew that his friend was right.

"Can I have your attention, lads?" Stead called. The room fell silent instantly. "I've just got off the telephone. A Halifax bought it last week." He paused. "It was Mark Wolsey's."

The three vampires shared a glance. Wing Commander Wolsey, the previous squadron commander. It was clear from the reactions around them that the name meant a lot, especially to the survivors of the original squadron. Crowe saw Geordie Hulse bow his head, and a couple of the younger pilots looked close to tears.

"I'm sorry," Stead said. "We all liked him."

"How did it happen, Harry?" one of the pilots asked softly. Stead hesitated, as if unsure whether to answer.

"They reckon the Vulture got him."

The name meant nothing to Crowe, but from the sudden chorus of muttering it clearly bore huge significance for the regular crews. Crowe saw the looks they exchanged amongst themselves.

"The Vulture?" Morgan whispered.

"I've no idea," Crowe said.

"Another good man gone," Clark said. He was looking at Crowe and Morgan with obvious loathing.

"Shall we go?" Morgan said quietly. "Our aircraft should be nearly ready."

They got up and walked out of the room to grab their flying kit, Crowe aware of more unfriendly looks. They were not lost on Morgan, either.

"Why were they all looking at us like that?" he said as they headed for the waiting transport.

"Isn't it obvious?" Crowe said. "They're used to losing friends. We turn up and we haven't lost a man yet. And we're not part of the old squadron. We're still outsiders, even if we do wear the same uniform."

They collected their navigators, and drove out to the dispersal hut to grab their oxygen masks, helmets and goggles, only to be told to hold there. To make matters worse, the sound of a car engine a few minutes later heralded the arrival of Clark and Hulse with their own navigators.

"What do you want?" Crowe said from the doorway of the dispersal hut. Clark ignored him as he brushed past.

"Group Captain's orders," Hulse said. "He wants us flying as many sorties as possible."

"Which 'us' does he mean?" Werner said as Hulse followed Clark to get ready.

"Well, here we go again," Morgan said as they reached the Mosquitoes that were parked side by side on the grass by the tiny wooden hut. "Be lucky."

"I don't feel lucky right now," Crowe said sadly.

Three times fighter controllers directed them onto possible radar contacts, but all turned out to be false alarms. Two hours of empty skies left Crowe annoyed, and with nothing to take it out on. The fact that he spent much of his time thinking about Cassie Noone didn't help, either. He'd seen her a few times in the bar since they'd talked. She was always friendly, despite his abruptness. He wondered briefly whether he should seek her out when they returned, but then reality hit him and he angrily dismissed the idea. Jones wisely kept quiet throughout the flight, sensing his pilot's mood.

"Mosquito Leader to all callsigns, let's call it a night." It was almost the first time any of them had spoken in two hours. Hulse landed first, with Crowe next behind him in the circuit. He was vaguely aware that Clark was flying very close behind him as he made his final approach, but thought little of it. Clark was probably just keen to get back to the bar, and Crowe couldn't blame him. It had been that kind of evening.

"What a waste of time," Morgan said when he and Baggers joined Crowe and Jones near the parked aircraft. He looked up in disgust as the first drops of rain fell on his dark hair.

"Transport's late," Crowe said.

"Our perfect night continues," Morgan said. Away in the darkness they could see the crew vehicle slowly making its way across the airfield. "What do you reckon, Baggers? Drinking contest? Might as well salvage something from the night."

"Aye, skipper, if you think you're up to it. Crowe tells me you're a bit of a lightweight."

Morgan smiled. "We both know Crowe never said that."

"Yeah, I did. I just wasn't that polite."

Morgan turned as if to say something, but instead his face took on a resigned expression. "Look out," he said quietly, "arsehole at six o'clock."

"Well, well," Clark said. Bobby Barton trailed in his wake, carrying both men's kit. "It's our illustrious guides. Good job leading us to the targets tonight, boys. Very slick."

"Feel free to go up without us, Clark," Morgan said brightly. "You never know, maybe you'll run into something. A hillside, perhaps."

Clark ignored him. "Crowe, I noticed something odd on that flight. I was right behind you on approach. I don't think you were looking at me."

"I try not to," Crowe said, turning away. Their transport was still some distance away.

"The funny thing is," Clark said, "in the dark your Mosquito looked just like a German bomber. I had you in my sights for a long time. It would have been so easy to squeeze that trigger."

Crowe turned to face him. He could see the shock on the faces of Morgan and the navigators.

"Accidents happen all the time," Clark smirked. "No one would have blamed me."

"Is that a threat?" Morgan said.

"Just something to bear in mind."

"What's going on?" Hulse said, joining them with Lomax.

Crowe ignored all of them. His eyes were purely on Clark. In his mind he knew that Clark could have killed them. They had been vulnerable, their wheels down and their airspeed too low for evasive manoeuvres. Even if Clark had missed with his first shot, they would have had no choice but to maintain their course or plough into the ground.

Clark wouldn't have missed. He was too good a shot for that.

"You're seriously out of order, Clark," Morgan said. There was the slightest catch in his voice, and Crowe knew that he too had reached the same conclusion. He could sense the fear in Baggers and Jones, the knowledge that the biggest threat to them might not be the Germans, but one of their own squadron. Clark might even be able to convince others that, in the heat of some future battle, he had made a genuine mistake. Clark was a bully, and he was good at it.

That left Crowe with only one option.

"Why didn't you do it?"

Clark blinked. "What?"

"Why didn't you take the shot?"

"You think I couldn't?"

"I know you couldn't," Crowe said, dropping the lightness from his tone. "And you know why? Because you're a gutless prick. If you missed, I'd kill you. If you hit us, I'd walk straight out of the wreckage and rip your fucking throat out."

Silence. The menace in his voice had seen to that.

Clark had gone white, as white as the vampires. He recovered well, though, and gave a laugh that was almost convincing. "Well," he said, looking around him for support, "I try to share some friendly advice and that's the thanks I get."

"Besides," Morgan said as their transport finally pulled to a halt next to them, "I've seen your shooting. You'd be lucky if you managed to find the trigger."

Crowe waited for Jones, Baggers and Morgan to climb into the back before throwing in his crew bag and following them in. There was enough room inside for a dozen men. He didn't sit down, though. He waited until Clark's hand appeared at the rear ramp.

"Wait for the next one," he said, pushing his face to within an inch of Clark's. "This one's full."

"Drive on, driver," Morgan called. With a lurch they pulled away, leaving Clark cursing while his three colleagues stared at him.

Crowe sat back on the hard bench and took a deep breath. His hand was shaking, though with delayed nerves or anger he couldn't tell.

"What the hell was that about?" Morgan said.

"Just Clark trying to act tough."

"I don't mean that. I mean you, egging him on."

"What was I supposed to do, let him get away with it?"

"Do you think he would do it?" Jones asked quietly.

"He hasn't got the balls."

"And if you're wrong?" Morgan said.

"I'm not wrong."

"Have you even thought about what it would be like to be shot down?"

"No," Crowe lied.

"Or trapped in a burning aircraft with the sun coming up?"

"Leave it out, Morgan. You're scaring Jones."

Morgan didn't smile. Crowe followed his gaze beyond the tailgate, where four men were dwindling into the darkness, already long lost to normal eyes.

"Sooner or later, we're going to have to do something about Clark," Morgan said softly.

"Now that's something I have thought about."

Chapter Eight

By the time they reached the Mess most of the Spitfire crews had already returned, their night's work done. The mood remained subdued. Morgan walked straight over to join Hinde and Werner at the bar. By the time Crowe had ordered their drinks all three were bitterly complaining about their lack of success.

"It's been a week since our last decent scrap," Morgan said as Crowe passed out the drinks and Barry shuffled away, muttering to himself. "It's as if they just can't be bothered to turn up anymore."

"Nazi cowards," Werner spat.

"Still," Morgan said, "at least someone got a kill. Hinde was just about to tell us about it."

Hinde drew out a cigarette. "Well, there were six of us, Raithe and me and four others. We were keeping close to London, hoping to catch some bombers coming in, but of course there was nothing. We were heading home when we saw the Messerschmitt 110." He lit the cigarette and took a deep breath. "Of course Raithe claimed it for himself," he continued, breathing out a cloud of foul smoke. "But he didn't just shoot it down. First he told us all to follow him. There were six of us watching this one German. And Raithe was really taking his time, getting closer and closer but not taking the shot. I thought maybe he had a problem, but he was just looking for the right shot. He only fired once."

Hinde shuddered slightly and took another long drag. "It was horrible. The bullets hit the pilot, just like he wanted. There was this spray of blood that came out through the broken glass and left a trail in the air. I could see the crewman behind the pilot and he was panicking. He had blood all over his face. But the aircraft itself wasn't damaged, it just flew on. Raithe started laughing on the radio. He kept laughing for a long time and wouldn't stop."

"There's something very wrong with that man," Morgan said.

"What a shot," Werner murmured wistfully.

"Hey, Bags," Morgan said. "Over here."

Danny Baggers had walked in with a still pale looking Jones in tow. His eyes seemed abnormally large as he hurried over to join them. "I was looking for you fellers. Did you hear about the bombers that went down?"

"Yeah, we heard about it before we took off. Halifax. The old squadron boss from here was flying it."

"Halifax?" asked Baggers. "This wasn't a Halifax; it was nine Lancasters. In the circuit at Pentney about an hour ago."

"What's this?" Harry Stead asked, overhearing Baggers and moving closer.

"I just heard it, sir, from a mate who's a Lancaster nav. Three or four Jerries got into the main circuit just as they were coming in to land. The Jerries only hit about five of them. The others were at such low level that when they tried to avoid the fighters they all ploughed into the deck."

"Jesus," Morgan said.

"Bloody hell," echoed Stead. "Sixty-three men, just like that."

"My mate reckons the fighters were single-engined," Baggers added.

"What, at night and two hundred miles from home? That can't be right. Your friend must have made a mistake."

"Unless they had very good pilots," Crowe said. Something about the incident just didn't sound right, he thought as Stead left the room to make some phone calls. It stayed on his mind as he walked down the corridor to the bathroom, but the more he thought about it, the more it seemed that Stead was probably right.

As he was returning Crowe passed the door that led to the storage area behind the bar. From within he heard a feminine muttering, and saw it was Cassie, apparently having some difficulty with the large cardboard box she was trying to lift onto a shelf.

"Hi, Crowe," she said, breathing heavily.

"Hi," he said shortly. He started to walk on, but came to a halt when he heard her muttering again and the sound of her straining to get the box up above her head.

"Damn it." He turned and walked back in. She smiled in greeting. "Give it to me," he said.

"Thanks. It goes just up there."

He took the box from her, bracing himself a little for the weight. There was none. The box was ridiculously light, and when he lifted it and felt no movement inside he realised that it was, in all likelihood, empty. He placed the box on the shelf and turned, puzzled, to find that Cassie had moved to block his escape.

"Sorry to trick you," she said, "but it was nice of you to offer to help. Besides, how else was I supposed to get you alone?"

"Why would you want to get me alone?"

"A few reasons, but mostly because I want you to take me out for a drink."

Crowe stirred uneasily. "That's a bad idea."

"Why?" she asked, stepping closer to him. "Because my dad is your boss? He doesn't need to know."

She was very well dressed for lugging boxes around in the storeroom, he thought, noting her figure hugging skirt. Her perfume was subtle and made him slightly breathless. "I'm flying every night," he said.

She shook her head. "I've seen the forecast for tomorrow. Dear old Harry explained it to me. It's going to be cloudy and raining, with strong winds."

"I can still fly in that."

"That's what I told Harry. But he says it doesn't matter, because the Germans won't. So how about that drink?"

He put his hands lightly on her arms. She raised one eyebrow, eyes widening slightly. "Can I get past, please?" he managed to ask with some difficulty.

"That depends on your answer."

He took a deep breath. She looked stunning, and in that moment he wanted to say yes. It was the thought of Noone's reaction if he found out that swayed him. Yes, the Group Captain would be annoyed, which had to be a plus point, and there was only a slim chance that he would react by grounding Crowe and risking the ire of Quiet and even Churchill. But the risk was there, and it was one that he simply couldn't take.

"Sorry," he said gently. She couldn't fully hide the disappointment that rolled across her pretty features.

"Never mind," she said brightly, "it was just an idea." She stepped aside to let him leave.

"What's up now?" Morgan said as he rejoined the group.

"Nothing. Why?"

"You've got that pissed off look about you. I can always recognise it. It's the one you start every night with."

"I'm fine."

Shaun Clark walked in to the bar. He looked pleased with himself.

"How about now?" Morgan said, nudging Crowe.

"No hard feelings, eh?" Clark said, giving Crowe a cold smile.

"None at all," Crowe said, returning the smile. His, unlike Clark's, was genuine, and Clark knew it. Clark was the one who had tried to intimidate him, not the other way around, but it was Clark who had backed down. Regardless of whether anyone else ever knew that, Clark knew. That was all that mattered. It was Clark who broke eye contact first now, backing down again. Crowe kept smiling. No one else needed to know. It would be their little secret.

At least, that was the plan.

"Clark," Stead shouted as he limped back into the room, his walking stick pounding against the floor. "What the bloody hell do you think you're playing at?"

"What are you on about, Harry?" Clark said, barely glancing at the man coming towards him.

"You know what I'm bloody on about, and you can bloody well call me sir while you're at it."

That made Clark turn around. "What are you on about, sir?" he said with a barely disguised sneer to his voice. All eyes were on them now, the room absolutely silent.

"How dare you threaten another pilot?"

Clark looked around the room, his face a model of assumed innocence. "Me? I was just giving Crowe some professional advice. It's a dangerous business we're in, and these vampires aren't very experienced after all."

Behind him, Mills suppressed a giggle.

"Professional, my arse," Stead said. "If I ever hear that you've pulled a stunt like that in the air again I'll have you on a bloody charge."

"You think so, do you?" Clark said, looking at Stead with contempt. "Think you're special because you're a Squadron Leader? You're just a broken old man, Harry. They only promoted you because they felt sorry for you."

For a moment Crowe thought Stead was going to cast aside the stick and go for Clark. It seemed to take an age for him to bring his anger under control. "Get out of this room, right now," he said through gritted teeth.

"I'm going," Clark said. Nonchalantly finishing his pint, he smiled at Barnes and Mills and strolled towards the exit. He paused in the doorway. "The only reason I'm not a Squadron Leader," he said loftily, "is because these freaks arrived. They won't be around forever. Maybe you should think whether you're with us or with them, eh?"

"Get out," Stead repeated. The obvious smirk on Clark's face as he left suggested that he was more amused than concerned.

"Jesus, Harry," Morgan said cheerfully. "I didn't think you had it in you."

"Damn this bloody back of mine," Stead muttered. "God, I wanted to hit him. Now I know how you feel, eh, Crowe?"

"I'll get you a drink."

"Let me get you one, son," Stead said, shaking his head. "I shouldn't have lost my temper like that. No good criticising Clark for being unprofessional then acting like a bloody idiot myself. Barry!"

"Hopefully that will shut Clark up for a bit," Morgan said as the barman began pouring beers.

"I doubt it, but I'm not having anyone in this squadron threatening anyone else. That's not how it works. Why didn't you tell me?"

Crowe shrugged. "We don't need your protection, Harry."

"No, but Clark does. Better a bollocking from me than a pasting from you."

"How did you know about it anyway?"

"Oddly enough, someone told me."

"Who?" Crowe looked at Morgan accusingly.

"It wasn't me," Morgan said, hands spread innocently.

"It wasn't a vampire, son," Stead said. "That's all you need to know."

Conversation had returned to the room, but it was not to last. The next time the door opened it was the Group Captain, with Clark following close behind. With one curt word Noone summoned Stead to the corridor, allowing the door to shut behind them and leaving Clark to rejoin his smiling friends.

The door kept the two senior officers hidden from the drinkers in the bar, but the prefabricated walls were thin and could do little to disguise the sound of Group Captain Noone's shouting. They heard it all. Noone's voice rose in pitch as he berated Stead for disrespecting his authority, for being overly sympathetic to the vampires and for failing to keep them under control. Occasionally Stead would try to get a word in edgeways but that apparently only enraged Noone further. To hear the Group Captain describe the incident it was Clark who had been under threat, and no one else, the

101

big Flight Lieutenant who stood smiling smugly in the bar the apparent innocent victim. The looks on the faces of the other pilots were more varied. Stead was popular and respected. Noone was neither.

Eventually the voices fell silent.

"The Group Captain wants us all in the briefing room," Clark announced. "Now."

Five minutes later, the entire squadron gathered in the briefing room for the first time in two weeks. There was no mistaking the unhappiness in the room. Raithe had emerged from somewhere, looking disdainfully around as if the whole affair was beneath him. Noone kept them waiting for a further ten minutes before he swept in, a rather fake-looking smile on his face.

Crowe joined the others in standing to some degree of attention. He didn't even try to conceal his lack of effort.

"I'm sorry to disturb your relaxation," the Group Captain began, sounding anything but sorry. "I wanted to gather you all together to congratulate you on your efforts so far. After two weeks of operations Treble-Six Squadron now has a combined kill total of forty-six. Impressive, gentlemen, most impressive. Believe me, it has been noted by my chain of command." There was a slightly sick look on his face. Crowe thought of William Bale's comments. The reaction at Fighter Command could hardly have flattered Treble-Six Squadron's commander.

"While this has obviously been a team effort," Noone said, "I would like to single out one individual who in my opinion has consistently showed top drawer flying skills and bold leadership. I am referring of course to Flight Lieutenant Shaun Clark, with three kills to his name so far. You could all do well to follow his example and learn from him." If Noone had expected a round of applause to follow he would have been disappointed. A couple of the younger pilots offered their congratulations, but otherwise the room remained mostly silent, the glances exchanged between pilots saying more than words ever could. Geordie Hulse looked over at Morgan and smiled sympathetically.

"Okay," Crowe told Morgan, "now I'm pissed off." Three kills? Morgan alone had eight kills. Raithe had eleven. They'd found those kills for themselves, not been led to them like a leashed dog by the lights on the back of vampire aircraft. He looked at Raithe first. The Romanian gave him a cold smile. Morgan simply shrugged, apparently unconcerned by Noone's words, but Crowe knew his friend well enough to know how deeply they would hurt his pride. Besides, Morgan might not be angry, but Crowe certainly was. He saw the expression on Clark's slightly rounded face and had to physically calm the urge to walk over and smash the man's head into the wall until there was nothing left of his skull but a dripping bloody smear on the whitewashed walls.

A few more words and the Group Captain left, leaving Harry Stead looking bewildered. The pilots trooped out in small groups back to the bar. Crowe hung back, wanting to speak to Stead.

"I'm sorry," Stead said. "It's not as if he doesn't know about Raithe and Morgan and you. But Clark's his favourite and it would seem that's all there is to be said." It was not much of a response, but then it was not Stead's fault, and he had already suffered for going against Noone once today.

Crowe walked out into the corridor and decided he needed a strong drink. Most of the aircrew had already returned to the bar or left for their accommodation, and the only person he saw in the corridor was Cassie. She was carrying another large box, though from the dull clinking of bottles he could tell this one wasn't empty.

Clark stuck his head out through the bar door as she passed by. "That looks heavy," he told her smoothly. "Do you need a man to help?"

"Do you know any?" she responded without looking at him. His cheeks reddening, Clark disappeared wordlessly back into the bar. Cassie looked up and saw Crowe approaching, and lowered her eyes, giving him a slightly embarrassed smile as she carried the box into the storeroom.

It took him only three steps to make his decision. He knew he was being stupid and that it was his anger which was driving him, but Clark and Noone had made his decision for him.

"Okay," he told the surprised Cassie. "If the mission tomorrow is scrubbed, we'll go for a drink. But keep it to yourself, okay?"

"I can keep a secret if you can." She looked pleased.

"You realise your dad would kill us both if he knew we were having this conversation?"

"No," she said, "he'd just kill you. See you tomorrow, Crowe."

He shook his head in disbelief and stepped back into the corridor, and a moment later heard Cassie's short but joyous laugh of triumph. What on earth was he doing? "I really need that drink," he muttered as he walked away.

"I thought I'd find you here, old boy," a familiar voice said. "Could we find a quiet place to sit down and have a chat?"

Crowe let go of the bar door handle and turned.

"I just want a drink."

"It's important."

"So is my drink."

"Crowe," Dr Madeley said sternly, "I've been speaking to Catherine Bale."

"Good for you."

"She's worried about you. I'm worried about you. Now can you please stop being stubborn and talk to me?"

Dr Madeley's office was a small room crammed with thick medical tomes and journals. The walls were covered in charts and diagrams. By the time Dr Madeley had sat down at his desk and Crowe had sunk into the leather upholstered chair opposite him there was barely room to close the door.

Dr Madeley pushed aside some of the clutter in front of him and began filling two glasses from an unmarked bottle. He was humming softly to himself.

"Does it surprise you that I've been speaking to Catherine?"

"Not really. You're her doctor."

"Family physician," Dr Madeley corrected. "Twenty years, now, ever since I picked a shell splinter out of William's knee at Gallipoli."

"Twenty years. You must be pretty bored of the job."

"How could I be bored? I've spent most of that time studying one of the most fascinating people who ever lived."

"Catherine?"

"Morgan."

"I find Catherine more interesting myself."

Dr Madeley blushed a vivid red. "Are you being deliberately rude, Crowe?"

"Yes."

"Well, stop it. Please." The doctor pushed a glass across the desk. "Here," he said. "Savour it."

Crowe lifted it and sniffed at it tentatively.

"Cognac?" he asked doubtfully.

"Not just ordinary Cognac, either. It's Rémy Martin V.S.O.P, so don't even think about turning your nose up at it."

Crowe took a sip. It tasted a lot better than he'd expected.

"Simply wonderful, isn't it?"

Crowe looked up and saw the look of dreamy contentment on the doctor's face as he drank from his own glass. "What do you want, Doctor?"

"If you'll be civil for a few minutes, I'll tell you. Can you manage that?"

"Pass the Cognac and we'll see."

Dr Madeley filled his glass for him, but his plump fingers kept a tight grip on the bottle.

"I want to tell you a few things," the doctor said. "Some of them you may have heard before. I was there the day William Bale met Catherine. Budapest, Nineteen-Nineteen. She was a rare beauty, Crowe."

"She still is."

Dr Madeley blushed again. "Morgan was born not long after they moved to England, and Catherine was protective of him from the start. Of course I thought it was bizarre, the way she wouldn't let him out of her rooms in the middle of the house. For the first eight months of his life I had to examine him by candlelight. He was a sickly child, too. I tried speaking to William, but you know he dotes on her. Morgan kept getting weaker, until one day Catherine asked me to bring Morgan some fresh blood. I refused. In fact, I came close to quitting that day."

"Why didn't you?"

"Catherine, I guess. I have no idea how she managed to persuade me, but I gave in."

Crowe had a pretty good idea, but he said nothing. The Cognac felt good as it slipped down his throat. Warm.

"I couldn't watch Catherine feeding blood to Morgan. Even William looked sick. Somehow she'd persuaded him too. But that was the last time Morgan was ill in his life. I guess he became my life's work from then on."

"I bet you could see your name in lights. Dr Madeley, Vampire Expert."

Dr Madeley sipped delicately from his own glass. "I didn't know that then. In fact, if I'm honest, I didn't have a clue why the blood helped. It was an open door that did it."

"Did what?"

"Helped me understand. One of the servants left a door open that should have been shut. Morgan was about eight months old, and he crawled into a sunlit room."

Crowe took a sharp breath. Dr Madeley nodded. "Well, you know yourself what that meant. By the time I reached him he'd crawled back into the shadows. He was whimpering, and the skin on his arms was horribly blistered. Naturally I bandaged him up and took him to his mother. You can imagine my shock when I went back an hour later and there wasn't a mark on him.

"That was me hooked. From then on I divided my time between caring for Morgan and trying to learn everything I could about vampirism. I went all over Europe. Libraries, folklore," he paused for a moment, watching Crowe, "insane asylums, anyone who could help me. As Morgan grew older I helped William and Catherine to understand the limits Morgan's condition placed on travel and socialising, and I would accompany him on his trips to London's nightclubs."

"That sounds like hard work," Crowe noted dryly.

"You'd be surprised. Can you imagine trying to convince Morgan to keep a low profile?"

"Good point."

"Anyway, I failed. Once William bought Morgan that damned Hurricane and he started knocking German bombers out of the skies, it was only a matter of time before K Department came knocking on my door. It took some persuading to get me to work for them, you know, but in the end the chance to work with an entire squadron of vampires was just too good a chance to turn down."

Crowe drained his glass again and put it heavily down on the desk. "Well, you were right, Doc."

"About what?"

"I had heard most of that before."

Dr Madeley smiled. "I guess what I'm trying to tell you is that I'm not altogether unfamiliar with vampire problems." He pointed at the empty glass. "Did you enjoy that?"

Crowe shrugged.

"I could offer you something stronger," the doctor said softly, "but I assume you're still not taking blood?"

"You've spoken to Catherine. You tell me."

"I'm asking you, dear boy."

"You know I'm not."

Dr Madeley took a sip of his own drink, rubbing one podgy hand across his face. He looked tired, pale from months of nocturnal living. He clearly wasn't suited to the lifestyle that his charges took for granted.

"I don't think you understand the importance of blood in your diet," he said wearily.

Crowe smiled. "Do you?"

"Not entirely. There's a great deal I don't know about vampires. But I've seen the effect on Morgan when he doesn't drink it."

Crowe's mouth opened slightly to speak before he could stop it, and he could tell by the questioning look on Dr Madeley's face that the action had not gone unnoticed. But the barriers he had placed between himself and the past were still there. He didn't know what effect not drinking blood had on Morgan. He did know what drinking blood did to *him*.

Dr Madeley watched him expectantly for a few more seconds, but then leaned back. The ageing leather of his chair creaked as he did so, the noise just failing to conceal his sigh. "You weren't born a vampire," he said, almost apologetically. "Some of the symptoms are still relatively weak in you. For whatever reason, blood isn't as crucial for you as it is for others. Lieberwitz wasn't born a vampire either, but he still drinks blood and still suffers when he doesn't. He's had the condition longer, of course, and he's older."

"If I find I need to drink it when I get older, I'll start."

"No, you won't," Dr Madeley said sadly. "Besides, by then it may be too late. Who knows what effect your abstinence is having on you?"

"That would be one of those things you don't know about vampires, then?"

"I'm more than happy to admit it," the doctor said, clearly not offended by Crowe's surly manner. "I don't know very much about the ageing process in vampires, or the long term health effects of your need for blood. I'm not sure anybody does. Yes, the skin remains youthful and the outer body retains its ability to heal quickly, but beneath the skin? We just don't know."

"What about Raithe?"

Dr Madeley shook his head. "Raithe has never let me examine him."

Somehow that didn't surprise Crowe. "He probably doesn't want a mere human touching him."

"Perhaps. But I think it's more than that." To Crowe's surprise the doctor's voice dropped to a whisper, as if afraid of being overheard. "Do you ever get the impression that Raithe is hiding something?"

"Everybody has secrets," Crowe said. He knew that Dr Madeley was right, and not just about Raithe. He'd long known the Romanian was concealing something about his past, but if he chose not to speak of it, Crowe would choose not to care. He also knew that he might be risking his long term health by his refusal to drink blood, but better that than the alternative. And at that precise moment, all he could think of was the past, of the memory of a man, a fighter, lying broken and bleeding his life out on a filthy stone floor.

He shook his head to clear the images, and stood up. "Thanks for the drink."

Dr Madeley was looking at him with suspicious eyes. "Do you have somewhere better to be?"

Crowe thought back to the storeroom, to Cassie Noone, to the look in her eyes as she stood close to him, head tilted back. He thought of her perfume. And then he thought of her father, and his face hardened.

"I can tell you're angry about something. What is it?"

"How long have you got?"

"Probably not long enough," Dr Madeley said. "After all, my dear fellow, you're the angriest person I've ever met. You really do take it to ridiculous lengths sometimes. But let's be precise. What in particular is annoying you right now?"

"I don't know. Noone. That prick Clark. You. Quentin Quiet and his whole bloody special squadron. The last sortie I flew. The fact that however many kills we get we're still just going to be seen as some fucking novelty freak show act, while the likes of Clark get all the praise and probably the bloody medals too. Is that precise enough for you?"

Crowe took a deep breath. Dr Madeley sat, unconcerned at the vampire's rant. "Why don't you sit back down, Crowe?" he asked calmly.

Crowe shook his head, remaining standing. "I'm not angry with you. I know you're trying to help, just like Morgan is, and Catherine too." He pushed his chair away. "But I don't want your help."

"Wait," Dr Madeley said, and something about the way he said it made Crowe halt. "There's something I want to show you." The doctor opened the top drawer of his desk, drew something out and placed it on the piles of paperwork in front of him.

It was a silver hip flask, identical to Morgan's but without the adornments. It glittered in the light from the desk lamp.

"Why don't you put that away, doc?"

"It's yours."

"I don't want it."

The doctor gave him a serious, slightly sad look. "One day you might. I just want you to know it's here for you when you do."

"I'll bear that in mind." He turned to leave.

"Where are you going?"

Crowe smiled humourlessly, and looked down at his watch. "I've got about two hours before I go back to hiding from the sun, so I'm going to get drunk. If you have an issue with that, then I guess you don't understand vampire problems at all."

Chapter Nine

She put his pint down on the table, sat down opposite him with her own gin and tonic, and smiled. "Now aren't you glad you came?"

They'd chosen the least public table, a small booth in a dim corner of the pub. It had not stopped Crowe getting some strange looks from the locals. Even without the sunglasses he would have looked out of place, his broad torso squeezed into an unfamiliar shirt and his tie uncomfortable around his thick neck. He was all too aware of the mud on his shoes and on the ankles of his trousers. Cassie, by contrast, looked perfectly at ease, though the revealing tops she habitually wore had been replaced this evening by a soft woollen jumper and a conservative though fashionable skirt. The effect was both demure and startlingly pretty. He felt clumsily dressed by comparison, and admitted as much.

"Don't worry," she said. "I don't normally dress like this, but Daddy thinks I've gone out with some friends to a play. I don't think he'd approve of it, if he knew I was here with you."

"I shouldn't be here at all."

"Really? Am I that bad company?"

"I meant in Staverton. The town is off-limits."

"I know what you meant, Crowe." She smiled. "I just like teasing you. You're so serious all the time."

"Sorry."

"Crowe," she repeated thoughtfully. "Do you have a first name?"

"Not any more."

"Mysterious," she said, sipping her drink daintily, her eyes watching him over the glass.

He changed the subject. "Do you lie to your father a lot?"

"Only when I have to. Daddy can be sweet but he's also over-protective. He seems to think that if he lets me out of his sight for one moment I'll run away with the first man I set eyes on, and he's

110

very particular over the sort of men he wants to see me with. Why are you looking at me like that?"

"You said your father was sweet. I find that hard to believe. He's not very sweet when I'm around."

"I said he can be sweet. Anyway, of course he's not sweet to you. You're not his only daughter."

"I suppose you've got him wrapped around your little finger."

"He doesn't mind being wrapped. Besides, I'm good at getting what I want."

"I can tell."

She laughed, and looked out of the window at the foul weather that had descended on Norfolk. "I didn't make it rain, Crowe," she said. "I just took advantage of it when it did."

She'd been right about the weather, and she was right about him being glad he came. Once it became clear that the night's missions were going to be rained off he'd been desperate to avoid her, but she'd been waiting. In the end it had simply seemed to be less trouble to go with her than to try and talk his way out of it. Much to his surprise, though, he was enjoying himself. Even more surprising, he realised from the sparkle in her eye, it seemed she was too.

"Did your dad convince you to get the job in the Mess?"

"Are you joking? It's the only thing he'd let me do, and it was hard enough to persuade him to let me do that. He won't even let me work every night. It has its perks, but it's not exactly how I saw my life going at this point."

"How did you see it?"

"When I was a child I always wanted to be a nurse. Then I wanted to go to University. And when the war started, I wanted to join up. But I'll be twenty-two in six weeks and I've not done anything. Daddy keeps trying to set me up with nice rich pilots who can marry me and keep me in the manner I've become accustomed to." Her expression left little doubt as to what she thought of that particular manner.

"Is that how he keeps your mother?"

"Kept, yes," she said. "She died about five years ago." Before he could open his mouth she smiled and added, "Don't worry about saying you're sorry. I'm over it."

"And your father? Is he over it?"

She hesitated, and the smile faded. "I guess he had his work to keep him busy." She paused. "My father never lets his personal life interfere with his so-called duty to his country."

Two soaked farm workers entered the pub, with the rain trying to follow them in. They were greeted loudly by their friends at the bar.

"What happened to the men he tried to marry you off to?" Crowe said after a few awkward moments.

Cassie shuddered. "Now there's a subject I try to avoid."

"Tell me anyway."

"Well, the first one was Matthew Fontayne. He was the son of an Air-Vice Marshal, so it wouldn't exactly have harmed Daddy's career if we'd married."

"Why didn't you?"

"He was an arrogant, boring idiot," she said, "though it took me a while to realise it. What's more he thought my place was in the home raising our children, and nowhere else. No wonder Daddy liked him so much. I'd love to have a family one day, but I want a life of my own first. He couldn't see that."

"What happened to him?" Crowe said, taking a sip of beer.

"He got shot down over Dunkirk," she said happily.

He almost choked on his drink, and the shock must have been obvious on his face.

"Oh God," she laughed, blushing, "I didn't mean he was killed. The Germans captured him. Honestly," she added fervently, with a guilty look in her eyes, "he wasn't even scratched. Of course, I had to pretend to be distraught for weeks. I got a letter from him via the Red Cross about six months later, asking if I would wait for him." She laughed again, though she was clearly embarrassed.

"And he wanted to marry you?" Crowe asked incredulously. She simply laughed more. "What about the other one?"

"The other one?"

"You said Fontayne was the first one."

"Hmm," she murmured distractedly. "Well, let's just say Daddy and I have different ideas about the sort of men I like and leave it at that."

He shrugged and took another drink. The pub was getting busier, which suited him. With so many people in the room very few noticed the pale-skinned man who insisted on wearing sunglasses indoors.

"I'm fed up of talking about me," Cassie said. "What about your parents? Do you see them often?"

"No."

"Oh." She obviously sensed the tension. "Tell me about vampires, then."

Crowe looked hurriedly around them, but there was no one within earshot and their voices wouldn't carry in the noisy bar. "What do you want to know?"

"Everything."

"Dr Madeley's the expert…"

"Dr Madeley's not here. You are."

So he told her, but not everything. He told her how he had developed the condition when he was seven years old. How his skin had gradually become more painful when exposed to the sun, until it started blistering. How the doctors had been unable to explain it.

"They didn't know what to do with me, so they put me in an orphanage. I just kept getting worse. By the time I was ten I couldn't go out in any sort of daylight, and my eyes hurt all the time."

"You haven't seen daylight since then?"

"It's difficult," Crowe said. He thought about mentioning Morgan's daylight suit, but decided against it. That seemed too personal, and he didn't really know this girl. She was easy to talk to, and that meant he had to be careful. It would be simple to tell her too much, and there were things about him she wouldn't want to know. Or, he corrected himself, he didn't want her to know.

He knew from the look of expectation on her face that he had been silent too long. He smiled. "I stayed in the orphanage until I was fourteen and then I left. I lived on the streets for a bit, stealing food, sheltering during the day. And that," he added, deciding she really wouldn't want to hear how he'd made his living, "was pretty much that until I got signed up for this and met Morgan and the rest of them."

"In Wales?"

"Yeah. That was the hard part, trying to learn to fly during the summer."

"Why was it hard?"

"The nights were too short," he told her. His mind wandered away from the conversation, back to the summer months. They would have been better served learning to fly during the longer winter months, but the war had not given them the luxury of being able to wait. It had been a strange time. The days had been long and boring, cooped up inside the old farmhouse where they had lived and studied while the beautiful, fatal sunshine beat down on the grass of the

113

private airfield outside. For three long months, as soon as the sun set each night the vampires had made their way down to the assortment of ageing warplanes which K Department had procured for them. That was when all the endless lectures in the darkened building seemed worthwhile. It had taken Morgan three months of intensive, exhausting flying training to get them ready for operations, months where Crowe had collapsed every dawn into his bed as tired as he had ever known, his mind trying desperately to cope with the new knowledge of yet another night of constant instruction. They had been probably the best months of Crowe's life.

"Morgan was a good instructor," Crowe mused aloud. "We managed."

"Morgan," Cassie echoed, shaking her head slightly. "He's funny."

"Funny?"

"He makes me smile."

"He has that effect on most people."

"Is he always so eager to please?"

"It depends who wants pleasing. Do you like him?"

She looked at him, knowingly. "Do you mean do I like him as a person? Or are you asking if I want to sleep with him?"

He was surprised by her directness, and it required a great effort to keep his face expressionless.

"You seem to be very good friends with him," Cassie added when he didn't respond.

"Yes. We shared a room during training, and it started there. We both love flying, him even more than me, if that's possible. But you're trying to change the subject."

"No."

"You're not?"

"No, I don't want to sleep with him. He's very good looking, and he makes me laugh. But he's not my type."

"What is your type?" He paused, and then leaned forward. "Ignore that question. Why are you here, Cassie? With me?"

"Let me ask you a question first," she replied calmly. "Do you enjoy being here with me?"

"Yes."

"And would you like to do it again?"

"Yes."

"And would you have ever asked me to come here if I hadn't asked you?"

"No."

She leaned forward. Their table was small and the movement brought her very close to him, so close that he could smell her familiar perfume despite the smoky atmosphere.

"That's why I'm here with you," she whispered. He could feel her leg gently pressed against his own. She lifted her glass and drained the last of her drink, but her eyes never left his face.

The door of the pub swung open again, and as a chorus of voices cried "Shut the door," three men walked in.

"Shit," Crowe muttered.

"What?" Her back was to the door.

"Shaun Clark just walked in."

Cassie stiffened, but didn't turn around. "Has he seen us?"

Even as the words left her lips Clark stopped his two companions and the three men walked towards their table. Crowe recognised Clark's friends as Archie Mills and Liam Barnes. He didn't really know them, but he'd never had any problem with them either. Both were Spitfire pilots, both were Flying Officers and thus junior to Clark, and both flew in Raithe's flight.

"They've seen me," Crowe said in a low voice. "Don't turn around. Keep your back to them."

"Evening, Crowe," Clark said loftily. "Don't you know the town is out of bounds?"

"Maybe it's time you weren't here, then."

"The rule doesn't apply to me," Clark said. "Besides, we don't stand out the way you do."

"No," Crowe replied blandly. "You're pretty ordinary."

The three men looked at each other. They were all taller than Crowe. Mills was the lightest, dark-haired and skinny, while Barnes had Clark's size but looked soft, fat where Clark had the naturally heavy build of a rugby player. Mills smiled. "Perhaps all four of us should step outside together?" he said in a nasal voice with a sideways glance at Clark.

"Are you sure, Mills?" Crowe asked quietly. "It's very dark out there." The young man hesitated, and Crowe noted with satisfaction the way the bluster faded. He glanced at Cassie, who mouthed "no fighting" at him.

Clark noticed the exchange. "Who's your lady friend?" He took a step forward. Crowe started to rise, but Cassie turned in her chair with a sweet smile on her face.

"Hello, Shaun."

His shock was palpable. "What are you doing here?"

"What does it look like? I'm having a drink with a friend."

Clark looked incredulously from the girl to the vampire and back again. "Is that what he is then, a friend?"

"At this point, yes."

"Meaning?"

"Meaning it's none of your business."

"Does your father know you're here with," Clark pointed at Crowe, finally adding "him?"

"It's none of his business, either."

"Really?"

Cassie turned away from Clark, feigning boredom, and smiled at Crowe. "Shall we go?"

He nodded, and as she took down her coat from the nearby peg he slowly drained the last of his pint, staring the whole time at the three men. He could see that Mills and Barnes were anxious to leave, their initial aggression fading quickly. Clark, though, returned the vampire's gaze.

Other customers in the pub had noticed the confrontation now. Cassie buttoned up her coat and turned to Crowe, nodding her readiness. "Excuse me," she said as she walked past the three men. Clark grabbed her arm. Crowe closed on him, his fists clenching, knocking a chair over as he moved past. Clark turned to face him, letting go of Cassie as Barnes and Mills froze.

"Don't," Cassie said.

"Take it outside," someone called from the bar.

"How about it, Crowe?" Clark asked. "Shall we take this outside?"

"Oh yes," Crowe snarled.

"Forget it, Crowe," Cassie said. He was ready to ignore her, but then he felt her warm fingers close on his fist. Confusion hit him like a blow, and he looked down at her, his hand relaxing as Clark took his chance to step back. Cassie's fingers slipped between his, and Clark's eyes opened wider in sudden disgust.

"We're leaving now, Shaun," Cassie said. "Why don't you go home and play with yourself?" She looked him up and down. "If you have any trouble finding it I'm sure you're friends will help." She smiled again and led Crowe by the hand towards the door.

"Next time," Clark said as the vampire passed him.

116

"Any time," Crowe shot back. He gave Clark one last threatening stare and followed Cassie out of the door. The rain was still coming down but she didn't even flinch, turning towards the side street where she had left her car. The door swung shut behind them, too slowly to muffle Clark's shout of "bitch". Crowe tried to ignore the words, tried to concentrate on the girl with him, but it was no use.

He let go of her hand.

"What are you doing?"

"You should go home, Cassie."

She stopped him as he tried to turn. "Where are you going?"

"I'm going to do the bastard. Right here, right now. His mates, too."

"What will that prove?"

"It won't prove anything. It'll just put him in the hospital." He tried to get past her but she blocked his way. He could have pushed her aside and wanted to, but something stopped him.

"Did you hear what he called you?"

"Do you think I care? He's an idiot. Let it go. Come with me instead."

"I can't." He put his hands on her to push her aside. That was when she kissed him.

For the first few moments only he could feel the desperation in her kiss, the urgent need to stop him, but she must have sensed that all thoughts of violence had left him. She relaxed, and he felt her press her body closer to his. Her cheeks were wet with rainwater, her lips cool and soft.

He opened his eyes, conscious that they were still stood in the street. There was no sign of light breaking through the heavy curtains of the pub, no faces at the window.

She smiled up at him, her eyes slightly wide. "Come on." She ran, her feet splashing water onto her slim calves and soaking the hem of her skirt. He followed her, past the silent post office on the corner and then, to his surprise, past her small car.

"Where are we going?" he asked but she just laughed and ducked into an alley. He pulled her close as she turned and kissed her again. Her hands slid up his back and gripped him. He felt her breasts against his chest, even through the layers of clothing. Her mouth opened, her tongue flicking hungrily against his as his hands slipped inside her coat and gently closed upon her firm, taut buttocks. He was aroused now and she could feel it, grinding her lower body forward against him. He wanted to lift her up, press her against the alley wall, pull up her skirt and thrust into her. He'd never known desire like it, and she could obviously tell.

"Wait," she said, breathlessly. He kept his hands on her, keeping her close, but she didn't try to move away. She looked up at him. "I want to see your eyes."

He didn't hesitate. It never occurred to him to doubt her. He simply slid his right hand up her thigh, past her waist and the last fading traces of youthful plumpness, past her ribs, her eyes widening as his fingers brushed her left breast, and then he drew his hand out from under her coat and slowly lifted his sunglasses.

"Oh," she said, but her tone was one of wonderment rather than the shock or disgust that he had once feared. She touched his cheek with her hand, and simply gazed into his eyes, his heart thumping until she drew his head down towards her and kissed him again.

When he undressed two hours later he left the wet clothes where they lay, on the floor of his room. Things like that just seemed so trivial right now. Even the Clark incident was forgotten.

They hadn't made love in the alley, though he sensed she'd wanted to as much as he had. She'd driven them home, and they'd kissed again in the car when she dropped him off near the edge of the camp. And though he'd not wanted the evening to end it was close to midnight, and her father would be waiting for her, back in their big rented house a mile from the base. So he'd kissed her again and said goodbye, before going back in the way he'd left the base, over the fence where it passed close to the road. It wasn't hard to avoid the guards. He even managed it without getting any muddier. They only had flashlights, after all.

He showered and changed into dry clothes more or less without thinking about it. His mind was far from organised, and for a while he tried without success to work out why he felt so confused. When it finally came to him it was something of a surprise. He was feeling happy. He simply lay on his bed, remembering the way he had done so barely a week earlier, marvelling at how different he felt now. He could still smell her perfume, though he knew that at least was just in his head. But they had kissed. He'd felt her passion. Not the purchased kind that he'd known before, but much more than that. He wondered how Noone would react if he knew, and decided he didn't care.

Morgan finally came in about four o'clock, preceded fractionally by the smell of strong alcohol.

"Good night?" Crowe said casually.

"Dear God, yes. That Harry Stead can drink, let me tell you. Where have you been?" Morgan looked down at the pile of wet clothes.

"Just out for a walk. I needed some air."

"I've been looking for you half the night. That must have been a long walk."

"I needed a lot of air."

"Don't suppose you saw Cassie while you were out, did you?" Morgan said as he began to undress.

Crowe felt himself go cold. "No. Why do you ask?"

"She wasn't working tonight, which was a shame. I was itching to have another crack at her. I really think I'm starting to develop a thing for her, you know?"

"I thought you said she wasn't interested?"

"I did. But she doesn't know me yet. I reckon I can wear her down. She's worth the effort. She's a real beauty, all right. Besides, she's got to prefer me to her last boyfriend, hasn't she?"

"Why? Who was it?"

Morgan, climbing into bed, stopped and gave Crowe a quizzical look. "I thought you'd have heard by now."

"No."

Morgan shrugged. "Well, it's supposedly over now but no one seems quite sure." He lay on his bed and closed his eyes. "It was your old friend Shaun Clark. I hear they were pretty serious. Anyway, I hope you had a good night."

Chapter Ten

The mess hall was alive with gossip.

"Have you heard?" asked one pilot. "We're going into France tonight."

"Rubbish," the sergeant next to him told him bluntly. "The Jerries are throwing everything against London tonight and we're going to catch them on the way in."

"I heard we were going to bomb the U-Boat pens near Brest," suggested a navigator. "Didn't you see the Lancaster that landed this afternoon?"

"Listen to them," Morgan said disdainfully. "Not a clue, the lot of them."

"Where are we going, then?" Hinde asked him, nervously fingering an unlit cigarette with one eye on the scowling Werner. "Crowe?"

"Buggered if I know," Crowe told him, idly stirring his tea.

"What's up with you, anyway?" Morgan asked, nudging him.

"Nothing."

"Really? The last couple of nights you've been neither here nor there. I don't know whether to hug you or hit you. Is there something you want to talk about?"

"I'm fine," Crowe assured him, although Morgan looked dubious. Crowe felt a little guilty about lying to his friend. It didn't help that he hadn't seen Cassie since he'd got out of her car. He wanted to speak to her, needed to ask her about Clark, but she hadn't worked the night before and, although it was still early, there was no sign of her tonight either.

"Well, something is going on," Hinde said. "This is the best weather we have had for a week."

"And we are all just sitting around," Werner said, "when probably the skies are full with Nazis."

Crowe looked around the room. Everybody was there, even Raithe, making a rare appearance in the communal areas. He sat apart, of course, alone except for Lieberwitz. Both were silent. Raithe rarely spoke to anyone except when he had to or when he felt like announcing his superiority. Lieberwitz very rarely spoke at all, though his lined face hinted at a deep sadness which no one had ever known him to discuss. Clark was there too, but since the incident in the pub both he and the group he kept around him had made a point of ignoring Crowe at all times. That suited Crowe just fine.

Hinde tentatively pulled out a book of matches and rolled the cigarette between his fingers, looking hopefully at Werner.

"Light that," Werner said, "and I stub it out on your head."

Over Morgan's shoulder Crowe saw a tall, brown-haired Wing Commander walk into the room. Crowe did not know him, but he felt a strong sense of recognition. The man must have been in his late twenties, though the moustache he wore made him look older, as did the mature eyes in his gentle-looking face. He looked around for a few moments, and then smiled slightly. He walked slowly towards them, murmuring a quiet greeting as he passed a nearby table, until he stood behind the unsighted Morgan. Then, with a slow wink at Crowe, he reached out a hand and ruffled Morgan's hair.

"Who's that?" Morgan spluttered, turning in his chair and looking up, and then a huge smile crossed his face. "Jesus Christ."

"You can call me sir," the stranger said.

"Piss off," Morgan told him indignantly, leaping to his feet and embracing the man. "What the hell are you doing here?"

"Is that any way to greet a senior officer?" the man asked, smiling indulgently. "Surely Martin and I taught you better than that?"

Morgan laughed happily and clapped the man firmly on the shoulder. "Come on, I'll introduce you to the boys. Everyone, this is my older brother, John. Wing Commander John Bale, if you please," he added with a mock curtsey. "John, this is Werner, Hinde and Gorecki. The two fine gentlemen over at the next table are Raithe and Lieberwitz." John gave them a nod which Raithe, much to Crowe's surprise, returned.

"Haven't you forgotten someone?" John asked.

"Oh, yeah," Morgan said with a dismissive look at Crowe. "You don't want to know him."

"You must be Crowe," John said, offering a hand which the vampire rose to take. "I've heard a lot about you."

Crowe gave Morgan an aggrieved look. "It seems everybody has."

"My little brother speaks very highly of you."

"That's a vicious lie," Morgan said quickly.

"You are not vampire," Werner said.

"Technically we're half-brothers," John replied amiably, as if the thought had never occurred to him. "But who's quibbling?" He turned to Morgan again. "Martin sends his regards, by the way."

"Our eldest brother," Morgan explained. Martin and John were both sons of William Bale's first wife, Helen, Crowe remembered, dimly recalling that she had tragically died giving birth to John.

"How is Martin?" Morgan continued. "Still running the family business?"

"And doing a good job of it. I hear you've been making a name for yourself as well?"

"We've had a few successes."

"You're too modest. Ten for you alone at the last count, Harry Stead tells me. Isn't that right, Harry?" John asked as Stead approached. "You'll be beating your tally in the Hurricane soon," he added to Morgan.

"Hurricane? What Hurricane?" asked Stead.

"Don't tell me you've kept that to yourself, too?" John asked.

"Believe me," Crowe said, "he's not that modest."

"We are sick of hearing," Werner added.

"Morgan persuaded our father to get him a Hurricane during the autumn of 1940," John explained to Stead. "Dad's a big mover in the arms industry and he's also got a private airfield down in Hampshire. Next thing you know, my little brother is waging his own secret war every night over London. Did bloody well, really; sixteen kills in three weeks." He smiled at the admiring look on Stead's face. He might have smiled even more if he'd spotted the envy on Werner's. "Only problem is, of course, German bombers start turning up in Kent fields with point-three-oh-three machine gun holes in them, but no one is claiming any kills."

"Mum always told us it was rude to boast," Morgan said.

"You never listened," John responded fondly. "Anyway, one morning some big old fellow in a trilby turns up and asks to see Morgan."

"Quentin Quiet," Morgan explained. "The Observer Corps and the Home Guard, would you believe, were keeping an eye on me. Unusual aircraft movements or something like that, they called it. They traced me back to Hampshire one night, and Quiet stepped in. He found out who owned the airfield, and funny old thing, didn't

William Bale have a freak child back in the twenties who couldn't go out in the daylight? Quiet puts two and two together and makes vampire. But none of this answers my question, John. What are you doing here?"

"Well," Stead interjected, "if you come through to the main briefing room, we'll put an end to the rumours and let you all know where you're going tonight."

If the crews had been excited by the rumours, Harry Stead's opening remarks had them virtually breathless with anticipation.

"Tonight we start a new phase of ops. It seems the Germans have got tired of being slaughtered by us and don't want to come out to play, so we're going to take the fight to them. Wing Commander Bale will explain it all."

John Bale walked out to the front of the room and gave a signal to a colleague. An aerial photograph appeared, projected on to the wall behind him.

"Good evening, gents. For those of you who don't know me, I'm lucky enough to command the finest heavy bomber squadron in the RAF. I hear Treble-Six is the finest night fighter squadron going. I can believe it, too."

He turned to the photograph behind him. "This is a German barrack complex in Northern Belgium, about fifteen miles south of Ghent, where they dish out some pretty specialised training. It also houses an Abwehr listening post. Nobody likes a Jerry listening to their chat, so we're going in tonight with sixteen Lancasters to remind him to mind his own business. Sadly it's smack bang between three night fighter bases. That's where your Spitfires come in. You're going to hold our hands."

There were a few quiet words exchanged among the gathered aircrew. Morgan, Crowe noted, was looking at his brother with an expression close to adoration. John raised his hand again, and the picture changed to a different photograph.

"German *Himmelbett* radar station, about twelve miles down the road. There are seven hundred and fifty of these stations between Norway and the Italian border, each controlling a little box of sky twenty miles wide. Our target sits in this station's box, so we decided it might be nice to pay them a visit first. Six Mosquitoes, twelve two hundred and fifty pound bombs, and they won't know a thing about us. The German night fighters have their own radar, but they rely on this station to get them within range of us in the first place. The bad news is that if the Mossies do their job, the Spitfires and my gunners will have a very quiet night."

There were a few mutterings of disappointment from the single-seaters, made worse by the smiles on the Mosquito pilots' faces. John Bale quickly and efficiently ran through the details of the target locations and their route, while Jones and the other navigators frantically scribbled into their notebooks. The Spitfires were to rendezvous with Bale's Lancasters just off the coast.

"The Mosquitoes will go out last, and fly straight to the target," John concluded. "This should be a very straight forward mission, gents, but if it goes well we'll be doing it again. My crews have been briefed that you're operating with some new type of super-effective radar and they're looking forward to working with you. I know you won't let them down. Good luck. I'll see you up there."

"Nice speech," Morgan told him as the crews filed out. "You make it sound like we're in for an easy night."

"We probably are. To be honest, I think we're wasting your time with this, but Quentin Quiet insisted we use you. If I had my way you'd be out looking for the Vulture instead of nursemaiding us."

"That's the second time we've heard that name," Crowe said. "Who is he?"

John looked surprised. "You've never heard of him?"

"No. Should we have?"

"Well, the whole of Bomber Command talks about little else these days. The Vulture's probably the finest night fighter pilot the Germans have. They reckon he's got dozens of kills, maybe hundreds. Still, I don't suppose we'll run into him tonight."

"Why not?"

"Supposedly he picks only on damaged aircraft and stragglers, and then only on dark nights."

"Sounds sensible," Crowe said. "Why make yourself a target?"

"Not very sporting, though, is it?" Morgan said.

"There's nothing sporting about getting killed."

"Quite right," John said. "Still, we won't see any sign of him, more's the pity. It would be nice to even some scores. But I'm afraid this is probably going to be very bland and boring. Let's try to have fun, though, eh?"

"He's as bad as you," Crowe observed to Morgan as they headed for the waiting transport. "Listening to him you'd think we were having the time of our lives."

"Well, aren't we?"

"Yes, but we can see where we're going." He checked his thigh pocket. "Bugger it."

"What?"

"I left my gloves in the mess hall."

"Well, hurry up. I'll keep the transport waiting."

Crowe made his way back to the deserted mess hall, and found his black leather flying gloves lying on the floor by his chair. He slipped them into his pocket and hurried out to catch up with the others. Outside he could hear the engine of one truck as it pulled away, and another idling as he passed the open door of the stockroom.

"Hey," said a familiar voice. He turned and saw Cassie, standing in the room. "I thought I'd missed you."

Crowe looked up and down the empty corridor. There was no one to see him, but still he hesitated. The pain and anger he had felt when Morgan had mentioned her relationship with Shaun Clark was back.

"I've been looking for you," he said finally, checking both ways one more time before slowly walking into the room and closing the door behind him.

If she noticed his hesitation or his reserve, she gave no sign. "I wanted to see you too," she said. "But Daddy wanted me to stay home last night. I'm not sure he believed I'd been to that play."

"We need to talk."

"But not now." She wrapped her arm around his neck and pulled him in for a long, deep kiss. For a moment he tried to resist, but her tongue was insistent and her body felt warm and inviting against him. She broke away and nuzzled into his neck, kissing him softly. "I missed you."

"I missed you too," he said awkwardly. He wanted to ask about Clark, but now somehow couldn't find the words.

"And if you don't get a move on," she added, "you'll miss your take-off. I'll be in the bar when you get back. If you're lucky I might ask you to help me with some more boxes." She smiled suggestively. "Go and be a hero for me."

He paused a moment longer, letting his eyes stray over her body. She turned away before she could see his own smile fade from his face, replaced by the painful realisation that the confrontation was still to come.

"Got them," Crowe said as he clambered into the truck, brandishing his gloves.

"You took your time," Morgan said as he banged the roof of the truck and the vehicle lurched away from the building. Crowe saw the oddly suspicious look on his friend's face, and quickly turned away. Werner grinned wolfishly at him.

"Nervous?" Crowe asked Jones.

"A little bit, yes."

"Just get us close. I'll do the rest." He cracked his knuckles with a satisfying pop.

"Why do you always do that?" Morgan said.

"My hands haven't had it easy. Sometimes they get tight. It relieves the pressure."

"It's utterly revolting." He reached into his flying suit and pulled out his monogrammed hip flask. Werner also drew out a flask, though his was more plain and functional.

"What's that?" Jones asked.

"Blood," Werner said.

"Human?" the navigator said anxiously. Werner merely stared at him blankly.

"It aids concentration and reflexes," Crowe said.

"Where's yours?"

"I don't need it."

"Crowe doesn't drink blood," Werner said. "I never find out why. You don't like the taste, no?"

Crowe ignored him. He saw the look on Jones' face as the young navigator saw Morgan and Werner drink for the first time. Morgan's reaction, as always, was muted, a slight intake of breath and a low moan of pleasure. Werner's was more obvious. He shook violently, his fists clenching, and his lips peeled back to reveal his gritted teeth. There was the faintest trace of blood left on his lip. Jones shuddered. Even Ronnie Hall, who must have seen this process half a dozen times as Werner's navigator, looked away.

"Don't worry, Stevie," said Danny Baggers, laughing at the look on Jones's face. "You get used to it eventually."

"Every vampire reacts differently," Crowe explained. He knew that better than anyone. Above them they heard the combined roar of four Merlin engines as John Bale got airborne.

"Too much blood will hurt you," Morgan said. He looked at Crowe. "But not enough will kill you."

They were still loading the last of the bombs into the Mosquitoes when they pulled up, and Crowe watched as Dom and two other men rolled a bomb on a cart under his aircraft. With much sweating and cursing and the help of little more than a couple of pulleys they managed to fix it in place.

Morgan gathered the Mosquito crews in for a final brief. "We'll stay at low level all the way there," he said, shouting to make himself heard over the majestic sound of twelve Spitfires getting airborne. "It's going to be quite dark but watch out for flak all the same. Crowe and I will hit the target first to mark it. The rest of you drop your bombs where ours land. Any questions?"

"What if you miss?" Clark asked.

Morgan gave him a pitying look. "Any other questions?"

"What do we do when we've destroyed our target?" Hulse said.

"Once we're done we'll link up with the others and provide extra escort. Not that they'll need it. No German night fighter is going to have a chance against us."

The crews broke up and headed to their aircraft. Morgan sent Danny Baggers on. "Are you sure you're okay?" he asked Crowe when they were alone. "You've been acting pretty strange."

"Honestly, I'm fine," Crowe said, trying to hide the rush of deceit that flared up inside him.

"Okay," Morgan said. Crowe could tell he was far from convinced. "If you ever need to talk…"

"I'll come to you. You know that."

"Yeah, I know that. Well, we'd better get going. Be lucky."

"I've never been lucky," Crowe said. "But what could go wrong tonight?"

He walked over to his own aircraft, where Jones was waiting. He nodded to Dom and clambered up the ladder, cursing as he banged his head on the top of the hatch. "Why don't they make these bloody things bigger?"

"A Mossie is a bit like a virgin, Crowe," Dom said cheerfully. "It's difficult to get into but very satisfying once you're in."

Crowe clambered into his seat and helped Jones up after him. Away to his right two of the Mosquitoes were already taxiing. With a wave to Dom he started his own engines and followed them out.

"All call-signs, this is Mosquito Leader. Is everybody ready?" Five confirmations came back to Morgan. "Remember, low and fast all the way. Radio silence until we get to the target area. No one speaks until I do. There's no need to let that listening post know we're on our way."

They took off and adopted a staggered arrow formation, Morgan leading. At two hundred feet the ground rushed past them, and Crowe had some sympathy for the regular pilots and for his obviously nervous navigator. With his own eyesight he could see the ground ahead in plenty of time to avoid any buildings or rising ground, though here over the fens there was little sign of either. But he remembered enough from his childhood to know that the picture would be very different from ordinary eyes. A dark smudge ahead could as easily be the shadow of a cloud as a thick woodland or collection of farm buildings. A road or railway line would be nothing more than a faint string, barely lighter in colour than the fields on either side.

Within minutes they passed a thin strip of sand and gravel and were over the shifting waters of the English Channel. The sky was a patchwork of broken cloud and lighter sections where stars could be seen breaking through. The moon, still in its infancy, flashed its brightness occasionally, but as they neared the coast of Europe its appearances became more and more infrequent and the clouds started to close up.

Europe. He'd always known there was more to life than the narrow confines of the streets of London, but for so many years he had never dreamed he could reach them. How could he have hoped to travel the long miles to France or Austria or Italy when to move in the daylight was death? It still amazed him that the likes of Gorecki and Werner had managed to travel so far to reach the squadron. They'd had help from Raithe and his Westphalia Trust friends. Crowe had nothing, and yet here he was. The aircraft felt alive around him and he tried to suppress the grin on his face.

Jones was looking at him. "Are you okay?" he asked over the intercom.

"Shut up," Crowe said, scowling. Why did everyone keep asking him that?

Jones looked hurt and turned his attention to his map. "About three minutes to target," he said after a few moments.

The radio crackled into life. "Crowe, come with me," Morgan said. "The rest of you climb to three thousand feet and await my signal."

Accelerating, Crowe followed Morgan as the others began to climb. They passed over the crest of a wooded hill and he saw the target immediately. He recognised the Freya and Wurzburg radars from the brief and from the photographs. The Freya was for long range detection, looking like a squared-off mass of scaffolding. The two Wurzburgs which flanked the Freya were circular designs, intended for close in accuracy, and now they both turned their way. Around the radars he could see a scattering of small buildings, several parked vehicles and what was obviously the door to a bunker. Even from this distance he could make out tiny figures scurrying between the buildings.

"I'll take the radars, you take the buildings," Morgan said.

Crowe slowed to give Morgan space. He had little desire to fly through the explosions of his friend's bombs. He watched as Morgan swept in and stiffened slightly as two thin lines of tracer rose into the air from a position to Morgan's starboard. He guessed they were small-calibre weapons, possibly machine guns firing at the sound of the aircraft, and Morgan didn't alter his course. Crowe saw the bomb doors open and then blinked as two orange explosions ripped through the radar site and sent chunks of shattered metalwork spinning into the air.

"Did you see that, Crowe?" Morgan exulted. "God, I'm good!"

Crowe didn't respond, concentrating on his own attack run. He was still coming in quicker than he would have liked, his mind desperately going back to the nights spent practicing bombing against dummy targets in Wales. That had been in a much slower aircraft, though. The tracers started again, this time cued by the flames from the burning vehicles. Crowe watched them climb lazily towards him and then whip past with brutal venom. He felt very aware that the Mosquito was a thing of lightweight wood.

He reached down with his right hand and pulled the lever for the bomb doors. The aircraft shook satisfyingly as they fell open. The target was dead ahead. The aircraft twitched, another reminder that their speed was too high and that the bomb doors were protesting in the slipstream, but it was too late to worry about it now. He didn't even have time to worry about the tracers which were encroaching ever closer. He struggled to resist the urge to release the bombs too soon, waited until what he judged was the perfect moment, and pressed the bomb release.

He was still pulling away and didn't have a chance to look back at the explosions, but even as the aircraft rocked and the sky momentarily lightened he knew that he had missed the bunker. At least he had contributed to the mess Morgan had made of their capabilities.

"Nice effort, Crowe," Morgan said. "Okay, lads, go on in and finish the job. Werner, take out that machine gun nest, will you?"

"With pleasure."

Crowe climbed and banked in time to see Werner's Mosquito dive sharply in, firing constantly. The gun crew tried to bring their weapon to bear on the attacking aircraft but an instant later the sandbagged position disappeared in a cloud of dust and sand. Werner pulled out of his dive and, as if for good measure, dropped his bombs directly on top of the bunker.

"Not bad," Morgan said.

"I give you lessons some time if you like," the German responded archly.

The three remaining Mosquitoes came in at their leisure now, emptying their own bomb-loads one by one into the maelstrom of flames and broken bodies.

"Okay," Morgan said, "that was nice. The others should be hitting their target shortly. Let's get up high and watch the show."

It took less than five minutes flying to reach the target area, even with a steady climb. They turned away before they reached the barracks, reluctant to risk alerting the German flak defences to the incoming bombers and even more reluctant to risk finding themselves over the target but underneath the bombers. "Life's too short to be dodging British bombs," was Morgan's considered opinion.

"Shouldn't they be here by now?" Crowe asked Jones after they had circled for ten minutes.

Jones checked his watch. "Maybe the bombers were late taking off?"

"Maybe. Morgan? We're starting to look a bit silly out here."

"Perhaps your brother got lost?" Clark said.

"Shut up," Morgan snapped. The concern in his voice was obvious. "They should be here by now. I'm going to try and raise Raithe on his frequency."

"Won't they be observing radio silence?" Crowe said.

"Bugger radio silence. Something must have happened." He fell silent.

"Let me do it," Crowe said. "We need you in charge here." He gestured to Jones. "See if you can raise them."

At first the radio gave up nothing but static. "Hello, Spitfire Leader, this is Mosquito Three, can you hear me?" There was no response. He repeated the call as Jones fiddled with the radio switches.

"Crowe, this is Hinde," he heard faintly in his ears. The static flooded back, with only garbled fragments of the Swiss vampire's voice breaking through. One word came out clearly though, "fighters", and the note of fear in Hinde's voice was unmistakeable.

"Morgan," Crowe said, switching frequencies, "they've been attacked."

"Come on," Morgan said, instantly hurling his Mosquito into a tight turn and heading towards the target area. "All navigators plot their course. We'll follow it back until we find them."

"Morgan, wait," Crowe said as the barracks complex loomed into sight below them. "Don't take us over the target." But it was too late. The night was suddenly alive with light as three massively powerful beams shot up from the ground and began to sweep the sky.

"Searchlights," Werner said with a curse. "Get above the clouds, for Christ's sake."

There was a distant flash and then the crump of the first anti-aircraft shell. Crowe saw the cloud of smoke that appeared in the air a few hundred yards to their left. That would be the marker shell, helping the gunners get their range. There would be more to come. He'd never seen flak before, but he'd heard enough stories to know they needed to get away fast. He pushed the throttle all the way forward, knowing that they were clearing the target and that in just a few more seconds they would be out of range.

And then, in an instant, he was blind.

Pain tore through his body. He screwed his eyes shut but still light came in, burning and brutal.

"We're being coned," Jones blurted unnecessarily.

Crowe wanted to scream abuse at the navigator but it was all he could do to concentrate on flying the aircraft. The aircraft shook as they were bracketed by flak. He could hear the shells bursting around them as they hung suspended in the sky, illuminated by one or more searchlights, a sitting duck for every gun on the site. There was a smell in the cockpit, cordite from a cloud of smoke that they must have passed through a matter of moments after it had exploded in a deadly shower of red hot shrapnel. He fumbled for his flying goggles, but when he opened his eyes their tinted lenses barely took the edge off the pain.

"Break right!"

Crowe hurled the Mosquito to starboard.

"We almost hit one of the others," Jones said.

"I'm blind."

"Put the aircraft into a dive," Jones said. "I'll tell you if we get too low." Even as Crowe obeyed he could feel Jones's shoulder brushing against him. He opened his eyes for an instant, long enough to see the blurred outline of Jones, leaning over and pressing his face close to the instrument panel in front of Crowe, his hand over his eyes as he sought to watch the spinning altimeter. The aircraft vibrated from the trauma of the passing air, the dive as sharp as any it had been designed to cope with. The sounds of flak receded as they dropped in height too quickly for the gunners to adjust their fusing, and then the light was gone. They had broken free of the searchlights.

Crowe opened his eyes. His vision was blurred by shock and tears.

"Okay, pull her up straight and turn thirty degrees to starboard."

Crowe obeyed, blinking. Through the haze he saw the altimeter needle slowly come to a halt. They had lost seven thousand feet in a matter of seconds, though it seemed like the pain had lasted much longer than that.

The radio burst into life. "Crowe, are you okay?" There was a note of horror in Morgan's voice.

"Tip bloody top," Crowe said shortly.

It was several seconds before he even began to regain his full eyesight, while Jones calmly gave him course and altitude instructions.

"You did well back there," Crowe finally said, gruffly. He slipped the goggles back up onto his helmet.

"Thanks. How are your eyes?"

"Fried. But I can see. Morgan, where are you?"

"Your eleven o'clock high. You've lost a lot of height."

Crowe looked up. Sure enough he could just about make out the tiny speck in the distance, though his vision was still a little blotchy. "Okay, I see you and I'm climbing now. Where are the bombers?"

"Somewhere ahead, I don't know how far. Get up here quickly, the bombers have been hit by fighters, I don't know how many. I spoke to Raithe. He says there are at least twenty."

"What? That's impossible. The Germans don't operate in those sorts of numbers, not at night."

"Twenty's what Raithe told me. The bombers have turned back."

"What's that?" Jones asked, tapping Crowe's arm. There was a fire burning in a field six thousand feet below, the light powerful enough to alert Jones. The navigator could not see what was causing it, but Crowe could. Through the writhing smoke he caught a glimpse of strewn metal and two engines on a single wing, torn from the fuselage, their propellers stilled.

"I see them," Werner interrupted. "Five miles, dead ahead."

"Seen," Morgan told him.

"Nice that you are still with us, Crowe."

"Thanks, Werner. It was a bit close for comfort."

"Jesus," Morgan said, "Raithe was right. There's dozens of the bastards."

"That means more targets," Werner said exultantly.

"Focke-Wulfs, by the look of them," Morgan added.

"Shit," Crowe muttered. That was not good news. The Focke-Wulf 190 was small, fast and manoeuvrable, and Crowe knew that even the latest Spitfire was barely a match for it. But the RAF aircraft here had one crucial advantage; they could see in the dark, and that, thought Crowe, was what really didn't make sense. The German aircraft was a single-seat day fighter. It had no radar and no observer, and it certainly didn't operate in groups of twenty at night. The whole thing was absurd. But there above the horizon he could see the ongoing battle, and knew that Morgan was right. There were more aircraft then he'd ever seen before at one time. He could make out the large shapes of the Lancaster bombers, flying close together on a steady course while all around them smaller aircraft whirled and dived through the sky.

"Switching frequencies," he heard Morgan say, and followed suit. Instantly his ears were filled with comments and commands and voices of desperation. "Got one," he heard someone say, and an instant later he saw a trail of smoke that began high in the sky and then dropped, seemingly slowly but accelerating until the ground finally brought it to a halt.

"Hang on," Crowe told Jones. "This may get bumpy." At full speed, teeth bared and his pulse thudding in his temples, Crowe joined the battle. He had a sudden recollection of an earlier fight, of a man standing in front of him, face broken beyond recognition by repeated blows, but then a Focke-Wulf zipped past his starboard wing and he wrenched his attention back to the present. The sky all around him was a seething mass of fighters, Spitfires and Mosquitoes and Focke-Wulfs, and in the centre were the bombers, droning on with only the slightest variations. From every gun position Crowe saw tracers reaching out into the night in desperation. He knew the gunners would not be able to tell friend from foe in the dark. In their fear, they might not even care.

A Focke-Wulf passed in front of him and he turned sharply to get behind it. The German pilot was clearly unaware of his presence, concentrating on the bombers ahead, and Crowe closed the range in a matter of seconds. He knew the Focke-Wulf was a fast aircraft but it had bled too much of its momentum off in the battle and Crowe had the advantage of arriving into the melee at full pelt. At two hundred yards he fired and the Focke-Wulf simply exploded, the wreckage cartwheeling across the sky before plummeting out of sight.

"Crowe, watch your tail," he heard Raithe say. Crowe twisted in his seat and saw the flashes as the fighter behind him opened up. He banked sharply, cursing his own stupidity for flying straight and level in a dogfight even as the enemy's fire missed his tail by a matter of inches. The Focke-Wulf turned sharply with him, seeking to fire again, but then it burst into flames and dropped away. A Spitfire flew over the burning wreckage and turned away in a hunt for more pickings. It was Raithe. He could tell by the markings on the tail.

"They are running," Werner called. "I'm going after them."

"Stay with the bombers," Morgan said. "We're going home."

Werner muttered something foul into the radio, then must have realised his mistake and released the transmit button. For a few seconds the air was silent but for the drone of engines.

He looked over at the bombers. Sixteen had left England. He counted twelve now, spread out in a weary untidy column, John Bale's aircraft leading the way. Every one of them bore signs of damage, including their commander's. The Spitfires were harder to count, but his first count yielded only ten. Ten from twelve. Jesus. All the Mosquitoes were there, and Morgan came alongside him and nodded. He looked exhausted.

"Where is Hinde?" Werner asked.

"He's dead," Raithe said instantly. There was anger in his voice.

Crowe felt something turn cold in his chest. Hinde, with his nervous eyes, his foul cigarettes and perfect English. Hinde, the first of them to die. "Who else?" he managed to say, the words little more than a croak.

"Michael Rhys-Jones," said a voice that Crowe recognised as Geordie Hulse. Crowe thought of a thin, slightly soft looking pilot with floppy hair. Dead now, his body trapped in a burning wreck, somewhere far below them.

"How many did we kill?" Werner asked.

"Does it matter?" Morgan said heavily.

Crowe sighed and looked back behind them. Although distant now, he could still make out the columns of smoke rising from the silent countryside. A small flicker of flame still blinked on the horizon, and he followed the smoke trail upwards to where it finally dissipated. There was an aircraft there.

His first thought was that it was one of the Mosquitoes, but a quick glance around him confirmed that all six aircraft were accounted for. It was twin-engined, though, so that ruled out a Focke-Wulf or an errant Lancaster. Whatever it was, it was keeping pace with them.

"Morgan," he said, "someone's following us. He's about three miles back and about three thousand feet above."

He saw Morgan twist in his seat. "Probably another German night fighter. We'll keep an eye on it."

Crowe looked at Jones. "How much fuel do we have to spare?"

"Not much, but we'll make it home no problem."

"Morgan, I'm going to go and take a look."

"Ignore it, Crowe. Let's just go home, okay?"

"It won't take long." He pulled away and slowly turned away from the bomber stream.

"Crowe," Morgan began, and then seemed to change his mind. "Okay," he said, resigned, "kill it and catch us up."

Crowe climbed on full power towards the German aircraft. He could imagine the fighter's radar operator hunched over his seat, excited at the prospect of getting among the slow moving bombers and trying to make sense of the new contact that seemed to be getting closer. But as he watched the unknown aircraft turned slowly away and began to retreat.

"He spotted us," Crowe said, impressed. "He's got a good radar operator." Disappointed, he turned back towards the bombers.

"Did you know Hinde well?" Jones asked quietly.

"I suppose. Well enough to know he was a good man. Morgan will probably take it hardest."

"Why?"

"He trained Hinde. He trained all of us. I guess Morgan is the nearest thing to a leader we've got."

"What about Raithe?"

"Raithe? He's nobody's leader. He's nobody's follower either."

"Why don't you like him?"

"It's not that I don't like him. I don't like what he stands for."

"What's that?"

"Raithe believes vampires are different to other humans. He believes we're superior, like the next step of evolution or something."

"What do you believe, Crowe?" Jones squirmed as Crowe shot him a look. "I'm just asking."

"Don't. Just get us home. What's the bastard doing now?"

"Who?"

"That night fighter's back again." Crowe began to turn the aircraft again, but even as he did so the other aircraft slowly turned away and began to retreat again. Crowe pushed the throttles forward again, causing Jones to look anxiously at the fuel gauges.

"We don't have enough fuel to keep maximum speed for long."

"That's okay," Crowe said. "We'll pop up, kill the bastard, and then we'll cruise home at a nice efficient speed. Damn it, he's accelerating." The other aircraft was maintaining the distance between them, and even as Crowe watched the gap began to expand. "He's getting away from us."

Jones looked at him in surprise, and then checked their airspeed. "That's impossible," he said. "The Germans don't have anything that can outrun a Mosquito, do they?"

"I'm telling you, he's getting away." The other aircraft was dwindling into the distance. "First of all he sees us when he shouldn't, and then he outruns us. Something doesn't add up here."

Jones looked down at his notes and then looked with a certain amount of unease at the fuel gauge. "Um," he began, "my fuel figures won't add up unless we turn for home now. Please?"

For a long moment Crowe ignored him, concentrating on the unfamiliar shape of the aircraft ahead of them, four miles now and receding. Then, reluctantly, he turned for home. Below them the last flames of a burning Spitfire flickered and died.

Chapter Eleven

"Two of our aircraft gone, not to mention four bombers. Is this the kind of success I can expect from vampires?"

Group Captain Noone was in a rage. He paced up and down his office, ignoring Harry Stead's efforts to calm him. "How do you think this will look when I report it to my superiors?"

John Bale sat on the corner of Noone's desk, looking exhausted. His face was blackened by smoke and there was dried blood on his hands and neck from the wounded tail gunner he had helped to carry to the ambulance. The landing had come too late. The man had died in his arms.

"Sir," John said, "I don't blame Treble-Six for what happened."

"Oh, really?" Noone looked toward Crowe and Morgan who stood at attention with Hulse and Clark beside them. "Who do you blame, then? Who shall I say was to blame for young Rhys-Jones' death when I write to his parents?"

"Try the Germans," Crowe said angrily.

"We lost a pilot too," Morgan said as the Group Captain gave Crowe a dangerous look. "Hinde." Morgan looked calm and his voice was steady, but Crowe could tell how hard he was taking the loss.

"Oh, yes. Of course," Noone said casually. "The vampire. Those incredible eyes of his didn't do him much good, did they?"

Morgan stiffened. Crowe instantly opened his mouth to respond but John Bale shook his head. "Sir," the bomber commander said in a measured tone, "that German squadron hit us with more aircraft than I've ever seen operated at night, and they outnumbered our fighters by some distance. And we still got at least eight of them."

"You'll excuse me, John, if I don't consider eight of theirs to be worth our losses, especially when the target wasn't even damaged. The question is how did they find you? I thought the Mosquitoes destroyed the radar station?"

"We did," Morgan insisted.

"I wasn't talking to you, Bale. Mister Clark?"

"It was dark, sir," Clark said without looking at the vampires. "I couldn't tell if we hit the right target or not." Geordie Hulse gave him a contemptuous look.

"So you're saying it's possible that the radar station wasn't destroyed?" the Group Captain insisted.

"Yes, sir."

"Fuck you, Clark," Crowe said.

"Not now, Crowe," Harry Stead said, although it was clear that he understood Crowe's anger.

"It is my belief, as mission commander," John said, emphasising the last words, "that the Mosquitoes destroyed the radar station. I also believe it doesn't make any difference whether they did or not."

"What do you mean?"

"I mean that each of those *Himmelbett* boxes can control one fighter at a time. We destroyed it so that we could operate unseen over the target for as long as we wanted, not because we thought it would keep us safe from fighters. And no single radar station could possibly have controlled that many fighters onto us. It's impossible."

"Clearly it isn't. They found you."

"I'm well aware of that, sir," John said firmly, glancing at his blood-stained hands. "But I've been flying raids at night since early 1940, and I've never seen that many fighters at once. And these were day fighters. They didn't have radar. I don't know how they found us but they did, and we'd all have bought it if it wasn't for your boys."

Noone smiled, the expression looking faked and unpleasant. "Wing Commander Bale, I appreciate your comments. I'm sure you genuinely believe this and are not saying it out of some understandable though misguided desire to help your," he looked at Morgan, "brother. But I'm afraid I see no other possibility than that the vampires failed to indicate the right target and that the radar station was, consequently, still operational."

"May I speak to you alone, sir?" Crowe said.

"I'd prefer witnesses," Noone said. "There may still be a court-martial."

"Fair enough," Crowe said. "I'll tell you all, then."

"Tell us what, precisely?"

"There was another aircraft out there. A night fighter. German. Twin-engined."

138

"That one you followed?" Morgan asked him.

Crowe nodded. "He was flying above the battle."

"Probably waiting for easy pickings," Noone sneered. "It seems there were plenty, thanks to you."

"I tried to engage him. He outran me."

"Really?" Stead said. "What was it?"

"That's the point. I've never seen one of them before."

"It wasn't a Messerschmitt, or one of those converted Dorniers?"

"Outrunning a Mosquito?"

"No, of course not," Stead said, looking puzzled. "That's not right at all."

"Whatever it was," Crowe said, "it spotted me turning at three miles."

"Have you heard of radar, Crowe?" the Group Captain mocked.

"Yes, and I've killed men who were using it, or trying to." He couldn't resist a glance at Clark. "It wasn't radar. He couldn't have reacted that quickly."

"What are you suggesting, Crowe?" Stead said quietly.

"The Germans have got a vampire."

"Rubbish," Noone snapped.

"Hold on a minute," John Bale said. "It makes perfect sense. You have vampires directing non-vampire pilots onto targets, don't you? Why not the Nazis?"

"The idea is ludicrous," Noone said. "The reason we've got vampires in the first place is because they're fleeing from the Nazis. Besides, Quentin Quiet is the only person who would be insane enough to believe you could use vampires as a weapon. No, John," he said with a patronising smile, "I'm afraid Crowe is merely trying to wriggle his way out of trouble. Isn't that right?"

Crowe struggled to contain himself. He imagined leaping across the desk and slamming the Group Captain's face against his over-polished desk. But the thought only brought back unpleasant memories of another man, another time.

"Sir," said Stead, "we need to give this serious thought. If the Germans have got a vampire…"

"They haven't," Noone told him sharply. "I'm starting to worry about you, Harry. I wonder if you are becoming a little too fond of the vampires." He turned to Crowe and Morgan. "The only reason I'm not grounding you is because I can't yet prove that your negligence cost the lives of two dozen men. But another failure like tonight and I will not hesitate. You're dismissed. All of you."

Clark saluted smartly and walked from the room. The others followed in silence.

"Will you come for a drink?" Morgan asked his brother.

"I can't. I have to get back to my Squadron. I should be with them now."

"I'm sorry, John."

"It wasn't your fault. And for what it's worth, Crowe, I believe you." He smiled sadly. "I'm sorry about Hinde. Take care, both of you." And with a last pat of Morgan's shoulder he was gone, out to the car that was waiting to take him back to his own shattered squadron.

There was a brooding atmosphere in the bar. Werner and Gorecki sat at a table in the corner; to Crowe's surprise, both Raithe and Lieberwitz sat with them. From the empty glasses on the table it was clear that all except Raithe had been drinking heavily.

While Morgan joined them, Crowe went to the bar and waited until Cassie finished serving Owen and Slater at the other end of the counter. She walked down towards him.

"Are you okay?" she said immediately.

"A vampire died tonight. Hinde."

"I know. I'm sorry. If you need me to be with you…"

He shook his head. "I really should be with the others."

She smiled sadly. "What can I get you?"

"A bottle of whisky and seven glasses." He watched as she reached up to grab the whisky, and thought again of her and Clark. Her fingers brushed his as she passed him the bottle, and without thinking he recoiled from her touch. He saw the hurt, puzzled look in her eyes.

He made his way back to the table and poured the whisky. Even Raithe took a glass. One glass sat empty on the table.

Crowe raised his glass. "Anyone want to say anything?" No one spoke, so Crowe drained his glass, the others following suit. The whisky tasted smoky and burned in his throat. He refilled their glasses, all but Raithe's, which sat untouched.

"I have a toast," Raithe said. "To Hinde," he said, rising. "May he be the only fool amongst us to die fighting in servitude to humans."

"Why did you have to say that, Raithe?" Morgan said quietly without looking up. "That's not the way Hinde would have looked at it."

"You think so? Tell me, Morgan, why was Hinde here?"

"He made a choice."

"He chose to die in the company of these animals?"

"He chose to fly, and to fight for a cause he believed in."

"You would say that, of course," Raithe said. "Your love for humans baffles me, Morgan. No matter how much they despise you and spit on you and force you to live in the shadows, you still defend them."

"Do you really believe we're that different?"

"We are more than just different, Morgan. We're better than them."

"You arrogant bastard," Morgan said, loud enough for the whole room to hear. The few pockets of conversation elsewhere died in an instant, all eyes turning towards Raithe.

"Do you think your human brothers pity you for your condition? No. I watched your brother with you tonight. I saw the look in his eyes, the envy. You will know things he will never know. How it is to walk in the darkness and see everything. How it is to cut yourself and watch the wounds heal in a heartbeat. How it is to hunt men down like cattle and kill them as they blunder blindly through the night."

Morgan didn't reply. He simply stared at Raithe, his handsome face twitching as if he wanted to speak but was unable to get the words out. The thin vampire smiled.

"You say Hinde made a choice, to die fighting for the humans? Answer me this question, Morgan. How many humans would have died fighting for him?" With a last imperious look around the room Raithe left, his untouched whisky abandoned on the table.

"Any time anyone else feels like joining in these conversations feel free," Morgan said acidly, looking at Crowe.

"I've asked myself the same question," Crowe said quietly.

"Well, I guess we know now how vampires really think." Clark walked over to them. He was alone but behind him several others were standing too. Things had become very tense.

"Leave it," Crowe said in a low warning tone.

"Or what? Are you going to start a fight in here? I don't think so. I think you'd rather wait until you can get me somewhere dark and sneak up on me. Hunt me down like cattle, like your friend Raithe would say. Isn't that right?"

Crowe pushed his glass to one side and stood up. Morgan put a warning hand on his arm but Crowe simply shrugged him off. He could feel Werner moving into position behind his right shoulder,

Lieberwitz slowly stepping up alongside him. Several of the other pilots were shifting uneasily into position, outnumbering the vampires by far, but Crowe didn't care. His eyes picked up the other movements and instinctively worked out distances between them, who were threats, who would stay and fight and who would back away; but his focus was on Clark. He felt a sudden fierce exultation as he prepared to finally knock the bastard to the ground, and knew with absolute conviction that he would not stop until the man was broken or dead. His hand began to come up, his mouth twisting into a smile.

Gorecki stepped between them. The little Pole held his book of poetry in his hand, as it seemed he always did, but he did not look down at it. He stood barring Crowe's path to Clark. "Bow your head, please," he said quietly. He looked around at the others too, and one by one they put their drinks down and lowered their eyes.

Gorecki began to speak, the words unfamiliar to Crowe, who knew it must be Polish. He spoke slowly and calmly, but his voice carried through the room. When he finished he paused for a moment, and then switched to English.

"To the ground my body broke
And without a sound I shed this cloak.
My wings unfurled under the light
And the heart flies free of all this blight."

Clark giggled. The sound echoed hollowly in the silent room.

Gorecki look slowly up and raised his glass. "To fallen friends," he said.

"Fallen friends," a few of the pilots said quietly. Half a second later, the words echoed in a dozen or more voices.

"Human and vampire, united now," Gorecki said softly, and took his seat. One by one the others did the same.

Clark stood in the centre of the room, the vampires ignoring him on one side and his regular colleagues on the other. With a disbelieving shake of his head, he walked back to rejoin Mills and Barnes at the bar.

"Thank you," Morgan said. Gorecki smiled and gave a shy nod.

"Our little Swiss friend would like that, I think," Werner agreed. "But he would have been sorry not to see Crowe destroy Clark."

"Do you think that would have helped?" Morgan said.

"For sure, no." Werner paused. "But it would make me laugh. A lot."

"Some other time, perhaps," Morgan said dryly.

"You can count on that," Crowe promised.

"Keep your mind on the enemy, will you?" Morgan said. "It's bad enough having to fight the Germans, without making more enemies at home."

"I think he is already made," Werner said.

"Fine," Morgan snapped. "But let's not make it any worse. Maybe if we all ignore him he will just go away, preferably into the sea at four hundred knots. I've got more important things to think about right now, like a German vampire flying around out there."

"What is this?" Werner said, shocked. Morgan turned and quickly filled the other vampires in on the discussion in the Group Captain's office. Both Werner and Gorecki looked thoughtful when he had finished. Lieberwitz's face was as expressionless as ever.

"Wonderful thought, isn't it?" Morgan finished with a sour note to his voice.

"You really think this German pilot was a vampire?" Gorecki asked Crowe.

"I don't know. Maybe he did just have a good radar operator."

"I hope he was a vampire," Werner said. "For the challenge, ja?"

"Well, it certainly doesn't look like Noone thinks he was, does it?"

"He's a bastard too. Someone should cut his throat." The way Werner snarled the words suggested he would be first in line for the pleasure.

"Would he really ground you?" Gorecki said.

"Definitely," Morgan said. "He'd ground the whole squadron if he thought he could get away with it. Or the vampires, at least."

"But it wasn't our fault."

"Do you think that makes any difference to Noone? Whatever reputation we'd built up died tonight. All our kills mean nothing now." Morgan looked morosely down at his drink. "I don't know what I'd do if I got grounded."

"I do," Werner said. "I would kill Noone. Unless Crowe gets there first, of course."

"It's a nice thought," Crowe said absently. The idea of being grounded made him feel sick. He tried to push the thought to the back of his mind, without success, and with one quick grab took Raithe's abandoned whisky and swallowed it.

"I'll get another bottle," Morgan said, starting to rise. "Hello, what's this now?"

Crowe turned and saw that two of the regular aircrew, who he recognised as Peter Owen and Ian Sullivan, were walking over to them. Neither of them struck him as the fighting type, but all the same he slowly shifted his position in readiness.

"Hi," Owen said hesitantly.

"Hello, Peter," Morgan said easily. "Is everything okay?"

The two men looked at each other nervously, until finally Sullivan coughed.

"I just wanted to say," Sullivan began, "or rather we just wanted to say that we're sorry about Hinde. He was a decent bloke."

"We've got three kills each and we wouldn't have got them without him," Owen said. "He was really quiet but he did his job and you just felt, you know, that he was looking out for you in the air. He was a good man."

"It's good of you to say so," Morgan said, looking over towards Clark. "Thank you. I know you're taking a risk speaking to us."

"Well," Sullivan said, "we just wanted you to know that we were sorry."

"So," said Werner as the two men walked away, "that was not expected."

"I hope they don't get into trouble," Morgan said.

"Did Clark see them come over here?" Crowe said.

"I don't think so. If he did they'll probably be in Noone's office tomorrow. I wonder if he'd ground them. Nothing about that man would surprise me."

"I've been thinking about this grounding business," Crowe said, leaning forward and lowering his voice. "Never mind whether they've got a vampire or not. I've got an idea how we can get our reputations back."

"How?"

"Simple. We do the one thing that will make us look good in front of Bomber Command. With them behind the squadron, Noone would look like a fool to ground us, wouldn't he? And Noone doesn't want to look like a fool, even if it means tolerating us."

"What are you talking about, Crowe?"

"We catch the Vulture." He smiled at the look on their faces. "And I know exactly how to do it."

Chapter Twelve

"I'm not sure I can do that."

"Come on, John," Morgan implored. "All we're asking for is one aircraft."

They were sat in John Bale's staff car, parked in darkness outside the headquarters building. John, sat in the driver's seat, didn't look happy to be there. He'd been reluctant to leave his squadron so soon after the previous night's disaster, and had told them as much.

"I've already lost four aircraft this week," John said. "Group are asking me to explain what happened and what am I supposed to say? That I lost a quarter of my squadron flying with Treble-Six and now I'm sending another aircraft to operate with them? They'd have my job."

"Not if you deliver the Vulture," Crowe said from the back seat.

"Look," said Morgan, "you said yourself that this one aircraft has shot down dozens of our bombers. What will your bosses say if you bring him down? Surely it's got to be worth the risk?"

"Maybe."

"You know it is. Besides, you want revenge. How many of your men has he killed?"

"How many more will he get if we don't stop him?" Crowe added.

"Come on, John. Just one aircraft. You know I wouldn't ask if I didn't think we could do this."

John Bale put up his hand in an appeal for silence. The two vampires sat back in their seats, looking at each other.

"Okay, you can have your aircraft," John said wearily. "I won't order anyone to do it but I'll ask for volunteers. In my squadron that's as good as an order." There was a strong note of pride in his voice.

"You've made a good decision, big brother."

"Let's hope so. Don't let me down."

"We won't."

145

"When do you want the aircraft?"

Crowe looked at his watch. "About three hours from now?"

"Three hours? I thought you were talking about next week or something."

"He could have another half dozen kills by then."

"Okay, three hours." John sighed. "If you have to do this let's do it properly. Get me a map. I'll ring the squadron, and then I'll show you where the bastard normally operates."

John Bale was as good as his word. Shortly before midnight the circling Crowe and Morgan saw the single Lancaster approaching.

"Hello Mosquito Leader, this is Dancer Two-One. Are you receiving me?"

"Mosquito Leader, roger. Have you been fully briefed on the mission?"

"Dancer Two-One, all we've been told is that we're going to fly up and down the coast here with two engines out and try to look damaged. You're trying to draw the Vulture out, right?"

"Yes. Are you happy with that?"

"Well, we're feeling a bit like the cheese in the mousetrap down here, but we're game."

"Okay Dancer Two-One, we'll be above and behind you, about two miles away. Don't worry. We'll be able to see you just fine with this new radar of ours." Morgan said the lie easily, and exactly as his brother had told him to say it. "Good luck."

"Happy hunting," the bomber pilot replied cheerfully.

"Brave man," Crowe said when the two vampires had changed radio frequencies so that they could speak privately.

"They all are. John's really proud of them. He's done a great job there."

"He's proud of you, too."

"Yes he is, but then he's always had fine judgement."

"He admires your modesty most of all."

"Modesty is for cricketers and nuns, though probably not at the same time. But in my defence, Crowe, if you include my kills from Nineteen-Forty I am the leading night fighter ace in the RAF. Not that anyone is allowed to know it."

"Does that bother you?"

146

"No, not really; I'm lucky enough to be someone who really enjoys his work. Besides, I know, and so do you, and John and Mum and Dad. There's not a lot else that matters, really."

The time had come, Crowe decided, to be honest with his friend. He didn't know what was going to happen with Cassie. The thought of her with Shaun Clark appalled him, and he desperately needed to speak to her to clear things up. Whether or not anything ever came of it, though, he didn't want to lie to Morgan any more.

"Morgan, there's something I need to tell you."

"Yeah?"

"Not here. When we land."

"Okay." There was a note of wariness in Morgan's voice, as well as curiosity. "We'll talk about it when we're on the ground. But if it's a personal problem,and by that I mean some kind of nasty genital fungus, you'd be better off going straight to Doctor Madeley."

Below them, the Lancaster had killed its two port engines, and was beginning to weave erratically. As Crowe watched the bomber slipped to port, losing altitude steadily, and then righted itself and began a slow laborious climb, all the while struggling to maintain a straight course.

"Does he look damaged to you?"

"It doesn't have to be exact," Morgan told him. "He's just got to make enough of an impression on a radar screen to draw the Vulture in."

"If he needs radar," Crowe muttered. He looked over both shoulders, checking behind them, but there was no sign of any aircraft. The sky was empty, save for a few scattered clouds. Jones was looking like he was in danger of falling asleep, and Crowe gave him a forceful nudge.

"Don't forget to check behind us."

"Do you think we'll see him tonight? The Vulture, I mean?"

"Probably not."

"But I thought he'd got fifty kills or more in this area?"

"That leaves plenty of kills that he's got elsewhere. The sky's a big place." That was the drawback of the plan. It relied on the Vulture coming to them.

"Morgan thinks we might see him," Jones said.

"Morgan's an optimist."

"You make it sound like that's a bad thing."

"An optimist is just someone who hasn't worked out the odds." Crowe checked their six again and scanned the sky, but the three British aircraft were alone. "We don't know if he's even hunting tonight," he told Jones.

"Then why are we flying?"

Crowe looked at him, slightly confused. "Because we can." Surely, after all, that was reason enough? Even on a night like this, when the odds of encountering the enemy were low, there was nothing he would rather be doing.

Jones didn't seem convinced. "And if we don't see him?"

"Then we come back tomorrow night, and the night after. We keep coming back until John Bale takes away his bomber or the Group Captain grounds us. We'll see the bastard eventually and then we'll take him."

"Mosquito Leader, this is Dancer Two-One. We've reached the end of the search area. Shall we head back and start again?"

"Yes please, Dancer Two-One. That was good so far." The disappointment in Morgan's voice was plain.

The sky became busier as the night wore on and bombers started to return from targets all over Western Europe. This was the optimum time for the Vulture to be operating. At one point they saw a twin-engined fighter in the distance and Crowe's heart-rate began to speed up, but Morgan's sharper eyes identified it as another RAF Mosquito, returning home from a night intruder sortie. Both vampires kept an eye on the aircraft anyway. They'd heard too many stories of British aircraft accidentally shooting down their own colleagues in the darkness. There was also a persistent rumour that some of the top night fighter pilots were not overly concerned with identifying their targets before they opened fire, so consumed were they with the desire to improve their scores. But the intruder passed them by without interest, and they went back to maintaining their slow patrol, Jones dozing in his seat.

Finally, after four hours Morgan decided enough was enough. He thanked the bomber crew and told them they would be needed the next night too. The Lancaster turned for home. The two vampires escorted the bomber back to its home base before turning south to cruise the thirty-five miles to Charney Breach.

"We'll get him tomorrow," Morgan said, mistaking Crowe's silence for disappointment. Crowe felt a little deflated about their lack of success, but his silence was something else entirely. He was thinking about Cassie.

Morgan took the lead, landing as always at a higher speed than recommended. Crowe woke Jones. The young man came alert instantly, with a guilty look on his face.

"Sorry. I didn't mean to fall asleep."

"You didn't miss much. Check your straps." He reached down to the two low-mounted levers and pulled the right hand one. He felt the undercarriage entering the slipstream through the controls and looked for the light that would confirm the wheels were down and locked. It didn't come on.

"That's not good."

"What?"

Crowe pulled the lever again, with no effect. "Morgan, are you still on radio?"

"Yes. I'm just parking the kite. What's up?"

"Can you see if my gear's down?"

"Have you got a problem?"

"You tell me." He took the Mosquito through the normal approach procedures but instead of landing, he kept the aircraft at thirty feet and deliberately overshot.

"Looks fine," Morgan said from the cockpit of his taxiing Mosquito. That confirmed the wheels were down but there was no guarantee that they were locked. If they weren't the undercarriage would simply give way. It would be a crash landing in all but name.

Crowe tapped Jones to get his attention. "There's a button by your left heel that's part of the emergency hydraulics. Push it down."

"It won't go."

"What?"

"The button won't go down. It's stuck."

"Push it harder."

"I'm telling you it's stuck." There was a hint of panic in his voice.

"Relax." Crowe forced his own voice to remain calm, even as his mind raced to remember the correct emergency procedures. There was a vague notion running around his head. He should have paid more attention during training, he thought. The notion became more concrete. "Look around you, there should be a metal bar somewhere."

"Is this it?"

149

"Yes. Attach it to the emergency hydraulics. There, where I'm pointing."

Jones fumbled for a few seconds until the bar clicked into place. "Now what?" he asked.

"Pump up and down like your life depended on it." He didn't feel he needed to add that it did. Jones threw himself into the task, fear clearly giving strength to the maniacal pumping action. He unstrapped himself so that he could get more leverage. The light stayed off.

"Morgan, how's that gear looking?"

"It still looks alright. But I can't tell if it's locked."

"What are we going to do?" Jones said.

"We'll land on the grass. It will be softer if the wheels collapse."

"If the wheels what?" The hint of panic had became a lot more solid.

Crowe began his final approach. Beside him, Jones looked pale and his mouth was moving slowly in an inaudible muttering.

"Make yourself useful," Crowe said, "switch the fuel off the moment we touch down. Otherwise we'll burn."

"Burn?" Jones said, looking confused.

"Yes," Crowe said evenly. "As in fire."

Jones reached down towards the fuel switches as they passed over the end of the runway with their wheels less than three feet above the ground.

"This is it," Crowe said. "Hold on." He took a deep breath, braced himself, and put the aircraft down.

For a few moments it seemed as if everything was running to plan. The wheels rolled perfectly with barely a bump from the grass below. Then the belly and engines struck the ground almost simultaneously. The cockpit was filled with a horrific grinding noise as turf sprayed up from the props tearing into the dirt. With a sudden crack one of the propeller blades sheared in two. Crowe instinctively ducked as the top half spun towards his face and glanced off the Perspex an inch from his left ear. He could hear the sound of wood splintering as the aircraft began to break up, but somehow he kept the aircraft straight as it slid along the wet grass until finally the tail slewed round and the aircraft ground to a halt.

They sat in silence. Crowe realised he was still gripping hard on the controls and released them. His knuckles felt tight. Jones looked at the mud that covered the windscreen and the cracks in the Perspex.

He turned in his seat and looked back at the hundred metre long furrow behind them. Only then did he seem to remember their situation and fumble for the door. As Crowe waited impatiently the young navigator crawled out of the half buried door and sprinted away from the aircraft. Crowe followed him out and walked calmly back across the field towards dispersal.

The fire crew had already arrived and they passed Crowe at high speed on their way to the aircraft. Jones was sat on the grass by the time Crowe reached him, looking numb. Crowe sat down next to him and cracked his knuckles, releasing the tension in his hands.

"The Group Captain's not going to be happy," Jones said eventually. Crowe nodded silently, watching as the crew sprayed the aircraft down.

Another vehicle pulled up behind them and Morgan and Dom climbed out. Dom held two cups that steamed in the cold night air.

"Quality landing," Morgan said. "Perhaps just the tiniest bit heavy, though."

"Dom, you're a star," Jones said as he gratefully took an offered cup from the engineer.

"Never mind that," Dom said, "what have you done to my sodding aircraft?"

Morgan took a sip of tea from his own cup. "They do say that any landing you walk away from is a good one," he said.

"They might well say that, sir, but I bleeding well don't. What happened?"

"Undercarriage problem," Crowe said. "The gear wouldn't lock itself down."

"Did you try the emergency hydraulics button on the floor?"

"Jones did."

"It was stuck," Jones said. "It wouldn't go down."

"Even after you pulled out the safety catch underneath? The one that stops you pressing it down accidentally?"

Jones looked at Crowe, his mouth slightly open with horror. "Even then," Crowe said firmly, before the navigator had a chance to speak. Out of the corner of his eye he saw Morgan smile and hurriedly hide the gesture behind his mug. He sipped at his tea. It was strong and sweet, but he felt the need for something stronger still.

"Well," Dom said, "I'd better check on the damage. It doesn't look good from here. Lucky for you we had a spare aircraft arrive this afternoon." He walked away with a last despairing look at the two men seated on the sodden turf.

"Will he be able to tell I'm lying?" Jones whispered.

Morgan glanced over at the forlorn shape of the wrecked Mosquito, and then pointedly back at the trail of debris that stretched back across the grass to the original impact point. "I think you'll be fine."

"Sorry, Crowe."

"You'll know next time."

"I'm hoping there won't be a next time."

"Don't hope too hard," Morgan told them, a half-smile on his face. "Noone may not let you have the spare. I heard he doesn't like you, Crowe."

"You heard that, eh?"

"You can ask him yourself in a moment," Morgan added, pointing to the staff car that was racing over the field towards them, bouncing alarmingly with each rut and rise in the ground. Rear wheels spinning in the mud, it slid around the back of the fire truck and came to a halt. The Group Captain emerged from the rear of the car and made an admonishing comment to the driver.

"Told you," Morgan observed. "Face like a smacked arse."

Noone looked with a mixture of rage and horror at the shattered Mosquito.

"A fine night's work, gentlemen," he sneered as Harry Stead limped up behind him. "So much for your great plan to catch the Vulture. An entire night of patrolling wasted and what do we have to show for it? One wrecked Mosquito."

"We had an undercarriage problem, sir," Jones said quietly.

"Sir," Stead said, "mechanical failures do happen. It's hardly Crowe's fault."

"Squadron Leader Stead, I'll thank you to kindly shut up. I see, Bale, that you manage as always to be at the scene of the problem. You're lucky your brother has more influence than I had given him credit for. While you were flying I received orders to give John Bale all assistance possible in catching the Vulture. Of course, that order arrived before they realised Crowe had destroyed one of my aircraft."

"We do have a spare, sir."

"I am fully aware of what aircraft we have, Bale. You may recall that it is my squadron. You may also recall that our brand-new Mosquitoes are not even supposed to be in service yet. We are lucky to have received any at all and we certainly won't be getting any more, so it is as simple as this. Crash that spare and I'd advise you not to survive the landing. Come on, Harry." He turned and walked back to the car.

Stead hesitated. "Don't worry," he said, "I'll speak to him."

"Don't waste your breath," Crowe said.

"There's no point in you getting into trouble too," Morgan agreed.

"Squadron Leader Stead!"

Stead rolled his eyes, and with a last exasperated shake of his head he turned away to join the waiting Group Captain. "Damn this bloody back of mine," he muttered as he slowly hobbled in obvious pain towards the car.

"That could have been worse," Morgan said.

"I need a drink."

"You need flying lessons."

"Do you want a slap?"

"John must have dropped Father's name into conversation with someone," Morgan said, pensively. "He hates doing that."

"He won't mind so much when we get the Vulture."

Morgan looked over at the twisted remnants of Crowe's Mosquito, and the disgruntled engineers who were already starting to pick at the remains like carrion birds. He turned to Crowe, and shook his head in silent disapproval.

"So," he said, "what did you want to tell me?"

At first he thought the noise at the window was part of his nightmare. It was the old dream, of a dimly-lit ring in a derelict factory. It was as vivid as ever, but this time when his opponent fell beneath his hands and lay motionless on the cold stone floor, it wasn't a boxer. The bloodied face was that of the rear gunner from the first Dornier he had shot down over the Channel, what seemed like a hundred years ago.

But he was awake now. He knew instinctively that it was not yet dawn, and he could only have been asleep for a matter of minutes. The noise came again, a soft insistent knocking. He swung silently out of bed, looking over at the sleeping Morgan, glad that his friend had hit the drinks so heavily before they turned in. He walked across the room and drew the heavy blackout curtain to one side.

"What are you doing here?" he asked incredulously when, having quickly dressed and pulled on his boots, he crept out of the barrack block.

"I heard about the crash. I wanted to see you."

"Come here," he whispered sharply, pulling her into the shadows behind the building. "Are you out of your mind?"

Cassie looked a little hurt. It quickly gave way to indignation. "I thought you'd want to see me, too. I guess I was wrong."

"It's not a question of wanting. Do you have any idea of the risk you're taking? What if you'd woken Morgan instead of me?"

She smiled. "I was going to tell him I was in love with him."

"I guess he would have believed that." It was not long to dawn now, and the camp was almost silent. On the far side of the airfield he could see and hear the ground crew with a small tractor removing the last of the wreckage of his aircraft.

"Haven't you told him about us?"

"I told him tonight," Crowe said.

"How did he take it?"

"Okay," Crowe said shortly. "But so far no one else knows, and I'd like to keep it that way." Even that was not true, he knew. Clark knew they'd been together in Staverton, though he hadn't mentioned it. He probably hadn't said anything because he didn't want the embarrassment of people knowing his ex-girlfriend had gone out with a vampire.

"I didn't realise you were so worried about being caught," Cassie said.

"I'm not worried about me," he lied, though the fear of being grounded was all too fresh in his mind. "I'm worried about the squadron. Your father already has a thing about vampires."

Cassie stepped in close to him, sliding her left arm around his waist, the fingers of her right hand walking down his chest and stomach. "I have a thing for vampires, too. One of them, at least."

Crowe took a deep breath. "Like you had a thing for Shaun Clark?" he said quietly. He felt her body stiffen, and then she pulled away from him.

"Excuse me?"

"I know all about it, Cassie. You and Clark."

"Who told you? Him?"

"It doesn't matter."

"Clearly it does matter."

"Why didn't you tell me?"

"Because it was none of your business." She was annoyed now, but so was he.

"You didn't think it was any of my business that you were sleeping with that prick?"

"That's right, I didn't. And for your information, I wasn't sleeping with him. I slept with him. Once. We split up two days later."

"Why?"

"You mean besides the fact that he's arrogant, rude, and totally self-centred?"

"I mean why did you sleep with him?" He found his voice rising, and forced himself to bring it down to a whisper again. "What the hell possessed you to have anything to do with him?"

"Because I wanted to! Because believe it or not sometimes I want to have fun. Sometimes I want to have sex. Sometimes I want to be closer to someone than simply serving them drinks and then watching them go out to die!"

"Is that why you're with me?" he asked grimly.

"Yes, Crowe, that's exactly why I'm with you. The difference is that I never cared for Clark, and I do care for you." She walked away, leaving him alone in the shadows. When she turned, he could see the moisture in her eyes that reflected the faint glow of the sky. "Even if," she said, "sometimes, you can be just as big a prick as he is."

Chapter Thirteen

This time they flew higher. The bomber crew were still enthusiastic, despite the previous night's disappointment. They weaved erratically as before, dropping altitude and side-slipping, the big aircraft handling the rough treatment with aplomb. Crowe had half a mind to tell them not to waste their time. Although it was heavily overcast and therefore much darker than the previous night, reducing visibility for the two vampires to less than two miles, he could still tell that there were no enemy fighters in range. The show, expert though it was, was being played out without an audience.

His mood, as dark as the storm clouds gathering to the east of them, was not helped by the new aircraft. The spare Mosquito was clearly not fully flight-worthy yet. Dom had not been keen to let Crowe take it so soon. Now, with the aircraft feeling sluggish, Crowe regretted the brusque way he had brushed aside the engineer's concerns. He could tell by the way Jones nervously watched the starboard engine that the navigator was no happier.

Morgan had taken the news of Cassie surprisingly well, Crowe thought. He was obviously not happy with it, though he'd laughed at the suggestion it was because he wanted her himself.

"She's a nice girl," Morgan had admitted as they walked slowly back to the Mess the previous night, "but there are a lot of nice girls. Don't you think that maybe it might have been better to go for one who wasn't the Group Captain's daughter?"

"I didn't think about it."

"Is that supposed to surprise me?"

Crowe had smiled at that. "I mean, it just happened."

"I can't believe that even you would be daft enough to go to the pub with her. You must have stood out like a stiffy on a ballet dancer. Are you planning to see her again?"

"I don't know. There's the whole thing with Clark…"

"Over," Morgan said. "Definitely. I checked."

"I thought you weren't interested in her?"

"I'm not." He paused. "Well, not a lot," he admitted, "and certainly not now that you've had your repellent paws on her. But the thought of Clark being ditched by her makes me laugh. Let me rephrase the question. Do you want to see her again?"

"I think so."

"Why do I always feel so nervous when you talk about thinking? Who else knows?"

"No one."

"Good."

"Except Clark."

"What?"

"He came into the pub when we were together."

"That's fantastic," Morgan muttered. "Well, he obviously didn't tell her father or we'd both be in trouble."

"Why would you be in trouble?"

"We're all in this together, mate," Morgan said, and Crowe had been alarmed by the serious look on his face. "If one vampire pisses Noone off, we're all to blame. If you're going to keep this relationship going you need to be very careful, and not just for your sake. By all means, keep seeing her, but take some friendly advice. Think about what's at stake here. You could be grounded. Just to be sure you understand me, that means you won't be flying. Is she worth it? That's all I'm going to say. Think about it."

Not that it really mattered now, Crowe thought, his mind returning to the here and now of the Mosquito's cramped cockpit. After the previous night's conversation with Cassie he wasn't sure there was anything left to think about. He glanced over to the port side, where Morgan's aircraft was keeping formation barely fifty yards away. Beyond him, there was nothing but cloud and the approaching rain between them and the French coast.

"You're quiet," he said simply into the radio.

"Just thinking about John," Morgan replied after a few moments. "Well, worrying, really."

"Worrying?"

"I was speaking to him earlier. He's under a lot of pressure to get some results here. His reputation took a battering the other night and I guess some people think he's wasting his time trying to catch the Vulture."

"We'll prove them wrong."

"Maybe," Morgan said. Below them the Lancaster had feathered two engines, but even with its slow speed they were getting close to the southern end of their sweep area. In a few minutes they would be approaching Norwich and would have to make the turn north again. "I don't think he's coming, my friend. Not tonight, not with those clouds out there."

"I know."

"You still want to stay out here though?"

"I'm just not sure I can take another lecture from Noone."

"I know what you mean," Morgan said. I hate the way he makes me feel that we've let everyone down. Is that what worries you too?"

"I'm worried I might snap and smash his face in."

"Really? It's not like you to be violent."

"Besides," Crowe added, "those bomber lads are giving it everything."

"They do look like they're having fun, don't they?" Morgan conceded. "Oh, hell, why spoil their evening too? What do you say, one more sweep and then home?"

"One more sweep sounds about right," Crowe agreed with a glance at Jones, who gave a tired nod before resuming his anxious watch over the starboard engine. "Do you want to let them know?"

"Dancer Two-One, this is Mosquito Leader," Morgan began.

Jones gave a sudden squeal. "Fighter!"

Crowe's vampire reactions saved them. Without a moment's hesitation he yanked on the controls to bring the aircraft breaking up and right, even as bright tracers hurtled past the wingtip. The realisation of what had happened brought a bitter curse from his lips. The enemy fighter had approached from behind and above, and from the landward side of them. Their eyes had been so focused on the bomber below that they had neglected to check the unexpected direction. The fighter's first burst had missed but the Mosquitoes were in a desperate situation. They had kept their speed deliberately low to keep pace with the bomber. Now the Vulture had the devastating twin advantages of speed and altitude. Crowe rolled the Mosquito and dropped the nose to try and gain some momentum, desperately trying to spot the German aircraft.

"Morgan," he said in a warning tone.

"I'm working on it," Morgan said, excitement mingling with fear in his voice, but then Crowe saw the sleek shape of the fighter pass them by, and realised they weren't the target anymore. The German had fired a burst in passing but was now diving at great speed towards the Lancaster. The bomber crew must have seen the tracers above them, and as Crowe watched he could see the props on the bomber's starboard engines starting to turn as the pilot desperately strove to get back his surrendered power. Crowe pushed his aircraft into a dive, but even as he did so he knew it was too late. The gap between the night fighter and the bomber was closing rapidly. The Lancaster's rear gunner, firing virtually blind, opened up with his four machine guns but the German aircraft stuck to its course. The fighter seemed to slow in mid-air as its nose lit up with tiny flickering muzzle flashes, and then the bomber visibly rocked as round after round slammed home.

The effect was catastrophic. Even as the fighter swept past and began to climb out of its dive, Crowe saw large chunks of wing and fuselage fall away. One engine had taken a direct hit and a sheet of flame sprang instantly from the shattered powerplant and threatened to envelop the entire wing. A cloud of white spray appeared as the pilot operated his extinguishers, but it barely touched the fire. Fuel poured out into the slipstream from another engine, a faint dark trail against the troubled sea below. The rear turret had taken a direct hit, and as the range closed Crowe could make out, through the fragmented Perspex, the indescribable effect of the shells on the gunner.

"Jesus," Morgan muttered.

"Stay with the bomber," Crowe told him sharply as he pulled his aircraft into a climb, his eyes looking away from the carnage in the rear of the bomber to focus on the night fighter above.

"Crowe, wait," Morgan began in reply.

"Stay with the bomber," he repeated, shouting this time. His left hand was already on the black handles of the throttle, tugging viciously in an attempt to extract more power as he pulled away from the stricken bomber. He could see the night fighter well enough, and the recognition hit him hard. He did not know the type of aircraft, but he had seen it before, high above them the night of the raid over Belgium. He knew what was coming next. Even as the Mosquito's own engines screamed in protest at the strain they were under, the German fighter inexorably increased its lead.

"Is it him?" Jones asked.

"That's the bastard, all right."

"The Vulture."

"You've got speed," Crowe muttered as the German left them behind. "But one day it won't be enough to stop me killing you." With a final curse, he turned the Mosquito back towards home.

It did not take the eyes of a vampire to find the bomber again. Even Jones could see the fire, well before they drew close, the navigator's face draining of colour as they got nearer. The Lancaster was still flying, barely, but it was steadily losing height. He drew up alongside Morgan.

"Why aren't they bailing out?" Jones asked.

"They must have wounded onboard. How far to Charney Breach?"

"Four minutes. At the rate they're losing height it's going to be close." The combination of extinguishers and slipstream seemed to have prevented the fire from spreading to the fuselage but the flames were taking a toll on the control surfaces of the wing. Crowe looked over at the crew. The expression on the pilot's face was grim. A shell had passed through the window nearby and his hair was being ruffled by the breeze. The man looked shockingly young, and his eyes stared straight ahead. Next to him, the co-pilot was slumped in his seat. Most of his head was gone.

"Are we clear?" Morgan asked.

"He won't come back. Not now we're alert."

"His work is done, anyway," Morgan said sadly.

Ahead of them, the landing lights at Charney Breach appeared. The Lancaster lurched again, dropping a couple of hundred feet in an instant. Crowe wondered whether the pilot could see the tops of the trees below him, reaching up as if to tear the bomber from the sky.

"One minute," said Jones softly. Morgan began to calmly relay instructions to the bomber pilot, guiding him towards the darkened airfield. The undercarriage came down. The aircraft managed somehow to hold its course, arresting its slow slide downwards. Even so it was a close thing, the wheels passing less than ten feet above the trees at the end of the runway before the pilot managed to put them onto the deck with an ease and grace which was as astounding as it was incongruous. The aircraft began to slow.

With a sudden flash and a lethal shower of sparks the number two engine exploded, the wing tore free and the entire bomber collapsed sideways into the wet mud.

"Hold on," Crowe said sharply. Knowing it was dangerous and against regulations he put his own Mosquito straight into a fast approach and lowered the landing gear just in time to avoid a repeat

160

of the previous night. The landing was hard and fast, and he kept the speed up as he barrelled along the runway, braking only when he drew close to the growing ball of flame. Eighty yards away he stopped the Mosquito.

"Get out of my way," he snarled at Jones. The navigator took one look at the rage in the vampire's eyes and hurriedly clambered out of the aircraft, dropping to the soft ground below. Crowe pushed past him without a word and sprinted towards the bomber, shielding his eyes against the pain of the fire's glare until he could fumble for his goggles. There were figures silhouetted against the flames, crew members stumbling free and ground crew rushing to help them even as the fire spread and began to consume the fuselage.

"Get back," one of the fire crew was shouting. "Everyone get back. She's full of fuel." The heat of the flames became ever more painful as he got closer. He saw the pilot slumped on the turf, his head in his hands. Another crew member paced up and down as if dazed until he was unceremoniously bundled away by ground crew. Crowe ran over to the pilot, but Dom and another man were already there.

"We've got him, sir," Dom said grimly as they helped the young man up. The pilot looked around him, his eyes finally settling on Crowe. The vampire knew how he must look, with his tinted goggles worn in the dead of night, but the pilot's eyes betrayed no surprise, no emotion whatsoever. There was blood down one side of his face. Crowe felt his pulse quicken at the sight. Immediately his throat filled with the sickly taste of guilt. He turned away, shaking.

"You should get clear," Dom said. "There's nothing more we can do here now." Crowe hesitated for a moment, but he knew the engineer was right. He nodded and turned to leave, but then he froze. He had heard a voice.

At first he thought it was a trick of his imagination. No one else seemed to have heard anything. But then he heard it again, a low moan, a cry for help, and Crowe knew that his hearing, honed by his condition and his years in the dark, had not deceived him.

"There's still someone in there!" He sprinted towards the fire, ignoring the shouted warnings of the fire crew. His blood hammered in his temples. The heat of the flames intensified with each step and he took a final deep breath of night air before plunging through the rear cabin entrance into the smoke-filled fuselage. Even with his goggles the light from the flames was blinding, and he stumbled towards the cockpit, feeling his way with his gloved hands. His lungs already felt close to bursting with the effort of holding his breath, and he instinctively raised one hand to cover his mouth and nostrils. He could feel his skin beginning to burn and break from the heat of the flames that were all around him.

Outside, someone was desperately calling his name. He ignored them.

Through streaming tears he could just make out the stairs leading up to the cockpit and the body of a crew member, still strapped into his chair in front of an instrument console. His throat had been blown out by the same cannon shell which had destroyed most of the equipment.

Crowe stepped back, and as he did so a sheet of flame burst through from the wing and instantly took hold in the cramped confines of the fuselage. He gasped in pain. Sweat was running into his eyes, adding to his blindness.

He felt tired. There was nobody in here, nobody but the dead.

He was going to die too. Somehow the notion did not displease him. No more hiding in the dark. The flames would hurt, but if he was just to lie down, he could go to sleep, a sleep with no more nightmares. He dropped to one knee. The floor here was so soft.

The floor groaned.

In an instant he was alert again. He reached down and grabbed the wounded crewman, his eyes open just enough to see that the man's left leg was a shattered mess, his skin blistered from the heat. With an explosive effort that expelled the last of the oxygen from his lungs, Crowe dragged the man up and onto his shoulder and half fell towards where he knew the door must be. For a moment only he felt panic, the fear that he had gone the wrong way, but then there was a breeze blowing on his face and he leapt free of the wreckage, breaking into a lurching sprint even as he desperately gulped fresh air into his agonised lungs and a wave of flames flared through the open door.

There were people gathered some distance away, around the open doors of an ambulance. Crowe didn't stop running until he reached them. He didn't recognise any of them, but he knew the look of shock and horror on their faces.

"This man needs help," he said. He placed the crew man gently on the ground as people stood and stared at him. The man made no sound, and lay absolutely still.

"Now!" he screamed at the medical crew. "What are you waiting for? What the fuck are you staring at?"

"Come on, Crowe," he heard Morgan say as hands grabbed onto his arms and led him away. "It's okay."

"No, it's not."

Morgan and another man helped him away to the shadows and supported him as he slumped to the floor, his face cradled in his hands.

"He is okay?" a voice asked. He recognised it as Werner.

"I'm fine," Crowe said. He looked up and forced a smile, his eyes still half closed with the pain.

"Mein Gott," Werner exclaimed, staring.

"What?"

Morgan reached into his overalls and pulled out his silver hip flask. Crowe shook his head.

"No blood."

"Use it as a mirror," Morgan said.

Crowe took the flask and tilted it until, through the thin gap between his eyelids, he could see his face reflected. "Oh," he managed after a moment.

"You've looked better," Morgan said dryly.

Crowe's flame retardant clothing and helmet had prevented a lot of damage, and the goggles had saved his eyes. Nothing had been able to save his face. The skin around his eyes, across his upper cheeks and the bridge of his nose was reddened in places, blistered in others. He took off his gloves and touched the skin. It felt damp and bloated to the touch.

A car pulled to a halt next to them, its lights dazzling the three vampires until the driver switched them off. Dr Madeley clambered out and slammed the door behind him as he waddled over to join the pilots. There was a large medical bag swinging against the doctor's hip, and he looked concerned in the flickering glow from the burning aircraft.

"My God," he muttered as he saw Crowe's face.

"We've covered that, doc," Morgan said.

"Let me have a look at those burns," Dr Madeley said, kneeling down. Crowe waved him away impatiently and pointed towards the ambulance.

"Go to that crewman," he said, carefully removing his helmet. "He needs you."

"Well," the doctor said, reaching into the bag, "at least take this." He offered Crowe the metal bottle that had been in his study, but Crowe shook his head.

"Don't be a fool," Dr Madeley snapped. "Drink that and your skin will be healed in an hour. Ignore it and it will take a day or more, and you'll be in pain every minute of it."

"The pain's not that bad."

"Don't lie to me."

"Just bloody go and help that man, will you?"

"Go on, doc," Morgan said. "I'll try and talk some sense into him." Dr Madeley stood up, looking at Crowe with a mixture of exasperation and concern, and walked away towards the ambulance. Morgan watched him go.

"Well?" Crowe demanded.

"Well what? I'm not going to waste my breath trying to convince you to drink. I would be wasting my breath now, wouldn't I?"

"Yes."

"There you go, then. If you want to suffer in silence, be my guest."

"There are many people over there," Werner said, looking over towards a crowd who had gathered to watch the drama unfolding. Crowe could just make out the familiar faces of their squadron colleagues as his eyes began to return to normal.

"How long have they been there?" Morgan said.

"All the time, I think."

"I hope they enjoyed the show," Crowe said, bitterly.

"What went wrong up there?"

"The Vulture," Morgan said. "He bounced us from above. We never even saw him coming."

"Jones did," Crowe said. "He saved us."

"Remind me to buy him a drink some time."

"Have you seen him since we landed?"

"Last I saw, he and Danny were helping survivors back towards the vehicles."

That reminder brought another furious curse spitting from Crowe's lips.

"Don't blame yourself."

"Who should I blame, Morgan? It was my plan. If we'd stayed closer to the bomber…"

"The Vulture would probably have killed us both," Morgan interrupted. "And he'd still be up there and that bomber would still have gone down. So how about you stop feeling sorry for yourself and start thinking about how we're going to get the bastard?" He helped Crowe up.

"I'll get him, all right," Crowe promised, squeezing his friend's hand, placing his left hand on Morgan's shoulder.

Morgan smiled grimly. "I'll be there with you when you do."

Dr Madeley walked back over to them. He looked tired. His eyes looked straight past towards the fading flames and the blackened, skeletal remains of the bomber.

"Is he okay?" Crowe asked.

For a long moment the doctor didn't reply. His hands and his white pullover were soaked with blood.

"I need to get back to the other casualties," he said finally. "We really don't have the medics for something like this. We need to get them to a proper hospital."

"Is he okay?" Crowe repeated.

Dr Madeley shook his head. "I'm sorry, Crowe." He seemed about to say something more, but then with a sigh he walked back to his car. A hundred yards away the firemen had done their work, and the last of the flames flickered and died, leaving the night dark once more.

They refused the offer of a lift home. The cool night air felt soothing against Crowe's skin, not that he really cared. He walked a few yards behind the others as they crossed the sodden ground back to the Mess. The crowd had long since dissipated, and he was dimly aware of Morgan and Werner talking, discussing the bomber engagement, but he didn't listen. His only thoughts were of a twin-engined fighter dwindling into the distance while his own aircraft proved unable to match its speed.

"I ought to call John," Morgan said when they reached the steps outside the HQ building. "He deserves an explanation."

"You will have a drink?" Werner asked Crowe.

"No. I need to rest." Behind them the door of the Mess opened and Clark emerged, a group of other men behind him.

"Well, look at this," Clark said. "Crowe and Morgan, our heroes. Jesus," he added, seeming to notice Crowe's appearance for the first time, "you're looking even rougher than usual tonight, Crowe." He sounded a little drunk.

"Let me handle this," Morgan murmured to Crowe. "You go on back to the room."

"I'm staying."

"Good piece of flying tonight," Clark mocked. "Really top notch. What does your brother reckon to you killing some more of his men, Bale?"

Morgan didn't reply. He simply stared coldly at the man.

"First Rhys-Jones, then three more tonight," Clark continued. "Is anyone else wondering who is going to be next? Here's me thinking the vampires were supposed to be on our side. Our new super-weapon? Don't make me laugh."

"Please tell me you will hit him now," Werner said quietly.

"He's right, isn't he?" Crowe answered, and saw the slight look of incredulity in the German's eyes.

"Who is caring? Hit him anyway."

Clark smiled, and turned to the men gathered behind him. There were six of them, not a vampire amongst them. They were looking at Clark, but none stepped forward to join him. Instead they shifted uneasily on the stairs. One of the men turned back towards the door. Crowe recognised the man as Steve Slater. He'd never particularly noticed him before, just another of Clark's vampire-hating friends.

"Where are you going, Steve?" Clark asked. "Don't you want to know how many more of us the vampires plan to kill with their incompetence? It's your necks too."

"All I know," Slater said slowly, pausing in the doorway but not turning, "is that I saw Crowe run back into that aircraft to get that lad out, and it was the bravest thing I ever saw in my life."

"Didn't do the poor bastard much good now, did it? He's still dead."

"I know what I saw," Slater said, and walked back into the building.

"Hey, where are you all going?" Clark called.

"Leave it out, Shaun," Kev Masters told him. "The beer's getting warm." Within seconds Clark was alone. The big man, looking a lot smaller now, turned to face the three vampires.

"Is it me," Werner said to Clark with a grin, "or is it colder out here now?" He took a step forward, and Clark half stumbled as he stepped back so quickly that he was almost struck by the door opening behind him.

Harry Stead stuck his head out and took one stern look at them. "Inside, all of you. Quentin Quiet is here."

166

Chapter Fourteen

"Who is he, Quiet?" Crowe said, ignoring the gasps from the gathered crews at the horrific burns across his face. "Who is the Vulture?"

Quentin Quiet simply looked him up and down, his eyes hidden in the shadows under his hat but his face impassive. Beneath the brown suit his chest rose and fell slowly with his unconcerned breathing. "Why don't you sit down with the others, Crowe?" he said softly.

"You know, don't you?"

"Come on," Morgan said, tugging at his arm. Crowe stared at Quiet for a moment longer and then followed Morgan to their usual seats at the back. Every man he passed looked at him with a mixture of disgust and awe.

"I did not expect to be back here so soon," Quiet said, his voice filling the room and yet not raised in the slightest. "I had hoped you would have time to practice working together as a Squadron before the time arrived for a brief like this." He gave a signal to Harry Stead, who flicked the switch on the projector. With a whirr, the machine burst into life and a photograph appeared on the wall behind him. Crowe drew in his breath sharply.

"Are you alright?" Morgan asked, confused.

"That's him." The image on the wall showed a sleek twin-engined fighter with a thin fuselage and a clean, rounded nose. The photograph had been taken from above and to one side, the aircraft parked on a grass runway with its Luftwaffe markings clearly visible. On the nearer of the twin tail fins there was an emblem, a highly stylised bird of prey.

"It's an Arado Ar-440," Quiet said. "Don't worry if you've never heard of it; not many people have. It's manoeuvrable and very heavily armed, with four cannon. That's not all. Do you see that nodule above the rear fuselage? It contains two rear facing 13mm machine guns, remote controlled by the pilot, and there's another nodule like it underneath. This aircraft is not an easy kill. And it's very, very fast," he added, "as Crowe will testify."

"That's the thing that outran you?" Stead said. Crowe nodded. "How come we've never seen them before?" the Squadron Leader asked, turning to Quiet.

"It's a test aircraft, pretty new. Only about half a dozen have ever been built, and the Luftwaffe are still evaluating them in southern Germany. This is one of the only photographs we have, taken by a photo-reconnaissance Spitfire two weeks ago."

"Over Germany?"

"Belgium. One aircraft was flown out of Germany about six weeks ago. They skipped the testing and put it straight into service as a night fighter. The Spit that took this picture got shot to pieces over the airfield by extremely heavy flak. The pilot didn't survive the landing. Fortunately for us, the film did."

Geordie Hulse raised his hand. "It's a night fighter?"

"Yes."

"With no radar antenna?"

"So it would seem."

"Bloody hell," Hulse muttered, shaking his head. "Crowe was right."

Quiet smiled, his teeth momentarily visible in the shadows under his hat, giving him a predatory look. "Yes, Mr Hulse, he was. Crowe has seen this aircraft twice now, once over Belgium, and again, I suspect, earlier tonight."

"I don't get it," said Clark. He sounded bored. "What are we getting so excited about? So what if it's fast and manoeuvrable. It's still just one aircraft."

"This one aircraft," said Quiet, "is worth any hundred of Germany's other night fighters."

"The Germans have got a vampire," said Stead quietly.

Quiet nodded. "Yes. And it gets worse. You'll notice the markings on the tail?"

"A hawk?"

"A Falcon, Harry. It's the emblem of Jagdstaffel Falke, or Falcon Squadron to you and me. But if you look at it a certain way, it's reminiscent of a vulture, don't you think?"

"Hang on a minute," Clark said, looking confused as he leaned forward in his seat. "The Vulture?"

Quiet looked at him disdainfully. "Try and keep up, lad," he said. "I know it's hard." There were smiles around the room, not just amongst the vampires.

"How many kills does the bastard have now?" Stead asked. He wasn't smiling.

"Sixty that we've confirmed. Another one hundred plus suspected. That's just him personally, mostly in a Bf-110. He's even more dangerous in this faster and better-armed aircraft. Now for the bad news."

"Didn't we just get that?" Morgan said with an air of fatalistic amusement.

"Did anyone," Quiet said, "other than Crowe, wonder how those Focke-Wulfs managed to hit you so hard over Belgium? They're day-fighters, aren't they? No radar."

"They're doing the same thing as us," said Stead. "Using vampires to guide the fighters onto their targets."

"Precisely. Except the Germans only have one vampire." He paused. "That's the good news."

"I feel better now," said Morgan brightly. "Thanks."

Crowe sat back in his chair, barely listening now, his thoughts elsewhere. He felt no happiness, no triumph, that he had been proved right. He wanted to have his Mosquito rearmed and refuelled. He wanted to fly against the Vulture right away, take them all on, but dawn was coming fast. An image flashed into his mind of the burning Lancaster, of the Vulture accelerating away from them.

"How many Focke-Wulfs in the squadron?" Stead said, pressing. "How good are they?"

"We think about twenty. How good are they? Ask Rhys-Jones or Hinde." There were a few unhappy looks exchanged around the briefing room before Quiet continued. "Do not misunderstand me, gentlemen. We are talking about an extremely formidable foe. The days of easy pickings over the Channel are behind you. This is your new focus now. Jagdstaffel Falke is killing more of our bombers each night than the rest of the German night fighter force combined. If we try to fly anywhere near them, we die. If we try to avoid them, they come after us in our home bases, like those Lancasters they got at Pentney."

"But if this vampire and the Vulture are one and the same, what about all those kills the Vulture has got operating on his own?"

169

"Like tonight?" Clark said with a smirk and a mocking look towards Crowe.

"Even a lone wolf may hunt with a pack, Harry," said Quiet, seemingly ignoring Clark. "If the night is too dark, or the bombers don't come their way, the Vulture hunts alone."

"He must be more effective that way, too," Hulse interjected thoughtfully. "Look at us. We've got a couple of kills each, yes?"

"I've got four," Clark said haughtily.

"Raithe, on his own, has sixteen," said Hulse evenly. "That's more than most of us put together. They see better than us, and they fly better than us."

"What are we bothering with this bloody squadron for, then, if they're so good? Why do they even need us?"

"I have been wondering that myself," Raithe said.

"Enough," said Quiet. "You have your new mission. In a few nights time, weather permitting, we will begin our effort to engage and destroy the Vulture and his squadron."

"How?" said Crowe.

"You'll find out soon enough."

Clark stood up, looking first at Stead and then around at his colleagues before finally staring at Quiet. "Why are you telling us what our mission is? Why isn't Group Captain Noone here?"

"The Group Captain is sleeping," Quiet said.

"I suppose flying a desk must get tiring," Morgan said. The comment was made to Crowe, but with more than enough volume to reach the rest of the room.

Clark rounded on him angrily. "Show some respect," he snapped.

"Respect?" Morgan said incredulously. "For him? If that's an attempt at wit you're only half way there."

"That's enough, Morgan," Stead said sternly.

"It's getting late," Quiet said as Clark retook his seat, "and I have business elsewhere. Are there any questions?"

"Yes," Hulse said. "Why we don't send in half a dozen squadrons of Lancasters and flatten the airfield?"

"I could give you fifty reasons," Quiet said, "but three will suffice. Firstly, you saw what happened the last time bombers went near that base."

"We could escort them."

"You mean so we could meet the Vulture in battle? True, in which case we could leave the bombers behind and do the job ourselves.

Secondly, the airfield is built on top of an old Belgian bunker complex. It took the Germans four days fighting to capture it in the first place. Some of those bunkers are one hundred feet or more below the surface, and it's a fair bet that the aircrew sleep underground. It would take a thousand heavy bombers with more accuracy than has ever been seen just to put a dent in that place. And thirdly, we would just scare the Vulture away to a new base, and we'd lose another two hundred bombers before we could find him again. Does that answer your question?"

Hulse nodded, looking thoughtful. Quiet started to turn away.

"You never answered my question," Crowe said.

Quiet turned slowly back towards him, and Crowe felt the man's stare from beneath the brim of the fedora. "That's right, I didn't. Why don't you ask Lieberwitz?"

"Lieberwitz?" Crowe could not hide his surprise. There was a flicker of alarm on Lieberwitz's face as every man in the room turned in expectation towards him. The tired, morose expression soon returned to his craggy face.

"There's not a lot to tell," Lieberwitz said finally, his voice soft. "Just rumours, really. You hear stories from time to time. Gossip in Paris, a newspaper column in Budapest. They talked of a German nobleman, a gifted sportsman and hunter who developed a strange condition. His family were wealthy. Their money protected him when his condition became worse. He became a vampire, and the rumours say that he chose to embrace the life. The rumours say that he murdered children, drank their blood."

"And now he flies for the Luftwaffe?" Crowe said. "How did they recruit him?"

"They didn't," Quiet said, "just as the RAF didn't recruit you. He flies with Luftwaffe markings, but the Vulture answers to a different master."

"Who?"

"Have you ever heard of the Eckartstrasse?"

"No," Crowe said. Werner was sitting bolt upright, a shocked expression on his face like he had been struck.

"Good," Quiet said. "Pray they never hear of you."

"Who are they?"

"They are not nice people. They take their security very seriously indeed. The Eckartstrasse are named for the street in Berlin where

171

their offices are, except there is no Eckartstrasse in Berlin. It is a cover name."

"A cover name like K Department?" Morgan said.

"Perhaps."

"I have heard of them," Werner said darkly.

"Who are they?" Morgan said.

At first it seemed as if Werner hadn't heard him. His mouth twitched slightly, and Crowe saw that his hands seemed to shake slightly. The moment passed. Even as the other pilots looked at him in anticipation, his hands slowly came up to remove his sunglasses.

Crowe had caught glimpses of Werner's missing eye before, but even he was not prepared to see it fully now, deprived of all concealment. The ravaged eye socket glistened in the glare of the briefing room lights. The skin of the upper cheek and forehead was pristine, unmarked, testimony to the recuperative properties of the Favri bloodline. Even vampire healing powers could do nothing to hide the hideous damage within the shadows beneath his brow.

"They were the ones who did this," Werner said. His good eye blinked repeatedly in the light until he replaced the sunglasses. Crowe could see the expressions on the faces around him, but there was little or no disgust. The overwhelming emotion seemed to be sorrow, and even anger.

"What happened?" Quiet said softly. His voice was neutral, but Crowe knew the man in the hat must have known the story already.

"After the Nazis kill my family, they hunt me down. At first it seems they do not wish to hurt me, but soon it changes. When the man from the Eckartstrasse arrived I think I will soon be killed. No." He took a deep breath. "First they take my eye. I do not know why. They use sharp tools, then hot metal to stop the bleeding."

"How did you escape?" Jones whispered, his eyes wide and his mouth slightly open as he stared at Werner's sunglasses as if still seeing the horror behind them.

There was the ghost of a smile on the German's face. "British bombers caused a power cut," he said with a shrug. "When the lights return I am free and they are all dead. I was lucky. They were not."

"There are only two things you need to know about the Eckartstrasse," Quiet said, addressing them all. "The first is that the British Government is not the only one to devote effort towards unusual methods. The other is that it is sometimes better not to know anything at all."

Quiet left it at that, his tone suggesting he would not be drawn further.

Crowe's eyes had never once left Quiet's face. "How long have you known about the Vulture?"

"Harry told me about your theory after the Belgium raid. It seemed possible. I made enquiries and the pieces fell into place."

"Belgium was less than a week ago. That's some pretty fast enquiring."

"The department I run can be most," Quiet paused, "efficient."

"You're not bloody kidding," Crowe said, his mind racing. Although it was clear that many were confused by the new developments, there were no more questions; Quiet's manner did not encourage further interrogation, and the meeting broke up. Dawn was less than an hour away.

Quiet stopped Morgan and Crowe as they left. "Give your report to Harry Stead," he said. "He'll pass it on to me. And get Dr Madeley to look at those burns."

"I don't need a doctor."

"Don't think of it as a suggestion," Quiet said with a slight smile. The two vampires watched as he walked away towards his waiting car and the long drive back to London.

"Well, you were right," Morgan said.

"Not that it helped," Crowe replied, more harshly than he'd intended. Morgan, thick-skinned as always, seemed not to notice. He looked thoughtful as they walked towards Harry Stead's office for their debriefing.

"It's a good job you told Harry that you thought they had a vampire," he said. "K Department must be pretty good to find out so much about that German squadron so quickly. How do you think they did it?"

"I don't think they did," Crowe replied. "The question is why is Quiet lying to us about it?"

They wouldn't get the chance to find out the next night, nor would they start their new mission. The steady fall of rain and the miasma of low cloud ended that hope from the moment Crowe and Morgan awoke at nightfall. For a while the crews hung around the Mess, waiting for the call, but one by one they drifted away. Even the bar was quiet, Barry idly reading a newspaper while Cassie leaned over the till with her chin resting on her arm, forlornly waiting for custom.

Her father, predictably, had been apoplectic when he learned of the previous night's events. Noone launched into a furious tirade against Quentin Quiet and his department, but as Quiet was nowhere to be seen it fell on the long-suffering Harry Stead to bear the brunt of the squadron commander's rage. The rest of the squadron were not left in the dark, though, the thin walls of the HQ proving entirely incapable of withstanding Noone's ranting. He threatened to ban Quiet from the base; he poured scorn on Crowe's competence and threatened again to ground him; he was scathing about Stead's ability to keep Treble-Six Squadron running in his absence. Crucially, though, despite all his threats and bluster, Group Captain Noone did nothing. Within an hour he had left, to drive home in the rain.

"Oh, my God," Cassie said as Crowe and Morgan walked into the bar, "what happened to your face?"

"If you think it looks bad now, you should have seen it yesterday," Morgan said. "Fortunately we didn't recruit Crowe for his looks, or the war would be lost by now."

"Stuff it," Crowe told him, but he couldn't muster any real venom. His mood had lightened the moment he had seen the look of genuine concern on Cassie's face, but now it seemed her expression changed in front of him, the concern mixing with something else. He began to feel uneasy. He looked over Cassie's shoulder at the mirrored surface on the wall. The skin damage around the nose and eyes was still visible, with discolouration and the faintest traces of blistering, but the improvement in less than eighteen hours was incredible. Even a trace of fresh blood in his system would have finished the job by now, he knew. He'd ignored all offers.

"Does it hurt?" Cassie asked him, her eyes searching.

"It looks worse than it is."

"I'm fine too," Morgan said. "And it was sweet of you to ask."

"Instead of making smart remarks," Crowe said, "why don't you buy me a pint?"

"No need to be grumpy. Two pints of Best please, Cassie."

"Barry?" she called. "Can you serve these two gentlemen?" Barry ten feet away, was oblivious to her calls. She called again, louder, and when he turned to stare at her she mimed pulling a pint and pointed impatiently to Morgan. "Please excuse me," she murmured.

"What do you want?" Barry said gruffly as he shuffled down to them. Behind him Cassie took one quick look back at Crowe and then disappeared out of the back door. Now Crowe really didn't like the look on her face.

Morgan had noticed it too. "I'll get these," he said quietly. "Go and speak to her."

Leaving Morgan's increasingly indignant attempts to order a drink behind, Crowe walked into the corridor. The storeroom behind the bar was empty. She was not in the crew room, either. When he eventually found her, she was sat on the steps of the staff door at the back of the kitchens. The rain had briefly dissipated but there was still an unpleasant chill to the air and the stone felt damp when he sat down next to her.

"Are you okay?"

"Sorry," she said. "I just felt like I needed some air." She looked up at the cloudy night sky. "Do you wish you were up there now?"

"Always."

"Do you ever worry that you might get hurt?"

He smiled. "Worse than this, you mean?" he said, touching his face.

"It looks bad," she said, still without looking at him.

"Like Morgan said, it looked a lot worse yesterday. By tomorrow it will be completely gone."

She nodded, her eyes still on the leaden sky.

"But that's part of the problem, isn't it?" he said. He understood. He took his healing powers for granted. For Cassie they were just another sign of how different they were.

She turned and gave him an apologetic smile. "It just takes a little getting used to."

"Some people never get used to it at all."

"Sorry."

"Don't be. Besides, I owe you an apology."

"Yes, you probably do," she agreed. "You were right, though; I should have told you about Shaun. It's just...I was worried about how you might take it. I already knew you didn't like each other."

"I can't help it," he said defensively.

"I know. You're not alone, either. But we had such a nice time the other night that I didn't want to ruin it by mentioning him." She gave him a slightly dangerous look. "We did have a good time, didn't we?"

"Honestly?" he said. "I had a great time."

"And I'm forgiven?"

"You're forgiven."

"We can do it again, then?"

"I think we'd be pushing our luck if we went into Staverton again."

"There are lots of other places we can go," she said, with a slightly coquettish smile. She reached up and pulled the kitchen door closed, leaving them alone on the step in the darkness.

"Here?" he said as she edged closer. "It's a bit cold, isn't it?"

"It won't be when you put your arms around me," she replied, leaning forward to kiss him.

It was a good twenty minutes before he was able to untangle himself from Cassie's embrace and return to the bar. While Cassie disappeared to make herself presentable, Crowe rejoined Morgan, who was already on his second pint.

"What on earth have you been doing?" Morgan said. He took a long look at Crowe. "On second thoughts, don't tell me."

Crowe took a seat and a sip. "This beer's a little warm."

"Now whose fault can that be? Cheeky bugger. Hey Lieberwitz, do you want to join us?"

Crowe turned to see that the Austrian was standing in the doorway.

"You've got lipstick on your face," Morgan told Crowe in a rapid whisper.

Lieberwitz shook his head and started to turn away.

"Come on," Morgan persisted as Crowe wiped his mouth with the sleeve of his flight suit, "just a quick one? I'm buying."

"Okay," Lieberwitz said reluctantly after a long pause, and sat down as Morgan downed his pint and rushed to the bar to get new drinks. Crowe wondered how much of his friend's urgency was down to the fact that Cassie was back and serving the drinks again. Lieberwitz didn't offer any conversation, and for a few minutes they sat in silence listening to the beating of the rain beyond the heavy curtains.

"Gents," Morgan called from the bar, "I don't mean to interrupt your fascinating conversation, but seeing as it's just us in tonight shall I knock off the lights?" He took a quick step to the single master switch on the wall by the doorway and flicked it, instantly turning off each of the dim lights along the walls as well as the four shielded bulbs behind the bar. Barry gave a cry of anger and directed some choice words at Morgan, who looked amused as he flicked the switch back. Ignoring Barry's continued muttering he stepped back over to Cassie, took their drinks with a smile, and walked over to the table.

The young vampire sat down. He looked at Crowe and Lieberwitz in turn, opened his mouth as if to say something, and then took a drink instead.

"Dismal weather," Morgan said finally. He received a silent nod from Lieberwitz in reply. "Shame," he persisted, "You must be looking forward to having a go at that German squadron."

"Yes," Lieberwitz said, with apparently limited enthusiasm.

"It's fortunate that you've heard those rumours," Morgan added. "Otherwise all we'd know about the Vulture is that he's very good at picking off damaged bombers. Quentin Quiet must have been overjoyed when he found out how much you knew."

For a long moment the Austrian was silent, looking down into his pint as if confused by it. He had always been the quietest of them, though unlike Gorecki it wasn't because of his poor English. There was simply something ineffably sad about Lieberwitz, and Crowe had never felt it more than now. No one really knew him, or how he had come to be recruited by K Department. All Crowe knew was that Lieberwitz, like him, had not been born a vampire. When it came to sadness, perhaps that was enough.

"He should have asked Raithe," he said finally, as much to his drink as to them.

Crowe glanced at Morgan, who shrugged, just as confused as him.

"Why's that?" Morgan said.

Lieberwitz looked up at them. His face was as unreadable as always, but somehow, in that instant, Crowe knew exactly what he was going to say.

"Raithe knows him."

Chapter Fifteen

"What?"

Lieberwitz missed the look that Crowe and Morgan exchanged. "They were in the Westphalia Trust together." The Austrian shrugged slightly and took a mouthful of beer.

"Raithe knows the Vulture?" Morgan repeated.

In Crowe's mind a number of questions had just been answered. He didn't know much about Raithe, and the tall, haughty vampire didn't allow any of them to know much about him. Dr Madeley had been right when he said that Raithe was hiding something. It wasn't a surprise that he had kept secrets from them, but this? Crowe knew enough about the Romanian to know that he had been high in the Westphalia Trust, and that a wealthy German nobleman developing vampirism was not the sort of thing they would have missed. They had to have known.

And yet Raithe hadn't said a thing.

"Well, isn't that interesting?" Morgan mused aloud.

Squadron Leader Stead limped into the room, discomfort etched across his face, his eyes searching out Crowe. "Are you busy, son?"

"What's up, Harry?" Crowe pushed out a chair for him and Stead slumped into it, smiling gratefully.

"Oh, I've just had the engineers on the telephone. They've been doing some work to your Mosquito and they need an air-test done. The weather is pretty bad out there, so I won't order you to go."

"It's not a problem. I'll go now."

"I knew you would," Stead said, wincing. "I've arranged for transport to pick you and Jones up from here in ten minutes. Don't worry, lad; I'll take care of the rest of your beer." He smiled as he took the pint glass from Crowe's hand.

"How's your back, Harry?" Morgan said, looking concerned.

"I've had better days," Stead admitted. "But the Group Captain's talking about grounding me permanently if it gets any worse."

"Give it a few weeks and we'll all be grounded," Crowe heard Morgan say as he left the room. Jones arrived a minute before the transport and Crowe greeted him warmly. The combination of his conversation with Cassie and the unexpected chance to fly had left him happy. Twenty minutes after leaving the bar he was signing for the aircraft.

It was a mark of how unusually good his mood was that the air-test did little to dent his spirits. It was not a pleasant flight, but just the chance to fly alone without the need to hunt for the enemy brought a simple pleasure for Crowe. He took the aircraft up through the low cloud base, climbing until he cleared the weather and was looking down at an unbroken field of grey that spread as far as he could see in all directions. He swung the aircraft through a series of hard manoeuvres, assessing the extent of the engineers' success, and then carried out the in-flight tests one by one as laid out on the sheet Dom had given him. It seemed all too soon that they were descending again, breaking through the clouds less than a mile from Charney Breach. The rain, mercifully, seemed to have stopped.

"I was a little worried I wouldn't be able to find our way back," Jones admitted when they had safely landed and were taxiing back to the waiting ground crew.

"I wasn't."

"Really?" Jones looked at him. "That was probably the worst weather I've ever flown in. Didn't it bother you at all?"

"No. You're a good navigator," Crowe said simply. He ignored the grin that spread across the young man's face.

"What did you think?" Dom asked after engine shutdown.

"Better," Crowe admitted. "That starboard engine is still running a little rough. The rudder is a bit sticky, particularly to starboard. Oh, and the bomb doors don't work."

"Not at all?" Dom asked, surprised.

"No. Not unless I was pulling the wrong lever." He noticed the look on the engineer's face. "I wasn't pulling the wrong lever, Dom."

"No," Dom said hurriedly. "Course not. Never thought you were."

"It's all on the sheet," Crowe said, passing it to him. The transport was already waiting to take them back. With Jones in tow and his flying kit slung over one shoulder, Crowe walked towards the vehicle. It was a flash of movement in the trees a hundred yards from them that made him stop.

"What's up?" Jones asked.

"Nothing," Crowe said. "You go ahead. I'll meet you in the bar." Jones gave him a puzzled look and clambered into the transport, and Crowe waited until it was well on its way back to the distant buildings before checking no one was watching him and making his way to the trees.

"What are you doing here?"

"Well," Cassie replied, "I thought that seeing as we're friends again and it's stopped raining, you might like to sit out with me for a little while."

"The ground's wet."

"That's alright," she said with a smile. "I brought a blanket." She laid it out on the ground and sat down. With the trees behind them they were virtually invisible, and as he sat down next to her they had a good view of most of the airfield.

"Won't Barry miss you in the bar?"

"There's no one in tonight," Cassie said. "I was just sitting there, bored. Even Morgan only stayed for a little while after you left."

"Did he say anything?"

"I don't think he likes me much."

"He does," Crowe said. "He's just not sure we should be seeing each other."

"Because of my father?"

"Because of what your father can do. Morgan's worried he might ground me. He thinks I should choose between you and flying."

"What do you think?"

He looked at her. Her hair was slightly damp and her shoes were muddy from the long walk across the airfield, and her breath hung in faint clouds in the cold night air. She looked beautiful. "I think I want both," he told her.

"I'm flattered that you would take the risk for me. You do know that, don't you?"

"I think you're worth the risk."

She smiled. "I think so, too." She leaned her head against his shoulder and he slipped his arm around hers.

Deep within the wood behind them Crowe could hear the faint shuffling sounds of some nocturnal animal, interspersed with the heavy thud of rain drops that had coalesced on leaves before falling to the ground. On the far side of the airfield a small truck drove slowly along the perimeter track, the noise of its engine carried to them on the wind. There was little sign of movement, though, just a small knot of engineers working away at the air-tested Mosquito. It was not the sort of night that encouraged people to go outside.

"This must be frustrating for you," Cassie said after a few minutes.

"The weather? Yes."

"At least you got to fly tonight. I think Morgan was annoyed that he didn't get the chance. I heard Harry talking about you two the other night, how you always want to get up there whatever the weather. He thinks you'd never bother landing if you didn't have to refuel."

"He's probably right," Crowe said. He turned to her. "There's something else that always brings me back, though."

"What's that?" she said, her mouth opening slightly as she moved in for the kiss.

"Well," he said, "the dawn, obviously."

That cost him the kiss. "Pig," she said, pouting. "I don't know why I bother with you, although it may be because you're very sexy, in a rugged and angry and weather-beaten kind of way."

"Is that a compliment? I can't tell."

She sighed contentedly. "I'm very happy, being here with you."

"I'm glad to hear it."

"You know," she said, "it's a very dark night. No one can see us." She gave him a look which could have been described as indecent. It was, nevertheless, most alluring. She lay back on the blanket and pulled him down on top of her for a long, lingering kiss, her skirt sliding down to reveal long stretches of creamy white thigh. He put his hand on her smooth skin, above the knee, and felt her smaller hand close over his and gently pull his hand beneath her skirt.

"Cut that out, you two," Morgan said. "I'd tell you to get yourselves a room, but it would probably be mine."

"Bastard," Crowe murmured. He hadn't heard or seen a thing to warn of Morgan's approach. Cassie gave him a disapproving look for his language as she sat up and smoothed down her skirt, swinging her legs under her and adopting a more demure position.

"Hi, Morgan," she said politely.

"Cassie," Morgan said, smiling. "Crowe," he added with theatrical disdain.

"What are you up to?" Crowe said.

"Just enjoying the night air, though apparently not as much as you two."

"That's nice. Are you going to keep walking, then?"

Morgan seemed oblivious to the hint in Crowe's voice. "This seems like a nice spot. Maybe I'll stay around for a bit. Oh, Cassie, Barry was after you. Something about stock-taking, I think." He shrugged. "I'm not sure, I was pretending to be deaf. Let's see how he likes it, the miserable bugger."

"I was just about to go anyway." She started to stand, and then turned to Crowe. "Bring my blanket back to me sometime," she said, kissing him chastely on his cheek. "I might get cold without it." She stood up, and smiled at them both. "Goodnight, boys."

"Satisfied?" Crowe said when she was out of earshot.

"What? You don't honestly think I came all this way just to break you two up?" Morgan sounded choked with emotion. "That hurts me, mate," he said, clutching at his heart, "right here."

"Why did you come, then?"

"To break you two up," he said cheerfully.

"Why? Oh, forget it," Crowe said shortly. "How did you know we were here?"

"Remember who you're talking to, mate. You're sitting right out here in the open. I could see you from half a mile away, and if I can see you here, you can be sure that Raithe and the others can, too. All it takes is for one of them to mention it in the wrong company and the whole thing falls apart." He made a peremptory motion of his hand. "Budge up."

"Have you seen Raithe?" Crowe asked as Morgan sat down.

"Not since Lieberwitz's little bombshell, no. What do you think?"

"I think I'd like to have a nice chat with him."

Cassie was a hundred yards away now, sticking close to the edge of the woods. Crowe wondered where she'd parked her car. She didn't look back. He watched the sway of her hips as she dwindled into the distance.

"She really is a good-looking girl," Morgan agreed without the need for Crowe to say it. "I can see why you're interested. I guess I don't have to ask if you're still seeing her. Still casual, eh?"

"Still casual."

"You wouldn't be falling in love, then?"

Crowe didn't answer, his eyes still on the girl. The thought had occurred to him. At the back of his mind was the thought that he'd never been in love, and probably wouldn't know it when it happened. But he knew for certain that he wanted this girl.

"I fell in love once," Morgan said after a few seconds. "Lord Aberbodie's daughter." He gave a lovestruck sigh and shook his head in wonder. "Now she was stunning. Making love to her was like taking a Hurricane into a pack of Dorniers."

"Sounds special," Crowe said dryly.

"I think the happiest times I ever spent on the ground were with her. I loved every minute, right up to the point where her father and brothers were chasing me with shotguns."

"You've never really told me what happened there."

"Well, some things are just personal," Morgan said. He gave Crowe a knowing look, which Crowe returned blankly. "So, have you?"

"Have I what?"

"Do I have to spell it out?" Morgan said. "Because I will if I have to. It's my favourite word."

"Sex? No. Anyway, what happened to some things being personal?"

"Different situation entirely. Do you want to?"

"Yes, but..."

"But she won't let you," Morgan interrupted, nodding sagely. "I don't blame her, my friend. There's a good reason I keep our beds so far apart."

Crowe shook his head. Cassie was gone from sight now. "I don't know where it's going to lead."

Morgan's smile faded, replaced by a serious expression which surprised Crowe with its sadness. "I do. Nowhere good."

They sat in silence.

"You know how happy I'd be to see you with someone you could love, don't you?"

"Yeah, I know."

"So you know when I tell you to walk away from this, I do it because I think it's what's best for you?"

"And for you, too?" Crowe said, unable to keep the bitter edge from the words.

Morgan didn't seem offended. "If you get grounded, you might take us all with you. So yes, guilty as charged. But what happens if it's just you? You love flying. You need to fly. I remember how you were when we met. I was there the first time you flew, remember? I know how much flying has changed you. And I know you would never forgive Cassie if that was taken away from you because of her."

Crowe didn't respond. It hurt him to admit it, but everything Morgan said was true. That didn't make it any easier to deal with, though.

"It hurts me to be the one who has to tell you this," Morgan said quietly. "More than you know." He punched Crowe playfully on the arm, but the gesture was half-hearted at best. "Come on, let's go back. It's starting to rain again."

The walk back to the Mess was uncomfortable, and not because of the rain. Crowe declined Morgan's offer of a drink, forcing a smile to try and soften the rejection. Morgan gave him a sad look and patted him on the shoulder, and then disappeared into the building, leaving Crowe to walk home alone along the waterlogged gravel path.

He first heard the footsteps as he turned the corner to see his building up ahead. It sounded like someone was moving at a good pace, possibly more than one person, and he distinctly heard the sound of feet splashing through a puddle. When he looked, though, he saw nothing. Whoever it was must have been on the other side of the long, low building that provided the accommodation for the ordinary pilots. He carried on.

He was reaching for his key when he heard the second noise. This time it was just one man, he was sure, moving slowly, much closer, the sound clearly audible over the impact of the rain on the puddles. He stopped, turning silently to look each way, and after a few seconds the noise, which had stopped when he had, resumed. Crowe took two quick steps to take him to the corner of the building, and then a third longer step brought him face to pale surprised face with the source of the noise.

"Hello, Crowe."

"Raithe," Crowe replied evenly. "Been out for a walk?"

"Evidently."

"Not a very nice night for it."

Raithe smiled coldly, the silver ring on his hand shining faintly. "What do you want, Crowe?"

"We were just talking about one of your old friends."

"Yes?"

"I know him as the Vulture. What do you know him as?"

"You've been talking to Lieberwitz," Raithe said calmly. If he was flustered by the question he didn't show it.

Crowe stepped closer. "It's strange that you didn't mention that you knew him back in the Westphalia Trust."

"Are you drunk, Crowe? Or merely stupid?"

Crowe cracked his knuckles. "Tell me about him."

"Are you threatening me?" Raithe asked, amused. "There are easier ways to answer my question."

"I've never liked you, Raithe."

"I've never cared."

"You really should."

"Goodnight," Raithe said. He tried to pass by. Crowe extended an arm gently but firmly.

"We're not finished," he said. For a second or more, Raithe simply looked down at the rain-soaked hand resting on his chest, as if amazed, and then he looked up at Crowe and smiled.

The veneer of lofty disdain, the unblinking calm that he cultivated and perfected was gone. Raithe's lips peeled back to reveal stained, uneven teeth, the gums vivid red against the alabaster white of his face.

"Evening, lads." Harry Stead smiled cheerily as he limped past, a walking stick in one hand and an open umbrella raised in the other. "How was your flight, Crowe?"

"Fine," Crowe said tersely, suppressing a curse as Raithe took the opportunity to slip past and disappear into the building.

"He's in a rush, isn't he?" Stead said, watching Raithe go. His words were slightly slurred. "I wish I could move that fast. Here, don't go telling Noone you saw me with this bloody stick, will you?"

"Goodnight, Harry." With Stead's cheerful farewell hanging in the night air behind him, Crowe walked into the building. Raithe's door was closed and, he guessed, locked, but the arrogant bastard wasn't going anywhere. They would have their conversation soon enough.

Unfortunately, though the squadron's pilots seemed enthused at the thought of taking on the Vulture, it appeared no one had explained the plan to the weather. The area of low pressure remained resolutely over south-east England and the Channel, and the next two nights saw the new mission left frustratingly on hold. Tempers started to rise, and it was all Harry Stead could do to keep the different petty arguments in check.

On the first night a break in the weather at least allowed the Mosquitoes to get airborne and join the northern bomber stream heading to targets in the Ruhr valley. They flew a few thousand feet above the mixed formation of Lancasters and Halifaxes, unseen by the bomber crews, hoping to catch a glimpse of the Vulture and his Focke-Wulfs. At one point they saw a dozen or more aircraft approaching the bombers, but it took only a few seconds for Morgan's excellent eye sight to identify them as British Stirlings, making their way back from an earlier raid. The crews were bitterly disappointed. Morgan did his best to remain cheerful and upbeat, but Crowe could tell that the decline in the squadron's fortunes was getting him down.

It was not just that, though. It wasn't that his friend had really acted any differently towards him, but Crowe could tell that Morgan wasn't happy about his relationship with Cassie. Crowe didn't blame him. To an extent he shared the younger vampire's slight air of foreboding, and wondered if anyone else had noticed. He doubted it. To most people, Morgan was probably his usual happy self, but Crowe knew him better than any of them.

Morgan said nothing, though, even when Crowe left the bar early after their flight. When he returned an hour later, his hair and flying clothing damp from the seemingly interminable rain, Morgan bought him a pint and welcomed him back into the conversation. He must have known where Crowe had been. Cassie had not been working that night. She'd picked Crowe up and they'd snatched thirty minutes together in her car, parked behind one of the less-frequented buildings. She couldn't stay any longer, but it was still enough to leave Crowe feeling less disappointed about the night's flying failures. His own happiness, though, just made him feel guiltier when Morgan didn't say anything.

The next night didn't begin particularly well.

"You're bloody lunatics if you go up in this," Harry Stead said, standing under the cover of the Mess doors and shaking his walking stick at the sheets of rain which drifted across the sodden airfield, obscuring their aircraft from view.

"You're absolutely right, Harry," Morgan responded with a grin. "I don't suppose you've seen our navigators, have you? The transport's due in two minutes."

"I could order you not to go?" Stead said, hopefully.

"You could, but that would just make everybody unhappy and we'd still end up flying. Besides, someone has to get airborne. We don't want to get a reputation for being lazy."

186

Stead shook his head in mock surrender. Even under the cover of the doorway, enough of the rain had reached him for fine droplets of water to fall from his hair. "At least you flew last night. The Spitfires haven't been airborne for three nights. The lads are getting tense."

"They'll get over it. I think everyone could just do with a good fight."

"Careful what you wish for," Crowe said.

"I meant with the Germans," Morgan retorted.

The navigators arrived moments before the transport. Danny Baggers took one look at the endless seeping clouds and laughed. It appeared that some of Morgan's enthusiasm was rubbing off on his navigator. Jones looked anxious at the prospect of navigating in such appalling weather, but said nothing.

Even the short walk from the transport lorry to the aircraft was enough to soak them. Jones ran ahead to join the miserable-looking ground crew hiding under their Mosquito's wing while Crowe and Morgan stopped to talk.

"He's right, you know?" Crowe said.

"Who?"

"Harry. This is lunacy."

"It'll stop in a minute," Morgan promised. "Trust me."

"There's a difference between optimistic and stupid."

"But they both make a man happy. Be lucky."

Crowe looked up at the descending rain, and gave Morgan a despairing look. He turned and walked towards the waiting Mosquito, feeling the ground squelch beneath his boots and the steady trickle of water running from the top of his helmet down the back of his neck. He shook his oxygen mask to get rid of the rain that clung to it, and looked up.

"I don't believe it," he muttered. The rain had stopped. He looked over at Morgan, and saw the smug expression on his friend's face. "It won't last," he called.

"Enjoy it while it does," Morgan replied after a second's pause. Crowe thought he heard the faintest traces of sadness in the words, but then Morgan gave a cheery wave and half ran to his own aircraft.

Crowe climbed into the cockpit, and settled damply into his seat. "Wet enough for you?" he asked Jones as the young navigator clambered awkwardly in behind him.

"This is insane," Jones said grumpily. "No one else is flying tonight."

"That's their loss."

The rain held off long enough for them to get airborne without any great problems, although Crowe was careful to give Morgan a good amount of clearance until they were above the low cloud. They headed directly east, flying close together with a certain amount of casual chat between them. Morgan seemed much happier now that they were airborne, and Crowe wondered if he had imagined the recent hint of tension between them. By the time they crossed the coast of France the weather had improved a little, although enough cloud still lingered to prevent the thick clusters of coastal artillery from firing at the two tiny aircraft high above. For over an hour they made their way from one German night fighter base to another, hoping for a glimpse of Luftwaffe aircraft, but it seemed that they were alone in the whole vast emptiness of the sky.

"You know," Morgan said after several minutes of silence, "the Vulture is probably hemmed in at home by cloud."

"We'll get him soon," Crowe said. His thoughts flickered back to the Lancaster from John Bale's squadron burning on the runway. There was a score to settle.

"I don't think you're following me," Morgan persisted. "If he can't get airborne, there's a good chance his aircraft is sitting on the deck."

"Meaning?"

"Meaning they'd never expect an attack in this sort of weather, would they? We could go in fast and low and strafe the buggery out of that aircraft of his. I doubt it would be that quick after we put a couple of hundred holes in it."

Crowe smiled. There was a boyish enthusiasm to Morgan's voice that was almost irresistible. Almost. "What about the flak gunners?"

"Asleep," Morgan said as conclusively as if he'd already heard their snoring. "What do you think?"

"I think you're a nutcase."

"That's harsh."

"You remember where I grew up?" Crowe asked. "There were people like you in there."

"Witty, handsome and charming?"

"Nutcases."

"You've changed, Crowe. What happened to your sense of adventure?"

"What happened to your sense?"

In the seat next to Crowe, Jones smiled. He was listening to the whole exchange on the radio. Somehow Crowe was sure that his smile was less amusement and more relief that a mere two Mosquitoes would not be attacking one of the most heavily defended airfields in Occupied Europe.

"Okay," Morgan sighed theatrically. "I give up. Be like that." Crowe wondered where they were. At eighteen thousand feet the land seemed little more than an endless smudge, interspersed with large stretches of dark cloud. There was enough cloud above them too to occasionally blot out the three-quarter moon.

By unspoken agreement, they turned towards home. Jones occasionally gave navigational updates, but Crowe was content to follow Morgan's lead. He wasn't sure at which point in the flight his thoughts had turned to Cassie, but in a strange way he was glad they hadn't encountered any German aircraft. He doubted whether he could have given them his full attention.

He knew he had to tell Morgan of his decision, or at least the fact that he hadn't made the decision Morgan wanted him to make. Morgan knew Crowe hadn't finished the relationship. That much was obvious. He looked out again at the expanse of the sky, realising that he still loved flying as much as ever. Despite the frustrations of the weather and the lack of opposition, simply being airborne made him happy. For the first time in his life, though, he had something that made him happy when he wasn't flying.

That was the problem.

"I'm bored," Morgan said. "Keep heading home, I'll catch you up in a minute."

"Where are you going?" Crowe said, confused, as Morgan's Mosquito plunged into a rapid dive and hurtled between two clouds towards the exposed French countryside below.

"Trainspotting," Morgan replied happily.

"Child," Crowe muttered. He noticed that Jones was giving him an amused look. "What?"

"Nothing."

"Good."

"It's just that I find it strange that you two are such good friends."

"You and me both," Crowe said, wishing he'd left the transmit switch pressed so that Morgan could have heard the conversation.

"You seem to bicker all the time."

189

Thousands of feet beneath them there were a series of flashes as Morgan apparently strafed some unseen target. If we ever stop bickering you'll know there's a problem, Crowe thought, but resisted the urge to say it. Instead they flew on in silence until Morgan rejoined them.

"Happy now?"

"I saw a train down there."

"I didn't see it."

"It's not your fault, your eyes are so much older than mine," Morgan told him. "Anyway, I thought I'd have a pop at it."

"Any luck?"

"Yes, the driver had buckets of it. Frankly, I made a complete arse of the whole business. Hitting a target on the ground seems much harder than hitting another aircraft. To be honest, I think you were in more danger than the train."

The rest of the journey home was uneventful, with Morgan apparently dissuaded from wasting any more ammunition on the European rail network. Crowe knew from experience that Morgan's ground crew would be excited on seeing the torn muzzle covers on Morgan's guns that would show they had been fired. They'd be disappointed to hear that the only things he'd hit were a couple of innocent French railway embankments.

There was still a fine drizzle in the air when they landed back at Charney Breach. They taxied back to dispersal, but even as they shut down their engines, Crowe's mind continued to run over the same question. When was he going to tell Morgan that he wasn't going to finish his relationship with Cassie?

"Another night wasted," a surprisingly cheerful Morgan called up to him as he climbed down the crew ladder. It never ceased to amaze Crowe how quickly his friend could abandon his aircraft once it had finished its purpose for the night. "Come on, let's get a drink."

Crowe shook his head. "I'll pass."

"Oh," Morgan said. "Did you have a better offer?" That answered one question, at least. The edge to his voice definitely wasn't in Crowe's imagination.

"No," Crowe said, honestly. "I just don't fancy a drink. You go, though. Tell them how your great shooting destroyed that train."

"Hmm," Morgan said. He did not smile. "Well, I guess I'll see you later." He turned to walk towards the transport.

"Morgan?" Crowe waited until his friend turned around, and then held out his open hands. "I just don't fancy a drink," he repeated.

Morgan looked at him for a few seconds, nodded, and climbed into the transport. "Come on," his voice called, disembodied, from within the interior of the lorry. "You're getting wet and, more importantly, my beer's getting warm."

He hadn't exactly lied to Morgan, Crowe thought as he walked through the rain-soaked undergrowth of the woods. He hadn't wanted a drink. There was another reason, though, why he had chosen to leave Morgan to go into the bar on his own.

Group Captain Noone's temporary home was a large manor house rented by the Air Ministry. It was set back from the road that ran along the outside of the airfield, far enough that the barbed wire of the fence was hidden from view by trees. Crowe knew nothing of architecture, though at another time he might have been impressed by the simple beauty of the building. At that moment, though, its elegant, ivy-cloaked exterior was simply another obstacle between him and Cassie. He had some serious doubts about coming to see the girl, but the time he had spent thinking about her during the flight had filled him with a desire to see her again. She'd told him her room was the one above the front door. He took a deep breath and crossed the lane.

There was a thick hedge surrounding the house on three sides, with a five foot wall at the front broken by a metal gate and, a little further on, a larger wooden gate at the foot of the driveway. Cassie's tiny Austin was parked along the side of the house, with no sign of the Group Captain's much larger staff car. No lights were visible, and without breaking stride he reached up and vaulted the wall. Slowly and carefully, he closed the distance until he was only a few feet below Cassie's window.

It was the work of a moment to find a suitable stone and to throw it up in a gentle trajectory. It caught the window pane the merest of glancing blows. The crunch the stone made when it hit the ground sounded horribly loud in the quiet of the night. He repeated the process three times before the curtains twitched and opened slightly, and Cassie's face appeared at the window. There must have been enough moonlight breaking through the cloud cover for her to be able to see him. Her surprised look was still there when she opened the door.

"What are you doing here?" she whispered.

"Just saying hello. Is your Dad around?"

She ushered him in, looking suspiciously each way across the silent grounds before closing the door behind him. "No, he's working late tonight."

"Why are you whispering, then?"

"I don't know." They were standing in a wide hallway at the foot of a staircase. She stood on the lowest step to kiss him. She had a heavy shawl pulled about her shoulders but Crowe was more interested in the thin linen night dress beneath it. "You're wet," she said, disapprovingly.

"You're cold," he replied, feeling her shiver as he put his hands on her sides.

She smiled coquettishly and looked up at him with eyes that didn't match her attempted look of innocence. "Maybe you could try to warm me up a little?"

"Maybe…" he began, but then he heard a noise outside, faint at first but rapidly growing louder. He stifled a curse. "Maybe some other time," he finished sourly.

"Oh," she said, looking disappointed, but then she heard the noise too. Her hearing was not quite as sensitive as his but her mind was even quicker to recognise the sound of her father's car. "Oh," she repeated, loudly.

"Is there a back door?"

"Down the end of the hall there," she said with an exaggerated gesture, and kissed him again before turning to run back up the stairs.

"Is that it?"

"Unless you want to explain to Daddy why I'm up and about," she said, blowing him a kiss. "Hurry, and next time come earlier."

"Next time," he muttered to himself, finding the back door in the kitchen and slipping through it just as the front door opened. Seeing her hadn't gone quite how he'd planned it, and as he silently crossed the lane and clambered back over the fence it started to rain again, washing away whatever little remained of his good humour.

It was only about two hours until dawn when Crowe got to his own door, unlocking it silently to avoid disturbing Morgan. Unsurprisingly the room was empty, and he thought briefly about going to join his friend for a drink after all. The sound of the rain on the window, though, convinced him otherwise. He started to peel off his sodden clothes.

192

There were steady footsteps in the corridor, and then a loud knock. He felt a sudden surge of excitement. His first thought was that only one person had ever knocked at this room, at the window. It had taken him a fair amount of time to walk back, more than enough for Cassie to have driven onto the airfield.

His second thought was bitter disappointment. The person at the door was Geordie Hulse.

"I'm not sure I like you, Crowe," the Northumbrian said before Crowe could speak.

"There's a lot of it going about," Crowe said warily.

"I think you're a nasty bastard, and a bit of a thug."

"Don't sit on the fence. Say what you think."

"Morgan's a different matter, though," Hulse said. "He's a good lad. Sound as a pound. That's why I'm here."

"Is there something on your mind, Geordie?"

"Clark, Barnes and Mills were planning to beat you up tonight once everyone had left the bar. They asked me if I'd like to join in."

"Would you?"

"I may not like you all that much, but I've got no grudge with you, and you get the job done right enough. Besides, I reckon you're big enough and ugly enough to handle Clark and his little friends."

"You reckon right."

"Problem is it's not you they've got. It's Morgan."

The chill that Crowe suddenly felt had nothing to do with his wet clothes. "What?"

"In the bar."

"What are they going to do?" Crowe asked. He was already pulling his gloves on. He felt a cold fury beginning to rise in him. He let it grow, instinctively knowing that it would stop him feeling concern for Morgan now, when it could weaken him. Do the job, sort the situation, worry later. Walking over to his bedside table, he opened the top drawer and rummaged under the clothes inside until he found what he was looking for.

"They reckon they can rough him up a bit," Hulse said. "He's a vampire; he'll be fine in the morning. But it's going to hurt."

"And you didn't try to stop them?"

"I thought you'd want the pleasure."

"Thanks, Geordie. I won't mention to Clark that you were here."

Hulse shrugged. "Clark doesn't worry me." The Yorkshireman's eyes opened wider, but even though he was sensible and down to earth and not one to show his emotions, he still did well to keep the alarm from his voice. "Are you planning to use that?" he asked, pointing at the pistol in Crowe's hands.

Crowe simply grinned.

Chapter Sixteen

It took the merest of moments to get their attention. The pistol saw to that.

Crowe stood in the doorway, his arms loose and relaxed by his side, the pistol pointing at the floor but with enough flex to indicate that could change in an instant. From behind sunglasses that dripped rainwater he took in the scene. There were four men in the dimly-lit room. Barnes stood at the bar, a pint glass raised in his hand but poised short of his lips. His mouth hung open in surprise. Mills, his jacket off and the sleeves of his light blue shirt rolled neatly up above his elbows, stood with his side to Crowe but looking at him over his shoulder with wide eyes. Clark had his back to Crowe, feet spread in a stance designed to provide a stable base for the heavy punches he had been raining down a few moments earlier. There were traces of blood on the floor at his feet and he was breathing heavily.

"Shaun," Mills said quietly. There was fear in that nasal whine.

Clark looked up at his friend and turned around. For a moment the big Flight Lieutenant could not hide the concern that followed the shock of seeing the vampire, but he recovered instantly and hid the anxiety well behind a sneer.

"Nice of you to join us, Crowe," he said mockingly. "We were expecting you a little earlier."

"I'm sorry I'm late," Crowe told them, meaning it. "Are you okay, Morgan?"

The men's victim was slumped on the floor, his back to the wall below the thick black curtains. He raised his head, and Crowe felt anger flare within him. Both Morgan's eyes were already swelling. There was blood on his chin where his lip had been ruptured, and a ring on someone's finger had torn a nasty cut across his left upper cheek. He was almost unrecognisable.

"Peachy," he said, the word sounding thick through his swollen mouth. "These three fine gentlemen were just showing me a good time. I tried to tell them I'm not that kind of girl."

"You ready to leave?"

"But it's just getting fun."

"Shaun," Mills repeated, a little more urgently.

"What?" said Clark.

"He's got a gun."

"I can see that."

"It looks like you lads have had fun tonight," Crowe said calmly. "Fun's over. Where are you going, Barnes?" The pilot, his pint glass still clenched in a slightly trembling hand, had started to edge away towards the door that led to the back storeroom. The pistol in Crowe's hand twitched, just slightly, and Barnes stopped, as if frozen to the spot.

"Morgan, why don't you leave now? I'll see you in a few minutes."

Nodding amiably, but with a dazed expression, Morgan put out one hand onto the carpet that was spattered with his blood. He tried to push himself up. His strength failed him, and he sat heavily back down, resting his head against the curtain.

"I might stay here a little while," he slurred, as if drunk. "I don't feel very well. I must have had a bad pint."

"I'm sorry," said Clark, his eyes on Crowe. "I think we may have been a little rough."

"It happens."

"Shaun," Mills repeated a third time. "He's got a gun."

"I know," Clark said sharply, and then smiled. "But he's not going to use it, are you Crowe?"

"No."

Clark smirked. He looked over to his left at the wide eyed Mills, and then towards Barnes. His face suggested he was reassured by the superior numbers as he looked back at Crowe.

Crowe pushed the door behind him closed with his foot. He stepped slowly to his left, reaching smoothly out to place the pistol on the wooden counter of the bar. He kept his eyes on Clark throughout the movement, watching how the bigger man's eyes flickered, giving out their confusion as if in Morse code. Crowe could sense his fear, the way he had that first night in the bar, even if Clark hid it well. He had, Crowe reflected, been wrong about Clark that first night. Clark was a bully. He surrounded himself with weaker friends because it made him feel stronger. Barnes and Mills would have been nothing without Clark. But he had been wrong about one thing. Clark, unlike Mills, wasn't a coward. He wasn't bright enough for that.

"So," Clark said finally, looking at the pistol with perplexed eyes, "what are you going to do?"

For a few seconds Crowe didn't respond. He slowly turned his head to stare at each of them in turn, savouring their fear. He reached slowly up with both hands until he held the thin metal frames of his sunglasses between his fingers, and then tilted them inch by measured inch to reveal the eyes below. Crowe noted the way Mills' anxiety turned to panic. He noted how Barnes involuntarily stepped back another foot and glanced towards that back door. Most of all, he noted the way Clark's eyes widened with sudden realisation, minutes, hours, weeks too late.

"This," Crowe said.

He turned off the lights.

The darkness was instant and near-absolute. The blackout curtains had done their job. The tiny sliver of light which passed under the door from the corridor beyond was less than insignificant. No normal human eye could have hoped to have seen more than a few inches in that gloom. Crowe saw everything.

The sound of his knuckles cracking was like a gunshot in the silence of the room.

Barnes first. Of the three men he had reacted quickest, turning to run for the side door, but the darkness had disorientated him and he had instead stumbled into a bar stool. Crowe's mind told him that Barnes posed the biggest threat of raising the alarm or bringing attention. Crowe's rage simply saw that Barnes was nearest.

By the time the man could right himself, it was too late. Barnes gave a startled groan as Crowe pivoted on his toes and dug a hurtful hook into the pilot's soft midsection. Barnes fell heavily against the dark wood counter, catching himself with one arm as he pawed out blindly with the other. Crowe smiled and then punched him in the kidneys. Barnes cried out in pain, his legs giving way beneath him, his chin dropping forward and bouncing off the counter. He fell heavily to the floor.

Crowe turned around. Both Clark and Mills were where he had left them, both circling with their arms outstretched. Clark's posture was one of defence. Mills, on the other hand, was making soft noises, sobbing with fear as he reached out with open trembling palms in front of him. Crowe walked towards him, making no attempt to conceal the noise of his approach.

Clark heard the approaching footsteps and turned in roughly the right direction, only to stagger quickly backwards as Crowe hit him with a hard jab above the right eye. Crowe followed him. After so many weeks it felt good to finally strike the man, and the anger within him wanted more, but even as he closed on the blustering Clark he felt Mills brush blindly against his shoulder. The skinny man's eyes were wide open, though it did him little good. As they made contact he whimpered, and gave a childlike squeal of terror as Crowe's fingers closed about his throat.

"I'm sorry, I'm sorry," Mills rasped as the grip tightened, making no attempt to fight off his attacker. Clark heard the noise and began to move towards the sound, swinging his arms violently but randomly in front of him. Crowe kept his left hand tight on Mills' windpipe, and shoved the man back against the wall. He smiled at the look of relief on Mills' face when he released his grip. The look didn't last long. Before Mills could even draw a proper breath, Crowe punched him hard in the solar plexus, finishing the job the choking had started. Utterly winded, Mills slumped to all fours, gasping loudly while tears streamed down his face. Crowe gave him a few seconds and then kicked him twice hard in the ribs. Mills dropped to the floor and lay curled into a foetal position, sobbing.

Crowe turned away, and looked down at Morgan. His friend was still slumped against the wall, watching him. Crowe smiled. The gesture was not returned. Morgan looked away, just as Clark swung a big right hand which missed Crowe by at least half a yard.

Clark. Crowe looked over at the big man, circling him in the darkness as Clark stumbled into a table. He wanted to hurt him badly. As Clark began to back away Crowe stepped forward and hit him across the jaw with a short, chopping right hook. It dropped Clark, as intended, though he could tell instantly that he had not caught him flush enough for the knockout. That suited Crowe fine. He wasn't quite ready for it to be over. Across the other side of the room Barnes was starting to stand up, using his arms on the counter to pull himself slowly to his feet. Crowe let him reach a standing position and then kicked his legs from under him. Barnes' chin cannoned off the bar top again.

Clark was trying to climb to his feet. He heard Crowe coming, his eyes blindly darting about, filled with panic. By the time he was

198

upright Crowe was already behind him, his arm reaching around to clamp across his throat, forcing the bone of his forearm into Clark's windpipe. Clark struggled. He was a strong man, but Crowe was already tightening the choke hold and knew Clark was losing consciousness. Another few seconds and the bastard would be dead, and Crowe smiled again even as he tensed the muscles of his back and shoulders and prepared to pull the gasping, desperate man into a final killing embrace.

"Crowe," Morgan said sharply.

"I'm finishing this now," Crowe said through gritted teeth.

"If you kill him, it's over. For all of us."

Clark dropped to his knees, his hands feebly clutching at Crowe's arm, their strength all but gone. The anger was still in him. A few moments more. That was all it would take.

"Crowe!"

With a curse, he reluctantly released his grip. Clark pitched forward onto the cheap carpet, gulping air, his agonised gasping competing with Mills' crying in the darkness.

Crowe knelt down next to Morgan. "Can you stand?"

"I think so. I'm not sure I want to, though."

"We should get you back to our room. Have you got any blood there?"

"Of course. Clark is crawling towards the door, by the way."

"I know."

Morgan looked sharply at him, his eyes becoming focused for the first time since Crowe had entered the room. "Are you having fun?" he asked. Something about his tone seemed strange. Aggressive.

"What do you mean?" he asked, but Morgan simply looked away, his eyes distant, his swollen lips resolutely still. Crowe looked back over his shoulder. Clark had reached the door and was starting to push himself up, using the wall for support.

"Excuse me," Crowe said quietly to Morgan.

Clark managed to get to his feet. His questing hand slowly made its way up the cheap wallpaper until it found what it was looking for. With a grunt of triumph, Clark switched on the light, turned to face Crowe, and then dropped to the floor with a girlish whimper as Crowe's head butt splintered his nose across his face.

"Easy now." Crowe helped Morgan lower himself onto his bed. His friend winced as he lay back, leaving Crowe worrying that beneath the mottled and damaged skin, there was something broken. That would slow the healing process considerably. It would also leave Morgan in pain for much longer. The vampire condition might heal skin in a matter of minutes, if properly supplied with blood, but bones and internal injuries weren't so simple.

"Where do you keep your blood?" Crowe asked, looking around their room.

"Top drawer." Morgan nodded towards the nearer of the two bed side cabinets.

"I should have killed him."

"Who?"

"Clark," Crowe said, as he pulled the distinctive monogrammed silver hip flask out of the drawer. "I should have finished him off. Mills and Barnes, too." With the slightest feeling of regret, he placed his pistol back in his own top drawer and passed the flask to Morgan.

"What good would that have done us? Quiet would have had you killed. The rest of us too, most likely."

"What, for the sake of Clark? We're too valuable for that."

Morgan shook his head, wincing as he did so. The bottle sat unopened in his hand. "Not if we turn on our own. You've said it before, we're only valuable as long as we're doing the job and killing the enemy. Once we become too big a risk, he'd finish us in a second. You know it."

"Yeah, I know it. But it's not like you to talk like that."

Morgan gave a grim smile. "It's been that kind of a day." The smile faded, and his eyes remained firmly downcast. "Besides, I don't blame Clark. Not entirely, anyway."

"What do you mean?"

"Well, it's been coming for a while, hasn't it? We always knew sooner or later he'd have a pop at one of us. Keep poking a dog with a stick and one day it will bite you. We all hoped he'd go for you, of course. Ever wonder why he chose to go after me?"

"Hulse said it was me they wanted to get, but I wasn't there."

"You rarely are, I find." Morgan's tone was odd, with no hint of his usual banter, and Crowe began to feel uncomfortable. "Did you wonder what I was doing there alone tonight?"

Crowe shrugged. "You went for a drink after we landed."

"Did you see anyone else there? Everyone went home hours ago. Here." Morgan reached into his blood-spattered overalls and pulled out a piece of crumpled yellow note paper. "You might find this interesting. I did."

"What is it?" Crowe took it and carefully unfolded it.

"It had been slipped under the door when I came in. It's the reason I went back."

Crowe felt the oddest sense of foreboding which he could not have explained. A few seconds later he knew it was justified. *I must see you. The bar at 0300. Come alone. Cassie.*

"It's not real," Morgan said quietly. "But with hindsight I guess you've been with Cassie tonight, so you already know that. Clark wrote it, but I thought it was from her. That's why I went."

"Didn't you guess it was for me?"

"You weren't here. I didn't want to leave her sitting there on her own. I was trying to be a gentleman. It didn't turn out too well, did it?"

"I'm sorry," Crowe said.

"Of course you are," Morgan said shortly.

"You knew that note was supposed to be for me." He didn't like Morgan's tone and felt his own temper starting to get the better of him. "Did it ever occur to you that it was none of your business?"

For a second Morgan simply looked stunned, and then he laughed. The sound shocked Crowe. All traces of Morgan's usual bonhomie and light-heartedness had gone. "Clark just made it my business," he said. "He also told me what he thought of you and Cassie. I take it you are still seeing her, despite everything we talked about?"

"Yes."

Morgan sighed and looked away. It was the disappointment in his sigh that disturbed Crowe the most. He knew he had let his friend down, but still this was not like Morgan at all.

"I know you're angry…"

"You have no idea."

"Will you hear me out?" Crowe said, his anger flaring again.

"Go on. Seriously, go for it. I'm all ears."

"I know you don't approve…"

"You noticed that?"

"I know you don't approve of me seeing Cassie," Crowe continued, gritting his teeth in irritation at the interruption. "I also know I'm taking a risk by seeing her. But the fact is it's my risk to take."

"Your risk?" Morgan said incredulously, letting the unopened flask of blood drop onto the bed sheets. "Let me fill you in on some recent

201

events." He pointed to his battered face. One eye was swollen shut. The other looked at Crowe with ill-concealed anger. "Take a look at this. Was this your risk to take?"

"I said I'm sorry."

"For Christ's sake, Crowe," Morgan said angrily, "flying is your life! What do you think Noone would do if he found out you were sleeping with his daughter?"

"I haven't slept with her."

"Not yet, maybe, but it doesn't matter anyway. The fact that you've even touched her would be enough for him to ground you."

"He could try."

Morgan laughed again, the sound dripping with bitterness. "Listen to yourself, will you? Quiet will only step in if he thinks it's worth his effort. You're an asset to him, nothing more. That goes for the rest of us, too. If we become more trouble than we're worth he'll cut us loose, and you know what that means. Do you think Quiet approves of this little liaison with Cassie?"

"I don't care what he thinks," Crowe said hotly.

"Yeah, I guess that sums it up, doesn't it? I don't suppose you care about putting the rest of us in danger, either. It's not just about you. You're risking everything you've achieved and putting us all in danger, and for what? A quick fling?"

"It's more than that."

"For you, maybe," Morgan said, and for a moment there was a hint of sadness and sympathy in his expression. It didn't last. The anger flooded back. "Have you asked her? I tried to warn you it would come to this. I thought you were going to end it."

"I never said that."

"Yeah, that's my fault," Morgan admitted sarcastically. "It never occurred to me how stupid you could be."

"Now I'm stupid, is that it?"

"Carrying on with the Group Captain's daughter right under his nose? Letting Clark see you together in Staverton? Do these sound like clever things to do? Clark hates you enough without you rubbing his nose in it."

"You're a fine one to talk. You reckon you've never wound Clark up?"

"I admit I had great fun pissing him off," Morgan said with open hands that were shaking with suppressed and unaccustomed rage.

"But take a look at my face. Whatever liberties I took, I've paid for them tonight. I don't see any marks on your face."

"Maybe that's because I can look after myself."

"Oh yes, Crowe the hard man. I'm so sorry that I've never felt the need to go around picking fights every single day."

"Every day? Morgan, you've never had to fight anytime in your entire life, except from a nice warm cockpit." Crowe struggled to contain himself. He knew he should take a deep breath, accept the criticism and walk away, but he could not do it. It just wasn't his way. "Maybe if you'd actually had to fight once or twice when you were living in Daddy's mansion with your own personal doctor and all the money and fresh blood you could ever need, maybe Clark wouldn't have had such an easy time with you."

"Is that how it is? I've had an easy life?"

"That's how it looks to me."

"It's all becoming clear now. Morgan the rich kid, with his money and nice house and all the advantages life can bring." The momentary hurt in Morgan's eyes was replaced by fury beyond anything Crowe had known him capable of. "I've never noticed this jealous streak in you before, Crowe," he said coldly, the words all the more disturbing for the softness of his voice. "I'm wondering what else I've missed, because right now I feel like I don't know you. And to be honest, that's doesn't bother me."

He reached out and lifted up the hip flask, turning it in his hand as he looked at the speechless Crowe. "You might want to leave now," he said. "I know how much you hate having to watch me do this." He looked away dismissively, unscrewed the bottle and began to drink. A thin trickle of blood escaped his mouth and ran down his chin before dripping slowly onto his clothes, to mix with the already drying spots of his own.

Chapter Seventeen

There was a tangible air of excitement in the briefing room. The weather was clear and they knew that there would be flying tonight.

Crowe sat with Lieberwitz, and looked around the room. There was so much enthusiasm there, pilots vying with each other to appear the most keen to engage the enemy. Maybe they even believed it themselves, sometimes at least, but he could sense the fear beneath the bravado. He'd heard it said that the thing pilots were most scared of was letting their fear show. He saw the young looking aircrew laughing and joking, and wondered which among them was thinking of Michael Rhys-Jones, dead in his smoking Spitfire.

He saw Werner looking at him. The German was sat with Morgan a few rows ahead, and gave Crowe a quizzical look. Morgan gave no indication that he was aware Crowe was in the room.

"Room 'shun," someone called, and the assembled aircrew stood up as the Group Captain strode in. Crowe couldn't help noticing that it was not just the vampires who showed little enthusiasm for the squadron commander's arrival. Harry Stead and Quentin Quiet followed close behind.

"At ease," Noone muttered, watching impassively as they took their seats. "Tonight," he began, "we begin our mission to destroy the Vulture and his special squadron. I do not need to remind you how important this mission is. I will, however, say this. Treble-Six Squadron began operations with great success and created an excellent reputation. In the last ten days this reputation has been somewhat tarnished. I expect better tonight. That is all."

Stead, standing by a large map that had been pinned to the wall, waited until Noone had left and the door was closed behind him. "Well," he said, "if that didn't boost your bloody morale, I don't know what will."

There was a general ripple of laughter through the room. Clark did not share in it. The big Flight Lieutenant was looking at Stead with what seemed to be pure hatred. That said, Crowe decided, it could have just been pain. He could not resist a slight smile at the sight of Clark, with his broken nose strapped down and the discolouration around his left eye. Barnes and Mills did not look quite so bad, though there was a raw scab under Barnes' chin and a pale Mills shifted uncomfortably in his seat with the pain of his bruised ribs. He wondered what Dr Madeley had made of their injuries when he had been called to attend to them.

Morgan, by contrast, looked fresh-faced and unmarked.

"Right, lads," Stead said, "I won't keep you long. I know how keen you are to have a proper crack at them, and God knows I'd love to be with you. We've had a couple of false starts, but the plan tonight is very simple." He turned to the map. "In one hour's time the whole squadron will take off together, climb to twelve thousand feet, and fly at slow speed towards this point here." He indicated the map.

"Why slow speed, sir?" Peter Owen asked.

"We're trying to fool their radar operators into thinking we're a bomber formation. The main bomber effort tonight has been routed over Denmark, so we'll have the skies pretty much to ourselves."

"Apart from the Nazis," Werner said with a smile.

"Quite so. Jagdstaffel Falke are too far west to be sent against the main stream, but a smaller formation coming right at them should be too juicy a target to ignore. That said, if they don't react to the bait by the time you're one hundred miles inland, you're to turn back and return to base."

"Why?" Werner asked sharply. "Why not fly on and kill the scum on the ground?"

"Because the nearer you get to them, the more the odds are in their favour. We already know how much flak they can put up around that airfield and there's a good moon tonight to help the gunners. Even worse, they'll be fresh and close to home while our Spitfires will be running short on fuel. And it's a long way to get back if you are damaged."

Werner seemed barely satisfied, but accepted the decision with only a few mutters.

"Are there any questions?" Stead asked, once he had run through the details. "Mr Quiet, have you got anything to add?"

Quiet looked around the room from beneath the brim of his hat. For a moment only his eyes lingered on Clark, Barnes and Mills. He shook his head.

"Transport will be arriving in twenty-five minutes," Stead said with a glance at his watch. "Until then I suggest you grab a mug of tea and relax. Flight Commanders on me, please."

The assembled crews dispersed as Morgan and Raithe walked over to the map for further instructions from Stead. Crowe tried to listen in, but Geordie Hulse walked over and sat next to him.

"I'm surprised," Hulse said with a nod towards the departing Clark. "I didn't think you'd be that lenient."

"I couldn't afford to hurt them too badly. We need every pilot we can get up there tonight."

"I suppose so. How's Morgan?"

Crowe hesitated. "He's okay," he said finally. "Not a mark on him."

"I see that. The same can't be said for Clark."

"I thought the Group Captain would say something."

"He doesn't know. Clark told him it was an accident playing Mess rugby while they were drunk."

"Why did he tell him that?"

Hulse smiled. "Because Harry Stead told him to keep his mouth shut, and most of us agree. Believe it or not, Crowe, Shaun Clark really isn't that popular. Everyone knows the sort of bloke he is. I'm a little surprised Mills and Barnes got involved, but..."

"But they're Clark's friends, and they follow his lead."

"That's partly it," Hulse said thoughtfully, "but I think there's more to it than that. You know who their Flight Commander is."

"Raithe."

"I don't think that helped matters. The boys like Morgan. Some of them even think that you're okay. Nobody likes Raithe."

"I wonder why," Crowe said dryly, with a look towards the tall pale Romanian. Morgan noticed Crowe looking and for a moment returned the gaze before turning dismissively away.

"Well, I'm going to get a brew before take off," Hulse said. "But I think you've got more company on the way."

"Will you join me for a drink, Crowe?" Quentin Quiet said. Crowe could smell a faint trace of alcohol on his breath.

"I should get ready. The transport..."

"The transport will wait, Crowe. I won't."

With a shrug Crowe stood and followed Quiet out of the room and into the bar. The room was empty except for Barry. Without asking Crowe's preference Quiet ordered a double measure of single malt and a pint of Best. To Crowe's surprise, Barry immediately nodded and produced the drinks with a minimum of fuss.

"Cheers." Quiet took his seat at the corner table and raised his glass. Crowe returned the gesture. Both put their glasses down without touching the drink.

"Did you want something in particular?" Crowe asked. "Or is this a social drink?"

"You've been making friends, haven't you, Crowe?"

"I can't help being popular."

"Did you enjoy your evening in Staverton with Cassie Noone?"

"You're well informed," Crowe said evenly.

"Of course. It's my business to be."

"I was just taking the offer of a free drink."

Quiet gave him an odd look, one that seemed almost sad. "There's no such thing. They all cost you in the end. But I'm not here to comment on your relationship with Cassie Noone, so long as it doesn't affect your flying."

"It doesn't," Crowe said casually.

"I'll be the judge of that, and I'll decide when it goes too far. Right now your relationship with Shaun Clark is more worrying. How are your hands, by the way? I'd hate to think you hurt them last night."

"Didn't you hear?" Crowe said, trying to look innocent. "Clark and his friends hurt themselves accidentally."

"Oh, yes, Mess rugby. I heard the official story. No one believes it, though. Not even the Group Captain."

"I'm glad to hear it," Crowe said. "I'd hate to think I wasn't getting the credit."

"Don't be flippant," Quiet said. The words were delivered casually, but the warning tone was unmistakeable. "I'm starting to become a little...concerned. Many people seem to think that you have problems controlling your anger, including Dr Madeley. Harry Stead tells me that before you paid Clark a visit, he saw you confronting Raithe."

"There's a reason for that," Crowe interjected. "Did you know that Raithe knows the Vulture?"

"I know everything about Raithe that I need to know," Quiet said. "Let me make this perfectly clear, Crowe. I know what Clark and his friends did to Morgan, and I can forgive your actions this once, but do not let it become a habit. I will not tolerate anything that disrupts the mission of this squadron. Anything, or anyone. Do you understand me?"

"Yes," Crowe said. Quiet was right about one thing, he realised as the anger swept through him. "Now let me make sure you understand something. I didn't come looking for you. You asked me. I've killed a lot of men for you. And I will kill the Vulture."

He stood up, leaving his pint untouched. "Thanks for the drink. And don't worry about your mission," he said. "I've got my own." He walked away towards the door and the waiting transport, pausing only to glance at the mirror behind the bar. Quiet's reflection downed its drink in one and stared thoughtfully into space.

Morgan didn't tell him to be lucky. It was, Crowe decided as the six Mosquitoes climbed steadily into the clear sky, a small issue. But somehow he couldn't get it from his mind.

Treble-Six Squadron, flying as one single formation for the first time, was an impressive sight. At twelve thousand feet there was just the faintest scattering of cloud. To Crowe's right, he could see the five Mosquitoes extending in a loose line, Morgan's aircraft slightly ahead of them. A thousand feet below the Spitfires clustered in their individual flights, three or four in a group. A single Spitfire led the way, aloof. Crowe did not need to be able to see the markings on the fuselage to know who it was.

"We're approaching the French coast," Morgan said. "Radio silence from now." The occasional smatterings of chatter stopped and each crew retreated into their own solitary cocoon. Below them, on the calm waters of the Channel, a pair of German E-Boats prowled offshore along the Pas de Calais, oblivious to the eyes watching them from the moonlit sky above.

The first flak came almost as soon as they passed over the wide beach. It was an innocuous looking puff of smoke which appeared in the sky well ahead and above them, blossoming for an instant like a drab winter flower before fading to nothing. The effect was misleading. Crowe knew full well how deadly those innocent explosions could be. He thought of the searchlights that had coned them over Belgium. The memory was not a welcome one.

More air bursts followed. They were fairly desultory, as if the flak unit below was only a small one. For the most part the rounds were exploding well above them as the gunners misjudged the range, more used to engaging large and heavy bombers and confused by the small size of their targets.

The shot which hit Steve Slater's Spitfire Eight, then, could only have been a fluke. Perhaps, Crowe thought, it had been badly fused. Either way, the outcome was the same. There was a brief flare as the shell went off eight hundred feet below them. At first Slater's aircraft, a hundred feet from the dirty white smoke, flew on without any noticeable reaction. After a few seconds, though, a thin trail of fuel began to stream from one of the internal tanks. The liquid sparkled gently in the moonlight as it hung suspended in the air.

"I've been hit," Slater announced, breaking radio silence.

"Can you make it home?" Raithe asked, sounding like he didn't care either way.

"I think so," Slater replied. There was a tremor in his voice.

"Go, then."

"Good luck," Morgan added hurriedly. Crowe could hear the concern in his friend's voice but, as Slater's aircraft banked slowly away and turned for home, the words only served to remind him that, for the first time he could remember, Morgan had not wished him that same fortune.

A few seconds more and they were beyond the flak, the gunners choosing to conserve their ammunition as the small, evasive targets slipped out of range. Jones had not spoken since take-off except to provide simple navigation instructions. The navigator was still busily poring over his maps, but beyond him Crowe saw a sight which made him forget his tension in an instant.

"There's a fighter over there," he said.

"Is it him?" Jones said excitedly, looking optimistically in the same direction as Crowe. The aircraft was still at least five miles away, though, about two thousand feet higher than them. There was no chance that Jones could see it.

"I don't know," Crowe said. "It's twin-engined but I can't tell. Oh, hang on. Shit."

"What?"

"It's not him. It's just another Messerschmitt."

"Damn it," Jones said with real annoyance. Crowe gave him a surprised smile, and turned back towards the rest of the formation. He wondered whether to break radio silence again to report the sighting, knowing that Morgan would want to engage the aircraft, but there was clearly no need. Morgan started to turn but then, without warning, Raithe's lone Spitfire broke sharply to starboard and began to climb towards the German aircraft, accelerating as it did so. Crowe could imagine the varied responses of the rest of the pilots. Morgan would be annoyed with Raithe for breaking formation, and the Spitfire pilots would hate him for his arrogant disregard for his flight. Werner would simply be jealous that the Romanian would get a kill that he would have wanted for himself. Crowe glanced over towards the Favrio's aircraft, and could clearly see Werner's mouth moving as he subjected poor Ronnie Hall to a stream of frustrated Teutonic vitriol.

It did not take long. Even as the rest of the squadron droned on at their simulated bomber speed, Raithe closed the gap and swung around to bring his fighter behind and below the unsuspecting German aircraft. As Crowe watched there was a brief burst of tracers. The Messerschmitt's fuel tanks ignited, and the flaming fragments of the night fighter plummeted towards the silent countryside below. A minute more and Raithe swept down to rejoin the formation. No one said a word.

"We're at the abort point," Jones said quietly through the intercom a few minutes later. Crowe resisted the urge to snap at him. He knew where they were. The countryside below them was familiar, though it was amazing, Crowe decided, how different it looked from twelve thousand feet compared to the extreme low level they had adopted on their last visit to this part of Belgium. Rhys-Jones had died somewhere below them.

The problem was that with the exception of one random fighter there had been no sign of the enemy. The Vulture's airfield was less than forty miles away and the complex which had been their target that fateful night was even closer, but clearly the Vulture hadn't been drawn by their feint. It was time to turn back.

The radio crackled into life. "This is Mosquito Leader. Let's call it a night." The reluctance and disappointment in Morgan's voice was obvious.

"We should press on," Crowe said, earning a shocked look from Jones.

"We're going back," Morgan said, with just a hint of annoyance.

"I agree with Crowe," Werner said. "If the Vulture won't fly, we hit him on the ground."

"Hey," interrupted Clark. "You heard the briefing. We'll get creamed if we go in against that flak, not to mention all those fighters."

"Go home, then," Crowe said. "Leave the fighting to the rest of us."

"Or do you always need three against one, Clark?" Werner added.

"If you two want to go on, be my guest," Clark retorted. "Hopefully the Vulture will kill both of you and do us all a favour."

"We're all going home," Morgan snapped. "This isn't a bloody democracy."

"All Spitfires," Raithe said in his emotionless voice, "this is Spitfire Leader. Increase to cruising speed and turn for home."

"We're missing our chance here, Morgan," Crowe protested. "We've caught the bastard napping. It's not just you and me tonight, either." There was no reply. For a few seconds the Mosquitoes flew on as one by one the Spitfires peeled away below them and accelerated towards the distant Channel. Then, with a slow, almost reluctant bank, Morgan's lead Mosquito turned towards England, the others slowly following suit. Crowe cursed silently and followed. For a few seconds Werner's aircraft continued on towards the distant enemy airfield, as if planning to take them on alone, until finally it banked sharply and joined the rest of the flight. Werner's exclamation of contempt was emphatically not silent. On a command from Raithe the Spitfires merged into two files and streamed away, leaving the Mosquitoes to cruise along behind them.

Crowe opened the throttle and closed up to Morgan's aircraft, pulling into formation only a few yards off the Mosquito's dark painted port wing. He leaned forward in his seat to look past the slightly bewildered Jones towards Mosquito Leader.

"Morgan," he began, "I have a suggestion."

"I don't want to hear it."

"Yes you do. I know the Squadron is going home. Just hear me out."

Morgan was looking back at him now. Without sunglasses or goggles, Crowe was able to look into Morgan's eyes. From the look on the younger vampire's face it was clear that he had not forgiven Crowe for the previous night. His handsome features were as open and honest as ever, showing his hurt and wounded pride more clearly than the now-vanished bruising could ever have achieved. The anger was clearly still there, too, poorly hidden beneath the surface.

Finally, Morgan sighed. "What is it?" he asked wearily.

"Look, maybe the Vulture didn't fall for it. Maybe his whole squadron went north to hit the real bombers. I'm not ready to give up just yet, though. Are you?"

"It's not a question of giving up. We'll try again tomorrow."

"Of course. But in the meantime, why don't you and I hang back a little?"

"What are you thinking?" Morgan said slowly.

"The Vulture may decide to put in an appearance after all. It can't hurt to see."

"I stay with you," Werner said brightly.

Morgan ignored the German. His eyes remained fixed on Crowe.

"Okay," he said finally. "We'll slow down and let the others get ahead. But if we don't see anything by the time we reach the Channel, we're heading straight back to Charney Breach."

"Agreed."

"Werner, take the rest of the squadron home."

"But I want to…"

"Take them home, Werner," Morgan said testily. "We won't be far behind you." Werner muttered his displeasure but kept to his course. The rest of the Mosquitoes silently accepted the decision, their crews probably keen simply to be given the chance to fly home without further risk. As Morgan and Crowe slowed their aircraft, the other four drew quickly away. Jones stared wistfully after them.

"How much flying time have we got left?" Crowe asked.

Jones gave him a faintly resentful look, and then looked down at his notes. "Plenty," he said, his tone making it clear that he wished it were otherwise. He looked like he wanted to say more, but evidently decided not to waste his breath.

"Keep an eye out behind us," Crowe told him. The memory of the Vulture ambushing them just a few nights previously was still vivid in his mind. He had a sudden recollection of the burning Lancaster. He twisted in his seat, feeling his seat straps rubbing against his neck as he scanned the sky behind them. "God, I hope he comes," he muttered.

"So do I," Morgan said. "But I don't think he will."

"What's happened to your optimism? Where's your faith?"

"It's taken a battering recently," Morgan admitted, with an unmistakeable edge to his voice.

"Morgan," Crowe said with an intake of breath, "we need to talk."

"Not right now, we don't."

They flew on in silence, Crowe occasionally banking one way or the other to gain a better view behind them, constantly turning in his seat. His back and neck hurt from the effort, a reminder of the years of strain he had put on his body. His skin was young, he reflected ruefully, but the muscles and bones beneath were old before their time, damaged by too many nights spent sleeping rough on cold stone floors. Conscious of the approaching Channel coast, he began to let the Mosquito drift one way then the other, buying a little more time with each zigzag. Jones was constantly checking behind them, but it was largely pointless, his own eyes rendered redundant by the alertness of both vampires. Crowe could see Morgan effortlessly and lithely turning in his own seat. He was younger, after all, Crowe thought with a hint of jealousy.

Morgan's eyes were younger too. His sudden exclamation was full of boyish excitement. "Got him!"

"Where?"

"He's at six o'clock high, about five miles."

Careful not to let the aircraft change course and possibly alert the enemy fighter, Crowe twisted again, wincing slightly. It took him a few seconds to spot the aircraft, about four thousand feet above them, and a minute more before he could tell that it was twin-engined and moving reasonably fast. At this range it was impossible to make out any more than that, even with the help of the moon.

"It could just be another Messerschmitt," Crowe said warily, trying to suppress his growing optimism.

"It's him," Morgan said firmly. The gap was closing rapidly. Even as the Mosquitoes kept to their course, the fighter began to descend and the details began to become more clear.

"Is it him?" Jones said.

Crowe ignored him. "Morgan, let's lose some altitude. Maybe at low level he won't be able to run so fast."

"Should we turn towards him?"

"Let's drag him in a little first." He pushed the control column forward and took the Mosquito into a gentle dive. His airspeed began to increase, but Crowe hardly noticed. He was barely even aware of Morgan's aircraft next to him, because another quick glance had confirmed that the approaching aircraft had no radar aerials. It had no need for them. It was the Vulture.

This time they knew he was coming.

Chapter Eighteen

"Now!"

"Hold on." Crowe threw the aircraft into a violent turn to port, accelerating as he did so. Beyond his pale-looking navigator he saw Morgan drop into a similar manoeuvre to starboard, but then all his attention was devoted to the enemy fighter.

The Vulture was running. With instant reflexes and disturbing manoeuvrability the German had turned sharply away and was diving towards the French countryside below, his nose already pointed towards his distant base. This time, Crowe saw to his pleasure, the gap was not opening. They'd let the night fighter get to within a mile of them before they'd turned, and the distance between them remained that. If anything, it was decreasing as the three aircraft plunged towards the ground.

The Vulture pulled up at five hundred feet. With its dark grey and black paint scheme the German aircraft should have been invisible from above at night. Against vampire eyes, though, its camouflage was next to useless.

"Stay above him," Morgan said sharply. "Don't let him climb." At high altitude the Vulture could outpace the Mosquitoes. At low level they might have a chance. The Vulture descended further, until he was less than twenty feet above the scattered trees and hedgerows. They swept over a sleeping village, where a solitary dog barked at the sudden noise, its sound lost in the roar of Merlin engines on full power. The Vulture jinked from side to side, trying to lose them, but the pursuing aircraft continued to close the distance. It was less than eight hundred yards now.

They passed over a ridgeline of bare soil, the Vulture low enough that a spray of dust was thrown into the air in his wake.

"We can't keep up this pace for long," Jones warned.

"It will be long enough."

For a moment the Vulture was silhouetted against the sky as he passed over a second ridge, and Crowe's finger began to involuntarily close on the firing stud before the German dropped sharply down again. Conserve your ammo, he told himself. In a few seconds more the Vulture would surely creep into kill range. He guessed the range to the target again. Still eight hundred yards.

Either they were slowing, or the Vulture had accelerated, which would mean they weren't closing in on him at all. He looked quickly down at his air speed, and began to feel a little uneasy.

"Crowe," Morgan began in a concerned voice.

"I know," Crowe interrupted.

"He's toying with us. He may be leading us into an ambush."

"I'm not giving up now."

"Who said anything about giving up? I just thought you should know."

The Vulture made a sudden sharp turn to starboard, heading south now towards a small town. The Mosquitoes were alert to the manoeuvre and instantly corrected their course to keep close to the German. The turn had achieved nothing, except to lose the Vulture a little of his lead. Crowe wondered if the Vulture had any idea that the two British fighters behind him were piloted by vampires too. Probably. There was a tiny puff of exhaust fumes from their quarry's engines, and in a few seconds the Vulture had increased his lead back to eight hundred yards.

"That proves it," Morgan said.

"Ambush," Crowe agreed.

"Here they come, right on cue," Morgan said. "Two o'clock high, two Focke-Wulfs."

"Have they seen us?"

"I don't think so. They're above the town. They're starting to descend now."

Crowe took his eyes off the fleeing Vulture and took a quick scan of the sky. The two Focke-Wulfs were definitely diving towards them, although still a few miles away. A further flash of movement caught his eye, further east.

"Two more coming in, ten o'clock."

"I see them. This is getting sporting, eh?" Morgan sounded pleased. Crowe could see the smile on his face when he looked across towards the other aircraft.

"We can still turn back," Crowe ventured.

215

"Do you want to?"

"It's your decision, Mosquito Leader."

"Well," Morgan said quickly, "it would be a shame to go home without a few kills, now that we've come all this way."

"We're not seriously going to take on four fighters?" Jones asked, reaching down, apparently unconsciously, to check that his parachute was close to hand.

"Five," Crowe said. "Don't forget the Vulture."

"How could I?"

The Focke-Wulfs were less than three miles away now and closing fast, but the Vulture was no longer with them. Without warning it had pulled its nose up into a near-vertical ascent.

"Jesus, that thing can climb!" Morgan exploded as the two Mosquitoes followed.

"What's your plan?" Crowe asked. "Do we split up or stick together?"

"Split up," Morgan replied without hesitation. "I don't want you getting in my way." He laughed happily. Crowe felt the tension between them evaporate, however temporarily it might prove to be. His friend, he knew, was feeling the wild exultation he did every time he flew, magnified ten-fold because of the odds against them. Crowe felt his own adrenaline flowing, burning through his veins. At that moment he knew that he would kill today. The thought brought him joy. The guilt would wait.

"I'm going to be busy for a few minutes," he told Jones. "Keep an eye out behind us, okay?" Jones made a noise which could have been a strangled attempt at a reply. The navigator might have been nervous, but his eyes were already scanning the skies around them.

At a closing speed of six hundred miles an hour the Mosquitoes and Focke-Wulfs passed, wingtips missing by only a few yards. One of the single-seaters fired at Morgan but the tracers missed by some distance, the Mosquito a vague shadow against the dull backdrop of the land. The Vulture was still climbing away, leaving the melee below. Crowe knew that he couldn't hope to keep pace with the Arado. He broke hard to port and turned his nose and its silent, patient armament towards the four aircraft from Jagdstaffel Falke.

He picked his first target quickly, for no other reason than that it was the nearest. The German had obviously become disorientated, his eyes struggling to pick out the target in the darkness without detailed instructions from the Vulture. Another Focke-Wulf swept across Crowe's vision but he ignored it, concentrating on the first aircraft. He was above it and descended fast, the enemy pilot circling as he tried to get his bearings. The sky to Crowe's right was illuminated momentarily by a stream of tracer rounds, but he knew instinctively they weren't aimed at him and dismissed them as irrelevant. The cockpit seemed to grow quiet around him. The target was less than four hundred yards away as he dropped down behind it and slightly above. His mind calculated the correct angle of deflection as calmly as he might order a pint. Time seemed to slow, the familiar distortion he experienced every time he fought. His black leather flying gloves felt like they were just another part of his skin as he gently caressed the firing stud, waiting for the right instant. Beside him Jones was still, his duty to watch behind them momentarily forgotten as he watched the enemy fighter grow closer and closer.

Crowe fired.

The wooden frame of the Mosquito shuddered. It seemed to try to arrest its forward motion as the four machine guns and four cannon opened up simultaneously, hurling a maelstrom of steel and lead towards the hapless fighter. Perhaps the enemy pilot saw the rounds coming towards him, experiencing his own form of slowing time as the tracers hung momentarily in the air before springing towards him. More likely he saw nothing, and died without even the slightest knowledge of his fate. The heavy cannon shells ripped through his fuselage and cockpit, the lighter machine gun rounds adding to the damage as the aircraft broke apart, the two wings collapsing despairingly to centre like a snapped kite. The whole incident, from acquiring the target to firing, had taken less than six seconds. It was forgotten in less than one.

Crowe turned sharply, peering briefly over his shoulder and noticing with some satisfaction that Jones was doing the same. They had flown in a straight line for too long, but they had been lucky. There were still three fighters out there, but none had followed Crowe. They were all clustered around Morgan about a mile away, the Vulture nowhere to be seen. A flash caused him to blink.

"Did you see that?" Morgan called gleefully. "What a shot that was!" A piece of burning wreckage flared once as it plummeted towards earth and was extinguished in the same instant as the life of the young man who had piloted it. Morgan's Mosquito rolled in familiar celebration of victory. A Focke-Wulf drifted across Morgan's sights and he fired briefly, one of the rounds clipping the

German's wing and leaving a thin trail of smoke in the air as it hurtled over Morgan's head and climbed towards Crowe.

"I'll take that one," Crowe said, diving head on towards the damaged fighter.

"Where's the other?" Morgan said. Crowe caught a flicker of movement, looked up to his right and saw the fourth Focke-Wulf closing in on Morgan's six o'clock position, unseen.

"It's behind you," he warned.

"This is a dogfight, Crowe, not a pantomime." With effortless grace Mosquito Leader flicked his aircraft to starboard, avoiding an ill-timed burst of fire from the pursuing German. A few seconds later and Morgan was behind it. Crowe didn't have time to marvel at his friend's skill. His own target was closing.

They were head on now and less than half a mile apart when to Crowe's surprise the German opened fire. A detached and reasonable part of Crowe's mind calmly informed him that he had made a mistake by allowing himself to be silhouetted against the scattered stars. This time there was no illusion of slowness about the tracers. They zipped past Crowe's cockpit, seemingly inches from the Perspex. He felt as much as heard Jones' sharp intake of breath. He pressed his own trigger and felt the reassuring shaking of the aircraft as the powerful cannons fired, but the German was still coming, less than two hundred yards away, and Crowe all too belatedly realised that one way or another the German was about to hit them.

And then it exploded.

Crowe thought he saw fragments of engine, wing, fuselage and pilot slicing through the air on either side of them before his eyes closed in agony. He pulled up and unleashed the most venomous string of curses he could think of, the words tumbling out until he was almost breathless.

"Sorry," he said finally to Jones as he opened his eyes and tried to blink away the multi-coloured splashes of light that distorted his vision.

"Forget it," Jones said, slumping back in his seat and closing his own eyes in relief. "I agree with every word."

"Crowe, are you okay?" Morgan asked urgently.

"Fantastic," Crowe said. Some distance above them Morgan was on the tail of the last Focke-Wulf, which was twisting and jinking with increasing desperation. "Haven't you finished him off yet?" For some reason he felt uneasy.

"He's a tricky bugger," Morgan admitted. "But I suppose we should think about heading home." The Mosquito levelled out, adjusted its aim, and sent a short burst hammering into the fighter. A thick snake of black smoke erupted from the aircraft's engine. Crowe saw something fall away from the cockpit, and then the distinctive flare of a parachute. His unease increased, but the skies around them seemed empty and free of threats. Seeing the pilot abandoning the stricken aircraft, Morgan pulled up and with a joyful laugh put the Mosquito into a victory roll.

Crowe turned to Jones, and froze. Past his navigator's head he saw the sleek, shark-like form, closing at an incredible rate. But it was not headed for them.

"Morgan!" he shouted.

Morgan reacted with the speed that only vampire reflexes could bring. Breaking hard to starboard he evaded the onrushing attack of the Vulture, and the German fighter couldn't help but overshoot. In an instant Morgan was on his tail. The Vulture jinked and dived, and Crowe realised with joy that the German's need to keep out of the way of Morgan's guns was nullifying his speed advantage.

"He's mine now," Morgan exulted.

In a tight banking dive the Vulture rushed towards the ground, but Morgan stuck close to him, his nose manoeuvring inexorably towards the killing angle. The Arado pulled out of its dive at two thousand feet, desperately turning east, but Morgan had anticipated the manoeuvre brilliantly and was now on the German's tail, barely two hundred yards short.

"Say goodbye to the Vulture, Crowe," Morgan said happily, his aircraft poised to deliver the final short burst of fire that would finish it. Crowe looked past the Mosquito and saw the now-vulnerable looking shape of the German fighter stop its jinking and fly straight and level. That confused Crowe. He tried to spot the pilot but from this angle he saw nothing but the distinctive twin tail and the thin shape of the fuselage. He noted the two small barbettes that marred its clean lines both dorsally and ventrally. A fraction of a second later he realised the intent behind the German's lack of manoeuvring but by then it was already too late.

Four rear facing machine gun barrels flashed simultaneously. Tracers tore into the nose and cockpit of the pursuing Mosquito, smashing the cockpit canopy. There was a flash as the starboard engine burst into flames. Half a second later the port engine flared too, smoke streaming forth. Like a wounded animal trailing twin streams of blood the Mosquito started to slip away, even as the Vulture slowed and began to turn in towards it with practised ease.

"Oh, please, no," Crowe heard Jones murmur over and over again as the flames from the stricken Mosquito lit up the sky. He didn't hesitate. Although they were at least a thousand yards away he pulled the nose of his Mosquito up and fired.

It was luck, pure and simple. The burst could have gone anywhere. With no time to aim and at such a distance, he could as easily have hit Morgan as his pursuer. But though none of the rounds hit the Arado, they flew across its path and above its cockpit, and within just a few feet of the spinning props of his twin engines. It was good enough. With the practised response of self-preservation, the Vulture turned and dived away towards the waiting safety of the distant, heavily guarded airfield.

Crowe had no thoughts of pursuit. He would never have been able to keep up, and something told him the Vulture would not be back, not even for his damaged victim.

It was incredible that Morgan's Mosquito was still flying. As Crowe flew up alongside it the scale of the damage made him gasp. The starboard engine was silent and smoking. The fire extinguishers had done their work, but so had the shells. The props stood forlornly still, stark against the night sky. The propellers of the port engine were still turning but the metal around the exhaust was glowing white, the paintwork on the wing around it scorched and peeling away. Crowe barely dared look at the cockpit. The massive rends in the Perspex were unmistakeable.

"Morgan, are you okay?" The words felt hollow and stupid in his mouth.

"Yes," the reply came finally. The voice sounded distant.

"Are you wounded?"

"My leg's a bit of a mess," Morgan said wearily. "I forgot the barbettes. Who'd have thought it, eh?" He paused. "Bags is dead."

Crowe looked over at Jones. The young man had gone pale and looked close to tears. "I'm sorry," Crowe said. He meant it for both of them.

"If I hadn't been taking my sweet time about it I'd have finished him before he got the chance to fire. My mother always said that one day I'd be too cocky for my own good."

"She'll probably nag you about it when you get back."

Morgan laughed, the sound descending into a pained groan. "Not going to be an issue, my friend."

"Don't quit on me. If anyone can get that aircraft back it's you."

"Thanks for the compliment," Morgan said. "But I've got one engine out, another engine that is about to fall apart and a leg that's pissing blood all over the floor. Things, as they say, look bleak."

"We're only fifteen minutes from the Channel. We'll be back at Charney Breach in half an hour." Even as he said it, though, Crowe knew there was no chance. Morgan's aircraft was losing height steadily, the solitary damaged engine unable to maintain even their limited altitude. In another few minutes it would all be over.

Morgan knew it too. "I guess I'll pick a field and land this thing." The pain was evident in every syllable, even as Morgan tried to sound unconcerned. "Assuming I still have an undercarriage, that is," he added. "Mind you, having no wheels to land on never stopped you, did it?"

"Will you be able to get out and undercover with that leg of yours?" Crowe asked, then instantly regretted it.

"It will be dawn soon," Morgan said, ignoring the question. "You probably shouldn't hang around."

"I'm staying," Crowe said firmly, trying to hide the helplessness in his voice. He swallowed, his mouth dry. "I'm sorry," he said again.

"It wasn't your fault."

"No, I mean I'm sorry about last night. About what I said, and for lying to you."

"I should think so," Morgan said with a cough, and then added "Forget it. I have."

The Mosquito was at less than two thousand feet now, and Crowe could see Morgan in the shattered cockpit, scanning the ground ahead for a suitable landing place. There was blood on his face. Crowe couldn't tell whether it had come from him or Baggers.

"I think I see a couple of good spots ahead," Morgan said, as they passed over a small village. Ahead of them was an unusually grand village church with a needle-like spire. There was a large cross at its peak. Beyond it the woodland ended and the ground became more open. "I don't suppose I'll get a better chance. Look, do me a couple of favours, will you?"

"Anything."

"Get that bloody Vulture, will you? I'm starting to find him annoying. I'd hate him to miss out on a painful death."

221

Crowe smiled sadly. "Consider it done," he replied, meaning it. A thousand feet now, and the trail of smoke from the port engine was becoming thicker and darker. The aircraft weaved erratically, and with a sudden lurch fell two hundred feet.

"Morgan!" Crowe snapped.

"Sorry," Morgan said. "I fell asleep a bit there."

"Where's your flask?"

"In my pocket. If I survive the landing, I might have a drink to celebrate. Oh, that reminds me of the other favour."

"What is it?"

"If by some miracle I do survive the landing, tell my parents I died in the crash. I don't want them to think the sun got me." Morgan turned in his seat and smiled out at Crowe. "At least I'll get to see the sun rise properly for once in my life." The smile faded slowly. Morgan looked what he was, a frightened young man. As Crowe watched he blinked, turned away and reached down. A few seconds later the undercarriage descended. Five hundred feet. Crowe kept his Mosquito level, looking down as Morgan's aircraft slowly dropped away towards the waiting field. There were silent tears streaming down Jones' face. Crowe's face was dry, and he hated himself for it. Couldn't he be like a normal human being, just once?

In a barely audible voice, Morgan said "Be lucky." Crowe tried to reply but no words would come as the now burning Mosquito touched down in the field.

The wheels held. The Mosquito bounced once and then ran smoothly across the field. From the air Crowe couldn't see the narrow drainage ditch, just as Morgan hadn't seen it. The port wheel dropped in first. Crowe watched with horror as the aircraft flipped, seeming to stand poised for an instant on one wingtip before smashing into the wet earth, sending large clods of mud and grass into the air. Still its momentum carried it forward. The aircraft rolled twice more before finally coming to rest, the mud-covered cockpit facing away from them.

The fire had been extinguished in the crash, and the wreckage lay still. Faint curls of smoke rose from the smouldering wing. Crowe circled above it, but there was no sign of movement. A wing, snapped in the middle, reached out of the mud and pointed towards the solitary aircraft in the vast emptiness of the sky.

"Crowe," Jones said quietly.

Below them a night bird, disturbed by the noise of the crash, slowly returned, gliding down to settle on the broken wing.

"Crowe."

"What?"

"We need to go," Jones said. The damp streaks on his face glistened in the moonlight. He pointed to the fuel gauge. He didn't need to say that dawn was closing in on them. Looking down at the stillness of the field below, Crowe knew it all too well.

They made it back to Charney Breach with a low fuel light which flashed an urgent red. They had beaten the dawn, but as a shocked Dr Madeley and Harry Stead hustled Crowe out of the aircrew truck and into the protective embrace of the headquarters building, Crowe almost wished they hadn't.

Chapter Nineteen

The man lay on the cold stones, his mouth moving silently, his eyes begging the boy to run through the open door, but Crowe could only see the blood. It seemed it was everywhere, slick on the walls and streaming across the floor. The medical orderlies were trying to stem the flow but the knife had done its work, the arteries open, butchered. They weren't even watching him. He knew he should run now, just as he knew he wasn't going to run, just as he knew that the blood would keep him there. He was aware that he was dreaming, but it didn't matter. He touched the floor, feeling the hot blood on the cold stone. It ran over his fingers. He wanted to stop but he couldn't help himself. He never could. He raised his hand to his mouth and felt the blood touch his lips, heard the gasps of disgust, heard the single word burst from the lips of an orderly's face, contorted with horror. *Monster.*

Older now, locked in a tiny cell without light and with only a tiny window high above, open to the night air. There was comfort in the darkness, but he had been here before and knew it could not last. The empty square of the window began to change, the black sky starting to shift and brighten. Crowe banged on the door, shouting, but the solid iron seemed mute to his cries. Below the window a spot of gentle light appeared. It began to grow, casting glowing tentacles across the walls. The boy tried to back away. He pushed his body against the unyielding wall in the hope that it might relent, but the stone paid no attention. They never left him too long and he resolved not to scream or cry out, not to give them the satisfaction of knowing how they hurt him. The pain began as little more than itching across his naked frame, but it grew worse. His eyes were clenched so he could not see the smoke which rose from his skin, but he could not block out the smell. He bit his lip to try and stop the scream that rose, unbidden. Still it came. Even as he dropped to the floor he heard the door open, and felt the sharper agony as gloved hands gripped flesh burnt raw in seconds. Darkness enveloped him again, until there was only the feel of the cold metal table beneath his back as the doctors talked and the pens scribbled and the cold, dispassionate voice spoke its one simple word. *Monster.*

The man's name was Porter. He was from Luton, not that Crowe cared. He was just another opponent in another nondescript London ring. The baying of the crowd reverberated through the abandoned shoe factory, reaching a peak as Crowe blocked a clumsy swing and landed three quick, hard punches of his own. The man's face was already ruined, awash with his own blood from the gaping cuts above each eye. He blinked constantly to try and clear the liquid from his vision. Crowe drove a right hand into the man's solar plexus, feeling the fine spray of blood land across his face as the air was expelled from the fighter's lungs. The crowd wanted a big finish and he would not deny them, punching again and again, feeling the flesh soften under each blow. The man slumped back against the ropes, limp. Crowe knew he should stop. He didn't. His unprotected knuckles hurt from the force of landing repeated blows on skull and jaw. He was aware of the crowd falling silent and the referee's tentative, frightened hands pawing at his forearms, trying to draw him away. He turned away and let the man slide to the ground, unnaturally relaxed now. The crowd stared at him with loathing and horror. He let them stare. They had got what they paid for. He smiled as he raised his blood dripping knuckles to his mouth, smiled as the riot began, as he heard the single word that seemed to spit at him from every mouth. *Monster.*

Still he would not wake. The dreams kept coming, over and over, until he wondered if he would ever awaken again.

No one blamed Crowe, or at least that was what they said. They let him sleep in the HQ building, wrapped in blankets that barely kept the winter chill at bay. Then came the trauma of the inevitable debrief. Harry Stead asked mechanically the necessary questions about the number of enemy aircraft, their markings, the location of the dogfight. Morgan's death. Dr Madeley, sitting behind him with red eyes and an untouched cup of coffee, was only interested in the last.

Meeting Catherine and William Bale was the worst. They arrived in a staff car in the late afternoon, as the sun was beginning to set. John Bale, his own features struggling to hide his grief, led them in to the bar where Crowe had been left alone most of the day, trapped inside by even the weak winter sun. Crowe stood up when they entered, seeing the formal dress uniforms that both John and his father wore and ashamed of his own stinking flying clothes.

At first, as night finally came and the other pilots began to arrive, Group Captain Noone wanted all sorties to continue as normal. Crowe would have been happy to fly. He just wanted to be distracted, even if only for a minute. But William Bale spoke privately to Noone, and although no one heard the conversation, the result was clear. Harry Stead emerged a few minutes later to say that Crowe was excused flying for the night, leaving the vampire to watch wistfully as the crews trooped out towards their waiting transport. He caught a glimpse of Raithe speaking to Catherine, but he could not hear their words. Raithe did not speak to him. None of them did. Clark wouldn't meet Crowe's gaze, but there were unmistakeable traces of a smirk around his mouth.

With an oddly affectionate touch of Catherine's arm, Raithe turned and disappeared towards his waiting aircraft. Catherine walked back into the room.

"It is dark now," she said softly, her accent seeming stronger than he remembered. "Will you walk with me a little?"

"Of course," he said, his tongue feeling bloated and dry in his mouth.

"Morgan always loved flying," Catherine said hesitantly as they walked out into the cold night. "Even as a boy he was envious of the birds. Of course, the moment the war started he couldn't think of anything else except doing his bit. I suppose I could have tried to stop him. I could have told William not to buy him that damned plane."

"It wouldn't have worked," Crowe said. "He would only have found some other way."

"I know. There never was any point in trying to stop Morgan doing something. If would only make him want to do it more. I remember the first time he put on his daylight suit. I was horrified and begged Byron not to let him go outside in it, but Morgan just laughed and ran out of the door. He wasn't afraid at all."

Crowe smiled. "Why doesn't that surprise me?"

She looked up at him, and he was struck again by how extraordinarily beautiful she was. "You are his best friend, you know? He had his brothers of course, but although he loved them dearly he always knew he was different. I think that's why he loved you. You knew what he was going through."

"Yes," Crowe replied absently. He thought of the rising sun, and hoped that he didn't know. If Morgan had survived the crash, trapped inside the wreckage? Not for the first time Crowe found himself hoping that Morgan had been killed in the impact. It made him ashamed to think it.

"Byron told me that you blame yourself," Catherine said. He'd forgotten the unnerving way she could read his thoughts. "Don't. Everybody's blaming themselves. Byron blames himself for allowing Morgan to join the squadron. William blames himself for encouraging him to fly. And I..."

"None of you were there last night. I was."

"Yes, you were. And I thank you for it. He wasn't alone."

Out on the field a Merlin engine gave an almost apologetic misfire and kicked into life. Crowe looked past Catherine as more pilots climbed into the aircraft. One of the Mosquitoes was already taxiing. "He was an incredible pilot," he told her. "Last night he took two of them with him."

"Please," she said gently, "don't. I'm his mother, Crowe. One day you'll find a beautiful woman and marry her and you'll realise that a mother doesn't really care whether her sons died bravely. They're still dead. That's all that matters. Did you see him? At the end, I mean?"

"Yes. His aircraft was badly damaged. He had to crash land."

"Would he have been killed instantly?"

"Yes. I think so." He hoped it was true.

She looked into his eyes, and once more he felt that familiar feeling of vulnerability, that she was reading him. "But you didn't see him die?"

"No," he said honestly.

"It's strange. I always thought I would know the instant my child died. But this morning I woke up and I didn't feel any different. What do you think that means?"

"I..." he began, and stopped, realising what she was suggesting. The first warning signs had been there earlier. He'd hoped he'd been mistaken, but it was clear from her hopeful eyes that she hadn't accepted it. He wanted to say something to reassure her, but there was nothing that could be said. Morgan was dead.

"I don't think it means anything," he said simply.

She looked away. "That's what Raithe said too. He was a little harsher about it, of course, but that's Raithe."

"How long have you known him?"

"Since I was a little girl. I haven't seen him in over twenty years, but he hasn't changed a bit. He doesn't look a day older."

"How old is he?"

"I don't know. Older than my father, though."

That surprised Crowe. He knew Raithe was the oldest of them, of course, and not just because of the way the Romanian looked down on all of them as if they were children. The thought of how old he might actually be, though, opened up all manner of possibilities.

"He was a good friend to our family," Catherine said. "My father respected him, and deferred to his wishes. I suppose I was raised to see him as an uncle, but even as a child I knew he was powerful."

"I can't imagine Raithe being anybody's uncle. Was he as arrogant back then?"

She nodded, the slightest of smiles playing across her face. "More so. Arrogant, conceited and passionate. I once told you that my father wanted me to marry a Favrio and keep the bloodline intact. That was also Raithe's hope. When I told my father I was leaving with William, he sent for Raithe. He tried to stop me. He tried to reason with me, he threatened me, he even begged me, but when I left he turned his back on me. They all did, all the Favri. I'd known him my whole life, but the day I left for England was the last time I ever spoke to him, until today."

"What did he say to you?"

"That he was sorry for our loss," she said simply, gazing down at the damp ground. "Don't judge him too harshly, Crowe. He believes absolutely that vampires shouldn't have to hide away. He'd do anything for another vampire. And he's one of the bravest men I ever met." She looked up at him again, and to his surprise reached out a slim hand and placed it on his face. "So are you," she said.

He turned away, feeling his cheek warm where she had touched him. "When have I ever been brave?"

"I know the life you've led, Crowe, and you've survived it. I've known a lot of vampires. Most of them have never had to deal with the pain you've faced. They've had loving families or people like Dr Madeley or Raithe to help them. You could never have become the person you are without great courage. Morgan knew it. I think that's why you meant so much to him, because of your strength, because you were a survivor, and because you were brave. He envied you for it."

"Morgan envied me?"

"Of course he did. Believe me, I know. And I know he would have wanted you to be there when…" She stopped, and he saw the tears welling in her eyes. The first of the Mosquitoes, Werner and Hall, hurtled down the runway and lifted off into the night sky. She turned away. One by one, the squadron followed, climbing away and turning towards distant patrol areas. Crowe watched them enviously, and wondered how many would come home. Catherine watched them too, continuing to gaze into the noise-filled sky long after her eyes would have lost the Spitfires and the dwindling handful of Mosquitoes in the darkness of the night.

"He would have wanted you to be there," she said.

He was already well on the way to being drunk by the time the crews started arriving back, two or three aircraft at a time. A concerned Harry Stead had tried to drink with him but even the squadron leader had baulked at the pace Crowe set as he poured whisky after whisky down his throat. Dr Madeley had left with the Bales, concerned about them.

"I think William's taking it worst," the doctor had confided as they left. "I guess he always hid the depth of his love for Morgan. Now I don't suppose he'll ever get the chance to tell him." John Bale had shaken Crowe's hand as the family left, and the lack of accusation in John's eyes had somehow only added to Crowe's feelings of guilt.

Owen and Sullivan were the first to return, followed shortly by Gorecki. The Pole had taken command of their flight after Hinde's death. With a sympathetic glance towards Crowe he ordered another round of whiskies. He barely needed to bother asking, as Barry produced the bottle immediately from the counter where it had sat, already half-empty.

"Any joy, lads?" Stead said. It was the first time he'd spoken in an hour. He sounded relieved to have new company.

"One seaplane," Owen said. There was no triumph in his voice. Gorecki passed full glasses to each of them, hesitating slightly before topping up Crowe's glass from the nearly empty bottle. Others began to arrive in quick succession, casting concerned looks at Crowe. He ignored them, just as he ignored the despairing look that Stead gave them each in return. The whisky didn't seem to taste of anything, but Crowe continued to return to the bottle again and again.

Raithe walked in with Mills and Barnes close behind him. The moment they were through the door the two Flying Officers quickly moved away towards the far side of the bar. Raithe ordered more whisky, and when Barry produced a fresh bottle he simply took it from the barman. He did not touch it himself, but pushed the still full bottle straight along the bar towards where Crowe sat and then leaned back against the counter, eyes calmly scanning the room.

"That's another one for me, lads," Clark said loudly as he walked through the door. Beneath the strip of tape that supported his broken nose there was a huge smile on his face, which faded only slightly when he saw the looks on the faces of the people in the room. Still grinning, he walked over to join Mills and Barnes, who began to loudly congratulate him.

Werner walked in, looking apologetic.

"It is my fault," he confessed. "The arsehole flies with me tonight because," he hesitated, "because you were not here to mother him. I try to talk Kev Masters onto a Junkers and Clark got there first."

"Well," said Stead, "I didn't expect any kills, so I guess it's been a good night." He looked at Crowe. "Relatively speaking," he added hurriedly.

"Sir," Geordie Hulse said, "can I have a quick word?" The two men walked away towards the door. The noise in the bar, although still muted, was beginning to increase as people started to drink, but Crowe could still hear the two men talking. They had clearly forgotten the sensitivity of even a drunken vampire's hearing.

"Is he okay?" he heard Hulse ask.

"I don't know," Stead admitted. "I think he just needs to work this through his system."

"I hope so. We need him. Bloody hell, why did it have to be Morgan? And poor Danny Baggers, of course. They were both good lads."

"I know. We all feel the same way, Geordie."

From the far side of the room came a boisterous laugh.

"Not everyone," Hulse muttered darkly. Crowe turned in his chair to look over at the laughing Clark, who briefly returned his gaze. The big man's eyes danced with amusement.

More drinks came and went, merging into one. Crowe wondered where Cassie was. He felt that he desperately wanted to see her, and the more he drank the more the need grew. He kept looking up in the hope that she might have arrived, but there was only Barry, muttering as he collected empty glasses. Crowe saw Raithe looking at him with an odd expression before the cold blank expression descended over the Romanian's features once more. Crowe was dimly aware that all the vampires were drinking with him now. They were not alone, though. He didn't look up from his drink very often, but when he did he saw that Hulse, Stead, Owen, Sullivan and many of the others were close at hand. Jones was sitting a few feet away, his face showing even more concern than most.

Clark, a full glass in his hand, walked unsteadily into the centre of the room and coughed. "Can I have everyone's attention for a few moments?" he asked in a firm voice.

"What does he want?" muttered Werner. Crowe turned in his seat, placing his whisky glass down on the bar. Clark waited a few moments for the silence to take hold. The smirk had gone, and he stood tall in the centre of the room, his eyes serious.

"None of us here," he said, slurring only slightly, "are strangers to death. It's the business we're in. Sometimes, though, it hits you harder than others." He looked around at the silent, sombre faces and bowed heads. "I know you'll all agree that a part of Treble-Six died last night when that Mosquito went down. That's why I want you all to pick up your glasses, and raise a toast with me to Danny Baggers."

"Oh God, here we go," Crowe heard a voice mutter. Someone placed a gentle restraining hand on his shoulder.

"We lost two good men last night, Clark," Hulse said coldly.

"I count one." He smiled. "As for Bale, I reckon he got what he deserved."

"You're fucking dead!" Crowe shouted, shaking off the hand and stepping up from his stool in one fluid motion. He took a step but already there were hands on him, holding him back. Someone pulled his arms behind his back and took a firm grip, but it still took several others to stop him reaching Clark.

"Are you watching this?" Clark said, looking around the walls with a triumphant expression and open, questioning hands. "This man is dangerous. Does anyone even want him on this squadron? You're a monster, Crowe."

"Hold him," Stead barked, as Crowe struggled to break free.

"You'd better shut up right now, Clark, I swear to God," Hulse said, his face red with anger.

"Hey, come on Geordie, I'm just saying what we're all thinking."

"You're on your own," Slater snapped to a chorus of agreement.

Crowe tried to shake off the hands holding him. "Get off me," he shouted.

"Not here," Raithe murmured in his ear. It was the Romanian who held him back with his thin arms, his grip surprisingly strong. "Not like this."

"Take him back to his room," Stead ordered.

"You see what I mean, sir?" Clark said in a reasonable and all too sober tone, pointing at the violently struggling Crowe.

"Get out of my sight right now."

"Sir?"

"You heard me," Stead growled as the press of men half dragged, half carried Crowe out through the door. The vampire caught a last glimpse of a crestfallen Clark looking in shock at the contemptuous expressions on the faces of the remaining pilots.

"Raithe, let him go," Werner said as they stumbled down the steps outside into the chill of the night. "If he does not kill Clark, I will."

"You'll do nothing," Raithe said, his voice shaking with anger and unmistakeable authority. "This night is over. Do you understand me?"

Crowe, exhausted, let them take him back to his room. His head was pounding and spinning from the whisky and he felt the urgent need to vomit, holding it back only with difficulty. He tried to ignore the empty bed that had once been Morgan's and fell back onto his own. Werner passed him a glass of water. The liquid tasted bitter and he pushed it aside after a single sip.

Werner paced up and down the room, muttering while his fists clenched and unclenched rhythmically.

"Goddamn Raithe," the German spat. "Why does he stop me? You see the other pilots. They would not care if I cut Clark's heart out in front of them."

"Noone would," Crowe told him. His voice sounded distant in his ears, like an echo through salt water.

"I kill him too, then. And Barnes and Mills, the bastards. You should not have been so easy on them, my friend."

"It won't happen again."

"Next time I take care of it myself," Werner said as Raithe entered the room. He had a bottle in his hand, wrapped in brown cloth with only the neck visible.

"What do you want, Raithe?" Crowe asked.

"Why do you stop us killing him?" Werner demanded.

"It was not for the good of his health," Raithe said calmly.

"Then whose?"

"Mine," Raithe said simply. "I don't believe this is your room," he continued, looking sharply at Werner. "Why are you still here?"

"Someone should watch Crowe."

"Someone will," Raithe said. "Me. There are a dozen other places you could be. I don't care which you choose."

The German looked at him incredulously. "Who do you think..." he began to ask, but Raithe cut him off, speaking quickly in a low voice in a language Crowe could not understand. Werner hesitated with his face showing surprise, but then he responded, and Crowe knew they were speaking the ancient language of the Favri. For a minute or more they spoke, while Crowe stood and watched as Werner's face grew more respectful and the anger faded from his expression.

Finally the German gave Raithe a small, odd bow and turned to Crowe. "We talk tomorrow."

Raithe closed the door, and looked down at the prone Crowe.

"I don't need a nursemaid," Crowe said.

"You're not getting one."

"What did you say to Werner?"

"Nothing you could begin to understand, whatever Catherine Bale has told you. Drink this." He offered the bottle.

"What is it?"

"You know what it is."

"Yeah, I do, and you know I won't drink it."

"Perhaps you'd like some more whisky?" Raithe said dryly.

"Perhaps you'd like to piss off?"

"You refuse to drink the blood because it reminds you of what you are, yes? You are a vampire, Crowe. You are *Mulo*. That is a blessing, and yet you are ashamed. I pity you. Even the humans do not despise themselves for what they are."

"You know where you can stick your pity."

"You are angry with me because I stopped you attacking Clark? It is what he wanted you to do."

"He wanted me to kill him?"

"He wanted you to try." Raithe placed the bottle on the table next to Crowe's bed. "He knew you wouldn't have time to seriously hurt him. There were twenty men there to pull you away if you had got to him. Twelve hours later you would have been out of the squadron and back living on the streets. That is what he wanted. He was sober, he planned his trap and you walked into it. It seems this is becoming a habit."

"What's that supposed to mean?"

Raithe pulled up the flimsy wooden chair and sat down on it, unconcerned by Crowe's anger. "What happened last night?"

"Try reading the debrief notes."

"I have." Raithe leaned forward, the wood creaking beneath him. "Tell me anyway."

For a few seconds Crowe thought about telling Raithe exactly where he could go with his questions, but he was too exhausted for further confrontation. Besides, it could wait. Instead he talked Raithe through the engagement. He felt no emotion, as if someone else were telling the story. He described everything that had happened from the point he and Morgan had turned away from the main squadron. Raithe asked only occasional questions, focusing on minor details that the debriefing had not covered. His detached and clinical expression didn't change once, not even when Crowe described how Morgan had been hit.

"What about the Vulture himself?" he asked when Crowe had finished.

"What about him?"

"Would you describe him as a good pilot?"

"Didn't you hear?" Crowe said, knowing he was being facetious. "He's got nearly two hundred kills now."

"So you would say yes?" Raithe said. His voice seemed to pulsate with interest.

Crowe thought about it, replaying it again in his head, thinking back as well to the attack on the Lancaster. "No," he said finally. "He's cunning. He uses the night well, he keeps his distance and he has that bloody plane of his to get him out of trouble. He's got good reflexes and he has a knack of catching you with your back turned. But I'm not sure he's a good pilot."

"He has no need to be," Raithe said simply, sitting back with a strange expression on his face. It was not quite amusement, nor even smugness, but it made Crowe uncomfortable.

"Does this sound like the man you know?" Crowe said.

"Yes."

That surprised Crowe. "So you admit you know him?"

"Of course I know him," Raithe said. "But I've never flown against him. You have."

"Who is he?"

"He has gone by many names. The Vulture suits him best."

"Were you friends?"

"I prefer not to have friends. They are too often a liability. But we shared certain views."

"Such as vampires being superior to humans?" Crowe sneered.

"An obvious fact," Raithe said without hesitation. "He, however, took it too far."

"You mean killing people and drinking their blood, that sort of thing?"

"Those were not the worst of his crimes."

"There are worst crimes than murder?" Crowe said.

Raithe picked up Crowe's discarded water glass, sniffed at it, and took a sip before fixing him with an emotionless stare. "Do you know why vampires from all over Europe have gathered here in this squadron?"

"Apparently the Nazis didn't have much time for them in their home countries," Crowe said, off-handed.

"Ten years ago," Raithe said slowly, "the Westphalia Trust was protecting the interests of over a thousand vampires, Crowe, throughout Europe, in Poland, in France, in Austria, in Germany. More than seven hundred of them are dead now, killed by the Nazis." Raithe breathed deeply through his nose. There was unaccustomed colour in his pale cheeks, vivid against the whiteness of his flesh. "I knew every one of them," he said quietly, his voice burning with suppressed anger. "You will show them respect."

"I'm sorry." Raithe's anger had surprised Crowe, but he knew he deserved it. He hadn't meant to be so flippant.

"We tried to get them out, of course," Raithe said, outward composure returning in an instant. "At first we were successful, before the war. We had a vampire in Germany. He wasn't a pure blood vampire, though of course he had Favri blood, like you. He developed the condition as he grew older, like you. But he was cruel and vicious."

"Like me?"

Raithe didn't smile. "Believe me when I say that you would never wish to meet a man like this one. The only difference between him and the ones who took Werner's eye is that they can walk in the sun."

"Then why use him?"

"He had connections. He had money, and influence, and charm. He had a way of getting his own way, and most of the time that was our way too. Sometimes he did things for his own pleasure that I knew were wrong."

"But you were happy to overlook them as long as he was helping your people?"

"Our people," Raithe corrected. "Yours too. And yes, as long as he was helping vampires I did not care about his other habits. I was working from Paris, he from Stuttgart. We were successful. Sometimes we were unlucky and the Nazis caught one of us." Raithe paused briefly, a shadow of a horrible regret passing across his face. "But we got most of them away from Germany to safe houses in France and Holland."

"What went wrong?"

"Our man in Germany was captured by the Eckartstrasse less than a week before the German Army struck to the west."

Crowe thought of Werner, and the German's family being burned alive in their home. He'd known that the Nazis had hunted down the Favri wherever they had conquered new territory, but he'd never heard the figures before. Seven hundred was a staggering number. He'd never thought for a moment that there were so many vampires alive. How would the Germans have killed them? Firing squad? Hanging? Burning them alive, trapped like Werner's mother and brothers? Or would the German soldiers simply have dragged them from their sheltered hiding places, out into the daylight? He'd never thought about it before. He didn't want to think about it now. He swallowed, and tried to push from his mind once more the recurring thoughts of Morgan trapped in his shattered aircraft's cockpit as the sun rose.

"Couldn't you have found a replacement?" he managed to say finally.

"There was no time," Raithe said. "A few weeks later the Germans entered Paris. I was lucky enough to escape to England. Three weeks after I arrived in London, I heard the news that every one of the vampires we had helped escape from Germany had been taken by the Nazis."

Seven hundred vampires, all over Western Europe. "Your man who was captured in Stuttgart," Crowe said. "He gave them up, didn't he?"

Raithe nodded. "He knew it all. Names, addresses, descriptions. He gave it all to the Eckartstrasse."

"But he was a vampire. How could he give them up like that?"

"You ask that, after everything I have told you about him? Yes, he was a vampire, but he was also alive. In the end one was more important to him than the other. He told them everything they wanted to know." Raithe looked at him, and with a slow numbing realisation Crowe knew exactly what was coming. "Later, when they spared his life, he flew for them."

"The Vulture," Crowe said quietly.

"They offered him the choice, Crowe. Die in the sunlight, or kill for them. Would you have chosen differently?"

Crowe looked at him. There was no accusation in the Romanian's voice, and no malice. His face remained impassive, but Crowe barely saw him. Somehow, he could see nothing but a man in a brown hat, standing in the doorway of a prison cell, and a solitary window that would soon see the dawn.

He looked away.

"Morgan was not the first vampire the Vulture has killed," Raithe said.

"He'll be the last."

Raithe gave him a half-smile, as if he desperately wanted to believe him, but the smile faded and the Romanian stood up. Crowe could sense the sadness about him, close enough and real enough to touch, but the strangest thing of all was the feeling of age that hung about the vampire. It did not show on his face, but it was in the tired movement of his limbs and in the muted sigh that slipped unbidden from his lips.

"I'm sorry about Morgan," Raithe said, and the genuineness of the words left Crowe surprised again. "We didn't always agree. He was a naïve fool when it came to humans." Raithe took a deep breath. "But he was the best of us."

"Yes," Crowe said, looking up at him and nodding. There seemed nothing else to say.

"Soon it will be dawn," Raithe said. He motioned towards the neglected cloth-wrapped bottle. "Drink that. It will take all the bad memories away. Believe me. I know." For an instant it seemed like he would say something more, but then he walked from the room, closing the door gently and leaving his sadness hanging in the air behind him.

The soft footsteps in the hallway woke Crowe from a fitful doze.

He was wide awake in an instant, with the speed of mind of a man who had spent too many years fearing the vulnerability that sleep brought. Without even having to think about it his right hand snaked slowly out, found the handle of the table drawer and pulled it carefully open. The footsteps came slowly closer, the unmistakeable sound of someone trying to conceal their presence and movement. He instinctively knew it was almost dawn. His first thought had been that it was one of the other vampires finally returning from the bar, but no vampire would risk being outside now. Not so close to dawn.

He sensed rather than heard the hand on the door handle. Reaching under the top layer of clothes in the drawer, he pulled out his already-cocked pistol. The door slowly opened and a slim figure in a dark coat slipped into the room.

Chapter Twenty

"Cassie?"

Cassie smiled shyly. "It's dark in here," she said simply. With his free hand Crowe switched on the lamp for her, and her expression turned into a slight frown when she saw the pistol in his hand. "Were you expecting someone else?"

"I wasn't expecting anyone." Crowe put the pistol quickly away and closed the drawer again. He blinked painfully in the unaccustomed light of the dim lamp, and rubbed his eyes while his free hand searched for his sunglasses and put them on.

"Can I come in?" she said after a few seconds. When he nodded she closed the door behind her and took off her coat and scarf. She wore the same soft wool jumper she'd worn the night they had gone to Staverton, though the skirt was different, more practical. Her shoes were wet from the walk through the winter night.

"You don't have to wear those," she said, seeing his sunglasses. He put them on anyway. He was aware that he was almost naked, but didn't care.

"Are you okay?" she said, with a neutral glance at the unopened bottle of blood on the bedside table.

"I don't know," he told her honestly. He was still drunk, his mouth was dry, and his head was beginning to hurt, but that wasn't what either of them meant.

"I heard about Morgan. I know it won't help, but I'm sorry."

"Your dad told you, did he?"

"No," she said, flinching slightly at the hostile edge to his voice. "Harry called me a few hours ago. He always calls me when we lose someone. It's a pretty horrible tradition, really."

For the first time, Crowe saw that her eyes were very slightly puffy and discoloured. "Have you been crying?"

"It's part of the same tradition," she said. "He calls, I cry. You'd think I'd be used to it by now, but I don't suppose you ever get used to losing people you care about." Her voice dwindled away and she looked down at the floor.

"I wouldn't know," he told her quietly. "I never lost anyone I cared about, until last night."

She shuffled uncomfortably. "I shouldn't be here," she said. "If Dad knew I was here..."

"I'm glad you came."

She looked back up at him, and he was shocked to see the tears streaming down her face. He could see the pleading in her eyes and took a step forward to meet her, putting his arms around her and feeling the wetness of her face against the skin of his chest.

"I'm sorry," she said, sobbing now as he stroked her hair. The awkward feeling he had felt when she had begun to cry had evaporated, gone the instant he had held her. She felt delicate, her body shaking slightly with each sob.

"Look at the state of me," she sniffed. "I came here to comfort you, not the other way around. I hardly knew him, did I? But since Harry called I can't stop crying."

"Knowing Morgan, he would think that was the very least he was due."

"It's not just him," she said quietly. She didn't say any more, but he knew what she meant. In the last year she would have seen dozens of men walk out of the bar, never to return. He held her for what seemed a long time before she spoke again.

"What will you do now?"

"Carry on, I guess."

"Why?" she said, still not looking up at him, the words muffled by his chest. "Can't you just leave?"

"Leave?"

"Leave Charney Breach, the RAF. Go back to the life you had."

He wondered if she would have asked that question if she understood what that life had been. He kissed her forehead and hair. "Do you want me to leave?"

"I don't want you to die."

"I'm not going anywhere."

Her eyes met his. In that instant, all his fears and caution disappeared, replaced with an animalistic passion that drove every other thought from his mind. He leaned down and kissed her hard, pulling her tight against him. For an instant only she was surprised but then she returned his kiss, the salt taste of her tears on their lips.

She slid one hand over his cheek to lift his sunglasses from his head and tossed them aside. He winced in the sudden light, but then he half-sat, half-fell onto the bed and pulled her down on top of him. Her left hand fumbled for the lamp and plunged the room into darkness.

"I'm sorry," she whispered as they lay together afterwards in the blackened room.

"Why?"

"I didn't come here for this. I came to see if you were okay. I don't want you to feel like I took advantage of you."

Crowe laughed. "I've been taken advantage of most of my life. If that's what just happened, it's the first time I ever enjoyed it."

She smiled. Crowe knew she couldn't see him. There wasn't even a trace of light through the blackout curtains. Her hands stayed on him instead, as if reassuring herself where he was.

He kissed her gently. "Do you regret coming?"

Now it was her turn to laugh. "God, no," she said, still breathing heavily. "That was incredible." She hummed to herself happily for a few seconds. "What time is it?"

"Just before dawn. Do you need to get home?"

"Not really. Daddy's gone to a meeting at Biggin Hill. He'll be gone all day. That's good, isn't it?"

"Yes," he told her, and it wasn't a lie. But as she slipped into a contented doze, he lay alert, his eyes on the ceiling. He was sobering up now, and the slow realisation of what had happened scared him. Cassie seemed peaceful, and he wondered if she really knew what she had been doing all these weeks. He wanted her more than ever now, but Morgan had been right. This was dangerous ground. If Noone found out, if the news leaked to the rest of the squadron or someone had seen her coming here, what then? How would Morgan have reacted if he'd known they'd come to this?

"I'm cold," Cassie said, stirring. She was shivering as the sweat cooled on her smooth skin. He sat up, ignoring her slight moan of protest, and retrieved the blankets from amongst their discarded clothing. She reached out one exploratory hand, searching for him. He laid the sheets over her, but instead of lying down sat on the edge of the bed.

"What are you doing?" she said.

"Just thinking about something Morgan said."

"What did he say?"

"That this would end badly."

"The squadron?"

"Us."

She propped herself up on her elbow, the sheets wrapped around her, concealing her nakedness as the dark concealed his. "Do you think it has ended badly?" she said with the same note of alarm in her voice as before.

"I think it's been wonderful," he told her. "But it's not over yet."

"He was your best friend?"

"He was my only friend. The only one that counted, anyway."

"What about the other vampires?"

"I suppose. They're my own kind, after all." He couldn't keep the edge of bitterness from that statement, but Cassie didn't seem to notice. He thought about it a moment longer. "I'd fight for any one of them, even Raithe," he added. "But the day the war ends we'll all shake hands and walk away and that will be it."

"They must be friends if you'd fight for them."

"They're good men." He shrugged. "But maybe I just like fighting. I even used to fight with Morgan."

"Really?" she said, amused. "What about?"

"It's funny. I didn't like him when we first met. I took him for a spoiled rich brat who thought he was the best pilot ever." For a moment it was as if he was back in the classroom at that isolated, secretive airfield in Wales where they had done their training, listening to Morgan standing up in front of the group and telling them how they could all be as good as him if they put the effort in. He remembered the look on the regular instructor's face, the man whose name he could never remember, and sharing that same feeling of contempt for the young upstart that the experienced RAF instructor was clearly feeling. "I wanted to learn to fly better than him just to shut him up."

"And did you?"

"I never came close. He's the best pilot ever." She laughed. "Was," he added quietly after a few moments.

She reached out her hand again, and this time he moved closer and let her fingers find his. "He was lucky to have a friend like you," she said, squeezing his callused hand. "You're a good man, Crowe."

He took a deep breath. "I wonder if you'd still say that if you knew more about me."

"I want to know more about you."

"I'm not sure you do." He felt the conversation beginning to run away from him. He knew he should take control of it and keep it benign, possibly even end it by returning to the bed and kissing her. But there was too much she didn't know. He had to be honest. He had to tell her everything.

"Are you afraid I'll run away?" she said with a playful lilt to her voice.

"Yes."

Her eyes widened slightly at the seriousness of his voice. She leaned towards him. Almost despite himself he didn't shy away. She gently kissed him, her fingers reaching out to lightly stroke his face.

"Tell me," she said.

He looked at her, at the affection and fearlessness in her eyes, and wondered how long either emotion would last when she had heard his story. He took a deep breath.

"I didn't tell you the whole truth when we were in Staverton," he began. "When I was eleven years old the authorities took me out of the orphanage where I'd been living, if you can call it that, and put me in an asylum."

"Oh," she said quietly.

"There were no other children there. I spent my time surrounded by adults. Some of them were very intelligent people, teachers, lawyers, artists. I wasn't going to school, so the asylum became my school. I read every book I could get my hands on. I listened and learned anything people would tell me. Professor Bill used to tell me I was the brightest boy in my class." He paused, remembering Bedford Sands and the thin, grey-haired man. "Problem was Bill was insane. They all were, the ones who talked to me. The orderlies never talked to me, nor the doctors."

"They never came to see you?"

"I didn't say that. They came to see me a lot. They only ever took notes."

"Notes?" Her fingers were idly stroking the back of his hand. "On what?"

"On how much exposure to sunlight a child with my condition can take before he stops screaming and goes limp. Or how long it takes the burns to heal afterwards."

She didn't gasp, though her face suggested she wanted to. "They tortured you?"

"They would call it experimenting," he said with a shrug. "They probably thought it would advance the cause of medical science. It's amazing the evil people will do if they think it's in a good cause. Even the Nazis think they're in the right. Who knows? Maybe they are."

"I can't believe they could do that to a child."

"I don't suppose they saw me as a child. They just saw me as a thing."

"Didn't your parents try to stop them?"

"My parents?" He laughed bitterly. "My loving, horrified, disgusted parents? They dropped me off at the orphanage one day, and that was that. The last word I ever heard my father say was 'monster'. I don't even know where they are now. Professor Bill said they were afraid of me."

"You've mentioned him before. Who is he?"

"His real name was William Hunter. He was a teacher at one of the big public schools. A good one, too, until one day something just snapped in his head. Every chance we got we'd sit down with books from the asylum library, and he'd teach me English, maths, science, geography, anything I could handle. From the age of eight I never went to school, but he gave me an education. We used to spend most days in the asylum together. I think I reminded him of happier times."

"What happened to him?"

"He slashed both his wrists so that I could escape in the confusion."

"Oh, my God," she whispered.

"God," he said quietly. "Some of the inmates thought they could talk to God, you know? They were insane, of course. God never went anywhere near that place until the day they shut it down."

"But you escaped?"

"Yes. Two years later. If I'd escaped that day, maybe Bill's death would have meant something. No, come to think of it, it did mean something. It meant that day became the first day I ever drank blood."

"I don't understand," she said. She hadn't pulled away from him yet, but there was still plenty of time.

"Yes, you do," he told her gently. "Bill lay there with his veins open, and I drank his blood." He felt the fingers caressing his hand go still.

"I couldn't help myself. Sometimes I think I can still taste it. I wanted to throw up, but then the rush hit me and I just kept on drinking. He was still alive, too. I can still see the look in his eyes. They were sad." He looked away from her, towards the floor. "Accusing I could have coped with. The reason I feel so guilty about it is that he didn't want me to feel guilty."

"Of course he didn't want you to feel guilty," she said, her voice firm and certain. "You didn't do anything. He killed himself."

"To help me."

"That doesn't make you a bad person. You have nothing to feel guilty about."

"It gets worse." He watched her eyes and wondered if somehow, even in the darkness, she could see him. "Believe me, it gets worse. Do you still want to hear?"

She didn't blink. "Yes."

Outside, he knew that dawn had come and gone. The new day brought little change to the room, its deadly light held at bay by the thick blackout curtains.

"When I was thirteen, I did what I should have done for Bill. I escaped."

"How?" Slowly, almost without either of them realising it, her fingers had begun to trace their circuit on his skin again.

"I waited until night, and then broke every light bulb on my wing of the building. When the orderly came to find out what was happening, I was waiting for him in the dark. After I'd beaten him unconscious, I took his keys. That was seventeen years ago. Did you ever wonder what I've been doing since then?"

"I hoped you'd tell me someday, when you felt ready. And if you didn't, I was going to ask Quentin Quiet."

"I didn't realise you knew him," he said. The note of familiarity in her voice had surprised him.

"He was down here fairly often when he was setting up the squadron. I used to serve him drinks."

"He does like a drink."

"He likes a lot more than one," she told him bluntly.

"What makes you think he would tell you anything?"

She smiled, a little guiltily. "I thought you knew me better than that. He's a middle aged man. Men his age are easy. Give them a smile and wear a nice skirt and they'll give you anything you want."

"It's been known to work on me, too," he said wryly, thinking back to the storeroom where she had trapped him and asked him to take her out for a drink. It seemed so long ago now. So much had changed since then.

"Lie down with me again," she said. "Please?"

He looked at her, wanting her desperately but reluctant to let this moment of levity pass. To do so meant continuing the story, and although he knew it had to be done, he still didn't want to. Only when she kept her hands on him, her eyes large and warm and unafraid, did he finally get back into the bed. She moved back to give him space. He put his arm across her, pulling the sheet up to cover them both as they lay facing each other, noses almost touching.

"Tell me what you did after you escaped," she said softly.

From her voice Crowe knew that she really wanted to hear. He also knew that she expected to fall asleep afterwards in his arms, but he knew more than she did. He knew how the story went. That was why he expected the night to end very differently.

"Well," he said finally, slowly, "at first, I survived. Sometimes I'd kill animals for blood. Rats, mostly. Usually I just scavenged. When I kept growing and started to get hungry, I began mugging people." He felt her twitch slightly, as if a little shocked, but her warm hands were still on him and didn't move away. "Don't worry," he said, "I never seriously hurt them, though sometimes I wanted to. But eventually I got sloppy, and drew too much attention to myself."

"The police?"

"Criminals. From then on I was working for them. Things started to get more serious, the criminals started to get more serious. I was strong, I was quick and I could fight. They could make money out of me, and me out of them. Have you ever been to a bare-knuckle boxing match?"

"It's never really appealed," she said dryly.

"I had fifty fights in three years. No one could touch me. I was actually proud of that, until I went to sleep, and dreamed, and hated myself a little bit more each time. By the time the war started I was fighting twice a month. My employers even rented a flat for me, at three times the normal rate. I barely noticed the war starting. What did I care about Britain and Germany being at war, other than that it meant a few less punters at the fights? Of course, there was the blackout. I loved the blackout."

He paused. She seemed satisfied, her body and breathing relaxed, as if she knew nothing he could say could cause her to leave the bed and walk away from him. He put his right hand against the soft skin of her cheek. She smiled, and tilted her head further towards his fingers, kissing his palm.

He left his hand there a moment longer, and then pulled it away.

"And then I beat a guy to death in Clapham," he told her. He felt the involuntary tightening of her grip. "I beat him to a pulp, and then I just kept punching. I don't even know his name, but I killed him with my fists for thirty-five quid."

The words had come out more quickly than he'd expected, but at least it was over now. Her face was unreadable, but she hadn't moved, and slowly her grip on his hand relaxed.

"I never told anyone that before," he said.

"So that's the big dark secret in your past?" she said softly. "That you drank blood, because of a medical condition you never asked for, and that you accidentally killed a man in a fight, because that was your job and the only way you could make money to survive?"

"I didn't have to kill him."

"And you didn't mean to."

He shrugged. "Maybe I didn't, but he's still dead. I sometimes wonder if my parents were right. About me being a monster."

"Your parents?" she said, and he was surprised to hear the sudden burning anger in her voice. "Who cares what your parents think? They deserted you when you needed them. They let all those horrible things happen to you, and they probably didn't even care. They're the monsters, and the doctors, and the men who put you in that ring. Not you."

"I'm a vampire…" he began to say. She cut him off with a finger pressed against his lips.

"Yes, you are," she said gently. "You are a vampire. Why can't you just accept that and be happy with what you are? Raithe manages it, poor Hinde and the others too. What about Morgan? Did you think he was a monster?"

"That's different," he murmured.

"Why?" There was confusion in her voice now. "Because he was born with it? Or because he was lucky enough to be surrounded by people who understood him and you weren't? What about me? Do you think I am here because I want to be with a monster?"

"Cassie…"

She kissed him, her body close to his. "I want you. You may be different, but you're a good man." And whether the rest of the world believed it or not, Crowe knew that for her it was true.

He awoke briefly a few hours later, this time groggy with sleep and briefly confused and wondering what it was that had awoken him. It took him a few seconds to realise that there was no threat, only the girl who still lay in his arms, head resting on the pillow over his left arm, her back to him and her soft naked body curled up against his. He kissed the back of her neck gently, and she gave the tiniest moan.

"You're still here," he whispered.

She shifted slightly, pressing her body further back against his. "I'm not going anywhere," she said sleepily, reaching out as if automatically to pull his right arm tighter about her body and place his hand on her firm breast. A few seconds more and he felt her chest rise and fall once again with the gentle rhythm of sleep. He kissed her again, and closed his eyes.

The next time he awoke he was screaming, in the greatest agony he had ever known.

Chapter Twenty-One

Clark was laughing, but Crowe couldn't see him. He was blind, his eyes the source of a nightmarish pain that lanced through his entire body, bringing hot tears streaming down his face. They felt like acid against his burning skin. Though he had never felt it so agonisingly intense before, he recognised the pain. He rolled from the bed, hardly noticing the impact as he fell heavily onto the floor and his head bounced from the thin carpet. He could see nothing except the desperate white glare that threatened to tear out his eyes. All he could hear was Cassie's hysterical screaming drowning out Clark's giggling. By instinct alone he managed to roll under the bed.

Clark had opened the curtains. For the first time in fifteen years he had been subjected to the full light of the sun. The smell of his own burnt skin filled the room, suffocating him with its stench.

"How are you feeling, Crowe?" Clark mocked. "My God, Madeley wasn't lying when he told us what sunlight did to you things."

"Clark, get away from him!" he heard Cassie scream. "Close the curtains." The bed shook as the two struggled, and he heard her whimper as Clark pushed her hard back down to the bed.

"Stay down, slut," Clark snapped. "Hello, Crowe, what are you doing under the bed, eh? Is it a bit bright for you?"

Crowe managed to open his eyes slightly, just in time to see the onrushing black shadow. Clark's boot caught him above the eye. It was a glancing blow, but more pain shot through him as the sole of the boot scraped his temple, tearing blistered and bloody skin away with it.

"You're out of here, Crowe," Clark mocked. "Even if you stay cowering under that bed until the sun goes down, you're still out. The boss has had enough. Why don't you come on out? Make it easy for everyone?" He swung another foot at Crowe, missing as the vampire rolled further under the bed.

"You know," Clark mused, "I should have done this weeks ago. If only I'd realised how easy it would be." He casually propped his foot up on the bed and used a blanket to wipe the blood from his boot.

"Shaun," Cassie began.

"Shut up," he said harshly, and then laughed again. "You know, Cassie, you should really come and have a look at Crowe now. I'd like to know if you still want to fuck him now his skin's all gone."

Crowe opened his eyes. The room beyond the underside of the bed was still painfully bright, but he knew it must have been a cloudy day outside or he would have been dead already. Clark knelt down, a dark blur against a sea of shifting colours. Crowe almost welcomed his presence, if only for the shadow he cast.

"Have you got anything to say, Crowe? I'd ask how you are but I think I can tell from here." Clark tilted his head to one side with a sympathetic expression, and then threw a spiteful short punch that hit Crowe in the shoulder. There was no real power in the blow, but the contact of the knuckles with his raw flesh sent renewed paroxysms of agony through the vampire.

"You're a coward," Cassie hissed. "You wouldn't dare hit him if it wasn't for the daylight."

"What a hypocrite you are, darling," Clark said, amused. "Do you really think what I'm doing is any worse than him attacking me in the dark?" He looked down. "Wouldn't you agree, Crowe? Where are your threats now?"

"Do you want a threat?" Cassie said fiercely. "When my father hears about what you've done..."

"He already knows. But before he comes in, can I just say how nice it is to see you naked again? I'd forgotten how gorgeous you are out of your clothes. Not that I'd touch you now." He looked back at Crowe. "I hope you enjoyed her," he said quietly. "I did, and I was there first."

Crowe tried to speak, but the pain was too great. Opening his mouth only allowed a long groan to escape. For an instant he thought that he should not give the man the satisfaction of hearing his pain, but the thought disappeared, drowned by the urgent tortured dismay of exposed nerves.

Clark stood up. Crowe heard him walk over to the door and open it. Cassie ran to close the curtains, sobbing as she did so.

The room went dark for a moment, but then the newcomer walked in, switching on the lights as he entered. In the shadows under the

250

bed Crowe rolled to his side to look towards the door, and although the movement caused fresh pain, he could see impeccably shined shoes through the tears that clouded his eyes.

"Daddy," he heard Cassie gasp.

For a long time, Group Captain Noone didn't speak. When he finally did, his voice sounded as calm and civil as if discussing the weather with a stranger.

"Well, Shaun, it appears I was wrong to doubt you. I always believed you about Crowe, but I hoped you would be mistaken about Cassie."

"I think he may have used force," Clark said.

"You know that's not true," Cassie said scornfully.

"Rape, you mean?" Noone mused, ignoring his naked daughter. "Where is he?"

"Hiding under the bed," Clark said with a note of satisfaction.

"Ah, yes," Noone said. "Sunlight."

"I found these on the floor."

"His sunglasses?"

"I imagine he could really do with them now."

"Daddy, please," Cassie sobbed. Her voice sounded like a little girl's, but the masterful wheedling she could adopt to manipulate her father was absent. The trembling and begging in her voice was real.

"What?"

"He's dying. We need to get him to Doctor Madeley."

"Don't worry, Madeley will get to hear everything in time. But not just yet." Noone leaned down to look under the bed. "So, Crowe," he said reasonably, "did you enjoy having sex with my daughter?"

"Yes, he did," Cassie said immediately, the words angry amongst her tears. "And I enjoyed it too. Now call the doctor."

Noone looked away from Crowe. "You always looked like your mother, Cassie, but I'd hoped you wouldn't turn out like her. She didn't care about my career, either. Do you have any idea how much damage you could do to my reputation?"

"Your reputation? Don't you understand? There's a man dying on the floor and you're talking about your reputation."

"That's not a man," Noone said. "You could have any man you want, Cassie. Why on earth would you even let that thing touch you?"

"Oh, I'm sorry, Daddy," she retorted. "I'm sorry that he isn't more like your trained monkey here."

"Shut up, Cassie," Clark said.

251

"Watch your tongue when speaking to my daughter," Noone snapped.

"Sorry, sir."

"Get your clothes on," Noone told her.

"No."

"Get your clothes on, or I'll drag you out of here naked."

"What would that do for your reputation?"

"Cassie, I am your father. How could you do this to yourself?" Noone's voice sounded unsure and hurt. The whining note simply made Crowe despise him more. "How could you do this to me?"

"I'm not leaving until the doctor comes."

"I promise he will be fetched as soon as we leave. The longer you stay, the longer it will be before he arrives. Now get dressed. Shaun, avert your eyes please."

Clark turned away, slowly and with clear reluctance. Crowe heard the sound of her clothes being hurriedly pulled on, and saw her slim hand reach down to retrieve her discarded underwear from the floor. He wanted to reach out to her, but his hand stayed where it was, trembling.

"Crowe?" She leaned down, her face appearing upside down to him at the edge of the bed. She looked shockingly young, her hair falling down to rest on the carpet as it framed her face. He saw the horror in her eyes as she saw his glistening, raw naked body, and he recoiled further into the shadows, pressing his bloody skin against the cold wall and feeling the blood stick to the cheap paint.

"He's fine," Noone said. "Shaun, escort my daughter out to the car. I will just be a few moments."

Cassie reached under the bed, trying to hold Crowe's hand. Clark pulled her away. She gave a sob of protest and Crowe saw her still naked feet moving away as she was half-dragged towards the door and disappeared into the corridor.

Noone watched her go, and then spoke briefly to two soldiers in the corridor outside before he closed the door. He did not bother to kneel down to address Crowe.

"I don't think we'll be seeing each other again," he said. "Nor will you ever see my daughter again. You are grounded, permanently, pending dismissal from Treble-Six Squadron. You will never fly again for this squadron or any other. The soldiers outside will remain by your door, it will be locked, and you will not be allowed to speak to any of your friends. Tonight, when I am ready, I will let Doctor

252

Madeley see you, and then you will be escorted off this airfield. Where you go then, I don't care. I suggest you crawl back to the London gutter and die. I think that would be best for all of us, don't you?" There was the faintest sound of something landing on the carpet, and then the crack of splintering glass as Noone stepped on the sunglasses and ground them into the carpet.

He turned smartly on his heel and opened the door. "Goodbye, Crowe." The door shut behind him, the finality of the sound mocking in the stillness of the room.

Crowe did not know how long he lay alone under the bed in the silent room, his eyes closed against the pain and the intruding glow of the electrical light. The agony slowly subsided but remained there, emerging to send jolting shocks into him every time he moved and his raw flesh rubbed against the coarse carpet. Although Cassie had closed the curtains, Crowe instinctively knew that the weak winter sun had reached its zenith. Even with his eyes tightly shut, though, it took him a long time to generate the courage to move out from the shelter of the bed.

The pain came back simultaneously with his first movement, but with a sharp gasp he clenched his teeth and rolled to the side, feeling clumps of his remaining skin tear away, stuck to carpet fibres. His eyes remained closed as he managed to rise to his feet and stumbled blindly across the room, his hand slapping wetly against the wall until he found the light switch and flicked it off. He thought of Morgan's insistence on keeping the light intact that first day at Charney Breach, muttered a curse, and smashed the light bulb with his fist. Fragments of broken glass lodged in his already blood-soaked hand, but he barely noticed. He swore through gritted teeth. The girl in his arms had relaxed him, made him feel safe for the first time in years, made him unwary enough that he hadn't woken when Clark entered. It was not a mistake he could afford to make again.

Slowly his eyes adjusted, returned to normal, and he looked over at the table and saw the cloth-wrapped bottle that Raithe had left.

He didn't hesitate, not even for a moment. He took two quick steps and picked up the bottle with both hands. Ignoring the chafing of the rough cloth against his blistered palms, he flung the cork against the wall and began to drink. Head back, mouth wide, he let the blood rush out, splashing against his throat and bubbling down his chin, running in thin streams down his chest. His throat worked mechanically, rapidly, gulping the now-cold liquid down in great swallows even as he felt the spillage splashing against his feet and onto the carpet. He emptied the bottle in seconds, spun on his feet and hurled the bottle against the wall, watching as it shattered and fell to the floor, splintered into tiny fragments bound together by the cloth. A last few drops of dark blood ran slowly down the broken glass.

For a few seconds only, he felt nothing.

When it hit him it came hard and fast, more painful even then his immolated flesh, and yet bringing with it a surge of almost unbearable pleasure. He snapped rigidly into a pose of crucifixion as every muscle sprang taut, his cheeks pulling back to bare the blood-stained teeth beneath, his body shaking with sensation greater than any orgasm. He screamed in horrified delight, barely hearing the concerned voices of the guards outside over the noise of his own blood pulsing in his ears. His fists clenched into tight balls, the knuckles popping and his fingernails digging into his palms. He breathed quickly and shallowly, hyperventilating as the human blood from the bottle mixed with his own and coursed through his entire body, bringing with it pain and release and rage until he dropped heavily to one knee.

The guards. He could hear them talking outside, their voices strained and confused. He wanted to kick the door down and kill them both, rip out their throats with his teeth, snap their necks between his fingers. Patience, he told himself. The guards were nothing.

Clark and Noone were the enemy. They would die. First, though, let the blood do its work.

Already his skin was tingling. He held up his hand and saw the first signs of healing, the skin shuddering into place over glistening red flesh and exposed tendons. He could no longer feel any pain. The blood was anaesthesia. The blood was power. He could feel the strength coursing through his muscles, leaving him imbued with a force he hadn't felt in years. His eyes were hypersensitive and saw everything, every last detail of the room, from the tiniest fragment of broken glass to the quickly drying remnants of his own blood on wall and floor. His whole form sang with its need for action. He turned to the wall and with a twist of the hips smashed his fist into it. The cheap plaster seemed to dissolve beneath the blow. For a few moments blood pulsed from the fresh wounds on his knuckles, and then stopped. He laughed as the cuts healed even as he watched.

In just over four hours, he knew with absolute certainty, it would be dark enough to walk outside. Four hours until he could hunt for Clark and Noone. It didn't matter where they were, or how many witnesses stood around them. They would both die. If anyone tried to stop him, even another vampire, they would die too. He yanked open the drawer of his bedside table and retrieved his loaded pistol. They had been fools to leave it with him. He closed the drawer delicately, then lifted up his leg and brought his foot down hard onto the table, splitting it into two with a crack. Outside the guards muttered to each other again. He could sense their fear.

Crowe began to pace, up and down the room, his speed and footfall never varying. The minutes passed in a blur, his mind blank except for thoughts of the two men he would soon slaughter. After an hour his body was once again covered with a thin layer of skin, and the flesh beneath was invisible once more. Within two hours, there was no sign that he had ever been hurt. The pistol felt warm in his hand, held in a tight unyielding grip. The buzz was beginning to wear off now, but still he felt as healthy and alive as he had ever known, and his conviction didn't waver for even a second as two hours turned to three, and three slowly to four.

There was the sound of voices in the corridor outside, and then the sound of a key turning in the lock. Crowe smiled and turned to face the door, his body preparing to attack.

The door opened, and the light from the corridor flooded into the room. Crowe gasped and brought his hand up to cover his eyes, hissing his displeasure.

"Do I have to shoot you, Crowe?" Quentin Quiet said calmly. He stood silhouetted in the doorway, his distinctive hat casting a shadow onto the German-made semi-automatic pistol in his hand.

"It won't stop me," Crowe said. "Turn that light off."

"That would be...premature. Why don't you turn on your bedside lamp? I recall it casts a milder illumination."

Crowe stared at him, his eyes reduced to slits and his teeth bared.

"Please?" Quiet added in a reasonable tone, even as he cocked the pistol loudly. Crowe swore and reached out to turn the lamp on. Quiet motioned with the pistol for Crowe to step away, and then switched off the light in the hallway, reducing the ambient light to the dull glow of the heavily shaded lamp.

"That's better," Quiet said. "Why don't you take a seat? And put that gun down before you do something regrettable."

Crowe slowly placed his pistol on the bed, eyeing Quiet's warily. "You planning to kill me?"

"Only if I have to." Quiet's eyes darted for the briefest instant towards the broken glass on the floor, but were back and focused on Crowe before the vampire could even think of taking advantage of the distraction. "I see you've drunk all of the blood Raithe left you. He said you would. How do you feel?"

"Like you don't have enough bullets in that gun to stop me reaching you and tearing your head off."

Quiet returned his smile. "One between the eyes would be enough."

"You're sure you're that good a shot?"

"Yes," Quiet said simply. "Did you know," he added after a pause, "that it's been almost twenty years since K Department heard of you?"

Crowe didn't respond. The look of surprise that he couldn't quite keep from his face, however, clearly didn't go unnoticed.

"It's true," Quiet continued absently, as calmly as if there were no pistol in his hand and they were simply old friends discussing the past. "The doctors at Bedford Sands made a lot of notes. The subject wasn't called Crowe, of course, but it was you all the same. Their medical report would have made very interesting reading, if the Government hadn't suppressed it and passed it on to us. You'd be surprised how often that happens."

"I don't have time for this," Crowe said harshly. "Get out of my way." He started to step forward, but the look in Quiet's eyes made him stop again. The eyes beneath the hat never even blinked.

"It took us almost twenty years to find you, Crowe," he said. "I don't want to kill you but it would not trouble me to do so. I take it you plan to kill Clark and the Group Captain?"

"Do you have a problem with that?"

"It would be...unwise."

"Do you have any idea what they did to me?" Crowe said, his anger starting to shift towards the man in front of him.

Quiet seemed unruffled by Crowe's glaring eyes. "I know exactly what they did to you. Shaun Clark has been busy telling anyone who'll listen."

"I imagine that got a big laugh."

Quiet shook his head slightly, and then cocked it to one side, looking at Crowe as if seeing him for the first time. "You know,

Crowe," he said, "I'm rarely wrong about people but I'll admit you're an exception. When I recruited you I knew you were bitter. I knew you were damaged. I never took you for the sort who would wallow in self-pity."

"Be careful what you say to me right now."

"You really don't understand what's going on in this squadron, do you? Shaun Clark isn't popular. At best he was tolerated, and even that isn't the case anymore. Harry Stead told me that he had to physically restrain Geordie Hulse last night. Hulse wanted to help Clark swallow his own teeth after what he said about Morgan. The only reason Werner didn't attack those guards to get you out of here is because Raithe told him not to. The only reason Raithe didn't attack them himself is because I told him not to. Virtually this whole squadron supports you. You've won them over. Isn't that enough?"

Crowe shook his head. "It's still Noone's squadron."

"As you might say, his time will come."

"They hurt me."

"You don't look hurt to me," Quiet said calmly.

"Noone grounded me."

"You were a fool to sleep with Cassie." There was the faintest trace of anger in Quiet's voice, fading the instant he carried on speaking. "Unfortunately for Group Captain Noone, only one man on this airfield has the authority to ground you. It is not him."

"What are you saying?"

"The sun's down, and I want you to take a walk with me," Quiet said, casually making his pistol safe and slipping it inside his crumpled brown suit jacket. From the pocket he withdrew a pair of aircrew smoked goggles and threw them to Crowe. "You might want these."

"Where are we going?" Crowe's own pistol sat on the bed, forgotten. Quiet smiled slightly, the expression of a man for whom everything was going exactly according to plan.

"The briefing room," Quiet said. "Noone has called everyone together. He wants to break the good news of your dismissal. However, he's about to get some other news you may find…amusing."

"…for conduct unbecoming of an officer," Crowe heard Noone say as he followed in Quiet's unhurried wake down the corridor towards the briefing room. "And for a possible serious sexual assault."

257

"This is lunacy," he heard Hulse shout from amidst a babble of raised voices.

"It is bullshit." Werner's Teutonic accent was unmistakeable.

"I will have silence here," Noone snapped. "I am happy to ground more of you."

Quiet walked casually into the room. "I don't think there will be any more groundings today, Noone."

"May I remind you, Quiet, that this is my squadron?" Noone said, looking at him disdainfully. Then he saw Crowe following, and his eyes widened in shock. Crowe glanced around the room, past the Group Captain to where a disgusted looking Harry Stead stood by the blank chalkboard and the small table with its solitary telephone. Stead seemed to do a double take as he noticed Crowe for the first time. Crowe scanned the audience, seeing the same reaction on every face. Nearly every face, that was. Only Raithe seemed unsurprised.

"Take a seat, Crowe," Quiet said, as if he hadn't heard the Group Captain speak. Crowe, his eyes on Clark who had half-risen to his feet, walked slowly towards the back of the audience and sat down next to Werner. Jones was sat just in front of him and both men smiled as he sat, though they shared the same look of confusion with their happiness.

"What is he doing here?" Noone finally managed to say, regaining his composure.

"I asked him here," Quiet said.

"Who do you think you are? That man is under arrest."

"Do be quiet. You're becoming...tedious."

"How dare you speak to me that way?"

"Do you mind if I use your phone?" Quiet asked politely.

"What?"

"Harry, dial that number I gave you earlier."

"What the hell is going on here?" Clark said angrily, tearing his eyes away from Crowe and looking forward to where Harry Stead was busily dialling.

"Sit down, Clark," Quiet said coldly without turning to look at him. "You'll have less distance to fall."

"It's ringing," Stead said.

"Excellent."

"I'm warning you, Quiet," Noone said.

"Shush," Quiet said softly, taking the phone from Stead's outstretched hand. "Good afternoon, sir," he said. "Marvellous,

258

thank you. You'll recall I said I might call? Yes, I'm afraid it has come to that."

Noone looked perplexed as Quiet continued his conversation and Stead backed slowly away from him.

"He's standing right next to me," Quiet said, looking up at Noone. "Of course." He took the handset away from his ear and offered it to the speechless station commander.

"Who is this?" Noone said angrily, snatching the phone. "Is this a joke?" His face fell. "Oh," he said meekly. "Yes, sir."

Werner nudged Crowe and gave him a quizzical look. Crowe shrugged. He had no more idea than the German.

"Yes, sir, I understand," Noone continued, the colour draining visibly from his face. "Yes, Prime Minister." He slowly put the phone down. Murmurs spread through the stunned room. The Group Captain stepped slowly away from the phone, his eyes never leaving it. Crowe watched as the man seemed to slowly deflate in front of them, his shoulders dropping forward and his lower jaw opening slightly, the weak chin never more obvious.

"I've been posted," Noone said. It was almost a whimper.

"You've been sacked, I believe," Quiet corrected. "Don't try to dignify it with pretensions."

"I don't understand," Noone stammered. "I only did what was best for the Royal Air Force."

"Wrong audience, Noone," Quiet said. "Why don't you save your breath? Your driver is waiting."

For a few moments more Noone's eyes lingered on the phone. Then, without another word and without even the merest look towards the assembled pilots, he walked quickly from the room.

Stead took a deep breath, and pointed at the telephone. "That was really him?"

"The Fat Man has his uses," Quiet said. He turned to Stead. "Treble-Six is yours, Harry."

"Mine?"

"If you want it. I can't guarantee a promotion, and I can't guarantee you'll always be grateful for the job."

"I want it."

"Good. Everything is sorted, then."

Stead shook his head as if to shake off his dumbfounded expression. "Not quite everything," he said. He looked out into the audience. "Flight Lieutenant Clark?"

259

"Yes, sir?" Clark said, pulling his eyes away from the door that had closed behind the Group Captain.

"You're no longer needed here."

Clark stood stock still, his expression slowly morphing from uncomprehending to disbelieving. "You're grounding me?"

Stead shook his head. "Unfortunately," he began with what seemed like genuine regret, "Mr Quiet has already said there'll be no more groundings today, so I reckon we'll skip that part. You're dismissed."

"That means piss off," Stephen Jones said loudly, and then blushed. Crowe and Werner looked at each other for a moment, then burst out laughing.

Clark stared angrily at Harry Stead for several seconds, and then turned sharply, pushed his way past Archie Mills and walked quickly towards the door. Crowe stood up as the big Flight Lieutenant passed in front of him.

Clark stopped and turned towards him. "One day, Crowe…"

"If I ever see you again," Crowe said, simply, "I'll kill you."

"Unless I see you first," Werner added, rising from his own seat.

"No warnings," Crowe said, "no messing around. Just dead."

The fight faded from Clark's eyes. In an instant the bluster and bully was gone, and Crowe saw the fear that he'd seen in the bar the night they had arrived at Charney Breach. With his broken nose and bruised eyes, Clark no longer seemed intimidating, despite his size. He simply looked like a big, clumsy, stupid coward.

"Goodbye, Clark," Stead said firmly, and with that the big man turned, opened the door and was gone.

Stead waited for the door to swing shut again. "Now," he said cheerfully, "anybody else want to go with him? Mills, perhaps? Barnes?"

"No, sir," the two young Flying Officers mumbled together, shrinking in their seats.

"Good. Well, lads, I'm really not sure what to say." Stead looked around the room, clearly flustered. "Obviously it is a privilege to be given this opportunity…oh, dear…"

Steve Slater stood up. "Harry Stead," he said loudly and triumphantly, "Squadron Commander!"

The room erupted into cheering. Led by Geordie Hulse, the pilots and navigators of Treble-Six Squadron stood up almost en-masse and streamed down to surround the blushing and grinning Squadron Leader. Mills and Barnes hung back, looking sickly. Spitfire Leader sat alone at the back, calm, the faintest hint of a smile playing on his red lips.

Crowe joined Quiet at the edge of the scrum surrounding the new boss.

"Do you think it's wise, letting Clark go like that? He knows a lot about what goes on here. He could be dangerous."

"Don't worry," Quiet said. "We have ways of persuading people to keep silent about such matters that are…" and he paused again, seeming to look up and inward as he searched for the right word. Finally he looked at Crowe, gave him a slightly sinister smile, and said "humane."

Stead was merrily beaming as those hands he could not manage to shake reached from the throng to clap him on the back. Crowe joined the press, gripping Stead's hand firmly and receiving a wink in reply.

"Harry," Quiet said as the melee finally subsided, "you probably want a few hours to compose yourself and have a look at your new office."

"That would be appreciated. And thank you."

"Don't be too hasty," Quiet said softly. "Do you mind if I take over for tonight?"

"Not at all."

"Good man." Quiet turned to the audience, and waited for silence. There was definitely something about this man, Crowe thought once again. Within a matter of moments, and without Quiet having to say a word, the room had fallen silent and every single person was looking at him.

"It has been an interesting start to the night, hasn't it?" This got a nervous laugh, which Quiet allowed to dissipate without comment. "I ought to begin by congratulating Harry Stead on his new appointment."

There was more cheering at this. "Enough," Quiet said gently but firmly, and the room was silent again. "You don't need me to tell you there is still a lot of work to be done here. However, the Prime Minister has asked that I pass on his own, personal congratulations on your performance so far."

"The Prime Minister, eh?" Crowe said to Werner, feeling vindicated and inappropriately smug.

"He didn't mean you, of this I am sure," the German replied.

"I know," Quiet continued, "you'll be thinking of the Vulture and his squadron, some of you more than others." He gave Crowe the briefest sideways glance. "For the moment, you must be patient. We'll get to them."

"When?" Werner asked eagerly.

"Soon enough." Quiet reached into his inside pocket and pulled out a piece of paper even more crumpled than his jacket. "Here," he said, walking slowly forward and passing it to Werner, "read this."

"What is it?" Crowe said, leaning over. The words and figures on the page meant nothing to him.

"A German communications intercept," Quiet said. "Don't ask where we got it."

Werner scanned the note, his mouth moving slightly as he read the German text and tried to make sense of the numbers.

"Well?" Crowe said impatiently. "What does it say?"

Werner smiled. "There is a big raid tonight, leaving from Holland at 0100 hours. Twenty Nazi bombers."

"What's the target?"

"It does not say."

"Hull," Quiet said.

The excited chattering that instantly engulfed the room all but drowned out Jones' groan at the thought of yet another raid on his long-suffering home town.

"There will be twenty two bombers, to be precise," Quiet said, "and not a night fighter in sight." Only the slightest hint of his predatory smile was visible beneath the shadow of his hat.

"Have fun."

Chapter Twenty-Two

"Did you see my Heinkel explode?"

"That bastard of a rear gunner almost got me. Didn't do him much good though, did it?"

"He talked us right onto them. We couldn't miss! Brilliant."

"That's three kills for me now!"

"Who's for another beer?"

"Never mind beer, we need champagne!"

Crowe sat on his stool at the bar, sipping his pint of Best, and watched the pilots celebrate. Twenty two bombers had appeared over the Channel, exactly as forecast. They had been flying in loose formation, content that the darkness would provide enough cover for them to operate with impunity. They had been wrong, of course. An ill-timed break in the clouds and a sudden shaft of light from the quarter-moon had sealed their fate. Twenty two bombers, he thought, and not one crew member would ever see home again.

He saw Owen and Sullivan smiling happily as they chatted with Gorecki, occasionally reaching out to shake his hand. The Pole looked slightly embarrassed but his pride was evident in his shy smile. The squadron had worked together perfectly, and the resulting sense of achievement filled the bar. Even Liam Barnes and Archie Mills looked pleased. Thanks to Raithe's unusually selfless directions they had bagged a kill each tonight. Only two men did not seem to be entering into the spirit of the evening. One was Raithe himself, who had made his excuses early in his usual manner. The other was Jones, who was barely conscious on the stool to Crowe's left, slumped against the bar with the remnants of his fourth and final pint down the front of his uniform.

"Well, Crowe," Stead said, grinning as he sat down with two fresh pints in his hands, "did you enjoy that?"

"We were lucky," Crowe told him. "They should have scattered earlier."

"Rubbish," Werner said. "They scatter, and we hunt them down like animals. I feel strange now. I have this warm feeling in my stomach."

"That's pride," Stead beamed. "Pride in what we have achieved as a Squadron. I feel the same. We've come a long way."

The German shook his head. "I think the blood I drink before may not have been so fresh," he said.

Stead laughed and turned to Crowe. "So, another kill eh?"

Crowe grunted. The aircraft had been a Heinkel. Like all of the vampires, even Raithe, Crowe had first directed the non-vampire crews onto the target formation before beginning to hunt for his own kill. The Heinkel had escaped the initial rush, ditched its bomb load and turned for home. It hadn't made it very far, Crowe closing in quickly and firing. The shells had ripped off the bomber's starboard wing, sending it spinning rapidly and forlornly down.

"So you got one kill," Werner scoffed. "Big deal." He held up three fingers and smiled smugly. "*Ja,* it was a good night."

"How many is that for you now?" Stead asked Crowe, doing his best to ignore Werner.

"Nine and a half," Crowe said. The half score made him think of Morgan, who just a few weeks earlier had taken so much pleasure in publicly retelling the story of the Ju-88 which had ploughed into the factory wall. He guessed the thought must have showed on his face when Stead smiled sympathetically.

"My last kill was best," Werner said. "That Nazi bastard almost made it to the sea. He thinks he is safe. He does not know that I let him go there on purpose. Then bang! Five more dead Nazis."

"There's something bloody wrong with you," Stead said.

"There is nothing wrong with me that a million more dead Nazis would not make right."

"The strange thing is," Stead said to Crowe, "you'd have thought that the Germans would have learned not to send up their bombers in such big groups anymore. We've destroyed eighty of them in the last six weeks and they didn't have many to start with."

"Why do they keep doing it?"

"Revenge, I reckon. Bomber Command made two of its thousand bomber raids on Germany last week. Hitler thinks hitting Hull with twenty two bombers will have a comparable impact."

"Twenty-two," Werner said dismissively. "I wish they send a thousand. *Mein Gott,* what a night that would be."

264

"I just wish they would leave Hull alone," Crowe said. "Every time the Germans target Hull, Jones spends the whole flight whimpering like a schoolgirl."

"I don't whimper," Jones said hotly, trying unsuccessfully to rise from his stool before slumping back against the bar.

"I didn't even know he drank," Stead said, amused.

"Normally he doesn't," Crowe said.

"I do not think you can say drinking," Werner said. "Only four pints," he added, shaking his head in disgust.

"You've corrupted him," Stead accused.

"I've improved him," Crowe said.

Werner laughed. "Another few weeks and the boy starts fights in the bar too."

A young Sergeant walked hesitantly towards Crowe and Stead, nodding respectfully towards the new boss. Crowe recognised him, though it took him a few seconds to put a name to the face.

"Hello, sir," the man said, "I'm Bobby Barton."

"Clark's navigator," Crowe said. "Are you missing him yet?"

"Not at all, sir. I just thought I'd come over and thank you both. The man was a total shithouse. A fat, foul-smelling lazy shithouse. With the greatest respect to his rank, of course."

"You weren't an admirer, then?" Stead said dryly.

"Not really, sir. To be honest I wanted to punch him but there's not much you can do when you're a Sergeant and he's an officer."

"Crowe all the time would punch him," Werner said.

"That must have been fun," Barton said wistfully.

"Next time I hit him, I'll dedicate it to you," Crowe promised.

"That would be sweet of you, sir."

Geordie Hulse downed his pint and slammed it loudly on the nearest table. "Squadron Leader Stead, your men would like you to say a few words."

"Speech," several people shouted lustily. Behind them, Crowe saw Lieberwitz slip out of the room, his mouth moving inaudibly as he spoke to someone out of Crowe's sight in the corridor beyond.

"Oh, bloody hell," muttered Stead, "I knew it would come to this." He stood up and drained one of his pints. Holding the other as close as a comfort blanket, he limped into the centre of the room while the assembled aircrew cheered.

"Well, gentlemen," Stead said, leaning only slightly on his stick, "thank you for that reception. It brings a tear to an old man's eye.

And thank you for your efforts tonight. I've been in charge here less than twenty four hours and we've already set a new RAF record for night fighter kills in a single night!"

There was more cheering.

"That beats the previous record of twelve, which we set three weeks ago!"

This time the cheering was mingled with laughter.

"We've come a long way, gents. Six weeks ago I looked at the faces around this room, and I thought you could never work together. Well, I was wrong, and I couldn't be happier. Soon we'll be going up against the Vulture again." There was a sudden chorus of theatrical booing from the crowd. They were all well lubricated, to say the least. Stead waited for the noise to die down and the crowd to fall silent again.

"You all know how hard that will be," Stead said seriously. A thoughtful silence had descended on the room. "It won't be like shooting down German bombers who can't see who's attacking them. There's going to be a fight, a proper nasty bloody fight. Looking around this room, there's a few faces missing, friends and colleagues who won't be there to join in. Each and every one of them is a score we need to settle with the Vulture."

Crowe thought of Morgan. He knew how much his friend would have loved this evening, would have revelled in the atmosphere. This was, after all, what Morgan had always hoped would happen. The entire squadron, vampire and non-vampire, totally united. He would have laughed out loud to have seen Clark humbled and the Group Captain dismissed.

But Morgan was not here, just as Danny Baggers, Michael Rhys-Jones and the nervous, softly-spoken Hinde were not here.

For a moment he was certain that Stead was looking at him, but the Squadron Leader was just scanning his audience, looking at their bowed heads and serious expressions. Stead stood to his full height with a slight grimace of pain, and when he spoke his voice was full of the same conviction that shone in his face.

"We'll settle that score!"

"Kill them all!" Werner shouted, his voice just one among the cheers and war cries that filled the bar with their tumult, causing even half-deaf Barry to wince with the volume.

"Drinks are on me for the rest of the night, lads," Stead said. That got the biggest cheer of all.

Through the crowd Crowe saw Lieberwitz re-entering the bar and walking swiftly around the edges of the assembled aircrew towards him.

"Crowe," he said, "you should go to your room."

"Are you kidding?" Crowe said with a smile. "It's still two hours until dawn. Relax. Let me get you a drink." He turned around to gesture to Barry, but stopped as Lieberwitz rested one hand softly on his shoulder.

"Cassie Noone is waiting in your room."

He didn't run, but it was all he could do to keep to a walk, trying to act naturally and not to draw attention. The accommodation block was silent, with most of the vampires still in the bar enjoying the sense of drunken unity. He guessed that Raithe was in his room. After all, it must have been the Romanian who told Lieberwitz that Cassie was there, but if Raithe remained in the building then he was keeping quiet and out of sight.

The lamp was on when he entered the room. Its shaded light projected Cassie's slight shadow against the far wall, the wall that bore the mark of both his rage and his fist. She turned as he walked in. She was still pretty, but she looked more tired then he'd ever known her. She didn't speak. She simply looked at him, her eyes seeming huge and yet distant. She was wearing a woollen coat over a long skirt and practical shoes, her skin slightly flushed from the effects of the cold air outside.

"Hi," he said, stepping close to her and putting one hand onto her arm, feeling her warmth even through the thick material of the coat. She shied away from his touch, giving him a nervous smile to try and hide the rejection. It didn't work.

"Are you okay?" he said. He could not keep the pain from his voice.

"I'm fine," she said lightly. The words rang pitifully false. She looked him up and down as if seeing him for the first time. The brazen appraisal of their first meeting was gone, replaced by a faintly wary look in her eyes.

"You look good," she said finally.

"I feel good." It was true. Physically he could not remember the last time he had felt so strong, so healthy. The fresh human blood that had coursed into his system had always brought that effect, though it had surprised him this time. He had denied himself too long. He knew the guilt was still to come, of course. It would come with the dreams, when he finally slept.

"You drank the blood, then?"

"I..." he began, and hesitated. Her question was delivered in a neutral voice, and he searched her face, trying to see some sign of what she was thinking. Her eyes flickered once towards the broken glass and the blood stains on the carpet. "Yes, I did."

"Good."

That was unconvincing. He felt the sudden need to explain, knowing it was probably already too late. "I was in pain, Cassie. You saw how I looked."

"Yes," she replied. Her tone told him everything he needed to know. He did not need reminding of how he had looked the last time she had seen him, not sixteen hours ago, with his skin blistered and bubbling, curled in an agonised ball under the bed. She tried to correct herself, adding a light-hearted nonchalant quality to her voice. "It's fine, honestly. I'm glad."

"Really?"

"Why wouldn't I be?"

"I thought you might be disappointed."

"It's really none of my business."

"Why don't you sit down?" He turned to gesture towards the chair by the bedside, but the sight of the shattered wooden shards on the carpet reminded him that the chair had not survived his blood-fuelled rage. He motioned to the bed instead.

"I can't stay."

"It will be dawn in two hours. Surely two hours won't hurt." He reached out and placed his hand gently on her cheek, feeling how soft the skin felt. For a moment she softened, and he saw the warmth in her eyes. He began to lean forward, feeling the desperate need to kiss her.

"No." She pulled away violently, as if his skin still burned against hers. "You don't understand. I can't stay. We're leaving Charney Breach."

"Oh." He couldn't think of anything else to say.

"Daddy's been recalled to Fighter Command. We're leaving as soon as it gets light."

He should have known it was coming. There was no way the deposed Noone would have been allowed to stay at Charney Breach, in his large expensive house, even if he'd wanted to. Even if he'd not wanted to get as far as possible from the squadron he once commanded and the vampires he despised far more than the Germans.

"He doesn't know I'm here," she continued quietly. "I don't know what he'd do if he knew. Seeing me with you broke his heart."

"My heart bleeds for him."

"I just wanted to say goodbye."

He took a deep breath. "Don't go. Stay with me."

"I told you I can't."

"I don't mean for tonight. I mean, stay. Let him go alone." He saw her eyes widen as the realisation of what he was suggesting struck her. He looked for a sign that she would agree, even a glimmer that there was hope. There was none, just surprise and confusion, but he carried on anyway, the memory of the blood fuelling his confidence, alcohol giving him a foolish optimism that he could not bring himself to reject. "Harry Stead could find you somewhere to live. You could keep working in the bar. We could sleep through the day…"

She took a step back from him, and he felt his hope leave with her. Her eyes flashed her anger as she turned away and walked towards the door.

"That's a no, then?" he said softly.

"Crowe," she said, stopping but keeping her back to him, "do you have any idea what's happened? Dad's been sacked. He's been thrown out. He's lost his house, and he'll be lucky if he doesn't lose his career."

"I thought you didn't care about his career."

"I care about him!" She turned now, her face burning with the same anger that throbbed in her voice. "He's the only family I have. The two of us have been alone for the last six years. Since Mum died I've been all he has. Compared to that, you and I are nothing. What are we, a few dates? A one night stand? And you want me to give up my family and my future for that? I'm sorry, but no. No."

"You once asked me to risk my career for you," he told her, without anger.

She looked at him and shook her head sadly.

"This morning meant a lot to me," he said.

"Good. I'm glad. I really am."

"Did it mean anything at all to you?"

She paused for a long moment, and then looked away. "It was fun," she said. "Nothing more."

"You don't mean that."

"Yes," she said. A drop of moisture flickered in the dim light until she brushed one hand against her face. "Yes, I do."

There seemed little else to say. He could think of no response. They simply stood and looked at each other.

"Did you ever really think it could work?" she asked after a long pause. "You and me, I mean?"

"I'd hoped."

"I should have ended it when I saw the burns on your face that night," she said. There was no cruelty in her voice, just a matter-of-factness that hurt more than any harshness or mockery ever could. "It was the first time I really thought about it, how different we are, but I still wanted you. But do you really see us living our lives in the dark? Me watching you fly away every night, wondering if you would come home? What about when the war ended? Somehow I can't see us marrying and raising a family."

He'd tried to never think about it, but though he felt broken and rejected, he felt no surprise. He'd known this time would come. He'd known it the first time he'd looked at her in the bar, even before they spoke. He just never knew it would leave him feeling so hollow.

"No," he whispered. He looked down at the carpet, with its cheap worn fibres and tiny spatters of blood. He didn't want to look at her face.

"I'm sorry," she said, and he knew that she was crying a little now. It was not something he'd ever been able to do. She stood immobile, looking at him with eyes that knew it would be for the last time. Then she turned and walked to the door. He saw a single tear fall in her wake, tumbling slowly down onto the carpet.

"Cassie?" He lifted his head. She was already gone.

According to a hung-over Jones, Quentin Quiet had arrived in the early afternoon and gone immediately into a meeting with Harry Stead. The door to the Squadron Commander's office had stayed closed since then, opening only to allow Quiet to relieve the bar of a generous helping of whisky. Of course, none of the vampires saw him until after dark, when they trooped into the briefing room with the other crews and soberly took their seats, nursing a few sore heads from the night before. All of the vampires, though, had noted the Lysander that Quiet had arrived in. It sat like a squat hunchbacked gull amongst the sleek Mosquitoes and Spitfires at dispersal.

Crowe had never seen a Lysander before, but he had heard enough about them to know that it was a light observation aircraft, primarily designed for artillery spotting. More interestingly he'd heard stories of its usefulness in secretive flights into occupied Europe. Its incredibly short take off and landing distances made it ideal for flying into tiny unprepared runways and clearings in French woodland. Morgan had once claimed that the ugly, vulnerable looking aircraft could get airborne in two hundred yards or less. He'd never flown one himself, though, and Crowe had said he would believe it when he saw it. He felt no urge to fly one. Its only real defence against an enemy fighter would be its slow speed and the desperate hope that the fighter would overshoot.

He forgot about the visiting aircraft once they were seated ready for the briefing. The projector had been set up for the first time since the news was broken to them of the Vulture's existence. That alone was enough to start the rumour mill. He could hear men whispering theories to each other.

On the far side of the room, next to the comfortable armchairs for the senior officers, he could see Quiet and Stead talking. They were keeping their voices low. Beyond them, much to his surprise, he saw Dr Madeley. The doctor looked tired. There were bags under his eyes, visible even from across the room. Crowe made his way over and saw that at close range the portly doctor looked even worse. His eyes were bloodshot and showed little of their usual bonhomie.

"You okay?"

Dr Madeley nodded. "It's been a difficult couple of days, dear boy, but I'm surviving. How about you? You've had an interesting few days, I hear."

"I'm fine," Crowe said, forcing levity into his voice that he did not feel, trying to hide the damage that Cassie had done to him. Dr Madeley seemed to be about to ask something. The doctor, Crowe knew, wanted to hear about his drinking of the blood.

"What about the Bales?" Crowe asked quickly, before Dr Madeley could speak.

"Difficult to say. I'm concerned about Catherine. I don't think she's come to terms with it yet."

"I know what you mean. When I spoke to her it seemed like she thought he was still alive."

Dr Madeley looked at him, his eyes sad. "Catherine's always felt she had some sort of psychic gift. I don't know, maybe she does. She's always been able to look at me and tell me what I'm thinking."

"You too, eh?"

"It's quite disturbing the first time, isn't it? But she's gone one further this time, and that's what worries me. Last night she had a dream, and when she woke up she was convinced Morgan was alive. Absolutely certain of it. I'm afraid she became rather giddy. I ended up with no option but to sedate her." His face screwed up slightly. "I do hope she forgives me in the morning. She's a wonderful woman but she has the most tremendous temper."

Something about the way the doctor spoke and the way a half-smile played around the edges of his small mouth suggested that he was just a little bit in love with Morgan's mother. Crowe didn't blame him. Catherine Bale just inspired that sort of reaction in men.

"Couldn't you have stayed with them?" Crowe said. "Surely you're not needed that urgently here?"

"I was summoned," Dr Madeley said carefully, with a loaded look towards Quentin Quiet. Crowe looked over his shoulder. The last of the aircrew were taking their seats.

"I'd better go," he said. "I'll speak to you later." He turned to leave, but a thought struck him. "What happened in Catherine's dream?"

The doctor shrugged. "Something to do with Morgan being safe underground, waiting for night to fall so he could escape. Then she added that he was in a grave, but it wasn't his. Rather morbid stuff, and it quite upset William, I think. He's a lot more sensitive than he would ever admit. Do you think you might come and see them? I'm sure I could persuade Harry to give you a few days off, and I think it would help."

"I'll try," Crowe promised.

"Tonight is the night, *ja*," Werner said confidently to Crowe as he sat down, smiling at the nervous look on Jones' face. "I know it. I bet I outscore you. What is up with you?" he added, as Crowe merely grunted in reply.

"Just tired," he said. The blood rush of the previous day was now a long, aching depression and exhaustion.

"You feel better when I kill the Vulture," Werner said. "Hey, if you behave, maybe I let you watch."

Harry Stead called for silence, and stepped away to let Quentin Quiet take the stage. The assembled aircrew leaned forward almost as one. Every single man was keen to hear what Quiet had to say, though each was sure that tonight was the night that they would finally take on the Vulture again, and that there would be no surprises in the briefing.

They were half-right.

Standing at the front of the room, his suit more rumpled than ever and his eyes boring out from beneath his hat, Quentin Quiet looked around the room. It seemed an age before he finally spoke. When he did, it changed everything.

"Morgan Bale is alive."

Chapter Twenty-Three

Instant pandemonium.

Crowe was on his feet within a second, looking to Dr Madeley. The doctor was sitting bolt upright, every trace of tiredness gone.

"Alive?" Dr Madeley whispered. The word seemed to arc through the room like an electrical current, flicking from man to man even as they sat and stared dumbly. Quiet nodded.

"This had better not be some sort of joke, Quiet," Crowe growled.

"I don't joke," Quiet said.

"Where is he?" Dr Madeley said.

"How did he get out?" Crowe said. There were a thousand questions running through his mind, and he knew he was not the only one.

"Is he hurt?" Dr Madeley said.

Quiet smiled tolerantly. "Gentlemen, please." He held up his hand for silence, but the gesture went unnoticed or ignored.

"Have the Nazis got him?" Werner's face was alight with excitement.

"We need to get him back," Hulse added vehemently.

"Gentlemen," Quiet said, his voice rising slightly, "that is enough. Sit down, all of you. That includes you, Crowe."

For a moment Crowe stayed standing, his eyes locked on Quiet. The man from K Department returned his look without any expression other than the merest hint of impatience. Around the room the muttering slowly abated. Quiet reached out to switch on the projector. There was a low whirring sound and an image appeared on the large screen. It was oddly familiar. It took a few seconds for Crowe, his mind still racing, to remember the details.

"Recognise this place, Crowe?" Quiet asked.

He nodded. "It's about a mile from where Morgan went down."

"Full marks. It's the village of Eglise-sous-Bois, in north eastern France."

Quiet leaned over the projector, and a second later the image changed. This time Crowe's recognition was instant, and it felt like a blow. Up on the screen was a picture he had feared he would see in his nightmares until the day he died.

"This is the wreckage of Morgan's Mosquito," Quiet said. "As you can see, it is easy to believe that no one could walk away from this crash." That was an understatement. The damage was even worse than Crowe remembered. Small pieces of the aircraft were scattered over hundreds of yards. A photographic interpreter had circled the tiny fragments with a red pen, the annotations showing up on the photo. The broken wing still stood like a gravestone above the shattered fuselage.

"The Germans didn't take any risks," Quiet continued. "The morning after Morgan went down, they sent a patrol to search the wreckage, and found the body of Danny Baggers. The pilot was gone."

"Where?"

"No more interruptions," Quiet said shortly. He brought up the next picture. It showed the village church that Crowe had passed over seconds before Morgan's crash-landing, instantly recognisable with its tall, cross-adorned spire. "A PR Mosquito took this earlier today. It is an impressive church for such a small village, don't you think? Could anyone tell me what this is?" He reached out and pointed towards a small stone building in the midst of the cemetery.

"It's a crypt," Lieberwitz said immediately, his voice barely more than a murmur.

Quiet nodded. "The local landowners used to be very wealthy. They built this large and fine church. Fortunately for Morgan, they also built an equally large and fine crypt for the members of their family. Morgan is alive, and this is where he's hiding. What is it now, Crowe?"

Crowe had raised his hand, and now stared again at Quiet. "How do you know all this?"

"K Department has certain…advantages," Quiet said softly. "Maybe one day I'll tell you about them."

"So," Werner said, "we are going in to get him, *ja*?"

"Yes. There are problems, though. Morgan is very badly hurt."

"I don't understand," Hulse said. "I thought vampires healed quickly."

"They do," Quiet agreed, "superficially. The skin heals incredibly quickly, particularly if the vampire has access to fresh blood. Beneath the skin, though, there's much less difference between a vampire and any other man. Is that right, Byron?"

"What?" Dr Madeley said, tearing his gaze away from the image of the ruined Mosquito with a slightly wild look in his eyes. "Oh," he mumbled. "Yes."

"Morgan was wounded in the fight with the Vulture," Quiet said. "The crash compounded his injuries. The wounds are anything but superficial, and he has only a limited supply of fresh blood. If he isn't rescued soon, he will die."

"Then why do we wait?" Werner said.

"There are other obstacles. The Germans haven't found him yet, but the net is closing. Five miles away is the headquarters of an entire infantry regiment. Twelve hours ago they received a telephone call from Berlin. Now the whole area is crawling with very alert German soldiers."

"It gets better and better," the German muttered.

Hulse's open, honest face still wore a look of slight confusion. "They've deployed all those soldiers for one downed airman two days after he was shot down?"

"We think the Eckartstrasse have become involved," Quiet said simply.

"Verdammt," Werner spat.

"Quite," Quiet said blandly. "It gets worse. The Vulture knows it was a vampire that he shot down. By now he almost certainly knows Morgan survived. It won't take him long to realise that we will try to rescue him, and he will be waiting."

"Good," Crowe said. "What is the plan?"

Stead stepped forward. "This won't be easy," he said. "I'm sure you all saw the Lysander outside, and you'll have guessed by now why it's here. The Lysander will take off first and fly into this field here." He indicated a break in the trees, and a muted collective gasp spread around the room. "The Spitfires will provide fighter coverage," he added.

"That's a very small field," Crowe said, putting into words what they were all thinking. The word 'field' itself was misleading. It was a clearing, nothing more. He studied the image, his mind quickly racing through the variables. The aircraft would have to approach into the wind at a fairly steep angle and time its landing to perfection. A premature descent and the aircraft would clip the overhanging trees at one end. Too late, and it would not have room to come to a halt. The problems wouldn't end there, either. "Are you sure it will even be able to get airborne again?"

"With the right pilot, yes," Stead said confidently. He changed the slide again, this time bringing up one showing a number of large buildings clustered around an apparent parade square. Again a photographic interpreter had been busy, this time circling numerous flak and searchlight positions. "While the Lysander's on its way the Mosquitoes will hit the regimental headquarters here and cause as much carnage as possible. The Germans need to get a proper pasting. We want them too busy counting their dead to react to what's happening at the church."

"It will be a pleasure," Werner said. Crowe gave him a brief glance, half expecting to see the German licking his lips.

"Once that's done," Stead continued, "the Mosquitoes will join up with the Spitfires."

"I'm flying the Lysander," Crowe said.

"Not a chance. You've never flown one, and I need you in your Mosquito."

"Come on, Harry. I want the Vulture but he'll have to wait. You need a vampire in that aircraft if it's going to stand any chance of landing in that wood."

"We've got a vampire," Stead said. "The pilot will be Raithe."

"Raithe?" He twisted to look at the Romanian sitting behind him, and realised that every other pilot and navigator in the room was doing the same.

"Oh," Quiet said lightly, "did I forget to mention that Raithe was the first vampire I ever recruited for K Department? He's flown over fifty missions into occupied France to get out our people when they were compromised. There are dozens of SOE and K Department agents alive today who owe their lives to Raithe."

"I had no idea," Crowe said quietly.

Raithe gave him a faintly amused look. "You never were very bright, Crowe."

"You're still an arrogant bastard," Crowe said, smiling.

"And you're a thug. I will need you."

"I'll be there."

"Steve Slater will fly the spare Spitfire, and in Raithe's absence Spitfire Leader will be Gorecki," Stead said. "You'll provide top cover," he told the one-time poet. "Lieberwitz will help you direct the battle from above. As for Mosquito Leader, we've got two fine vampire pilots to choose from."

"I count one only," Werner said, sticking out his chest.

"Don't be so modest," Crowe retorted.

"Lads," Stead smiled, "I would trust either of you without hesitation. But I'm afraid sometimes an old man just has to pull rank."

The two vampires looked at him in surprise. "You're coming with us?"

"Since Clark left us there seems to be an empty seat. That means one less Mosquito, and we'll need every aircraft we can get." Stead grinned. "Besides, I wouldn't miss it for the world."

"Are you sure your back can take it, Harry?" Dr Madeley said.

"I might be a little bit sore in the morning," Stead admitted. "Raithe, how long do you think you'll need on the ground?"

"Five minutes to find him. Another five to get him back to the aircraft and taxi back to the other end of the clearing so I can take off into the wind."

"Ten minutes, boys," Stead said, looking around the room. There was a serious look on his face now. "That's how long the Lysander will be on the ground. That's when we'll be most vulnerable."

"I think you may have forgotten something, Harry," Quiet said gently.

"I didn't forget," Stead responded. There was a slight edge to his voice.

"What are you talking about?" Crowe said.

Stead paused before he replied, the hesitation long enough for him to give Quiet an accusatory look. "The moment that Lysander approaches the target the alarm will go out, and Jagdstaffel Falke will scramble every aircraft they've got. They're only fifteen minutes flying time away. If and when they arrive, the whole squadron's focus is the Vulture. That includes the aircraft providing cover for Raithe." He took a deep breath. "At that point, Morgan becomes the lowest priority."

"What?" Crowe said, rising to his feet. He could hear angry muttering from both sides of the room.

"You have to be joking," Hulse snapped.

Crowe's eyes flickered from Quiet to Stead, noting the apologetic look on the Squadron Leader's face, and how it contrasted with the emotionless calm on Quiet's. "If you think I'm going to leave Morgan and Raithe at the mercy of a whole bloody German regiment..."

"You will do as you're told, Crowe," Quiet said. "Harry, I'll take it from here. I think it's time they heard the whole truth."

"What is this truth?" Werner said.

Quiet stepped forward again, and looked around the briefing room. He must have been able to sense the hostility amongst the crews, but gave no sign of caring. His eyes were all but invisible beneath the shadow of his hat, the emotion within them impossible to divine. When he spoke, he did so in a low voice that carried to every corner of the silent room.

"The reason the Vulture is our highest priority," he said, "is because he has always been our highest priority. He and he alone is the reason Treble-Six Squadron was formed. Everything you have done so far has been done for the singular purpose of drawing out the Vulture and destroying him."

He paused for a moment, inviting them to dare to comment. No one spoke.

"The attacks on German bombers over England were practice," he continued, "but their real purpose was to get his attention when the bomber casualty rate went through the roof. The bombing raid on the Abwehr listening post was an attempt to draw him into battle. It worked, but we had underestimated his squadron's strength. Still, it cost him a lot of casualties, and it made him wary. That's why he didn't respond to our feint two nights ago. He recognised it for what it was."

"But he still couldn't resist coming up to have a look anyway," Crowe said, thinking of Morgan, of the Vulture's rounds pumping remorselessly into his friend's aircraft. He looked past Quiet at the image of the crypt where Morgan was hiding, perhaps dying even as they planned his rescue. Morgan had been used, just as they had all been used. They had been lied to from the very start.

"So you didn't just find out about him recently, after all," Crowe added bitterly.

"No."

"How long have you known?"

"Two years," Quiet said blandly.

"Two years?" Werner said incredulously. "Why are we not told before?"

"You didn't need to know before. The Eckartstrasse have ways of finding things out, just like we do. What you don't know, you can't spill."

"You think we will talk?"

Quiet smiled thinly. "You might not even need to." Crowe didn't know what that was supposed to mean, but right now it didn't matter. There were more important things to discuss. Geordie Hulse obviously agreed with him.

"How many aircraft does the Vulture have left?" Hulse said.

"They took quite a battering the night of the heavy bomber raid," Harry Stead told him. "We think they're down to about fifteen."

"We think, sir?"

Stead started to answer, but Quiet held up a hand and cut him off. "Geordie, before that raid you asked me a question," he said. "Do you remember?"

"I remember. I asked why you needed the rest of us to fly with the vampires when they could be more effective alone. You didn't give me an answer."

"And now I will. We knew that the Vulture had a whole squadron around him. Seven vampires, no matter how good, would be overwhelmed by sheer numbers, particularly on a moonlit night. That's where you come in."

"We're just here to make up the numbers?" Hulse said, stiffening slightly even as he kept his voice reasonable.

"Not quite. Last night you wiped out an entire formation of German bombers, but only a handful were destroyed by vampires. You couldn't have done your job without vampires. They can't do their job without you."

Hulse looked around the room, his eyes dwelling on the vampires, before shrugging. "Fair enough." He looked at Crowe and winked.

"That brings us to the last bit of bad news," Stead said. There was a muted groan of anticipation. "You may have noticed on your walk over, but it's almost a full moon tonight. It's going to be cold but clear over the target. Good visibility for all."

"Meaning the vampires won't be the only ones who can see in the dark," Hulse said. He turned in his seat, looking at the ordinary pilots around him, and smiled. "I reckon we'll be doing more than our fair share of making up the numbers tonight, lads," he said.

Crowe saw the smiles spread through the room. Most were nervous, the smiles of men who were about to fly out on a mission which would see some of them, perhaps even most of them, die. Crowe felt a sudden surge of emotion, and to his surprise he realised it was admiration. These were men who flew out every night into the unknown darkness knowing that they might never return. All of them had been doing it for longer than the vampires. Some had been flying almost every night for the last two or more years. They had seen their friends die around them. Often they had hidden from the sun themselves, fearful that the bright glare of the sun would damage their night vision and leave them more vulnerable. Most of them would never be aces. At night a successful kill was a rare thing, but the dangers were constant. Even if they evaded the enemy night intruders, there were all the normal risks of flying, magnified a hundredfold at night. There were mid-air collisions, crashes on take off or landing, disorientation leading to aircraft becoming lost before running out of fuel and ploughing into the sea. At night, in the darkness, even friends could become foes. The tail gunners of friendly bombers would not wait to recognise if an approaching fighter was British or German; they would simply fire, knowing that to hesitate might mean that they joined the sad roll of aircrew whose bodies would never be found, entombed in their shattered aircraft beneath the frigid waves of the Channel or burned alive in lonely agony. For a British night fighter, every aircraft in the sky could mean death, and yet they continued to fly night after night, and they did it without vampire reflexes and without vampire eyes that could see in the dark.

He was not like them, Crowe thought, and they were not like him. They would never be alike. But he no longer hated them.

"I want to go with Raithe," Dr Madeley said.

"Sorry?" Stead and Raithe said in unison.

"If Morgan is wounded, he will need medical attention. I can provide that on the ground and in the air."

"Mr Quiet?" Stead said.

"No."

"What do you mean no?" Dr Madeley protested, his hands shaking with emotion. "He could die."

"So could you. You're too valuable to risk."

"Besides," Raithe said, "we will need to be as light as possible to get off the ground in such a short distance."

"So you just expect me to stay here wringing my hands?"

"Yes," Quiet said bluntly, "I do. Go and pack whatever medical supplies you want Raithe to take."

Dr Byron Madeley stood up slowly, his whole heavy frame shaking. He looked imploringly at Crowe, and the vampire saw there were traces of tears in his eyes. Crowe nodded.

"We'll get him back, Doc."

The doctor swallowed, dabbed angrily at his damp cheeks, and walked quickly towards the door.

"Byron?" Quiet said, stopping him. "Make sure you pack lots of blood."

"Alright, gents," Stead said when Dr Madeley had gone. "Take off will be at midnight, and there's still a lot of planning to do. This may be the last time we're all together in one room. I don't need to tell you how dangerous this is going to be."

Crowe looked at the Squadron Leader, ignoring Quiet as the man from K Department took the opportunity to slip wordlessly out of the room. Stead seemed somehow younger than when they had first met. His eyes glowed with boyish enthusiasm and a deep affection for the men who sat before him.

"We've been through a lot together, and there have been differences between us, but I look around this room now and I see just one Squadron." His voice shook with pride. "We've got one of our lads missing, but we're going to get him back."

"Damn right," one of the regular pilots muttered from the front row.

"The Vulture will be waiting for us," Stead continued. "He won't be alone. He's going to have the best pilots the Germans can put in the sky alongside him. One way or the other this fight is going to end tonight." The nervousness and fear in the room was almost palpable, but so was the conviction. When Crowe looked at the faces of the men around him, both vampire and otherwise, he knew that none of them would admit to fear and none would let it control them.

"Lads," Stead said with a catch in his voice, "it's been a pleasure working with you, and it will be the greatest privilege of my life to fly with you tonight."

"Sir," Werner said, pretending to wipe away a tear, "please stop. You will make me cry."

The laughter that rang around the room was as much from the relief of tension as from the German's words, but it was genuine and heartfelt.

282

"Alright then," Stead said, laughing as his face went red, "bugger the lot of you. Grab your kit and sod off. I'll see you up there."

They gathered by Raithe's Lysander as the air began to fill with the sound of Merlin engines.

"I will bring him home," Raithe told Crowe. "He is your friend, but he is something even more important to me."

"What?"

"The future," Raithe replied simply.

It had occurred to Crowe that they were taking a huge risk trying to rescue Morgan when they knew the Vulture's squadron would intervene. He was surprised Quiet would take that risk. He was even more surprised when he found out why the man in the hat was willing to risk the mission to save one man. Raithe had given him no choice, just a simple ultimatum. Help us save Morgan, Raithe had told Quiet, or fight the rest of the war without us.

"Be careful," Crowe told him now as Raithe walked away towards the gull-winged Lysander.

"You don't get to my age by not being careful."

"Just how old are you, Raithe? Catherine Bale doesn't know." The Romanian didn't respond, and just carried on walking as if he hadn't heard. "Even Dr Madeley doesn't know," Crowe called after him.

That made Raithe stop, the thin fingers of one pale hand gleaming white in the moonlight as they curled around the handle of the aircraft door. He turned slowly to face Crowe, removing his sunglasses to reveal eyes that shined within the dark shadows of his face.

"Dr Madeley knows nothing about vampires," he said.

With a thin smile Raithe opened the door and climbed into his aircraft. Crowe watched him for a few seconds more. Then he walked over to join the others.

The vampires didn't bother with any long goodbyes or emotional speeches. It wasn't their way. They simply briefly wished each other luck, and shook hands.

And that was it.

"Well, it is time to go and get Morgan," Werner said to Crowe as they joined their navigators at the line of parked Mosquitoes. "He will be so sorry to miss this fighting tonight."

Behind them there was a whine as Raithe got airborne, the noise of the Lysander's engine drowned out almost instantly as Gorecki's

Spitfire began to taxi out onto the runway. Werner took a slug of blood and offered his flask to Crowe.

Crowe shook his head. "I have my own." He patted his flying suit, feeling the cold metal of his flask. The liquid inside shifted, and he imagined he could feel its warmth already. Dr Madeley had shown no reaction when Crowe had followed him to his office and asked for the flask. He had simply reached into his desk and passed it wordlessly across. Crowe had wanted to say something but couldn't think of anything. He had just placed the flask in his pocket and walked away.

Werner nodded gravely, his eyes invisible behind his sunglasses. Then he smiled. He clapped Crowe on the shoulder, before turning to ruffle the hair of a stunned Jones. "Have fun, my friends," he said.

"Be careful," Crowe said.

"Save your careful for the Nazis," Werner said. "I do not need it." He walked away towards his Mosquito, Ronnie Hall giving them a nervous wave before hurriedly following in the German's wake.

"You okay?" Crowe said to Jones.

The young man gave him a shy smile. "I was just wondering how many of them we'll ever see again."

Crowe walked towards his own aircraft. Dom was waiting with his clipboard.

"How's it looking, Dom?"

Dom passed him the clipboard and a pen. "You've got full ammunition and four two hundred and fifty pounders. Fuel's a little less than full because of the bomb load but you'll have plenty to get where you're going unless you're heading for Berlin." He paused. "You're not going to Berlin, are you?" he said in a tone of some concern.

"Not tonight, Dom," Crowe assured him. "Did you fix those bomb doors?"

"They seemed to be working fine when we were loading. We got the engines sorted too. But if I'm honest I'd feel a lot better if you could have done another air test."

"No time now," Crowe said, signing the paperwork and passing it to the engineer. "Let's get her started."

"Before you go," Dom began.

"Yes?"

"The boys just wanted to wish both of you good luck for tonight. Flight Lieutenant Bale always seemed a sound chap, and the lads who worked on his aircraft spoke very highly of him. They'd love to see him back with us again."

"Thanks. He'd appreciate that." He turned to the ladder that led up into the snug cockpit.

"There's one more thing, Crowe," Dom said. "I know you're not like the other pilots we've had. I mean, every pilot is different but you're, well, different."

Crowe raised one eyebrow behind his sunglasses.

"But," Dom continued, "you're our pilot. Every time you get a kill, we think of it as our kill. Every time you have a successful mission, we have a few drinks to celebrate. Some of the lads on our team here wanted to be pilots themselves, but they never made it. I think that when you fly, there's a little bit of them goes with you."

"Thanks," Crowe said, meaning it. He smiled at Jones, who was looking at him with fond amusement. "What about you?" he said to Dom.

"Me?"

"Did you want to be a pilot?"

"Bloody hell, no. I can't stand pilots. Bunch of overpaid nancy boys if you ask me. And navigators are no better." He smiled. "Good luck, sir. Give them hell from us."

"We will," Crowe promised. "And we'll see you in a few hours."

He turned and climbed up the ladder into the cockpit, awkwardly positioning himself in the pilot's seat and taking off his sunglasses as Jones followed him in. Dom waited until Jones was settled in and then closed and latched the door, leaving them alone in the cold silence of the cockpit.

To their left there was a roar of noise as Harry Stead's engines burst into life. The Squadron Leader looked over in their direction, and gave them a cheery wave. That was a bad sign. The sky above was clear, the moon was nearly full, and there was enough light for even normal eyes to make out details that would normally be lost to them in the gloom. He returned Stead's wave, but did not smile. He turned to Jones, who looked at him nervously.

"Are you ready?"

Jones nodded. "Let's do it," he said, as Crowe signalled to Dom, reached out and pressed the button to start the port engine.

"Contact," he said, and reached into his pocket for the silver flask.

Chapter Twenty-Four

At one hundred feet and four miles out, Squadron Leader Harry Stead broke radio silence for the first time since they had taken off. It was time.

"Spitfire Leader from Mosquito Leader. Take up your patrol area. Good luck."

"Acknowledged. This is Spitfire Leader. All Spitfires follow me please. Watch for fighters." Gorecki's aircraft pulled sharply up and away, towards the spire of the distant church that was visibly glinting in the strong moonlight. One by one the Spitfires peeled away after him, their slim frames both beautiful and deadly as they climbed powerfully, leaving the five Mosquitoes alone in a staggered arrowhead formation. Stead led the way, his Mosquito flying unerringly true. They had passed over the Lysander a few minutes earlier, slowly making its way towards the clearing.

"Climbing to attack altitude," Stead said. They climbed up to three thousand feet, the ground ahead opening up a little more with every foot of altitude gained. Somewhere out there Crowe knew German radar operators would be picking them up for the first time. He could imagine their confusion, knowing that the main bomber stream for the night had already passed far north of this area. The low lying fields and hedgerows spread out before them, coming abruptly to an end as the barracks complex came into view.

"Looks like we've caught them asleep," Crowe said with relish. He could feel the fresh blood coursing through him. The aircraft felt alive around him, part of him. His eyes seemed to see everything. Ahead of them the barracks seemed almost deserted, with only a single small vehicle moving slowly alongside one of the barrack blocks to disturb the stillness.

"Let's wake them up," Stead said. "Crowe, stay up here and provide cover. If you see anything we miss, kill it."

"Got it." He stifled a surge of disappointment. He wanted to join in the attack, felt the bloodlust and the familiar urge to kill and destroy raging within him, but he knew there would be time soon enough. For now he could control it.

"Five second intervals, I'll take the lead. Watch out for the bombs from the aircraft in front." Stead opened his throttle. With a hint of exhaust flare Mosquito Leader pulled away from the trailing aircraft. "Bomb doors open," Crowe heard him mutter. The noise of the Merlin engines must have reached the barracks, he thought. They had closed to within two miles and now Crowe could see that there were small figures darting between the buildings. The vehicle he'd seen was a staff car of some description, and it had parked outside a two storey building with a thin moonlit flagpole outside that glimmered like a beacon to Crowe's blood-fuelled eyesight.

"Now we kill everything," Werner shouted. Stead's Mosquito held its course for a second more, and then slid left and into a dive. Crowe pulled up, away from the aircraft positioning themselves in line, ready to take their turn. He let his port wing drop slightly to give himself a better view of the Mosquito diving towards the very centre of the barracks complex.

"I've missed this," Stead cried in exultation. Half a second later, Crowe saw the aircraft shudder as the bombs fell away and Stead yanked back hard on his controls. The Mosquito was as agile as ever and in the hands of a true expert. It was already climbing away when the four bombs smashed into the Headquarters. The target disappeared in a cloud of smoke, the shock wave briefly visible as it gutted the building and sent the staff car spinning away across the parade square. It was a wonderful piece of bombing, and he watched admiringly as Stead climbed away.

"Next man," the Squadron Leader said casually, as if he was doing nothing more taxing than a spot of practice on the range. Geordie Hulse was next, taking a slightly shallower dive towards the barrack blocks. For a few seconds it seemed he too would have an easy, unmolested approach, but then it was as if every flak and machine gun crew on the entire site had reached their weapons at the same time. The complex glowed with muzzle flashes and tracers that streamed up into the night sky, towards the single Mosquito that was silhouetted against the moon.

Hulse's aircraft didn't deviate even an inch. Levelling out at a thousand feet, he gave a terse call of "Bombs gone" and released the four two hundred and fifty pound high explosive bombs at short intervals. The first one struck just short of the largest of the barrack blocks, but the rest slammed home as he flew directly along the line of the narrow building, pulling up only as the last bomb hit home. Three heavy machine guns opened up and slowly inched their way towards Hulse's aircraft, grasping at it like claws, but then the Mosquito was clear and climbing up to join Stead.

"First rate, Geordie," the Squadron Commander congratulated him.

"I go in now," Werner said. "You watch and learn, Crowe."

"You watch out for that flak," Crowe responded. The night seemed to get a little brighter as a finger of intense light burst free from one of the flak positions and began to slowly sweep the sky. The searchlight could only mean one thing. The flak crews were ready to bring their heavier artillery into the battle.

Werner took his aircraft in at a very shallow angle and with a much slower approach speed than the others. For a moment Crowe thought the German had made a mistake, but then the Mosquito's nose lit up as Werner fired short bursts from his guns, adjusting slightly between each burst. The first landed harmlessly at the edges of the parade ground, kicking up great gouts of soil and gravel, but that was just Werner checking his aim. The second slightly longer burst annihilated the crew of a quad-barrelled heavy machine gun position. The third struck amongst a group of men who were running across the parade ground carrying ammunition boxes between them. Crowe saw them drop for cover, but it was too late for at least one. His lifeless body was flung limply several yards. Werner fired again, this time into one of the buildings, but he was saving his bombs for the vehicle park. There must have been a hundred vehicles or more, a mixture of trucks, half-tracks and light armour. Werner flew over them at low level, accelerating as he released his bombs and climbed away. Shrapnel and flames tore through the vehicle park. The last bomb must have hit a fuel bowser, and a huge ball of flame seemed to follow Werner into the sky.

"They are awake now, *ja?*" the German yelled.

"Werner, get out of there," Crowe warned urgently, as the searchlight swung ominously towards the massive fire left in the Mosquito's wake. They could not fail to see Werner's aircraft, illuminated by thousands of gallons of burning fuel, and the searchlight was on him in a second. Crowe heard him cry out in pain as the intense agonising brightness of the searchlight beam burned into his eyes.

"Werner," Crowe said, "close your eye and keep climbing. I'll take care of it." Without hesitation, he put his own aircraft into a dive, ignoring the tracers that were flickering across the sky. There were flames everywhere, and his eyes stung with the pain of their glare, but he focused on the base of the searchlight beam. No tracer seemed to be coming his way and he realised every weapon on the site was aimed at the beleaguered Werner.

"This is hurting," Werner remarked, trying to sound calm even as the words hissed from between clenched teeth. "Do it quickly, Crowe."

"Hurry," Jones urged. "They're going to hit him."

"No they're not." Crowe flew over the top of the ruined barrack block, individual tiles visible fifty feet below him. The Mosquito passed through a thick cloud of smoke, and for a moment they were blind. He felt no concern. Time seemed to be passing more slowly, as the blood in his system quickened his reflexes and raised every sense to a keen pitch. It never even occurred to him to use his bombs. The smoke cleared, and he took a deep breath before he squeezed the trigger. The Mosquito shuddered as four 20mm cannon and four .303inch machine guns fired in a gruesome symphony.

He didn't fire for long. He didn't need to. In half a second his rounds smashed through the searchlight and killed or wounded every one of the gun team. Darkness returned.

"*Danke*," Werner said.

"Werner, are you hit?" Stead asked.

"Only a little," the German said nonchalantly. Crowe climbed up to join him and realised he could see the moonlight through several holes in the Mosquito's wing.

"That looks bad," Crowe said.

"It's not," Werner said. "But my eye hurts. I am lucky. If I had two it would hurt two times more." He laughed at his own joke.

"You'll be better in a minute," Crowe said confidently. He looked to the south. Five miles away he could see the tiny circling Spitfires at seven thousand feet or so, waiting for their turn.

"You should turn for home," Stead told Werner.

Werner said something in German. The words meant nothing to Crowe, but the emotion was plain.

Beneath them there was a massive explosion, and all four of the circling Mosquitoes shook slightly from the blast. "Bloody hell," Stead said, "that was a good effort."

"Thank you, sir," said a voice that Crowe vaguely recognised as Kev Masters. He was one of Werner's flight and they had never really spoken. Clearly, though, Masters knew his business. "I think I hit the ammo dump," he said as his Mosquito joined them.

"I'll say you did," Stead said happily. Beneath them the barracks complex had been reduced to a shambles. Only a couple of light machine guns still fired, their staccato bursts reaching forlornly up towards targets that were already out of range. The vehicle park was a mass of still spreading flames. The main barrack block had been almost totally destroyed, with only a handful of tiny figures emerging and stumbling into the brightly lit parade ground.

"I don't think any of those buggers will be bothering us tonight," the Squadron Commander added. "Let's go and get Morgan."

Gorecki's soft voice reported no sign of any opposition when the Mosquitoes joined up once again with the Spitfires. They had briefly seen a German patrol a mile to the east of the church but they had retreated into woodland and the Spitfires had not sought to engage.

"That patrol may already have reported us. Any sign of Raithe?" Stead asked.

"He's coming now," Gorecki said.

Crowe looked to the west. It took him a few seconds to pick out the slow, camouflaged Lysander against the backdrop of the ground, five thousand feet below them. As Crowe watched it slowed even further, flaps shifting into place for landing. The Romanian must have miscalculated, he decided, because he hadn't yet reached the landing field. Crowe looked around, concerned now. He could not even see the landing field. This was definitely the right church, but there was no sign of anywhere an aircraft could land until it reached the fields where the wreckage of Morgan's aircraft could still be seen. The Lysander, though, was still descending, and Crowe realised it was about to plough into the trees next to a tiny clearing.

He swallowed hard. Next to him, he heard Jones gasp. The tiny clearing was the landing field.

With infinite precision, Raithe brought the Lysander down over the last of the trees and onto the ground. Seconds later, impossibly, he was bringing the Lysander to a halt.

"That," Crowe said honestly, "is the most amazing piece of flying I have ever seen."

"Ja."

"Is he down?" Stead said.

"He's down."

"Then we've got ten minutes," Stead said. "Keep your eyes peeled. Crowe, watch the ground. Tell me the minute you see anything." Crowe looked over at Jones. The young navigator was scanning the skies, his face alive with excitement. There was no trace of fear on his face.

Ten minutes passed, though it seemed like much longer. The Lysander sat in the clearing. The Squadron kept circling, five Mosquitoes at five thousand feet and seven Spitfires at eight thousand feet, the crews anxiously looking out towards the east and the distant base of Jagdstaffel Falke. Crowe felt a slight twinge of nervousness. He'd never truly realised how few they were now, with Morgan and Hinde and Rhys-Jones all gone, and with Raithe somewhere in the cemetery below them. Fifteen aircraft had been the estimate of enemy strength. He hoped they had not been wrong. He could feel the effects of the blood beginning to wear off, and reached into his pocket again. The bottle top was tight and his hands shook slightly as he unscrewed it, but then he put the flask to his lips and felt the warm blood slip into his mouth. He wanted to drink it all, but he knew now what he had done wrong before, what most of the vampires had always known. He took a few sips and put the bottle away.

"Too much blood will hurt you," he whispered, "but not enough will kill you."

"Did you say something?" Jones said, seeming to notice the bottle for the first time. An expression flickered over his face, but to Crowe's surprise it was not one of disgust. The young navigator seemed to give him a nod, though Crowe could not have been sure.

"I said I wonder what is taking Raithe so long," he lied. He looked at his watch. Fifteen minutes had now gone since the Lysander had come to a halt, and other than the briefest glimpse of the vampire as he entered the cemetery no one had seen anything of Raithe since then. He looked down at the church again. It seemed still.

There was a flash of movement.

"Shit," Crowe spat.

"What is it?" Stead said, alarmed.

"I think that German patrol is back."

"I see nothing," Werner said.

"They're approaching the cemetery."

"Have they seen Raithe or Morgan?"

"I don't know," Crowe said. "But they're deploying into line."

"Keep watching them, son," Stead said. "Hopefully our boys will get out before they reach them."

"I'm not taking that chance," Crowe said. He looked again to the east, where the skies remained empty. "I'm going in. Werner, take over my role."

"Stay where you are," Stead said sharply. Both vampires ignored him.

"I have it," Werner said. "Go, now."

"Damn it, Crowe," he heard Stead mutter as he pushed his Mosquito into a sharp dive. The German patrol must have been platoon-sized, he decided as he accelerated through two thousand feet. He could see about fifteen of the tiny figures, but more were emerging from the trees. They were within two hundred yards of the crypt and still there was no sign of Raithe. At five hundred feet Crowe pulled out of the dive, feeling the aircraft still sluggish with the weight of the bombs inside. He levelled off at three hundred feet, rushing towards the patrol less than a mile ahead of him now.

"Opening bomb doors," he said, and pulled the lever with his right hand. Nothing happened. He cursed and tried again, but from the serene unruffled progress of his aircraft he could tell that the doors hadn't shifted an inch.

"They're still stuck," he shouted at Jones as they swept over the German patrol. The infantry had gone to ground at the approach of the aircraft and one or two now fired ineffectually at him, their rounds passing harmlessly by in their wake. They swept over the edge of the woodland, Jones twisting in his seat to look behind them as Crowe swung the aircraft into a turn. The field below them was bathed in moonlight, the small dark figures unmistakeable as they resumed their advance.

"They're on the move," Jones warned.

"I'm coming around for a pass with guns," Crowe warned. "We're going in low."

"That doesn't sound like a good idea."

"Just say your prayers and clench everything."

At more than two hundred knots and less than one hundred feet, the Mosquito barrelled back over the trees, the ground a frantic blur

292

beneath them. The soldiers were out in the open, their attention on the cemetery ahead of them. Crowe was vaguely aware that his eyes were more focused and effective than he had ever known them. Even as he lined up his sights on the soldier at the nearest end of the German line, he saw the man turn and look up at them in fear. The soldier raised a hand, turning to his comrades to shout a warning.

Crowe fired.

The ground around the soldiers seemed to disintegrate. Great lumps of sod were tossed up into the air as the rounds tore into mud, grass and soft, vulnerable bodies. The image before him seemed almost frozen in time. Crowe kept the trigger depressed. He watched dispassionately as the heavy cannon shells and smaller machine gun rounds sliced with equal disinterest through bone and flesh. He saw a severed leg spin away into the night, and another man appeared to explode as a shell slammed directly into his chest. He watched men drop to the ground as if in slow motion. A soldier carrying a heavy weapon tried to run back to the cover of the trees. Crowe saw the impacting rounds lazily follow him, inexorably hunting him down, until one struck and the man stopped in his tracks, standing as if at attention before collapsing, decapitated in an instant. He heard Jones give a guttural howl of exultation as the German patrol was annihilated in a maelstrom of scything metal and brutalised flesh.

Still in slow time, Crowe looked to his right. He could see the cold stone of the crypt less than one hundred yards away. Two figures were making their way slowly from it, one seeming to half support, half drag the other.

"I see them!"

"Are they okay?" Stead asked.

"Crowe," Jones shouted urgently. Crowe looked back to his front and in an instant time returned to normal. The spire of the church was rushing towards them, the ground less than twenty feet below them now. Crowe pulled back hard on the stick, the aircraft feeling sluggish and unresponsive from the weight of the bombs still within it. The controls shook in his hands, and he grunted in exertion as with an explosive wrench of his back and shoulder muscles he pulled the aircraft up and into a steep banking climb. He heard Jones give a squeal of terror. It was surely going to be too late. The Mosquito's props clawed at the air, trying to gain height and separation. The spire was still onrushing. Crowe closed his eyes.

He sensed rather than saw the heavy wrought iron cross on top of the spire miss his port wing by inches, and opened his eyes again with a sharp exhalation of breath. The moonlit sky was ahead of them, and they were clear.

"Are you okay?" Crowe said.

"Fine," Jones snapped. "How are you?"

"You are trying to give us a bad name, Crowe?" Werner said.

"What do you mean?"

"You almost become the first vampire ever who is really killed by a cross."

Crowe climbed steadily away, banking as he did so and noting with satisfaction that the few survivors of his attack were enthusiastically retreating to the trees. He scanned the churchyard, looking for another glimpse of Raithe and Morgan. They had disappeared beneath the thick canopy of the woodland.

"Hello Mosquito Leader, this is Spitfire Leader, enemy sighted."

Crowe looked up past the circling Spitfires and Mosquitoes, towards the eastern horizon, and felt a sudden flicker of alarm.

"Where are they?" Stead demanded.

"Six miles east, closing fast," Gorecki said, "Angels Ten."

"How many?"

"I count thirteen."

"Unlucky for them," Werner said.

"No sign of Vulture yet," Gorecki added, almost apologetically.

"All aircraft to ten thousand feet, throttles open," Stead ordered. "Prepare to engage."

Crowe hesitated, torn between his urgent desire to engage the Vulture and his squadron, and the need to provide cover and support for Morgan and Raithe. He thought of the two figures he had seen in the cemetery, the way that they moved, one clearly badly hurt.

"Twenty bandits now," Gorecki said.

"Unlucky for us?" Werner said ruefully.

"Permission to stay and provide cover for Raithe?" Crowe asked.

"Negative."

"Come on Harry, they'll be sitting ducks down here."

"Do you think I don't know that?" Stead snapped. "But we need every aircraft up here now or none of us will get home."

"Twenty five," Gorecki said.

"Jesus," someone muttered on the radio.

"Crowe, get up here," Stead said, and with a curse Crowe pulled the Mosquito into a sluggish climb, the aircraft feeling every ounce of the thousand pounds of bombs in its belly. He could see the enemy fighters now, high above him as he passed five thousand feet. Their numbers dwarfed those of the Spitfires and Mosquitoes preparing to engage them. He silently screamed at his aircraft to climb faster.

"This will be wonderful," Werner said. His voice throbbed with genuine pleasure. "Remember our bet, Crowe. I will get more than you."

"Loser buys the drinks in the bar tonight," Crowe said, wondering if any of them would even be alive to have a drink.

"Positively identify your targets and make your rounds count," Stead said. "Don't fly straight and level for more than a few seconds and keep a watch on your tails. Good luck."

Less than a minute later, at a combined approach speed of 700 miles per hour, the German and British formations collided with shocking violence. In the chaos of over forty aircraft clashing, it was every aircraft for itself. There was no possibility of the vampires directing the battle, and no need either. The bright moon reduced vampire and non-vampire alike to the same level of terror and sheer survival instinct.

The fight was on.

Chapter Twenty-Five

A Focke-Wulf dived away from the fray with both wings burning intensely. Werner gave a shout of triumph, and his muttered Favri curse filled their ears.

"Jesus, there's a lot of them," Jones said.

"There'll be less soon," Crowe told him. They were barely two thousand feet below the fray now and still climbing, the radio net alive with the cries and warnings of British pilots. There was a flare above and another Focke-Wulf broke apart and began to tumble to earth. A scream filled his ears, the voice unrecognisable, reduced to a wail of agony which was abruptly cut short. A burning Spitfire plummeted past them. Crowe recognised the aircraft as that of Archie Mills before the flames spread further and reduced it to an incandescent ball of ravaged metal.

The fight was being conducted at lightning speed by some of the finest pilots either country could muster. Casualties were mounting quickly. Crowe saw Gorecki's Spitfire evade a Focke-Wulf's fire and quickly turn inside another before despatching it with a short burst of machine gun fire. All was confusion, aircraft darting about the sky at full pace, weaving and diving as the dogfight spread out to cover several thousand feet of altitude.

Two Focke-Wulfs broke away from the main dogfight and dived towards Crowe. Smiling, the vampire lined up the first in his sights and fired. The tracers hurtled up into the sky and tore through the night air inches from the German fighter's canopy. The Focke-Wulf sheared away in panic, and Crowe quickly pulled his own aircraft around onto its tail. The German pilot tried to climb, seeking the company of its comrades, but Crowe was too fast. He pulled up the nose of the Mosquito, judged the lead on the target perfectly, and fired a short burst. The heavy shells ripped through the aircraft's rear fuselage, and the tail broke away. For a few seconds the fighter flew on as if oblivious to the damage. Then it twisted onto its back and began to corkscrew wildly towards the ground, leaving a thin trail of smoke in the air above it.

"The other one's behind us," Jones said as a stream of tracers passed their port wingtip.

"Where?" Crowe twisted in his seat just in time to see the pursuing Focke-Wulf explode.

"Never mind," Jones said.

"That is one more for me," Werner exulted. "This is too easy."

"Have you seen the Vulture?" Crowe asked urgently.

"No."

"The bastard is here somewhere."

"What the hell is keeping Raithe?" Stead muttered irritably.

Crowe looked up again as a Spitfire, possibly Steve Slater's, passed by in a desperate dive. Crowe fired a long burst which killed the pilot of the Focke-Wulf that was following the young Brit. The aircraft never changed course, but simply continued its dive towards the waiting fields below.

"Thanks," Slater said. "I owe you one." Three seconds later he was dead, his aircraft destroyed in a burst of German cannon fire from another fighter which approached from his blind side. The sky around Crowe seemed alive with aircraft, but the numerous columns of smoke already rising from the French countryside below showed the rate of attrition more clearly than any count could ever hope to. He turned sharply towards a knot of three Focke-Wulfs half a mile beyond his starboard wing.

"The Vulture is here," he heard Lieberwitz say calmly. He looked up, scanning the sky above for any sign of the Nazis' vampire. He saw only the sudden, sickening flash as Lieberwitz's Mosquito burst into flames and began its slow final dive, starting to spin as one wing tore loose and fell away, burning. Through the cloud of smoke that marked Lieberwitz's passing, a thin predatory shape passed at high speed and began to climb away from the melee.

"Another you'll pay for," Crowe thought aloud. His bloodlust writhed within him, almost painful, shunting to one side any feelings of loss or regret over the death of the quiet vampire with the sad eyes. There simply wasn't time. He tried to climb to engage the Vulture but the Arado was too far away and retreating rapidly, and instead he turned his attention back to the three Focke-Wulfs. They scattered as they saw him approaching. One was a little slow to react and Crowe bore down on him. The German jinked desperately as the Mosquito closed on his tail. Crowe felt the burning of the blood in his system, knew that he would not miss, and fired a long burst, keeping the trigger depressed until the Focke-Wulf burst into flames. It flew on regardless for half a second more, and then disappeared in a brilliant explosion, sending smoking fragments outwards and downwards in an obscene glowing shower.

"Break right," Jones shouted, and as Crowe obeyed the smoking wreckage of a Focke-Wulf screamed past them. He caught a glimpse of the pilot, shaking lifelessly in the wind amongst the shattered remnants of his cockpit, his corpse straining even in death to be free of the straps that still held him.

"That is three for me," Werner said. "How many do you have, Crowe?"

"I got one," Kev Masters said.

"Owen, you have one to your port side."

"Thanks, Gorecki."

"How many more of these bastards are there?" someone called anxiously. The chatter of pilots was a near-constant noise as each man strove desperately not just to survive but to ensure that their friends survived with them.

The sky seemed to clear. Crowe looked rapidly around as he turned the Mosquito back towards the heart of the fray. Every sinew of his body strained with the urge to find more targets and kill them. He felt absolutely alive. The surge of blood filled his ears with its song of death and annihilation. Quickly and methodically he counted the aircraft he could see. Perhaps a dozen Germans were already dead, he estimated, but at least three British aircraft were gone with them. High above them he caught a glimpse of the Vulture, some distance away on the far side of the mass of swooping, writhing fighters.

"Yes," Stead shouted as he fired another long burst into a Focke-Wulf, and Crowe watched as it broke apart. "My God, I love this!"

"Harry," Crowe warned, seeing another fighter drifting onto the Squadron Commander's tail, "watch out behind you." Stead broke hard right to try and lose his pursuer, but magnificent though the Mosquito was, in a close fight it could not match the incredible manoeuvrability of the Focke-Wulf, a pure dogfighter. Crowe could tell from the economy of the German aircraft's positioning that the pilot was an expert. All the pilots of Jagdstaffel Falke were. The Vulture's squadron had been chosen carefully, and on this bright moonlit night and at this range, every pilot was a vampire. The

German fired. Crowe saw Stead's aircraft twitch and sparks and debris fall away from the fuselage and port engine.

"This is getting a bit bloody uncomfortable," Stead said calmly. Crowe was too far away to intervene, and vented his frustration by firing at a Focke-Wulf that was diving past, clipping its wing but not destroying it. There were thin streams of smoke coming from Stead's wing, and his efforts to evade the fighter were becoming more desperate. Still the German closed remorselessly in.

"I've got your back, sir," Hulse called. His Mosquito dropped down out of nowhere and the pilot of the Focke-Wulf on Stead's tail, expert or not, was too busy preparing to administer the coup de grace to notice the deadly form of the British fighter. He died before he could claim his victory. Without a word, Hulse rolled away and continued to hunt for more targets.

"Are you okay, Harry?" Crowe called. The Squadron Leader was a mile ahead of him, with smoke now pouring from his shattered port engine.

"We're in a pretty bad way, son," Stead admitted. "We might have to sit this one out for a bit."

"Geordie," Crowe said, "stick with him."

"Don't bother," Stead countermanded instantly. "You're in command now, Geordie. Stay in the fight. We'll be fine."

Crowe turned briefly away as the stricken Mosquito lurched away towards the distant coast, a trail of inky black smoke hanging in the air behind it. The dogfight was thinning out a little, spreading out as more and more aircraft were shot down and as the battle descended into desperate one-on-one contests. He scanned the sky for the Arado, his desire to find and kill the vampire so bitter he could taste it like tar in his mouth, but it was only when his eyes were drawn back to Stead's retreating aircraft that he saw it.

Crowe didn't even have time to utter a warning. The Vulture was on Stead in an instant. The Mosquito was raked nose to tail and plummeted downwards in flames, and Harry Stead and Bobby Barton died without a sound.

The Vulture climbed quickly away.

"Harry's gone."

"I saw," Hulse said shortly. "Werner, are you still at high level?"

"Yes."

"How's it looking?"

"We have eight," Werner said. "They have the Vulture and sixteen maybe. *Eine Minute, bitte*." There was a long pause, and high above them Crowe saw a flash. "The Vulture and fifteen," Werner corrected gleefully. "You cannot catch me now, Crowe."

Crowe barely heard him. He felt a cold rage burning through his entire body as he watched the column of smoke rising above the wreckage of Stead's aircraft. There was no chance of reaching the Vulture. The Arado was already a dwindling speck as it climbed away to high level. With a curse Crowe was again forced to choose another target, diving towards two Focke-Wulfs which were close on the tail of a Spitfire. He watched the British fighter trying to desperately avoid the fire from its two pursuers, but the German pilots were too good and Crowe still too far away. With a last desperate cry for help, Liam Barnes died in the fiery sarcophagus of his cockpit.

The two Focke-Wulfs began to turn, looking for another target. Crowe was above and behind them, and let the gap close to less than three hundred yards before he fired. His first burst must have ignited the fuel tank of the lead German, so intense and sudden was the explosion. The fighter simply disappeared, with little to mark its passing except a tiny oily cloud. The wingman hesitated, perhaps stunned by the ferocity of his colleagues demise. Whatever the reason, they were only parted for a matter of moments. With a touch of the controls, Crowe brought the Mosquito's nose to bear on the second aircraft. The eight barrels flared in synchrony and another German aircraft hurtled downwards to join the growing number of funeral pyres in the fields below.

"All aircraft, this is Mosquito Leader." Hulse sounded calm, only the faintest tremor in his gruff Northern voice revealing in him the fear that they all felt. "Everybody pair up with someone. Work together."

Crowe scanned the sky. It seemed empty now, more aircraft destroyed and pilots killed than left flying. His dive had taken him down to three thousand feet. A few thousand feet above him he could see Hulse, and in the distance he saw the Spitfires of Owen and Sullivan flying together, one covering the other as the lead aircraft closed in and destroyed another Focke-Wulf.

"Where's Kev Masters?" Hulse said.

"Dead," Gorecki told him.

"I didn't see it."

"Neither did he," Gorecki said sadly.

The radio crackled slightly, and a familiar voice filled their headsets, sounding faint and distant.

"I've got Morgan," Raithe said. "I'm preparing for take off."

Crowe felt his heart give a leap of joy. He looked briefly towards the clearing. The Lysander was still invisible, lost amongst the smudge of the forest.

"What is keeping you?" Werner chided.

"We ran into three soldiers in the dark," Raithe said. There was an edge to his voice, a hint of pleasure.

"Hurry," Hulse said urgently.

Crowe felt his harness straps bite into his shoulders as he checked the sky behind them. He looked carefully down, checking that there were no Focke-Wulfs in the area of the Lysander. Next to him, Jones was doing the same, but the only activity was high above them. Crowe, Hulse and Gorecki had the sky to themselves, but for a couple of Focke-Wulfs keeping a respectful distance from them. "I'm struggling to find targets," Crowe said.

"They are all up here," Werner said cheerfully.

Crowe put the Mosquito into a climb, glancing at the fuel gauge. Dogfighting used a tremendous amount of fuel but the Mosquito was an aircraft designed for endurance and they had a good amount of flying time left. His head was starting to hurt as the blood wore off, his neck muscles aching from the strain of keeping his head in place as they had hurtled around the sky. The distinctive shape of Werner's Mosquito was silhouetted briefly against the painful flame of the Moon, and Crowe realised that all of the aircraft around the vampire were identical.

"Jesus," he said, "you've got four of them on you."

"I can count," Werner said. "Stay away, Crowe. These are all mine."

"Don't be an idiot," Crowe said, as his aircraft's engines howled in outrage, pulling the bomb laden weight of the Mosquito higher towards the one-sided melee. They were still at least five thousand feet below the Favrio. Crowe knew they were climbing too slowly and watched in horror as tracers snaked out like malevolent tendrils towards the lone Mosquito. Somehow Werner was keeping all four German fighters at bay, hurling his outnumbered aircraft around the sky with desperate skill, and now, impossibly, the Mosquito was behind one of the Focke-Wulfs and fired a short burst that sent the Nazi away in a shallow smoking dive, but there were still three more of them, and it was only a matter of time. Even as Werner evaded one burst of fire, another struck him in the fuselage and port wing. There was a flash and a gout of smoke erupted to hang mockingly in the thin air.

"It is nothing," Werner said, answering an unasked question. Crowe watched speechlessly, powerless to intervene. It seemed like Werner might even have been right, as he flicked the Mosquito into a series of rolls and then into a tight bank which brought another Focke-Wulf into his sights. This time Werner fired a much longer burst. The rounds passed either side of the fighter before finally striking home. It flared sharply and broke apart.

"I haven't got the power to reach you," Crowe said. "Gorecki, can you get to him?"

"I'm already on my way," Gorecki said, and Crowe saw the shark-like shape of the Spitfire climbing steadily a mile to his left.

Crowe turned to Jones, whose mouth was moving silently. "You want to pray?" he said harshly. "Pray Gorecki gets there in time."

Werner let loose a stream of German. There was desperation in his voice, the universal language of fear and anger.

"I am out of ammunition," Werner said. Crowe heard the fear in his voice, and shared it.

Above him, mockingly out of his reach, one of the German fighters was closing in on Werner's tail, firing constantly. Werner's Mosquito must have been struck again because the Favrio's gasp of pain was heard by all of them, his radio still switched to transmit.

"Dive," Crowe said, watching as the second fighter dived towards the stricken Mossie to attack it head-on. "We can protect you."

"Protect Raithe instead," Werner said. The words were almost lost in his gasp of pain. "Ronnie is unconscious. His blood is everywhere. We will not make it."

Something about Werner's tone told Crowe everything. In an instant his plan was clear.

"Werner, don't do it," Crowe began, but he was cut off.

"Six kills for me," Werner said. "You buy the drinks." The German gave a painful laugh, and the radio went dead.

Two seconds later, with a last pull on the controls, Werner swung his Mosquito into the path of the approaching Focke-Wulf. The fighter ploughed through the Mosquito's wing between engine and fuselage, breaking apart as it did so and plummeting down without any trace of flame. For a few seconds the Mosquito continued to climb, one wing entirely gone, and then it seemed to collapse in on itself and spun in a slow pirouette towards the silent, waiting earth.

Crowe watched almost without conscious thought as Gorecki reached and killed the last Focke-Wulf. He felt lost, as if in a daze. The sky seemed empty now. To the east he thought he could make out the tiny speck of a distant aircraft, but he could not be sure. There were still three Focke-Wulfs a few miles away, keeping warily away from the British fighters circling over the clearing, but of the Vulture there was no sign. Even as he watched, the three German fighters turned and headed away to the east.

"The Focke-Wulfs are leaving," Crowe said. "I guess that means we won." He thought of Werner and felt no anger, just a deep sadness.

"I'm sorry," Jones said. "I know Werner was your friend."

"Yes," Crowe said. "He was a vampire." He paused. "Like me."

"I guess that just leaves me now," Jones said quietly, looking back at the smoke-stained horizon. "With Ronnie gone and Danny gone, I'm the only one of my class still alive. I know I should feel upset, but I just feel…" He fell silent.

"Empty?"

"Yes." They both fell silent as they followed the trails of smoke down towards the church.

The radio crackled again as they passed below eight thousand feet. "This is Raithe. We'll be airborne in thirty seconds."

"Are you sure you can make it?" Hulse said.

"I'll tell you in thirty seconds," Raithe replied calmly. Fifteen seconds later, Crowe saw the Lysander suddenly lurch forward, accelerating towards the trees. They couldn't possibly make it, there was absolutely no chance, and yet within scant seconds of beginning its forward motion the Lysander seemed to leap into the air, somehow clearing the trees. Crowe could not be sure, but he could have sworn he saw a cloud of leaves cascading to the ground, torn free from the upper branches.

"I'm airborne," Raithe said. "Crowe, stay close to me."

"How is Morgan?"

"Alive." The Romanian's tone worried Crowe. The wave of euphoria he had felt at the successful rescue dissipated in an instant. The thought that Morgan might be seriously hurt made his insides suddenly writhe.

"That take off was unbelievable," Hulse murmured in a tone of admiration. "I wouldn't believe it unless I'd seen it."

303

"Well," Owen said, "you've seen it. Can we go home now?" His pleading voice sounded very young.

"How are you doing for fuel?"

"Honestly? We'll be lucky if we don't have to swim back to England."

"Okay, lads, head for home. You too, Gorecki."

"What about you?"

"Me and Crowe will stay with Raithe. Don't worry. We'll not be far behind."

"You'll all be okay?"

"We'll be fine," Hulse assured him. "Just tell me one thing. Can anyone see any sign of the Vulture?"

"I think he has gone home," Gorecki said.

"He'll be back," Crowe warned as he descended and took up a position off Raithe's left wing.

"Well, we'll just have to deal with him if he shows up," Hulse said as he too closed on Raithe. "Where's everybody else?"

"There is no one else," Crowe said gently.

"This is it? This is all that survived?" Hulse's voice sounded disbelieving. "No one else made it?"

"No one else."

Above them, the three Spitfires cruised away towards the Channel and the waiting runway of Charney Breach. Crowe wondered if there would even be anyone there to meet them. Treble-Six Squadron was finished, that much was clear, whether or not they were deemed to have completed their mission. They had failed, Crowe realised suddenly. The Vulture was still alive, still at liberty to wreak havoc on those poor bastards in Bomber Command. Crowe resisted the urge to punch the instrument panel. His left hand still held the controls steadily, but his right fist rhythmically clenched and unclenched. He wanted to kill, and knew it wasn't just because of the blood that still lingered in his system.

"Crowe?"

He turned to Jones, who was looking at him with a mixture of fear and concern.

"Are you okay?"

"It was all for nothing," Crowe spat into the intercom. The anger and hollowness within him made him want to vomit. "Everything we've done, all those men we've lost were for nothing."

"What do you mean?"

"The Vulture is still out there. He's the only thing that mattered to Quiet. He's the reason they set this whole thing up, and he's still alive."

"At least his squadron's finished," Jones said. That much at least, Crowe conceded, was true. Treble-Six Squadron might have suffered heavy losses but so had Jagdstaffel Falke. The Germans had sent in at least twenty-five aircraft. Perhaps four had made it home. For an instant Crowe felt a grudging admiration for them, but then he thought of Werner and Lieberwitz and Harry Stead. With a last look back at the pillars of smoke, rising like headstones over a graveyard that spread five miles in each direction, he followed the Lysander.

Jones was still watching him with sad eyes. "And we rescued Morgan," he said gently.

"If he lives," Crowe said quietly, and looked over towards Raithe with renewed fear. The Lysander was a desperately slow aircraft, and it was all Crowe and Hulse could do to keep their Mosquitoes from leaving it behind. Hulse was seemingly lost in his thoughts, and Crowe knew that the northerner would be thinking of the men they had lost. He flew up alongside Raithe and looked into the cockpit. The Romanian glanced his way before turning back to his flying, his concentration clearly focused by the low level at which they were crossing the French countryside, hoping to evade any radar-controlled pursuit.

"How's Morgan doing?" Crowe asked.

Raithe paused a moment before responding. "He is not good," he said finally. "He was unconscious when I found him."

"Did you give him blood?"

"Yes. It woke him up for a few minutes, but getting him to the aircraft hurt him badly. He is in and out of consciousness now."

"But you've got plenty of blood on board," Crowe protested. "Isn't that helping?"

"Blood alone cannot help him now. His wounds are deeper than that. If I give him too much blood, it could push his body over the edge, you understand? He needs medical help."

"Dr Madeley will be standing by when we land."

"I hope so." There was the faintest catch in his voice. "Wait a minute." Crowe, while very conscious of their low altitude, risked another quick glance towards the Lysander and saw that Raithe was looking away, down to his right. Finally the Romanian looked up.

"Morgan wants to speak to you."

For what seemed an age Crowe held his breath, his hands painfully tight on the controls, until finally the sound of his friend's voice filled his ears. Even with all the worry and anger and grief, there was no stopping his smile.

"Crowe?"

"You gave us all quite a scare there, Morgan. How are you feeling?"

"Orgasmic," Morgan said, his voice sounding faint. "I'm a little bit sleepy. But I could murder a pint."

"Drinks are on me when we get back. You shouldn't be talking. Rest."

"I don't want to go to sleep. I might not wake up."

Crowe's smile faded. "Don't give me that," he said, trying to sound jovial. "You're going to be fine."

"Maybe." For a few seconds there was no sound, and Crowe and Jones exchanged worried looks. "Thanks for coming for me," Morgan said finally. "How are all the lads?"

Harry Stead. Bobby Barton. Ronnie Hall. Kev Masters. Cameron Nelson. Archie Mills. Liam Barnes. Steve Slater. Lieberwitz. Werner. Crowe thought of the burning, smoking hulks in the fields behind them and took a deep breath. "They're all looking forward to seeing you," he lied.

"We should have a party tonight," Morgan said, the words slightly slurred. "You could invite Cassie."

"I don't think she'd come."

"Of course she would. She likes you. Everybody likes you."

"He's delirious," Raithe said sarcastically, interrupting.

"I'm not delirious, I'm just really sleepy." His voice faded further, and Crowe looked over towards the Lysander and saw Raithe looking away, down towards where Morgan was slumped. "I do hope you'll be happy, Crowe," Morgan slurred. "Give her my regards, will you?"

"You can give her them yourself." There was no response. "Morgan?"

"He's unconscious," Raithe said, looking towards Crowe with his face unreadable.

"Then we need to get him back." He finally abandoned his restraint and punched the control panel, feeling the glass of the airspeed indicator display shatter beneath his gloved fist. "We're taking too long," he said angrily.

"Raithe can't make that Lysander fly any faster, Crowe," Hulse said.

"Goddamn it."

"He's going to be fine, I'm sure," Jones said soothingly. "We're already at the Channel." Beneath them a row of simple houses flashed by, and then the ground was sloping rapidly down towards a wide pebbled beach. A few more seconds and there was only the water of the Channel, a placid grey less than a hundred feet beneath them.

Crowe glanced at his watch. "Dawn isn't far off."

"We're going to be fine, too."

"Crowe," Raithe said, "I need you to check my landing gear for me."

"Have you got a problem?"

"Perhaps. We hit the trees on take off."

"It looks fine from here," Crowe said. "Hold on; I'll take a closer look." He pushed the controls gently to starboard and banked towards the Lysander.

He heard Jones's muffled exclamation at the same instant he saw the tracers. They zipped past the cockpit, flashing over the port engine. A second later a dark shadow passed just yards over the top of them and accelerated away.

"It's him," Hulse shouted.

"Stay with them!" Crowe shouted as he lifted the nose and fired a long hopeful burst after the retreating shape. His left hand slammed both throttle levers fully open and the Mosquito leaped forward even as his tracers missed the fleeing Vulture by three hundred yards or more.

"Crowe, wait," Hulse said. Crowe barely heard him above the roar of his heartbeat in his ears. If the attack had come a second earlier they would have been dead. The turn towards Raithe had saved their lives. The Vulture was already a mile ahead of them, the attack carried out at full speed. The Mosquito was accelerating too, but it still felt sluggish with the bomb load inside. Optimistically he pulled the lever to release the bomb doors. A mocking click was the only response.

"I don't get it," Jones said. "Why go for us? Why not attack the Lysander?"

"Because he knew we were the threat."

"He's leading us out to sea."

The Vulture was still climbing, but the gap was not opening. Crowe knew the Eckartstrasse's vampire was letting them keep up with it. "No ambush this time," Crowe said. "Everyone's dead."

"Is he planning to take us on alone?"

"Maybe he's getting brave. Or maybe he's desperate."

"Not that desperate. He's still faster and more manoeuvrable."

"That won't save him."

They flew directly north, steadily climbing while the Lysander and its escorting Mosquito dwindled and disappeared behind them. The gap between them remained a little more than a mile.

"How much fuel have we got?"

"Enough," Jones said. "But dawn's in thirty minutes."

"What's he playing at?" Crowe muttered. The Vulture's base was at least twenty minutes flying time away now, but the aircraft made no attempt to escape. The Arado turned suddenly, and its manoeuvrability appalled him. In moments it was in a dive towards them, the gap between them closing rapidly.

Both aircraft began firing at the same time, hurling cannon shells and machine gun bullets towards each other's cockpits. Crowe was only vaguely aware of the balls of deadly light eviscerating the air around him. His focus was entirely on the stubby nose of the German fighter, and he caught a glimpse of a black uniformed and helmeted figure sitting alone in the cockpit as the Arado flashed by. Somehow they'd both missed. Crowe threw the Mosquito into a tight bank, the muscles of his neck burning in outrage, but the controls still felt sluggish. The climb had cost them speed and energy, and he knew even before he had completed his turn that the Vulture held all the advantages now. He caught a glimpse of the German fighter pulling sharply out its dive and trying to get around behind him.

"Get those bomb doors open," he shouted at Jones. The navigator gave him a startled, hopeless look and began tugging at the lever. No response. Still weighed down, Crowe knew that there was nothing he could do to prevent the Arado getting behind him. Like the graceful bird of prey it was, it smoothly closed the gap even as Crowe frantically yanked at the controls and hammered the rudder pedals in a last attempt to keep it at bay.

The Vulture fired a long burst. It missed them, but only by a few feet. The next one, Crowe knew, would hit them. He thought of Morgan, of how his friend had once effortlessly evaded the Vulture and got behind him. It hadn't saved Morgan, though, and the Vulture had obviously learned his lesson. This time there would be no overshoot. Three hundred yards behind them, the Arado kept its position and waited for its moment. As Jones's efforts to free the bomb doors became ever more hopeless, Crowe turned to see muzzle flashes in the dark nose of the German fighter, and knew that they would be hit.

There was a sudden roaring noise as cannon shells tore through the Mosquito's wooden frame. Crowe felt a sharp pain in his neck as splinters tore into his skin. The aircraft bucked with the impact, and in desperation he threw the stick to the side as the Vulture prepared to fire again.

There was a sudden thud.

"They're open."

"What?"

"The bomb doors are open!"

Without hesitation Crowe reached out and jettisoned the four trapped bombs, sending them plummeting harmlessly and forlornly into the water below. The aircraft seemed to rise a hundred feet in an instant, freed of the useless weight. He pulled back on the stick, rolled over to port, and watched the Vulture fly underneath him and disappear out of view to his right. Turning after it, he reached out and grabbed the bomb door lever again.

Smoothly and without fuss, the doors closed again, as if there had never been a problem.

"He's running," Jones said excitedly as Crowe turned back towards the German aircraft. Sure enough the Arado was already accelerating away, heading for the coast.

"Thank God he didn't hit an engine," Jones added.

"He did."

"What?"

Crowe looked at him and smiled, and saw the colour drain from the young man's face.

"Don't..." Jones began, but Crowe didn't hesitate. He reached out his right hand to the large button on the upper console and feathered the port engine. For a few seconds the props spun regardless, and then, as if insulted by their treatment, they came to an obstinate halt and hung motionless in the slipstream.

"Are you insane?" Jones cried. Crowe ignored him. He let the Mosquito side slip to port, his eyes on the dwindling aircraft.

"Come on," he muttered. The Arado flew on regardless, two miles away now. He thought of Harry Stead's damaged Mosquito, of the wrecked Lancaster burning on the ground at Charney Breach, of the dying airman he had failed to save. He weaved erratically, still losing altitude, the waiting waters of the Channel seeming closer than the five thousand feet the altimeter stubbornly proclaimed it to be. But still the Vulture was retreating.

"Take the bait, you bastard."

Slowly, almost imperceptibly, the distant aircraft changed course and circled around towards them.

"He's coming."

"That's great," Jones said. "Now what?"

"We wait for him to attack."

"Oh. Smashing."

Crowe ignored him, feeling elation throughout his entire body, and reached into his pocket, feeling the hard metal within. He unscrewed the bottle and took the tiniest of sips. It was all he needed. He felt the warm glow, felt his muscles tense with pleasure and closed his eyes.

"Please watch where you're going," Jones begged. "I'm too young to die."

"He's going to overshoot," Crowe said calmly, his eyes still closed as the tremor spread through his body and then dissipated as quickly as it had come. He opened his eyes. Outside the night sky seemed clearer than ever. He looked over his shoulder again and saw that the Vulture was barely a mile away now.

"I'm still a virgin," Jones muttered.

"He thinks we're damaged," Crowe said, almost to himself. "He can't resist the chance for an easy kill."

"But if he takes his time…"

"He has no time. Dawn is in twenty minutes. He only has time for one quick pass. And the Mosquito can still fly on one engine." He turned to the navigator and winked.

"Oh God," Jones said, looking away in terror, "we're going to die."

Yard by yard Crowe watched as the Vulture closed the gap while the sound of Jones's frantic praying filled his ears. Not yet, he cautioned himself. Five hundred yards to go. Not yet. Four hundred, then three. Wait…

"Now," Crowe shouted aloud as he hurled the Mosquito to the side at the very instant the Vulture fired. The aircraft reacted as he knew it would, its response as wonderful on one engine as two. Overconfident and surprised and travelling at much greater speed, the Vulture overshot. The Arado went instantly into a climb and Crowe knew they could never hope to catch him, but for one glorious moment the German aircraft filled his sights.

Time seemed to stop, suddenly, the entire scene frozen before him. The all too familiar silhouette of the Arado Ar-440. The dying man in his arms as he stumbled from the burning bomber. The faces of every one of his friends who had died at the hands of this bastard vampire and his squadron. All these images played across his mind in an instant as his finger slowly squeezed. He fired.

The Vulture flew through the stream of tracer and emerged apparently unscathed.

"I missed," he whispered, stunned. The Vulture turned to climb away.

"No," Jones said, suddenly laughing as a flash lit up the sky, "you didn't."

Great chunks of metal fell away from the German's port wing. A sheet of flames burst from the port engine and spread quickly along the control surfaces, and then the entire wing was enveloped in smoke and the Arado lurched suddenly towards the sea. Crowe reached out and restarted the silent engine. It coughed just once, the props swung back into play, and he followed the Vulture down.

The Arado was desperately twisting and turning, trying to lose him. Crowe kept the gap at three hundred yards as the Vulture became more and more frantic. France was a long way from here, the Vulture's Belgian base even further, and Crowe looked at the aircraft's cockpit through the cloud of billowing smoke and wondered if the Vulture knew it was all over.

As if in response, the German aircraft stopped its manoeuvring, and flew straight and level, the barrels of the machine guns in the remote controlled barbettes shifting into position. Jones saw the movement, and gasped.

Crowe fired again.

He held the trigger as the Vulture's cockpit disappeared, as the aircraft exploded around him, as the wreckage simply disintegrated and plummeted in tiny fragments towards the final welcoming embrace of the water below, until the last rounds were gone and the weapons clicked empty and he watched the last of the wreckage splash into the Channel.

"*Mulo mukat tuv ratesa, bengu tuv anav.*" The *Mulo* takes your blood. May the Devil take the rest.

"Fifteen minutes until dawn," Jones said urgently.

With a last look back towards the distant French coast and an unseen church, Crowe swung the Mosquito around and headed for home.

It was the sight of the knot of figures around the Lysander that frightened Crowe, even more than the glow of the eastern sky. He put the Mosquito down onto the runway far too fast, half-expecting Jones to comment, but the navigator's eyes too were on the ambulance that was parked next to Raithe's aircraft. Minutes until dawn. They taxied quickly up as close as they could and saw that Dom was waiting for them with a covered truck.

Jones opened the door and cleared the aircraft without even waiting for the ladder. As Crowe dropped down his heart lurched and with Jones alongside him he sprinted towards the ambulance, his eyes on the open door and the blanket-covered figure on the stretcher that was being carried towards it. Raithe walked towards them, his arms outstretched, bringing them to a halt and for a few seconds they stood and gasped for air and watched Dr Madeley walking slowly alongside the stretcher. He didn't look at them.

Crowe opened his mouth to speak but the words would barely come.

"He's dead?"

"It is almost dawn, Crowe," Raithe said. And then he suddenly smiled.

"What?"

"The blanket is for the sun." Raithe's smile grew wider, and he reached out and placed one hand on Crowe's shoulder. "Morgan will be fine. He just needs a drink." The doors of the ambulance closed and the vehicle carried Morgan away.

Jones looked over to the east, where the first glow of dawn was lightening the sky. "It's going to be a beautiful day."

Crowe smiled. "They're all beautiful." And, as with a smile and a sigh the vampires lowered their smoked glasses and climbed into the vehicle that would take them back to the safety of the waiting empty bar, another day slowly began.

Epilogue

Christmas Eve, December 1942

The Fat Man coughed, gave his cigar an angry look, and looked up from his chair towards the man in the brown hat who stood by the fireplace.

"Treble-Six Squadron is to be disbanded, then?"

"It has served its purpose, sir. Half the crews are dead or missing. The remaining regular aircrew will be debriefed in the usual fashion, sworn to secrecy and dispatched to other squadrons."

The Fat Man glanced once more down at the single sheet of scrawled notes in his hand, sighed, and passed the paper back to the visitor, who wordlessly placed it into the fire.

"It was a failure, then?"

"I wouldn't say that. The Vulture is dead, and his squadron destroyed. There are a lot of our bomber crews alive today that wouldn't otherwise have been, and a lot less Germans. Overall, I would say the experiment was…interesting."

"And the vampires?"

"They will be taken care of, sir," the man from K Department said flatly, his eyes invisible below the shadow of the hat's brim.

"Good." The Fat Man placed his cigar in its personalised ashtray and started to rise, idly wondering what the visitor would look like without his hat. "Well," he said, "it was a brave effort. You'll stay for a drink, of course?"

"I'd love to, Prime Minister," his guest said, looking thoughtfully at his watch, "but I'm afraid I have some other business I must attend to."

"Of course. Thank you, Quentin."

There was a long moment of silence, broken only by the gentle crackling of the fire.

"Perhaps a quick one," said Quentin Quiet.

There had been no bombs that night to disturb the sleeping city. Some of the Air Raid Wardens talked in hushed voices of the possibility of an attack later, but few were seriously concerned. There had been little action for the crews of the heavy guns protecting London in weeks. It was almost as if the German bombers had simply stopped trying, they said, but it was probably the work of the RAF. Everyone knew the British night fighters were getting the upper hand now. It was in the cinemas and on the front pages, while away on the other side of the Channel, over Germany, Bomber Command was giving the Nazis a much-deserved taste of their own medicine. And so the unfortunate souls who had to work that night went quietly about their business, while the silence was disturbed only by the noise of a black Bentley with smoked, opaque windows and its lights dimmed pulling to a halt outside a nondescript Whitehall building.

"Christmas Eve," Crowe said wistfully.

"Always my favourite time of the year," Morgan said, his tall frame squeezed behind the steering wheel. "Not just the presents, although of course they were always fun. It's just that the nights are so long. So much time."

Crowe plucked at the collar of his ill-fitting suit and turned to his friend. Morgan looked well, he thought. In truth, Morgan's recovery had been nothing short of miraculous. His wounds had been severe, and the expensively carved walking stick lying on the leather back seat was a silent testament to the extent of the damage. His face and skin, of course, showed no sign of the injuries that had almost killed him. Dr Madeley reckoned that he would need the stick for six weeks or more. Crowe doubted his friend would submit to any doctor's advice for that long, even that of his beloved family physician.

Morgan looked through the window at the four stone steps and thick brown doors of the office building, and gave Crowe an expectant look.

"Are you sure about this?" he asked finally.

Crowe nodded. It had taken a lot of thought but he was sure. "When will you know what you're going to do?"

"I'll spend Christmas with my family, and then I'll decide. I'm not in any rush after all, not with this bloody leg. Raithe's talked Gorecki into doing Lysander runs with him, but I don't know." His face suddenly screwed up a little. "I didn't really enjoy my first flight in a

Lysander, to be honest. Come to think of it, I never really liked flying at all."

Crowe smiled, and Morgan suddenly laughed boyishly. "I'll never get used to seeing you smile, but it's always good to see. You will visit, won't you? We've got plenty of spare rooms, and Mum will be happy to see you. You don't even have to wear a day suit and go outside if you don't want to…"

"I'll visit," Crowe said. He reached into his pocket and pulled out the battered old sunglasses before sliding them on. He opened the car door, and stepped out. The night was already cold and the temperature still dropping, and the air felt as fresh as he had ever known it in London. To his surprise, he realised it had been more than a year since he had last been here. He looked back at Morgan. So much had changed in that time.

"Nice suit," Morgan said.

"Do you think so?"

"No." Morgan smiled and extended his hand. "Be lucky, my friend."

Crowe took the hand and shook it warmly. "What are the odds?"

Morgan winked. Crowe closed the car door and watched the Bentley drive quickly away into the night, tires squealing as it rounded the corner at the end of the street and headed off towards Westminster Bridge and the long drive down to Ravenswood and his waiting family.

A few hundred yards away Big Ben struck the note of ten, while somewhere high above the distinctive sound of twin Merlins betrayed the presence of a Mosquito night fighter, hoping their radar and the light of the fading moon would lead them to a target and the chance to claim a rare kill.

Crowe wished them luck, and walked up the steps into the building.

The large entrance hall was as bland as the exterior, with only a set of double doors, a single wooden bench and a reception counter, all on the far side. The walls were clean as if recently painted, but unadorned in any way. It was harshly lit, enough to make his eyes hurt slightly even with the sunglasses, and the heels of his shoes echoed loudly off the polished stone floor as he walked across the near empty room to the single, bored-looking woman behind the counter.

"Please take a seat, Mr Crowe," she said before he could speak. She didn't look up.

Crowe sat down on the bench and waited, shifting uncomfortably. The suit felt tight and constricting, the unaccustomed jacket seeming poised to split across his shoulder blades. Cassie must have thought it was hilarious when he had worn it into Staverton, even if she hadn't said anything. His tie, too, felt just as uncomfortable now as it had then, and he felt almost as nervous. He did not want to think of Cassie, though. Not now.

Forty minutes passed before the double doors finally opened.

"Sorry I'm late, Crowe," Quentin Quiet said. "Unavoidable, I'm afraid. Nice suit."

"Thanks."

"Shall we get started?"

His long brown coat draped loosely over one arm, Quiet led Crowe through the double doors and down a series of corridors. All were silent but for the echo of their footsteps. There were offices on each side of the corridors, but Quiet ignored them. They passed through a series of doors, until eventually there were no more offices and they were passing a kitchen area. Finally they stopped at a door with faded green paint. It was identical to many others, except for the small brass sign marked "Cleaning No 2". Quiet retrieved a key from his pocket and unlocked the door, and only then, as Crowe followed him down a dimly lit staircase, did he break the silence.

"You'll be pleased to hear that Raymond Noone is enjoying his new job as Assistant Director of RAF Communications," Quiet said. "Tea boy to an Air Vice Marshal."

Crowe said nothing. It seemed this staircase was rarely used. The walls were damp and filthy where water and accumulated dust had mixed to form grey clumps. A few inches above their heads, more dust clung to spiders' webs. Oddly, the tiles beneath their feet were well-worn and dust free.

"As for Shaun Clark," Quiet continued, "he's on his way to Malta to fly Hurricanes. You'll be pleased to hear the attrition rate out there is quite high."

"Is he still a prick?"

"Of course he is," Quiet said reasonably. "But he's also a useful pilot. And we can't afford to waste useful people."

They had reached the bottom of the stairs, their way barred by a thick-looking metal door with a combination lock. Quiet paused for a few seconds as if thinking and began turning the dial.

"What about Cassie Noone?" Crowe said quietly.

Quiet tensed slightly. "Cassie Noone. Hmm." He fumbled at the lock. "What's that damned combination again?" he muttered to himself.

"Mr Quiet?"

Quiet stopped. For a few moments he looked at the floor, Crowe wondering whether he had heard. But then he exhaled deeply.

"Unfortunately, Crowe," he said softly, "Cassie was a civilian, a civilian who knew a little too much about our operations." He looked up at Crowe, and despite the shadow of the hat, Crowe saw the calmness in his eyes. "And I took the decision that she knew too much to be allowed to walk away."

With a final click, the code was complete. Quiet reached down and pulled the heavy handle that opened the door.

Cassie Noone was sat in the small waiting room beyond.

She was sitting on a simple bench next to yet another set of double doors, in a plain skirt and white blouse, but Crowe barely noticed these details. For a few seconds all he saw was her face and the look of uncertainty in her eyes as she stood up and looked at him, and in an instant he knew that their future could never be easy. How could it be, when there were so many differences between them? So many compromises to make, so many problems to overcome. He was a vampire.

It didn't stop him smiling. He felt relief, he felt happiness, and both must have shown on his face, because suddenly she was smiling too.

"Like I said," Quiet said, "we can't afford to waste useful people."

"Couldn't you have told me?"

"You didn't need to know." Quiet suddenly smiled, and Crowe was shocked to realise that, for once, somewhere in that expression was a genuine hint of pleasure. It didn't last, of course.

"You never did tell me how you knew Morgan was in that cemetery either," Crowe said.

"Crowe, you cannot begin to imagine how much I haven't told you," Quiet said. "But at least some of the answers are through here."

He swung open the doors, and instantly there was a rush of sound. Beyond the obviously soundproofed doors was a huge open plan office. There must have been two dozen desks or more, some cluttered, others neatly arranged, a few looking like they had never been used and were simply waiting for someone to arrive and take on the role. Despite the late hour the room seemed to buzz with frantic activity. There were at least twenty people inside, all of whom seemed busy, going about their business without even seeming to notice the new arrivals. Every inch of wall space was covered, with maps, charts, strange images and diagrams. At regular intervals along the walls were plinths, some empty but others hosting various unusual items. Above each group of desks, hanging from the high ceiling, were the names of the different sections.

Artefacts. Remote Viewing. Revivification. ESP.

There were more, but even as Crowe heard Cassie give a tiny gasp of amazement, even as Crowe's mind raced to take in the possibilities he was seeing before him, Quentin Quiet was turning towards them once again.

"Welcome to K Department."

Printed in the United Kingdom by
Lightning Source UK Ltd., Milton Keynes
138855UK00001B/198/P